# THE IMAM

# OF TIME

# THE IMAM
# OF TIME

*A NOVEL OF THEN AND NOW*

## F. W. BURLEIGH

ZENGA
BOOKS

ISBN: 978-0-9960469-7-8

Published in the United States of America
Zenga Books, Portland, OR
zengabooks@protonmail.com

For more about *The Imam of Time*, visit:
www.itsallaboutmuhammad.com

This book should have been written by an Iranian, but to my knowledge no Iranian has ever written anything like it or perhaps even thought of it. *The Imam of Time*, therefore, is a default book. The people who should have written it didn't, so I did.

— F. W. Burleigh

The scenes in *The Imam of Time* involving Muhammad were inspired by events recorded in the original literature of Islam: the biographies of Muhammad by Ibn Ishaq, al-Waqidi, and Ibn Sa'd; the traditions about him by al-Bukhari, al-Muslim, and Abu Daoud; the Koran; and other important sources such as the Koran commentary of Ibn Kathir.

# PART I

# THE CAVE
# OF LIGHT

# Chapter 1

The cell phone rang, and Ahmed—the son of Abdollah of the town of Aliabad in the province of Golestan—knew who was calling, and more importantly, why.

It was Omid, commander of the Aliabad religious militia. Ahmed felt a rush of irritation and let the phone ring four times before answering.

Omid said, "The order has just come down from Tehran. We've been called up."

Ahmed was not surprised. He had been following the news of protests that had broken out in Tehran over the official results of the presidential election. With each passing day came reports of more demonstrations in Tehran, and in Mashhad, Isfahan, Tabriz, and other major cities. Foreign broadcasts that could be accessed even in a small provincial town like Aliabad predicted the ayatollahs would lose control of the streets and would be unable to hold on to power for much longer. The militias of outlying provinces had already been mobilized to beef up security forces across the land. The Golestan militia was still on alert, meaning: prepare for active duty.

"It will be your responsibility to contact the volunteers of your section and ensure they arrive on time at the assembly area."

Omid gave him the details: Two buses would take the Aliabad contingent to the militia headquarters in Gorgan, the provincial capital. There, they would be given anti-riot equipment and duty assignments.

"Where are we going?"

"Tehran. Our people will be spread out among different barracks. Tell everyone to come as they are, but bring a change of clothes and something to eat because nothing will be available while we're on the road."

Since his early teens, Ahmed had been a faithful member of the militia and an unwavering supporter of the Islamic Republic. How could it be otherwise? His father was remembered in Aliabad as one of the martyrs of the Sacred Defense, and Ahmed was honored as the son of a martyr. Nevertheless, he had been thinking about refusing to go if they were mobilized and even resigning from the militia if necessary. He could not bring himself to disagree with the demonstrators. It was certain that the election was rigged. Even before the voting closed, many polling stations trending in favor of the opposition candidates ran out of ballots, while in some stations, entire ballot boxes were found stuffed with fraudulent votes. The official count was the exact opposite of what almost everyone had been forecasting. Even worse, some of the opposition leaders, their staff, and student leaders from Tehran University had been jailed on charges of subversion. Some were beaten, and there were rumors of shootings.

"If they're not going to respect the vote, then why even hold an election?" he said to his mother, Amineh, a seamstress who lived above a cloth store in Aliabad.

He could leave the militia at any time because it was a volunteer organization. But he would face serious consequences. For one, he would lose the monthly stipend he received for organizing cultural meetings such as those honoring the martyrs of the Sacred Defense and patriotic rallies celebrating the victory of the Islamic Republic. To date, that had been his primary role. Even worse, he would be expelled from the agricultural university in Gorgan, where he was pursuing a degree in agronomy, a school that he attended tuition-free thanks to his membership in the militia.

But much worse was the fact that he lived in a conservative town in a province where most of the people believed the time was fast approaching when the Mahdi would emerge from a millennium of hiding to bring peace and justice to the world under the banner of Islam. The coming of the Imam of Time, as the Mahdi was called, was the rallying idea of the Islamic Republic, and he himself had been raised to believe in him and pray for his appearance. The purpose of the religious militia was to support the Islamic Republic; the purpose of the Islamic Republic was to facilitate the return of the Imam of Time. If he refused the mobilization order, he would be treated with suspicion that he was disloyal to the Republic, an enemy of the Imam himself.

He felt like a coward when he said, without enthusiasm, "I will do as you ask."

Even before the election, he had been struggling with doubts. It was not that he rejected the idea that the government should be guided by God or disbelieved that the hidden Imam would one day reappear. He had begun to question the goal of the religious leaders to create strife in the world in order to hasten his return. It was their dogma. The greater the chaos, the sooner the return of the Imam of Time, for it was prophesied that he would appear during a time of universal chaos.

"Isn't that evil?" he said to his mother, the only person to whom he dared trust with his doubts. "It means starting wars and bringing about the deaths of countless people. Isn't that what the Islamic Republic has been doing ever since the revolution? The Imam of Time is supposed to bring universal peace and justice, which is good, but how can evil be justified as a way of bringing about good?"

His mother was a good listener, but she had no answer other than to say that she agreed with him about everything. She cautioned him that he must keep his thoughts to himself. "Your own companions in the militia would turn on you if they heard you talking like this."

He also confided in her about a recurring dream that had been troubling him. These dreams started the year before. They were infrequent at first, but now they came almost every night, and it was always the same: He enters a cave; it is pitch black inside; he is fearful of going into the darkness, but he is compelled to go deep inside. At some point, a brilliant light appears, and he becomes frightened and awakens with a start. "This dream keeps coming back. What does it mean?"

"The light is the solution to what troubles you," she offered.

His doubts drove him to seek guidance from a cleric at the Aliabad mosque, whom he suspected might sympathize with his concerns. Mullah Koushiyar had a quality about him that led people to call him Baba—the affectionate word for father. During their Friday sermons, many clerics spoke in angry tones, wagging their fingers to warn of doom for those who, in their hearts, were disloyal to the Imam of Time, whereas his sermons were simple homilies that encouraged people to perform good works.

Baba Koushiyar had a roundish face, a trim gray beard, and cheerful eyes behind thick glasses. He invited Ahmed to sit on the carpet with him in a corner of the prayer area. He listened with polite nods of his turbaned head. When Ahmed was done explaining the reason for his visit, the cleric closed his eyes as if meditating, and after a moment said, "I'm confident the Imam will return when he chooses, and I'm certain he will reveal many good things to us. So instead of concerning yourself with such questions, wouldn't it be best to strive to perform good works here in our town and be forthright in your everyday dealings with people? That is the formula for contentment in these troubled times."

The cleric was being evasive. Ahmed tried to approach the subject from different angles, but the mullah kept going around it. "Baba Koushiyar," he finally said, "I would like nothing better than to perform good works, and I do so whenever I can, but I have a sincere concern that doing good works won't resolve. I can't resolve it on my own. I need your guidance. What we're called upon to do is evil. How can evil done in the name of the Imam of Time be justified as a way of bringing about good?"

The mullah shook his head and repeated what he said before. As they talked, Ahmed saw that the cleric avoided looking at him, staring instead at the carpet or the windows. He wondered if he was boring him, but then it hit him: the mullah didn't trust him. He was a member of the Basij, the religious militia. Everyone suspected that one of the roles of a *basiji* was to inform on people. Was the mullah afraid he would report him if he said anything that even hinted at disloyalty? Was Ahmed an agent trying to trip him up? He left the mosque feeling angry with himself that a man like Baba Koushiyar did not trust him.

The election came soon after his visit to the mosque, and it was followed by massive protests in the big cities and reports of shootings, arrests, and disappearances. And for Ahmed, it was followed by more dreams of a cave, and each time a burst of brilliant light deep inside caused him to awaken with a jolt.

"What does this mean?" he wondered.

Before he left for the buses that awaited the militiamen, he visited his mother to tell her that he would be gone for an unknown length of time.

"There's no telling where these protests are heading. Our country could spin out of control."

Amineh kissed him on the forehead. "Whatever you do, my son, don't hurt anyone."

# Chapter 2

Before they left for Tehran, Ahmed and the volunteers from across Golestan were issued black helmets and hard rubber truncheons at the militia headquarters in Gorgan and were assigned to one of dozens of buses. Most of the men on Ahmed's bus were from different towns, young agricultural workers with short dark beards and trim moustaches.

Several of the militiamen from Aliabad boarded Ahmed's bus after he did and followed him, hoping to sit next to him, but he slid into a window seat next to Behrouz. A crop-duster pilot and avid soccer player, he was popular among the paramilitaries for his jokes and the crazy acrobatics he sometimes performed in his airplane. Ahmed had been married to one of his cousins, who died the previous year as a result of an accident. They had remained close friends, but even so, Ahmed never dared to reveal his doubts to him.

Whenever their paths crossed, Behrouz had words of consolation for Ahmed's loss. Shadi had suffered from a severe form of epilepsy, but at times she refused to take medicine that kept it under control. She would do this over Ahmed's protests because her illness sometimes brought about experiences of such extraordinary joy that they made her feel like she was "wrapped in the arms of the divine," as she used to tell him. But one day, after she had not taken the medicine for more than a month, she suffered a grand mal seizure while descending a steep concrete stairwell in downtown Aliabad. She fell forward, striking her head on a sharp corner at the bottom, and died a few days later from the injury.

They spent a few minutes recalling fond memories of her, and after a long silence, Behrouz tapped his truncheon against the palm of his hand. He glanced at Ahmed. "Tell me the truth. Do you think you could hit someone with this?"

Ahmed shrugged.

Behrouz hit his palm with it, making a smacking sound. "Do you know what I said to them at headquarters? I said to them, 'Wouldn't it be better for you to make use of my talent as a pilot? Let me fly over the protesters and drop pamphlets that warn them of hellfire if they don't go home!'"

"What did they say?"

"One of them said, 'They don't have crop dusters in Tehran.' Then another one handed me this truncheon and said, 'Drop this on their heads.'"

Behrouz continued the patter for another hour before settling in for the long nighttime drive. Ahmed fought off sleep by leaning his forehead against the window and watching the road lights flash by. The lights were bright streaks and made him think of the "cave dream," as he now called it. It was always the same dream, except that each time there was more detail. In a recent dream, he had to climb a slope covered with broken rocks before reaching the cave entrance. In another, there were trees on one side of the opening. He wondered about the light. Maybe the explanation for it was prosaic: Someone was inside the cave with a flashlight who thought he was an intruder and frightened him by flashing the light in his eyes. He recalled a video about spelunkers with lamps built into their helmets. But dreams were never prosaic. The last time he had the dream, the light seemed more a translucent glow, brilliant in the center, yet not blinding. What was the meaning?

He resisted going to sleep out of fear of having the dream again, but the late hour, the drone of the bus, and the zipping lights soon lulled him into sleep. And once again he was in the cave; once again he was fearful as he stepped into the darkness; once again the brilliant light appeared, and he was startled into awakening.

He looked around the bus. The interior was dark, the motor was humming. Behrouz was asleep, everyone was asleep. The lights along the road continued to flash by. They were bright like the glow of the cave. "O cave," he groaned. "What do you want? Why don't you leave me alone?"

The bus arrived in Tehran in the early morning and stopped in front of a barracks near Niloufar Square. The words "Islamic Republic of Iran" were inscribed on the arch over the entrance to a courtyard that was filled with motorcycles. The barracks were a single-story building, laid out in a way that made Ahmed think it had once been a school. Instead of desks, the rooms were lined with military bunks. In the wide hallway were lockers, and on a bulletin board various notices were tacked, among them a list of "brotherings," as one of the commanders called it. Each Golestan militiaman was paired with a local *basiji*.

Ahmed heard his name called. A stocky man, older than most of the militiamen, motioned to him. He was shorter than Ahmed, gruff, with a salt-and-pepper beard, the leader of a squadron of ten motorcycles.

"I am Reza," he said without extending his hand when Ahmed came up to him. "You will ride with me. You will do everything I do, and you will do everything I tell you to do. Is that understood, bumpkin?"

Ahmed nodded. He was irked at being called a bumpkin, but kept it to himself.

"You have a few hours to relax and catch up on sleep," Reza continued. "Go find a bunk and stretch out. You need to be sharp when we go out. Do you understand me, bumpkin?"

"Yes, I understand."

When it was early afternoon, the entire barracks assembled in the prayer room. The room was packed. Most of the men wore street clothes and held black helmets and black truncheons at their sides. Some of the local militiamen also wore side arms.

After leading prayers, an older mullah, thin, with a sparse beard and a scholarly air, stepped onto the dais. He wore the garb of a cleric: a flowing tan tunic over a collarless white shirt buttoned at the neck. His turban was black, the symbol of descent from the bloodline of Muhammad. His voice shrill, he spoke into a microphone: "My greetings are first to Imam of Time,

16

the one whom all beings on earth and in heaven love without end. My greetings are then to all those who are preparing for his appearance, for they are those who await the rising of the sun. Our beloved Imam, the pure one who mirrors God's soul, the perfect human, the inheritor of all prophets from Adam to the last, our beloved Prophet Muhammad, may peace be upon him. The Imam of Time will fill the world with justice the same way the world is now filled with injustice."

The mullah surveyed the room, and it seemed for a moment to Ahmed that his gaze singled him out. "I am here to bring you good news, my brothers. Our Supreme Leader, may God inspire him with the greatest wisdom, has assured us that the Imam will soon make his appearance. I can tell you with the utmost confidence that the promise of God for his coming and for the establishment of the peace and justice of an Islamic civilization throughout the entire world will soon be fulfilled."

In a voice that sounded to Ahmed like it verged on hysteria, the mullah listed the portents that were unfolding, proofs that the appearance was at hand. Among the signs of his imminence were the protesters who now flooded the streets of Tehran. "They are the enemies of God, of the Imam, and of the Supreme Leader of our Islamic Republic."

When the mullah was finished, the barracks commander took the microphone. He had close-cropped gray hair, a narrow face, and an angry voice. "Soldiers of Islam," he began. "It is now time for us to perform our duty. Our duty is to defend the Islamic Revolution from its adversaries. Our duty is to hasten the coming of the Imam. You must obey your commanders in all things. Your commanders obey me just as I obey those who command me. And those who command me obey their righteous leaders. And through this chain, we all obey the Supreme Leader, who obeys the Imam. It is he who is infallible, and it is the Infallible One who is calling us to action today."

He denounced the enemies of the Islamic Revolution. It was the Zionists who were causing trouble in Iran. Their agents stirred up the populace against the revolution with false claims that the election was fraudulent.

"We are certain about the results," he went on, "but the people have been duped by these enemies, the same enemies who have promoted immorality in our cities and towns. But we have a word for these enemies, and the word is 'death.'" He shouted slogans that the militiamen repeated while thrusting their fists in the air: "Death to the enemies of God! Death to the Great Satan! Death to the Zionists! Death to enemies of the Revolution! Death to those who hate our beloved Imam and fear his coming!"

Ahmed had heard these slogans at rallies in Golestan, though at those events, people mouthed the words and never got carried away. But with expert cadences, the commander injected intense anger, and the room was swept up in electric rage. Ahmed felt himself being carried away too, and he had to pull himself back by breathing deeply. He glanced to the right and the left. Everywhere he saw angry mouths and inflamed eyes. He closed his eyes. "This isn't Islam," he kept repeating.

By the time the commander was finished, the men were pumped up for action. They jammed their helmets on and rushed to the motorcycles in the courtyard. Ahmed followed Reza and the others of his squadron. Dozens of motorbikes roared to life. Ahmed looked around for Behrouz, but could not see him. He had been assigned to a different squadron, and Ahmed could not tell where he was in the crowd of black helmets.

The burly Reza, his grizzled beard sticking through the helmet strap, jumped on one of the motorcycles and started it up. "Get on behind me, bumpkin, and hold onto the seat strap. These bikes go fast, and if you don't hold on, you're going to fall off and break a lot of bones. Save the breaking of bones for those filthy enemies of God."

Reza zoomed to the head of his squadron and drove through the courtyard entrance. The motorcycles raced into the street and sped through neighborhoods of apartment buildings. With each acceleration, Ahmed was propelled backward, and he had to clench his fingers around the strap to keep from falling. As they sped along the street, he noticed people spitting at them.

At a residential street corner a dozen blocks from the barracks, Reza signaled for the squadron to stop. Other squadrons had stopped at street corners farther up and farther down. Additional militiamen were jumping out of black vans and were forming into small groups on the sidewalks.

Reza tapped Ahmed's leg and pointed ahead of him. "The traitors are up another block, bumpkin, thousands of them on the boulevard. We will stampede them with our motorcycles, and if they don't budge, we get off and start swinging. Hit them hard so they'll never forget what God's punishment is like."

Ahmed's head began to hurt. It was all so unreal, like the worst of nightmares. The day before, he was in the comfortable, predictable world he had always known, and now he was thrown into the middle of chaos. He did not want to be part of it, but he had let himself get dragged into it. He should have had the courage to walk away. Now it was too late.

At Reza's signal, the squadron zoomed down the last remaining block before entering the wide boulevard. At the corner, a dumpster was ablaze, and stones were strewn about. When they turned onto the boulevard, they were faced with an enormous crowd. Ahmed had never seen so many people before, not even at regional soccer matches at the stadium in Gorgan. People filled the boulevard in loose groups from one side to the other and as far as he could see: young men, young women, the middle-aged, even grandmothers and elderly men. They looked no different from people he knew. His mother could have been among them. Many were thrusting their fists in the air while shouting, "Give us back our votes!" or, "Death to the dictator!" Others waved placards with the same slogans. They wore green as the color of protest: headbands, headscarves, wristbands, and T-shirts, all green. Some of the younger women had painted their faces green. Some women wore black chadors, but many were dressed in boutique finery and covered their hair with a loose headscarf.

A hundred feet from the line of protesters, Reza halted the squadron with a hand signal. In unison, the drivers revved their engines, sending out a menacing roar. A block farther up, riot police with plastic shields charged into the crowd from a side street, and it seemed the intention was to isolate the entire block of marchers from the main body that stretched farther up the boulevard. As the riot police bore down on them, the crowd panicked, and many of the protesters rushed for safety behind parked cars while others threw stones at the police. Yet others retreated in the direction of Reza's awaiting motorcycle squadron.

"Crack those hypocrite heads, bumpkin!" Reza shouted over his shoulder as he signaled to the motorbikes to advance on the protesters.

Ahmed saw what was about to happen and tried to jump off, but it was too late. All ten motorcycles dashed into the crowd, and with the exception of Ahmed, both drivers and riders struck anyone they could reach with their clubs.

It turned into a free-for-all. People ducked to avoid the blows. They cheered when two of the motorcycles were knocked over. Young protesters pummeled the riders and set the motorcycles on fire. By then, all of the militiamen had jumped off the motorbikes and were attacking small groups of men and women who had become separated from the main body of protesters. Everywhere he looked, Ahmed saw militiamen beating people while the ones being beaten protected their heads with their hands and arms, pleading to be left alone. Another motorcycle squadron arrived and joined the attack.

As the ferocity unfolded around him, Ahmed became frozen. Not far from him, Reza and four other *basijis* stood over a young man who was lying on the ground. A woman in a chador kneeling next to him pleaded, "Don't hit my son, please don't hit my son! He hasn't done anything wrong. We have a right to protest!"

Reza kicked the man in the side and dashed off with others toward a group of men and women near the sidewalk. As he turned to attack them, he spotted Ahmed and shouted, "What are you doing there dilly-dallying, bumpkin? I told you to do as I do. Give these traitors God's punishment." He pointed to a woman standing alone next to a car parked about twenty feet away. "Start with that whore. Beat the crap out of her!"

The woman stared at Ahmed. She was young, pretty, and terrified. In his entire life, he had never done anything that made anyone fear him, and it tore him to see the fear he was causing her. He wanted to protect her; he wanted to lead her away from danger, but if he took even one step toward her, she would become frightened. He raised his hand in a reassuring way. "I'm not going to hurt you. Run, save yourself!"

They were both distracted for an instant by the sound of gunfire, rapid popping sounds that echoed across the boulevard. The shooting seemed to come from the rooftops. Ahmed searched for a sniper, but he could not detect one. He looked back at the young woman and shouted again, "Run, save yourself!"

Another gunshot rang out, this time from behind him. The bullet hit the woman below her throat, and the impact threw her against the car. She touched the wound and looked in horror at the blood on her fingers. She slid to the asphalt and fell on her back. Several men ran up and dropped to their knees next to her. One of them pressed down where the bullet had struck in a vain effort to stop the blood.

It was a matter of seconds before her head rolled to one side, and it seemed to Ahmed she was looking at him, now with a quizzical look as if to demand why she had been shot. Blood began to spill from her mouth and nose and dripped to the pavement. Her eyes rolled upward.

"Those dirty assassins," one of the men shouted. He shook his fist at Ahmed and screamed, "You steal our votes, and now you steal our lives."

Ahmed felt dizzy. "This is not Islam!" he shouted. He threw his truncheon to the ground. He ripped his helmet off and let it fall to the pavement. "This is not Islam!" he shouted again, looking at various people who crowded nearby. He stumbled backward, shouting, "I am not a part of this. This is not Islam." He kept shouting it to everyone while shaking his head.

People were furious with him because he was with the militia. Several men shoved him, but a young woman, dressed in fashionable clothes and wearing a loose head scarf, stepped up to his defense. "Leave him alone. He's not the one who did it."

Another woman said, "At least one of them has come to his senses. Let him be."

He looked again at the woman bleeding onto the pavement and wished he could have stood in front of her so that the bullet struck him instead of her. Blood now covered the side of her face and pooled on the ground. He heard more gunfire and looked around the boulevard. Several people were crumpled on the pavement. The militiamen were swinging their clubs at people farther up. Clouds of stinging tear-gas mixed with the acrid smoke of burning tires rose a couple of blocks away and spilled in Ahmed's direction. Everywhere there was shouting, screaming, and panic. And again, more gunfire.

He had to get away. He saw people run down a side street and followed them. Some disappeared into apartment buildings; a few jumped into cars and drove off. Halfway down the long block, a woman threw open the entrance to a building and shouted to a group of men and women, "Come this way, hurry!" and shut the door after they ran inside.

He did not know where he was going. He felt dirty, and the only way to cleanse himself was to get as far away as possible. He kept running, but when he reached the first intersection, a group of *basijis* turned the corner. They were young, had stubby black beards, and wore street clothes with shirts hanging out, typical of the toughs who swelled the ranks of the local militia. He turned to run, but they were on him in seconds. Truncheon blows rained down on his shoulders and back. He stumbled to the ground and tried to protect his face and head with his arms, but one of the blows landed on his cheek. One of the militiamen kicked him in the side so hard it felt like his ribs caved in.

"Hit the bastard hard, hit the enemy of the Imam, crack his skull," cried one of them.

They had to be from the barracks. They had to have been in the same prayer room with him an hour before. He did not dare declare himself to be one of them. They would haul him back to the barracks for interrogation, and there was no telling what would happen to him. They did not let up until a motorcycle screeched to a stop right next to them and someone yelled, "Hey, what the hell do you think you're doing?"

Ahmed was relieved when he recognized Behrouz's voice. The militiamen straightened up, and one of them said, "What do you think? We're giving this traitor God's punishment."

"You idiots! You're beating one of your own."

The men looked at each other. One of them said, "He said nothing to us. Where's his helmet? This means he was running away, a deserter."

Behrouz got off the bike. He had an athletic build and a strong voice. "You're mistaken. The Zionist sympathizers knocked him off his bike and overpowered him. They ripped off his helmet and beat him. I rescued him and told him to get to this corner to wait for me so I can take him to a hospital. Now look what you've done. You've hurt him even more."

"Where's his ID then?" one of them said. "I want to see his ID."

Behrouz stepped toward them as if ready to take them all on. "I'm his ID. I'll vouch for him. Shame on you for hurting him. I can assure you that this matter will be brought before your commander if you don't let him go."

The men grumbled insults, and after hesitating, they walked away. Ahmed groaned and sat up.

Behrouz said, "Anything broken?"

"I don't know. Maybe a couple of ribs."

Behrouz grabbed him under the arms to help him to his feet and climbed on the motorcycle. "Get on. We have to get out of here. They might get wise and come back."

Ahmed got on and leaned against Behrouz. He hurt all over and felt weak and wanted to forget everything, but he could not get the chaos of the boulevard out of his head. He could not get the young woman out of his mind. He could see her face as clearly as if she were standing in front of him, first her shock at being shot, then the blood coming out of her mouth and nose, and then her eyes that seemed to plead with him to explain why this had been done to her.

"The dirty bastards," Ahmed said. "I don't care what anyone says, this is not Islam."

The motorcycle hummed. Building after building whizzed by. The farther away they got from the boulevard of death, the cleaner he felt.

# Chapter 3

As the motorcycle rumbled down a residential street lined with tall apartment buildings, Behrouz said over his shoulder, "I saw what happened to the girl. Someone behind you shot her. It wasn't anyone from Golestan. I saw you run, so I grabbed a motorcycle and followed to make sure you were all right."

"I don't want to go back to the barracks," Ahmed said. "I don't want anything more to do with the militia. I just want to go home. Take me to the train station."

Fifteen minutes later, they were at the railway station on the east side of Tehran. Ahmed bought a ticket, and they sat on a bench to wait for the train to depart. His cheek had become swollen and throbbed, and a tooth near the swelling felt loose. He was in pain everywhere, the sharpest in his ribs, and it was difficult to sit straight.

Revolutionary guardsmen were patrolling the station. Ahmed worried they would question him because of his swollen face, but Behrouz kept his black helmet in plain sight and smacked the truncheon against his palm whenever they came near, making it clear he was a *basiji*. The guardsmen stared at them, but left them alone.

"I couldn't hit anybody," Ahmed said.

"Me neither," Behrouz said. "I pretended. There's a way to do it that looks like you're hitting someone, but without touching them. I told people to run and let them get away."

"People were afraid of me," Ahmed said. "Nobody has ever been afraid of me before. It made me feel sick. When the girl was killed, I felt like I had died, too."

He was certain that by evening, he would be listed as missing and the next day tagged as a deserter. Before boarding the train, he told Behrouz to tell their commander that he intended to resign from the militia. "Tell them I will take care of it in Gorgan tomorrow."

The train was soon out of Tehran. He tried to empty his mind of the horrors of the boulevard by watching the countryside flash by. The rhythm of the rails soothed him. When the train slowed into Pishva, a half an hour out of Tehran, the turquoise dome of the mausoleum of Imam Zadeh Jafar, son of one of the twelve Imams, came into view. Ahmed could name all the Imams from memory, starting with Imam Ali, the cousin of Muhammad who married Muhammad's daughter Fatima and began the bloodline of the twelve Imams, the rightful successors to Muhammad. He knew their names ending with the last of the Imams—the Mahdi, the long-awaited Imam of Time.

The pale blue dome made him think of a bus trip his grade school class had made twenty years earlier to visit the mosque of the Imam of Time in Jamkaran. He remembered it as if it had taken place just the day before. There were thirty boys accompanied by a Quran teacher and several chaperones. He remembered the awe he felt when he saw the domes and twin minarets. They had arrived in Jamkaran on a Tuesday evening when the spirit of the Imam was believed to be present. The mosque was always filled that day with worshipers who had come with petitions for the Imam. During the bus ride, the Quran teacher repeated what they had been taught throughout their young lives: The Imam was hidden in a cellar when he was five years old for his safety. The eight previous Imams, all direct descendants of Imam Ali and Fatima, had been assassinated to keep the leadership of Islam out of the hands of the descendants of the holy family. The Imam remained in hiding throughout his life, and he was still in hiding the day Ahmed arrived at the Jamkaran mosque. He was present there in spirit form and guided believers who prayed to him. He would return in physical form one day, and when he did, he would emerge from the sacred well at the mosque. Jesus would return soon after, and together they would defeat the enemies of Islam and bring universal peace and justice to the world.

For Ahmed, it was a heartwarming story. His father, Abdollah, was killed during the Sacred Defense against the invading Iraqis while Ahmed was very young. He now had only vague memories of him, but as he grew up, he had felt his absence.

When he and his schoolmates got off the bus, he uttered a silent prayer for the Imam to come out of the well so he could rush up to him and tell him how much he missed his father and how much he longed for justice in the world. He would pledge then and there to fight for the Imam's cause. He would become a martyr for justice. As they went inside the mosque, he kept saying, "Please come! Please come, O Imam!"

He remembered that the students first performed prostrations between the pillars of the huge prayer room, and from there they were taken to the Well of the Mahdi on one side of a grand courtyard. Ahmed recalled how his heart leaped when he saw it. A rectangular receptacle had been built over the well with slits in the top that allowed people to drop petitions to the Imam. His class had composed a joint petition that they all signed. As the son of a martyr of the Sacred Defense, he was given the honor of dropping it through the slit. He remembered how his hand trembled as he inserted it, saying, "Please come! Please come, O Imam. Please come and bring peace and justice to the world!" He felt disappointment that the Imam didn't emerge, but it was said that if the hidden Imam was pleased with a petition, a cool breeze would come from the well, and Ahmed was certain he felt a slight breeze caress his cheek.

The visit to the Jamkaran mosque made such an impression on him that after returning to Aliabad, he worked hard to memorize much of the Quran. To better understand it, he devoted himself to the study of classical Arabic under the guidance of the Quran teachers at the Aliabad mosque. Over time, he learned how to write Arabic in classical script and earned regional recognition for his achievement. He excelled to such a degree that the clerics recommended he enter the seminary at Qom to pursue religious studies, but he decided against it. He had been raised with the soil under his fingernails, and he often spent hours sitting in fields to watch seeds germinate. "If you want proof of God's power, all you need to do is watch a seed become a plant," he used to say. Rather than becoming a cleric, he wanted more than anything to be an agronomist, and by joining the Golestan militia, he was given tuition-free entry to the Agricultural University of Gorgan.

As the train left the Pishva station and the mausoleum of Imam Zadeh Jafar disappeared in the distance, Ahmed felt throbbing pain build up in his cheek. He saw the swelling in his reflection in the window. He rolled up his sleeves and inspected the bruises on his forearms. They were deep purple with yellow blotches around them. His shoulders hurt. He was sure he would find bruises there, too. And on his rib cage. He felt stabbing pain where he had been kicked. The bruises were ugly, and people in the coach stared at him. He wanted to tell them his story; he wanted to tell them about the murder of the young woman; he wanted to shout to them about the injustice that was breaking out everywhere, that it wasn't true Islam. But he remained silent.

The train went east to Garmsar and veered north through the pass over the mountains toward Saria. After Saria, it was two hours to Gorgan. Before reaching Saria, he dozed off, and after a string of dreams of people running and screaming, he dreamed again of the cave, but this time it was different. The young woman was in the dream with him, and when they were near the cave, she looked at him and became frightened of him, just as she was frightened of him on the boulevard before she was shot. Then she was lying on the ground, staring at him with blood pouring from her nose and mouth. He climbed the loose rocks to the cave entrance. As he had dreamed so many times before, he saw the light, brilliant but not blinding. It made him afraid, and he backed away, but unlike previous dreams, it came rushing at him. He struggled to push it away, but it enveloped him and jolted him into awakening.

It took him a few seconds to remember he was on the train. People in the coach were looking at him, some amused, others with blank stares, and he didn't know what to make of it. Had he been thrashing out in his dream, or screaming?

A taxi took him from the Gorgan train station to Aliabad and left him in front of his mother's home, which consisted of several rooms above the cloth store. Amineh gasped when she saw him. She cupped his face in her hands. "My poor Ahmed," she said as she broke into tears. "What have they done to you?"

She sat him down on the sofa and ran to prepare a cold compress. While he held it to his cheek, he told her everything. She shook her head and wept when he described the shooting of the girl.

"We heard of people being killed. Everyone in Aliabad is talking about it. This is a portent, a sign of the Imam's coming. I have this certainty in me that he's about to appear."

"Mother, all my life I have been raised to love Islam, but what I saw wasn't Islam. I'm confused. I don't know what to think anymore."

He took off his shirt. Amineh broke into tears again when she saw the bruises. "Were they wild animals who attacked you? Only vicious animals would do something like this."

She prepared a balm of healing oils and applied it to the bruise. She fetched a length of black cloth that was cut into a wide strip and wound it around his chest. It was warm and tight and made him feel better.

Ahmed stretched out on the sofa and contemplated the portrait hanging on the wall of Imam Ali, the first cousin of Muhammad and the father of Hasan and Hossein. He had never visited a home in Aliabad that did not have an image of Ali with a green turban highlighting a manly face, the eyes half-open. His eyes were always enhanced with eye shadow, giving him an air of sensual spirituality. Often, there was a hint of a halo in the background. Ahmed wondered why it could not be like it was with Prophet Muhammad and Imams Ali, Hasan, and Hossein. "Theirs was the real Islam. How I wish I could know their Islam, the true Islam."

His mother warmed a bowl of stew for him. She sat next to him on the sofa so he could lean against her to relieve the pain in his side while he ate. As he ate, he told her about his talk with Baba Koushiyar, that he wanted to share his doubts with him and seek his guidance. "He didn't trust me and didn't answer my questions. I think it was because I was a member of the militia."

"Go to him again. Show him what happened to you. I think he'll trust you now."

The next day, he went to the mosque. After reciting Quran verses and performing sets of prostrations, he asked to speak with Baba Koushiyar.

The cleric was startled when he saw Ahmed. The swelling on his cheek had gone down, but the bruise remained. "What happened to you, Ahmed?"

"I need to speak with you, Baba, in private."

"Come this way then."

Ahmed followed him to a small office. On one side were shelves lined with books with gilded spines, a desk with a computer monitor, and a swivel chair, but on the other side was an open area with a large floral rug covering the floor and thick cushions propped against the wall. An oversized portrait of the Supreme Leader was on the wall along with another of Ayatollah Khomeini. The mullah gestured for him to sit against one of the cushions.

Ahmed sat down with difficulty. As an explanation, he rolled up his sleeves to display the bruises on his arms. He unbuttoned his shirt to show the tight wrap his mother had applied around his chest. "I'm black and blue all over."

He told the cleric everything, not leaving out any detail or any thought that had come to him or any emotion he had felt. When it came to the shooting of the young woman and other demonstrators, the mullah closed his eyes and shook his head. "There were reports about this in the foreign media."

Ahmed became heated. "This is not Islam, Baba. This isn't right! The Imam of Time is goodness. What they do is evil, and they say they do it to bring about his reappearance. How can they justify doing evil to bring about good?"

The cleric sighed. "You're right, there is no justification for any of this. People who understand what's right and what's wrong don't behave like this."

Ahmed repeated what he had tried to tell him weeks before.

"We've strayed from the Islam of Prophet Muhammad and Imam Ali. How I wish I could know the pure Islam of those days."

He pointed to the bookshelves. "You're learned in these matters, Baba. Please, please, give me guidance."

The mullah broke into a chuckle. He leaned forward and touched the bruise on Ahmed's cheek. "It looks like you've already learned what you want to know."

Ahmed tried to absorb what the cleric said. For a moment, he wondered if he was mocking him. "There's something else," Ahmed said. He told him about the recurring dream. As he spoke, the mullah looked down at the rug. At one point, he squeezed his eyes together and kept them shut. Ahmed wondered if he had made a mistake by talking about the dream. It was a stupid, boring dream. He was taking up the mullah's time. At any moment, Baba Koushiyar was going to glance at the wall clock or break into a yawn.

He kept talking about the dream. After he described how he would become frightened by the light and would run from the cave, the cleric opened his eyes. "Tell me more about the light, my dear Ahmed."

"When I first had the dream, I thought that someone was in the cave and that I was an intruder. Whoever it was shined a flashlight in my face to scare me away. But as I continued to have the dream, the light became different. It was translucent and brilliant in the center, but it wasn't blinding."

"Did it move?"

"Only once, yesterday, when I was on the train coming back from Tehran. The light rushed toward me, and I fought it off."

"When you went up to the cave, did you see trees?"

"A few, yes, on one side. Everything else was rocky."

The mullah's eyes became moist. He took off his glasses and dabbed his eyes with a handkerchief.

Ahmed became concerned. "Are you all right, Baba? I'm imposing on you. Perhaps I should leave."

"No, no, I'm fine." The mullah fell silent for a moment. "I know of a cave that matches what you described."

Ahmed brightened. "Where?"

"About half an hour from here. I have an open schedule for the next few hours. If you want, I can take you there, and we'll find out if it's what you saw in your dream."

The mullah owned an older black Paykan with bad suspension. He drove on the highway part of the way, turning onto a road going through the small town of Kordabad and continuing over a bridge to Zarringol, a village nestled in a fold of the Alborz Mountains. He parked where the road ended and a narrow trail up a canyon began. They followed the trail through dense trees until they reached a creek bed. The more they walked, the more Ahmed's rib cage ached, but he ignored the pain. With each step, he became more determined to find the cave. After hiking for fifteen minutes, they reached a steep slope covered with loose rocks. Above the slope was a sheer cliff. At the base of the cliff was a cave. To one side were three tall pine trees with thick branches.

"That's it! That's what I saw in my dream."

He scrambled up the loose rocks, but after going up a dozen yards, he became alarmed. The same fear he felt in his dreams swept over him. He looked back. Baba Koushiyar was still at the bottom, leaning against a boulder.

"Aren't you coming with me?"

"Whatever for? It's your dream. Go on up. I'll wait for you here."

Ahmed continued up the slope, slipping several times on loose stones. When he was in front of the cave entrance, he looked down the slope. Baba Koushiyar now appeared no bigger than the tip of his thumb. The mullah made a shooing motion for him to keep going. The entrance was narrow, forcing him to slide in sideways, but it opened up wider inside. Shafts of sunlight beaming through the entrance lit up the ground, but farther inside, it was total blackness. He shuffled his feet to avoid tripping and dragged his hand on the rough stone wall to guide himself. As in the dream, he dreaded going in deeper, but he felt the same compulsion to find out what was in there. Maybe there was no light. It was just a silly dream that meant nothing at all.

When he was twenty paces inside, he was startled by a light that appeared in front of him, first tiny like a star. With each second, it became larger and more brilliant, yet it didn't illuminate the cave.

"Who's there? What do you want of me?" he demanded as he backed against the wall. The light flared bigger and brighter. It did not float toward him as it had in the dream, but kept expanding so that it seemed it would encompass him. He struggled to keep it away. He felt panic rising from his chest into his head. He must be insane, first to have such dreams and then to go into this dark place. He was sure he heard a voice, but he couldn't make out the words. He backed up a few paces and turned to run toward the shaft of sunlight that came through the entrance. He squeezed between the narrow walls and scrambled down the slope, sliding several times on the loose rocks before reaching the bottom.

Baba Koushiyar was still leaning against the boulder. "Baba, I saw a light," Ahmed said, unable to contain his panic. "I must be going mad. It's one thing to have a dream, but it's another to see something like this when you're not in a dream. I think I was hallucinating. I'm sure I heard a voice. The light spoke to me."

"What makes you think it was a hallucination? You're wide awake."

"Whatever it was, it frightened me."

The mullah became stern. "You came to me with your dreams and your questions. Maybe you're afraid of getting answers? You must go back. If you don't, you may never have the opportunity again."

Ahmed took a deep breath and got a grip on himself. "You're right. I'm behaving like a child."

He climbed back up the slope. He took one last look at Baba Koushiyar way down below and slid through the cave opening. It was as dark as before. Maybe nothing was there. It was just his mind playing tricks on him. He had been having dreams of a light in a cave, so now that he went into a cave, his mind conjured up the light. That had to be the explanation. He went deep into the cave, shuffling his feet as before to keep from stumbling, and ran his fingers along the craggy wall as a guide.

When he was twenty paces inside, the light appeared again, at first as a dim glow, but it quickly flared. It was the same luminance as before, brilliant yet not blinding. He fell to his knees and raised his arms to the luminance.

His voice trembled. "Who are you?"

There was no answer.

"O light, what do you want of me?"

The cave was silent.

"I have dreamed of this, and I've had questions that I can't find answers for. Can you help me? Is that why I'm here? Will you help me to understand?"

Again, there was silence.

Ahmed said, "Who are you?"

After a moment, a voice said, "I am you, and you are me."

It was a voice unlike any that he had ever heard. He couldn't tell if it came from outside of him or inside, but it was clear and distinct: "I am you, and you are me."

He was surprised that he was no longer frightened. "O light, I don't understand what you mean. I want to know. I want to understand because there is so much that I don't understand. All of these things that have been happening are so confusing. Please, can you help me understand?"

Upon those words, the light expanded, encompassing him. He didn't fight it as he had done before, but surrendered to it. As he did, a feeling of joy unlike anything he had ever experienced swept over him.

After a moment in the embrace of the light, his head began to spin, and it seemed that the ground dissolved from under him. He reached out to steady himself, but he couldn't find anything to grab hold of. The light was gone. His body was in the midst of rushing air, and he was sure he was falling, as if from an airplane in the darkness of the night. The blackness was so total that he became fearful again. He was having a nightmare, but with his eyes wide open. Colorful lights flashed and disappeared just as quickly. Roars and whistles and grinding sounds assailed him.

And then he was wet, soaking wet. He was immersed in water, warm water. It wasn't a dream. There was no question about it.

He was underwater, and he had to hold his breath. He kicked his legs and stroked his arms to swim up. When he broke the surface, he reached out and felt a protruding stone. It was craggy like the wall of the cave and allowed him to take a firm hold to keep from sinking.

He looked around him. "Where am I?"

## Chapter 4

Ahmed looked up at a circle of light a dozen yards above him. Had he been deceived by the light? Were the dreams warnings?

He worried he was beyond help, but he shouted anyway. "Baba, help me! I've fallen into a well!"

His voice needed to reach outside the cave, and Baba Koushiyar was still a hundred yards down below. He kept yelling at the top of his lungs until at last a head appeared in the circular light. He could see a turban in silhouette against the light. "Baba," he shouted, "Am I ever glad to see you! Find a rope. Help me out of here."

A rope soon tumbled down, and the end splashed near him. He grabbed it and tugged. The rope felt frayed, but it seemed firm enough to hold his weight. He went hand over hand up the rope, but he also felt himself being pulled up and had to brace his feet against the side of the well to keep from swinging into it. As he ascended, the circle of light grew bigger and brighter.

When he neared the top, the light blinded him. He grabbed the rim of the well and pulled himself over. He scrambled to his feet and struggled to open his eyes. Above was a blue sky. Where was the cave? How could he be outside in the blazing sun?

A dozen men wearing turbans and long, dirty robes were staring at him. Behind them were camels with bulky loads strapped high. The camels, some with their necks lowered, were staring at him, too.

A burly man with a red turban and an unkempt beard waved a sword at him. He bellowed in Arabic, "What were you doing in that well?"

Though he understood, Ahmed replied in Persian, "Who are you? Where is Baba Koushiyar?"

The man turned to the other men and said with a gruff laugh, "He speaks Persian! He's from the land of the Persians! It's not enough for them to attack Arabs. Now they have to come and poison our wells with their stinking bodies!"

Ahmed stared at them, blinking against the sunlight. It took him a moment to think of words in Arabic. He said, "I was in a cave. I don't know how I got into the well."

The man with the red turban had a round, sweaty face and rotten teeth. He demanded, "Where is your caravan, Persian?"

"I don't know what you're talking about. I'm not part of any caravan. I'm from Aliabad. I came here with Baba Koushiyar."

"Persians don't come here except that they are slaves. Who is your master, Persian?"

"Nobody owns me," Ahmed said, bewildered and indignant. He looked around, searching for Baba Koushiyar. He did not recognize the surroundings. They were at the edge of a palm grove, and beyond the grove was an expanse of brown desert.

His heart beat faster when the man raised his sword as if taking aim. He brought the sword close to Ahmed's face and tapped the bruise on his cheek with the flat of the blade. The blade touched the top button on his soaked shirt and tapped against the wet trousers. The burly turned to the men around him and said, "This is what women wear in the harem." The men laughed.

Ahmed thought about running, but he didn't know where to go. Nothing was familiar. Aliabad was an agricultural province with rich farmlands stretching out from the foothills of the Alborz Mountains. He looked around at the palm trees and the bleak stretches of sand. Nothing like it existed in Golestan. The nearest desert he knew of was on the other side of the mountains in Semnan province. How could he escape? He was on foot. These people had camels, and they looked every bit as capable of violence as the *basijis*. He feigned indifference to the sword and demanded, "Who are you?"

The Arab ignored him. He pointed his sword at Ahmed's

shirt and trousers. "Take them off, and the shoes too." When he hesitated, the man raised his sword.

He stripped down to his underwear, exposing the bruises on his arms and shoulders and the black cloth his mother had wrapped around his chest. The Arab held up the trousers and shoes and showed them around. The men broke into guffaws.

"What is your name, Persian?" the man said.

"Ahmed."

"That is an Arab name, not a Persian name."

"I am Persian, and my name is Ahmed."

The Arab said, "I am Abdullah, son of Masud of the Kalbi tribe." He turned to his companions. "Let it be known to all that Ahmed the Persian is my slave."

Abdullah sheathed his sword and scrutinized the bruises on Ahmed's shoulders. He tugged on the long cloth around his rib cage until it loosened and unwound it. The bruises were still fresh and dark.

"What do you think he will fetch in Yathrib?" Abdullah said, looking at one of the men next to him. "Two hundred dirhams?"

The man had a thin face, a long beard, and a dirty, white turban. "Two hundred? Not with those bruises."

"He will heal by the time we get to Yathrib, unless I have to beat him." He glared at Ahmed. "You will do as I tell you. If you don't, I will put a ring in your nose and lead you like a camel. Do you understand me, slave?"

He carried Ahmed's clothes and shoes to one of the camels. He wound them into a ball, and after stuffing them into a saddlebag, he pulled out a long, brown garment and a pair of sandals. The garment was filthy, and the sandals worn.

"Put these on, slave."

After he dressed, Abdullah threw him the black cloth that had been wrapped around his chest. "Put his on your head or the sun will cook your Persian brain."

Ahmed stared at the various turbans. They were of different colors, mostly black or dirty white. Some, like Abdullah's, were red, others green, but they were all wrapped the same way, with the tail end hanging loose or draped over the shoulder. With the fingers of one hand, he pressed the end of the fabric to the side of his temple, and with the other hand, wound the long cloth around the top of his head. After it was wrapped, he tucked the trailing end in so it would not unravel. The cloth smelled of the balm his mother had spread over the bruise, and it made him long for home.

The men watched with amusement, and when he was done, they broke into side-splitting laughter. He didn't have a mirror, but from the reaction, it was clear he had not done it right.

"He's a jester," one of the men said, "Say he's a jester from the court of Khosrow. He'll fetch you four hundred dirhams, Abdullah, that's what he'll go for."

"The Jews will pay more than that if he can climb date trees," said another.

Ahmed prayed the authorities would show up to put an end to the indignity. He had heard that Arabs still practiced slavery, but how could they get away with it here in his own country? He couldn't be very far from home. Surely the Revolutionary Guard would intervene, or the army. He would even be relieved if a squadron of *basijis* drove up on motorcycles.

Abdullah clapped his hands and shouted something that Ahmed didn't understand. Soon, a boy ran up carrying a wooden neck shackle with a length of iron links attached. The boy clamped the shackle around Ahmed's neck.

"Put him with the others," Abdullah commanded.

He resisted, but the boy pulled hard on the chain, causing the shackle to dig into his neck. He had no choice except to follow. It was a long caravan with about a hundred camels packed high. Some of the camels were kneeling, and they groaned as he was led past them.

The caravan was readying to move out. Camels snorted and pulled against their harnesses when their handlers made them stand. One of the drivers kicked a stubborn camel in the flank, and it jumped up.

Trailing the last of the camels were horsemen guarding four dusty men who were also in neck shackles. The men stood in a line, hooked together by chains. Two of them were of Hindu appearance; the others appeared to be Arabs, one with gray hair sticking out from under his turban. The other was about Ahmed's age. The guards watched while the boy secured the chain of Ahmed's neck shackle to the shackle of the younger Arab.

"Don't fall behind or they'll beat us all," the younger Arab said while the boy attached the chains.

Ahmed said, "What's your name?

"I am Masruq, son of Fuqaym. And you?"

"Ahmed . . . My father was Abdollah, a martyr of the Sacred Defense."

"Where are you from?"

"Aliabad."

"Where's that?"

Ahmed was perplexed. How could he not know? Aliabad had the distinction of taking its name from Imam Ali. He gave more familiar place names, but Masruq didn't recognize any of them, not even when he mentioned Tehran.

The caravan leaders shouted to move out. Ahmed trudged behind the other captives, the chains of the shackles swinging with each step. He fell behind several times, causing the chain linked to Masruq's neck shackle to tighten, resulting in a string of curses from the other captives.

He looked in every direction to get his bearings, but he didn't see anything familiar: not a road, not a power line, not a fence. No airplanes were flying overhead, nor were trains or trucks sounding in the distance. At every opportunity, he questioned Masruq about their location, but he got nowhere. The man didn't know any of the names and places he mentioned, and Ahmed didn't recognize any of the places Masruq named.

"I heard them say you got robbed and were thrown down the well, and now you don't remember anything. Look at your head. You can't even remember how to wrap your turban."

"I've never worn one before."

Without breaking stride, Masruq showed him how to wrap it the right way. After a half-dozen attempts, Ahmed got it right.

After dusk, the caravan stopped at a small oasis with a clutch of thin palm trees that leaned to one side. The camel drivers formed the caravan into a tight circle next to a well. The captives were separated and put to work, still with the neck shackle on and the chain dangling. Ahmed was kept under the watchful eye of a guard while he set up tents, drew water from the well, and gathered firewood. Once the work was done, a guard gave him a handful of dates to eat and forced him to sit on the bare ground with the other captives. Only Masruq spoke to him. The older Arab was withdrawn; the Hindus didn't speak anything but their own language and were mistrustful and silent.

Ahmed was struck by the fact that the caravan had not once stopped during the day for prayer. After the camp was set up and Abdullah and the other cameleers settled around campfires, he was anticipating the call to prayer, but it didn't come. He had always been dutiful and prayed the requisite times a day, though not always at the prescribed time.

No matter what, he had to pray. Night had fallen, and the evening prayers had to be performed. The shackles made it awkward, but he was able to stand erect on his knees. Using water from a water skin, he went through the ritual cleansing and prayer movements, starting by reciting the opening lines of the Quran. Some of the cameleers turned from their campfires to look at him. The other captives stared.

When he was finished, Masruq said, "So, you are a follower of Muhammad's religion?"

Ahmed was surprised. "Isn't everyone?"

"I pray to al-Uzza and al-Lat to intercede for me with Allah, as do many people. Tell me about Muhammad's religion," said Masruq.

Ahmed explained the doctrines and recited the declaration of faith: There is but one God and Muhammad is His Messenger. "If you obey the Quran and follow the teachings of Prophet Muhammad, then you will find a place in paradise."

"I hear that Muhammad frees slaves when they convert. Do you think he will free me if I convert?"

Ahmed felt like he had just been hit on the head. Earlier in the day, Masruq told him they were going to be sold at the slave market of an oasis called Yathrib. It seemed he had heard the name before, but he couldn't remember anything about it. Now everything came together in a rush, yet he couldn't believe what it meant: Yathrib was the original name of Medina, the City of the Prophet. Masruq said he prayed to al-Uzza and al-Lat. Ahmed remembered that they were the names of goddesses the Meccans worshiped. Masruq had just spoken of Muhammad in the present tense.

He looked around at the rough people who had taken him captive. The amber light from their campfires flickered on their craggy faces and on the beasts of burden crouched nearby. Was he now—somehow—back in the days of the Messenger of God? How could it be? Such a thing was not possible, yet how else could everything he had experienced since coming out of the well be explained?

He asked Masruq questions at a rapid clip: "Who is the Supreme Leader of Iran? Who is the king of Saudi Arabia? Who is the king of Jordan? Who is the president of Syria?"

"You say strange words," Masruq said. "Khosrow is the emperor of Persia, Heraclius is the emperor of the Byzantines, the Negus rules over the Abyssinians, and the Quraysh are the lords of the Hijaz and the custodians of the Kabah."

Ahmed couldn't contain himself. Without waiting for answers, he said in a rush, "Have you ever driven a car, or ridden on a bus or a train? Have you ever flown in an airplane? Have you ever used the Internet? Tell me, what is your favorite television program? What movies have you liked?"

Masruq looked at him wide-eyed. "You say words I've never heard before."

Ahmed was almost delirious with excitement. He told his mother and Baba Koushiyar how much he wished he could experience the true Islam of Muhammad and Ali, and Ali's sons, Hasan and Hossein. Had God listened to him and granted his prayer? He pinched himself to make sure he was not dreaming.

"What year is it?"

"That depends. By whose reckoning?"

"How long has the Messenger of God been in Yathrib?"

Masruq scratched his scraggy beard. "I started hearing about him five years ago when he left Mecca."

Ahmed couldn't hold it in any longer. He cried out, *"Allahu Akbar!* Truly, God is the greatest. He can do all things!"

He had trouble falling asleep. All he could think about was that soon he would be near the Messenger of God. A miracle had happened: the miracle of the cave and the light that had enveloped him. It was the light of God that had embraced him. Perhaps he would have the chance to go to the mosque and hear the Messenger of God preach, to hear with his own ears the words of the most perfect man who had ever existed. How could he not be the most perfect man when he was chosen by God Almighty to bring the divine will to mankind? Ahmed thought of the Imam of Time. Muhammad prophesied that he would appear one day to bring about the peace and justice of true Islam to the entire world. Muhammad's perfection would then be the world's perfection. The Imam of Time would complete the perfection.

At dawn, he was eager to get going. When the guards separated the captives to put them to work preparing for the departure, he rushed in to help break down tents, reload baggage camels, and fill water skins. With a cheerful smile, he asked to be placed at the head of the captives. During the march, he walked at a rapid pace despite the digging of the shackles into his neck and the protests of the other captives strung out behind him. When he reached the head of the caravan, he said to Abdullah, who was atop his camel. "What's holding you up, O Master? Faster, faster!"

He kept it up day after day to the point that Abdullah, growing annoyed by his pestering, said, "Truly, I have never seen anyone so eager to be sold as a slave."

In the camps at night, he showed Masruq how to perform the ritual cleansing and taught him some of the verses believers recited during prayer. The Hindus looked on with scorn, but the older captive, Hamid, showed interest. Ahmed invited him to join in the prayers.

Over the previous days, he had learned that Masruq and Hamid were shepherds taken captive by Bedouin raiders. The raiders grabbed their herd of goats and sold the shepherds to an agent of Abdullah, who turned them over to him when his caravan, laden with Indian spices, went through Jeddah. The Hindus were the surviving crewmen of a trader vessel that sank in a storm off Jeddah and were enslaved when no one wanted to shelter them. Another agent of Abdullah acquired them. When they were not despondent, the Hindus were angry and rebellious, but the whips of the captors brought them back to despondency.

And he, Ahmed, son of Abdollah of the town of Aliabad in the province of Golestan, had been robbed and thrown down a well and made a slave by his rescuers. That was the story that circulated in the caravan. It was good enough for him. Who would believe the truth?

There had to be a purpose to it all. He kept hearing the voice in the cave: "I am you, and you are me."

He said to Masruq, "What do you think it would mean if I said to you, 'I am you, and you are me?'"

"It means we're both slaves."

Ahmed was a slave all right, but as he settled in for the night on the hard ground, he thought that he had to be the happiest slave on earth. Lying on his back, he gazed at the blaze of stars. The Creator of the vast universe chose a final messenger to explain creation and convey his will to his creatures. The name of the messenger was Muhammad, son of Abdullah.

Muhammad, son of Abdullah, was in Yathrib, the City of the Prophet, and the caravan would be there on the morrow!

# Chapter 5

Mountains and valleys and more mountains and valleys, all brown, barren, and boring. To break the monotony, the camel drivers often broke out in cameleer songs with improvised lyrics that caused laughter. Even the dullish camels seemed to perk up with the singing. When the caravan came near the valley of Yathrib, Ahmed was relieved that the long march was almost over. Word had spread through the column of their approach, but he saw nothing more than expanses of an ancient lava field on both sides of the caravan trail.

"There's Uhud," Abdullah shouted from atop his camel, pointing with his whip to a high mountain that soon came into view. "We're near the door to Yathrib."

They plodded onto a wide plain at the foot of the mountain that began where the lava field ended. They crossed a dry riverbed and headed deep into the valley. Soon they skirted fields where men with scythes were harvesting barley. They went by a fortified compound with two-story stone houses with flat roofs. Outside the walls of the compound was a modest village of low adobe shacks.

The trail led through a convergence of date plantations, and Ahmed soon lost count of the palm trees. When they came out on the other side, there were more and larger villages and high forts with battlements. The trail widened into a road bustling with turbaned men in long robes and women in various colorful garments, some with faces covered, some not. Everywhere, camels and donkeys moaned under heavy burdens. Excited boys commanded small herds of goats.

With each weary step, Ahmed rejoiced that he was closer to the Prophet. He walked alongside Abdullah's camel, his chain clinking and his neck sore from the shackle. Despite his lowly status, he kept up a conversation with Abdullah, who admitted to being so bored out of his mind by the long journey that he enjoyed talking even with a slave. He complained that, except for the Jewish territory, Yathrib had become a tedious stop. "With your prophet, no more wine, no more wine taverns, no more singing girls. At least with the Jews, you can still get wine." He admitted a fondness for fermented honey and crude barley beer. He described how it was fermented in a hollowed-out tree stump. "By God, is it potent. I got drunk on it once while riding and fell off my camel. Broke an arm."

The deeper they went into the valley, the more talkative he became. He spoke about an agreement with Muhammad that allowed him to enter for trade, but it required him to report everything he saw and heard during his travels.

"You will meet with him then?" said Ahmed, hoping he could talk Abdullah into bringing him along.

"That's not the first order of business. First comes the market, and that includes the slave market. I don't often take a liking to my slaves, but for you, I will get you a good master. I know a Jew who uses slaves in his date groves. Jews make good masters as long as you work hard and without complaint. Do you know how to climb trees?"

While the caravan passed through groves, Ahmed observed men high up in the palm trees cutting fronds laden with dates and lowering them by rope to the ground. If they could do it, he could do it.

"I can learn, but not with a shackle around my neck."

"Don't worry about it. No one runs away from his master. It means a severe beating once you're caught, or worse. So you won't be forced to wear a shackle and chain. They are for when you're in transport."

As they neared the center of the valley, Abdullah informed him that they would soon pass in front of Muhammad's mosque, but the caravan would not stop. Ahmed wished it would move along faster. He prayed that he would get a glimpse of Muhammad, or perhaps of one of his companions. Maybe even Imam Ali.

The caravan went between more palm groves and another village. Men, women, and children rushed to the roadside and waved at them.

"What do you bring us, O fat merchant?" one of the women said to Abdullah.

Abdullah gave her a lecherous smile, revealing his decayed teeth. "We bring spices from Yemen and fine silks from India. The spices to make your food tasty and the silks to hide your pretty faces from our evil gaze."

Some of the women giggled and tightened the veil covering their faces. The children kept waving and running alongside until the long column was far down the road.

As they entered yet another palm grove, Abdullah said to Ahmed, "We are now in the territory of the Najjars. I heard that your prophet's great-grandmother was of the Najjars, so that's why he built his prayer place here."

Soon, they were in what appeared to be more of a town than a village since it was denser than any of the villages Ahmed had seen so far. Many of the buildings were cubic, with two stories and flat roofs; some were even three stories. Alleys lined with one-story adobe homes went off in every direction. Screaming children played in mud puddles; donkeys brayed; women carrying water pots on their heads chattered as they went up the alleys and disappeared into courtyards. The caravan soon entered the open area of a busy marketplace lined on all sides with food and artisan booths shaded by palm-branch awnings. Scores of people milled in front of the stalls, haggling over merchandise. As the caravan passed through, people shouted questions about the cargo.

"All that your purses desire, my friends," Abdullah shouted back from atop his camel. "We're going to the Qaynuqa market, so you can join us there."

The caravan continued on. A hundred yards beyond the market was a long, high mud wall with architectural flourishes along the top. Abdullah raised his hand, and the caravan came to a halt. He pointed to the entrance and said to Ahmed, "That's the prayer place of your Messenger of God."

Ahmed's heart raced with excitement. The entrance was about four paces wide. The doors were thrown open, allowing Ahmed to see a large courtyard filled with men sitting cross-legged on the ground, their backs to the entrance. They wore white garments and turbans and were facing a platform. On one side was a group of women, also dressed in white. Seated in a pulpit chair on the platform was a middle-aged man wearing a white robe and a white turban. He was speaking to the assembly, but Ahmed could not hear what he was saying. Was that the Messenger of God? He wanted to go into the mosque to hear him speak and get close to him, but the shackle that bound him to Masruq and the other captives reminded him it was not possible.

"Isn't that the Messenger of God?" said Ahmed.

"I don't know if he's the Messenger of God, but that is Muhammad," said Abdullah.

Ahmed pleaded with him to allow him at least to go up to the entrance and linger there a moment.

"No. You're a slave. If Muhammad buys you, then you can linger there all you want."

He whacked the flank of his camel. The caravan resumed its stride and was soon beyond the mosque. An hour later, the long line of camels reached the slope of Upper Yathrib. Perched at the top was an imposing fortress that Ahmed learned had once belonged to a Jewish tribe, but it was now the property of Muhammad's followers. The fortress soared four stories, and Ahmed had to crane his neck to see the battlements. The caravan trudged up a wide path cut into the side of the slope, leading to a busy market in front of the fortress.

The market was even bigger than the one in the Najjar territory. It was lined with an assortment of artisan and food booths, and chatty crowds milled in front of them. Some of the stalls leaned against the fortress wall and were shaded with thick layers of palm fronds. Others extended from adobe buildings that surrounded the plaza. Turbaned men in small groups shouted greetings to Abdullah, who called out to them by name. The camels, exhausted from the long march, groaned and snapped their teeth as the cameleers brought them to the ground, forelegs folding first, followed by the hind legs.

For the next hour, Ahmed strained to lift bulky merchandise from the backs of the camels—sacks of spices, bolts of fabric, flasks of perfume wrapped in leather, and miscellaneous armaments such as shields, spearheads, arrowheads, and daggers. The merchant-cameleers uncovered their wares next to their camels, and buyers crowded around to inspect and haggle over prices. After the unloading, guards ordered Ahmed and the other captives into a low adobe hut and locked the door. Inside, it was dark and hot. The dirt floor smelled of manure and urine. The only light came through cracks in the door.

Ahmed and Masruq took turns peering through the cracks. "When they're done with the merchandise, they'll come for us," Masruq said. "I've heard about these things. The buyers will do something to get the slaves angry so that they spit or throw a punch. That lowers their value, so they get a better deal."

Ahmed couldn't see the Hindus in the near darkness, but he heard them weeping. He felt sorry for them. They were so far from home and in a strange land, destined to never see their loved ones again.

An hour later, the door swung open, filling the hut with blinding light. Abdullah called out all the men except for Ahmed. The door was locked again. Ahmed peered through a crack, straining to see their fate.

The four captives, squinting against the bright light, were made to stand next to one of the camels and told to strip. A group of men examined them from a distance, pointing to them and talking among themselves. Several approached, squeezing the men's biceps and forearms and inspecting their teeth. One of the buyers was rough with the taller of the Hindus, pushing him on the shoulder when he pulled his arm away. The Hindu tried to butt him with his forehead, but Abdullah stepped between them.

They were too far away for Ahmed to hear, but he saw that

the captives were being auctioned. Hands were raised; Abdullah pointed to people; more hands went up. The first to go was Masruq after one of the men shook out coins from a leather bag, and Abdullah counted them. The Hindus were led away together, leaving the older shepherd. After more haggling, someone handed Abdullah a bag of coins and led him away, too.

The sale over, Abdullah walked toward the hut and unlocked the door.

"Come out, I have to talk to you."

Ahmed stooped to get under the lintel and stepped into the sunlight, causing him to squeeze his eyes against the brightness.

"I have good news for you," Abdullah said. "I've got someone coming to look at you, Nabbash, a Jew from the Qurayzas. The Jews own big date plantations four miles from here. He's got a Persian slave that I sold him years ago, and I know he's pleased with him. He even made him a foreman. Just don't go telling him you are a believer in Muhammad because then he won't want you. This deal is good for me and for you. As far as masters go, you could get a lot worse."

Once locked back in the hut, Ahmed sat against a wall and pondered his fate. How could he hide his belief in the Messenger of God? He believed in him with a pure heart. When he prayed, he recited verses God had transmitted to Muhammad. How could he deny him? How could he hide that he wanted more than anything to be in his presence? He thought about the irony of a Jew owning him and almost burst out laughing. The Islamic Republic had turned hatred of Israel into a state religion, but though its leaders engaged in a constant diatribe against the Jews, Ahmed had never felt hatred for Jews, or anyone else for that matter. He had never known a Jew, so how could he form an opinion about them?

Three hours later, the door swung open. At Abdullah's command, Ahmed stepped out. The sun was now behind the fortress, and the light was not as blinding as before. An older man with a long, graying beard, whom Ahmed presumed to be Nabbash, was with Abdullah. Behind them, mounted on horses, were several turbaned men. Nabbash's clothes were different than what he had seen so far. He wore a tunic of fine fabric tightened at the waist with a sash. His turban was covered by a brown shawl that draped over his shoulders. He had an air of dignity, and his demeanor reminded Ahmed of Baba Koushiyar.

In a showman's voice, Abdullah pointed to Ahmed. "This is Ahmed the Persian."

Nabbash looked him over with a quick glance. "That's an unusual name for a Persian."

"That's the name I gave him," Abdullah said.

"Where in Persia are you from, Ahmed?" Nabbash said.

Ahmed was uncertain how to reply. Abdullah had already wrapped him in a lie. He had to be careful not to say too much. One question could lead to another, and if he revealed the truth, they would think he was a madman. "Golestan," he said.

"I'm not familiar with the name," Nabbash said.

Ahmed thought of an ancient landmark that would be known in the century of the Prophet. "It's near the Great Wall of Alexander."

Nabbash nodded. "I once visited it, a long time ago, on a commercial trip." He stared at Ahmed for a moment and said, "Come forward."

Ahmed stepped up to him.

"Show me your hands."

Nabbash took one of his hands and examined the palm. "Your hands are strong, but I see no calluses." He pushed up Ahmed's sleeve, exposing the bruises inflicted on him by the *basijis*. They were faded but still visible. Nabbash touched the bruise on his cheek. He turned and glared at Abdullah.

Abdullah interjected, "They're not from me! We found him in a well. I think he was robbed and thrown in it. I pulled him out. He doesn't remember how he got there."

"What do you know about the cultivation and harvesting of dates?" Nabbash asked.

Ahmed liked his eyes. They were the kind of eyes that inspired trust. He said, "I saw people working in trees when we got to Yathrib. I didn't see them doing anything that I couldn't learn to do."

"You should have seen him on the trail," Abdullah boomed. "He did the work of ten people!"

Abdullah and Nabbash stepped away and talked in a low voice. Several minutes later, the Jew handed Abdullah a small leather bag. Abdullah stuffed it into his tunic without examining the contents. He signaled to one of the caravan boys, who ran up and removed the shackle from Ahmed's neck. His neck felt raw where the wood had rubbed against his skin.

Abdullah beamed. "I will count myself blessed by the gods if I find more Ahmeds in wells!" He patted Ahmed on the shoulder. "Next time I'm in Yathrib, I'll look you up to see how you're doing."

He turned and walked away, soon disappearing amid a group of merchants near the entrance of the fortress.

Nabbash pointed to one of the horsemen. "You will ride with Salman."

# Chapter 6

As Nabbash turned around to get on his horse, Ahmed remained as if stuck in place. Salman? Abdullah had spoken
of a Persian slave. Could the Salman on the horse be the famed
Salman al-Farisi? Ahmed remembered seeing photographs of a
great mausoleum in Iraq named in honor of Salman. In the history books, it was said that he was a slave of the Jews in Yathrib,
but he purchased his freedom, joined Muhammad, and became
a companion of note. Shi'as and Sunnis revered him. So did the
Sufis and the Ismaelis. Ahmed remembered what he had been
taught about him, that he was tall and broad-shouldered, a very
strong man, and the man on the horse was of imposing build.

Ahmed snapped out of it when Nabbash said from the saddle,
"What is holding you up, Ahmed?"

Feeling timid, he stepped up to the horse. Salman was looking
at him with a steady gaze, neither smiling nor frowning. A blanket was the saddle, and there was room on the croup. Without a
word, Salman extended a flexed arm to Ahmed as a grip to hoist
himself onto the horse.

As the group plodded down the road, Nabbash carried on
a conversation about the date harvest with another horseman
dressed as he was, with a patterned shawl covering his turban
that draped over his shoulders. Salman and the other horsemen
rode behind in silence.

Riding with Salman made Ahmed think of Behrouz. Less than
two weeks before, he was on a motorcycle with Behrouz, zipping
through the streets of Tehran, fleeing from the violence of the
boulevard. Now he was on a horse with Salman al-Farisi on a

dusty road surrounded by crop fields and date plantations. It all seemed so unreal, yet it was real. It was not quite like being in the presence of the Messenger of God, but riding with one of his famous companions was the next best thing. He felt like shouting *"Allahu Akbar!"* but he remembered Abdullah's warning against revealing himself as a Muslim.

An hour later, after they had gone through a date plantation, Salman broke away from the group and headed the horse toward a village. As they rode away, Nabbash turned in his saddle and said, "Teach him what he needs to know, Salman."

Salman stopped in front of a clutch of low adobe huts. It was getting dark. Several men stepped out of one of the huts and stared at Ahmed. Farther up, children playing in a clearing next to a palm grove stopped to look at him, too.

He followed Salman into one of the huts, a room three yards in depth and width. Ahmed was taller than average, but Salman was even taller, and his head nearly reached the ceiling. The hut had an uneven dirt floor. A leather mattress was pushed up against a wall. Serving as a table was a wide section of a palm trunk. Ahmed thought of his home back in Aliabad. It was modest by Iranian standards, but it was a palace compared to the humble mud shack.

A boy came in after them and set an earthen bowl full of dates on the table. He left and came back minutes later with a lit oil lamp, holding his hand in front of the flame as he walked. Salman hung it from a hook extending from the wall, allowing the flame to cast a feeble light on the room.

Before going out the door, Salman spoke for the first time. He smiled, but the tone struck Ahmed as odd. "Welcome to the land of the Qurayza Jews, Ahmed of Golestan."

The leather mattress was stuffed with palm fibers. It was uneven, but it felt better than the bare ground he had been sleeping on. As he lay on the mattress, he pinched himself to make sure he was not in some strange dream. Certain it was real, he decided that when there could be no mistake about Salman's identity, he would admit his belief to him and ask him about getting to Muhammad.

Ahmed was agile and strong and learned to climb trees with the aid of a looped rope after watching how the slaves and the Jewish workers did it. Soon, he was sitting at the top of trees, cutting fronds that were heavy with ripe dates and lowering them to the ground by rope. The plantation was huge, and he went up and down two dozen trees every day. It was exhausting work from dawn to dusk with breaks for meals of bread dipped in black seed oil or olive oil and an occasional stew of lamb or camel meat. He performed the rituals of prayer in the privacy of his hut and beseeched God to bring about the day when he could join Muhammad.

Nabbash, wearing a work tunic and a black turban, ventured into the plantation several times to inspect the irrigation system and talk to the foremen. On one occasion, while Ahmed was high above in a tree with another slave, Nabbash arrived, accompanied by two men and three young women. The men were dressed for work while the women wore finer garments. The tallest was of striking appearance.

The slave with Ahmed said, "The tall one is the daughter of Nabbash—Maryam, a real beauty." Ahmed glanced at the other treetops and at the workers on the ground. Everyone was staring at her.

The group was soon gone. As they were leaving, Nabbash's daughter spotted Salman climbing down a nearby tree. In a confident voice, she said, "Salman, there is good news coming to you soon."

"May God's blessings be upon you, O daughter of Nabbash," Salman replied.

Ahmed continued to hide his faith until the day he became convinced it was the real Salman al-Farisi. This came about after asking him about his captivity. Ahmed already knew some of the historical details because he had studied them in his religious training. Salman confirmed them: He was in Syria trying to reach Mecca so that he could join Muhammad, but he was taken into captivity through treachery. He had placed his trust in some horse traders who said they were going to Mecca. He paid them to bring him there, but they betrayed him at a Jewish oasis north of Yathrib. The horse traders claimed Salman was their slave and sold him to a Jew. It didn't matter that it was untrue. Salman had no proof that he was not a slave, and their word prevailed. He identified one of the horse traders as the caravan master Abdullah, the same Abdullah who pulled Ahmed out of the well.

"He told me he sold you to Nabbash," said Ahmed, growing more joyful by the minute as it became indisputable that he was in the company of the famed companion of Muhammad.

"Satan is the father of liars like him," Salman said. "He didn't sell me to Nabbash. The Jew who bought me was an evil man who kept me and other slaves in chains. He sold me to his cousin here in the Jewish territory of Yathrib, and the cousin later sold me to Nabbash. That's how I came to be here, and it was about the same time that the Messenger of God arrived in Yathrib after he fled Mecca."

"Tell me about the Prophet," said Ahmed.

"To see him is to see the face of God. To hear him is to hear the voice of God. To know him is to know with certainty that God is merciful to man."

Ahmed was confident that he could now reveal his faith. He knew much of the Quran by heart and recited some verses. He told Salman that he had dreamed of living the Islam of the Prophet, and the dream brought him to Yathrib. He omitted saying anything about his past other than that he didn't remember it. He described his joy when he glimpsed through the mosque gate when Abdullah's caravan passed through the Najjar territory, and how torn he was that he couldn't go inside and be in the presence of Muhammad.

The next morning, he joined Salman for the dawn prayer and was surprised to see three of the other slaves. They met in Salman's adobe, which was bigger than Ahmed's. They also congregated there during the day and late evening in order to observe the obligatory prayers. Ahmed taught them several verses they didn't know.

As time went on, he lost the awe he had felt with Salman. Instead of the larger-than-life character whom he had learned about in his youth, Salman became three-dimensional, a man like any other who sweated while he labored on the plantation and prayed at every opportunity.

Salman never questioned him about how he knew so much of the Quran, but would smile at his recitals and compliment him on his intonation and pacing. To impress Salman further, Ahmed showed him that he knew how to write in the script of the period, an ability he had learned from the religious scholars at the Aliabad mosque. Using a stick, he traced out the words of the opening lines of the Quran in the sand.

Salman was pleased. "O Ahmed of Golestan," he said with the hint of irony he now used when he addressed Ahmed that way, "You don't remember how you got into the well, and you tell me you don't recall your life before then, but it's good enough that you remember the Quran and how to write the holy words. If you weren't a slave and the Prophet knew of your ability, he would surely make you one of his scribes."

A month after his arrival, Ahmed was stunned when Salman told him he was about to be given his freedom. That must have been the good news the daughter of Nabbash alluded to when she called out to him while they were at work in the trees.

"I didn't want to say anything until it was certain," Salman said.

Two years earlier, Nabbash had agreed to a freedom contract after Salman pleaded with him that his enslavement had been a gross injustice committed by evil people who had taken his money and lied about him. Nabbash agreed to release him, but he was obligated to purchase his freedom. The price he imposed was for Salman to plant three hundred palm saplings in a patch of cleared land next to the plantation where Ahmed worked, but Salman had to procure the plants. When Muhammad learned of this, he urged believers to donate them.

"They came to plant them," Salman said. "Even the Messenger of God came and planted some with his own hands."

He took Ahmed to the site. The planting started two years earlier, and those early saplings were already flourishing. The most recent saplings still had fresh straw spread around the base, and little fronds shot upward from them. Salman pointed to the ones that Muhammad put in the ground.

"He dug the holes with his bare hands and said a prayer over them."

"When was this?"

"Just last month."

Ahmed felt crushed. The saplings were a mere thousand yards from Nabbash's village on the other side of the date groves. The last of the plantings took place not long after he was bought at the slave market and was already at work in the trees. If he had known about Muhammad's presence, he would have run to the site, if only to catch a glimpse of him.

"You've been visiting him then?"

"Yes, but not so much of late because of the harvest. There's always work to do, but there's less work in the winter and summer. So yes, I go to the mosque. Do you know that I was one of the first to greet him when he came to Yathrib? He stopped at Quba, not far from here, and stayed there for a few weeks before moving on to the Najjar territory. I knew my previous master would beat me for this, but I left the plantation without permission and brought the Messenger of God a bag of dates."

"Will you bring me with you the next time you go to the mosque?"

Salman shook his head. "I doubt Nabbash would allow it. He's not pleased that I'm leaving, and I know that as a Jew, he has no fondness for the Prophet. But he's a fair-minded man, as you've seen. Maybe later, during winter, when the work slows down. I'll see if I can arrange it with him."

A week later, Salman was gone. Before leaving, he said, "I will tell the Messenger of God about you, Ahmed."

# Chapter 7

Not long after Salman gained his freedom, Ahmed saw the daughter of Nabbash again. It was on a day that he had to lead two donkeys pulling a cartload of dates to a sorting warehouse in the center of the village. The village began where the rows of palm trees ended, bordered by the lowly huts of the slaves. It expanded from there for a hundred yards through mazes of narrow lanes. Deeper in were homes of better and taller construction. The village abutted the high stone wall of a compound that rose above the village, the home of Nabbash and his extended family. Near the center of the village was an open area that served as a market and processing area for the date harvest.

Ahmed guided and sometimes tugged the donkeys through the tight lanes to the warehouse, a building that was open on the sides and had a roof of palm branches. In its shade, women with scarves tied under their chins were sorting piles of dates.

When he arrived at the warehouse, one of the workers, a woman who was given to flirting with him, put her hands on her hips and said, "More work for us, Ahmed. And you think maybe we don't have enough work already?"

He was well-liked. He worked hard and showed a keen interest in date cultivation. He learned all he could, including identifying the different varieties grown in Yathrib from their distinctive pits. Nabbash, he learned, specialized in growing three varieties. His inquisitiveness helped him keep his mind off his captivity and the fact that Muhammad was still as distant as ever, even though his mosque was but five miles away. Everywhere he went, he asked people about their work. His curiosity and his knowledge of agronomy endeared him to the workers. When he asked to be given a tour of the irrigation system, one of the foremen was pleased to show him the ingenious sluicing methods used to direct water where it was needed.

When Ahmed stopped the donkeys at the warehouse, two lanky teenagers came out to help him unload the cart. Most often, the cargo consisted of entire fronds laden with dates. This time, the cargo was of loose dates in sacks, each weighing more than a hundred pounds. He helped the teenagers lug the bags into the warehouse, open them, and smooth out the dates for the women to sort. These tasks completed, he helped them move batches of dates that needed more ripening into the sunlight outside the warehouse.

On this day, the daughter of Nabbash was among the workers. Like the others, she was wearing a colorful blouse and a long skirt, her hair covered by a red kerchief tied under her chin. The women were on their knees, picking out the dates that were spread before them, separating them into piles of ripe, unripe, and spoiled. He spotted Nabbash's daughter as he carried the loads into the warehouse, but when he looked at her, she averted her eyes. He thought there was something familiar about her face that he had noted when he first saw her in the palm grove, but he couldn't place it. As he turned the donkeys and the cart around to leave, he saw that she was looking at him. Her gaze lingered on him and ended when he pulled the donkeys onto the path back to the plantation.

Several days later, while he was at work in a section of the plantation farthest from the village, he saw her again. She was with another woman walking along the wide cart path that he used to haul loads of date fronds. He was climbing down a tree, and they approached him just as he reached the bottom.

"O Ahmed, may we speak with you?" she said.

He leaned against the tree while the women sat on the trunk of a fallen palm tree a few paces away. A breeze rustled the canopy of palm leaves above them.

The woman with her was older. "I am Maryam, daughter of Nabbash," she said. "This is my cousin, Esther."

Her cousin was silent, staring at the ground. Ahmed guessed she was there as a chaperone. He felt uncomfortable. It had to be unusual for the daughter of a slave owner to visit one of her father's slaves, and it put him in a difficult position.

Maryam sensed his unease. "What brings me to speak with you, O Ahmed, is that there is something different about you. There is a mystery surrounding you."

He shrugged. "I'm the slave of your father. That makes me different because most of the people I work with aren't slaves, but are men of your tribe."

He wondered about her purpose for being there. His mind told him there was nothing duplicitous about her, nor was there anything haughty in her demeanor or her voice. Her father struck him as a righteous man, so how could his daughter be anything but righteous? He waited for her to continue.

"It is said that you were found in a well. Will you permit me to ask how you got there?"

He hesitated a moment, wondering how to answer without making up a story. "That is something I can't explain. I was not there, and then I was."

"They say that you were robbed and thrown down the well."

"If they say that, maybe they know more than I know."

"Where were you before you were in the well?"

He couldn't reveal the truth. How could she understand when even he couldn't understand? Moments before struggling in water deep in a well, he was in a different world. All he had to do for that world to come back was to close his eyes, and he would have visions of Aliabad, his late wife Shadi, his mother and friends, and the violence in the streets of Tehran. That world ended the moment he opened his eyes.

"I was in a cave. There was a brilliant light, and then I was in the well."

A look of surprise appeared on her face, and in an instant, he realized what had seemed familiar about her: Her face was like that of the girl in Tehran who was shot. Her face had the same shape, and her eyes and mouth were similar, but her face was not marred by fear. A gleam appeared in her eyes.

She leaned forward. "Please, tell me about the light."

He told her about the recurring dream of the cave, that each time he had the dream, he went into the cave and encountered the light. He always became fearful, and the fear always woke him up. "I found the cave that I had seen in my dreams, and I went in. The brilliant light appeared to me, just as it had in the dream. I was frightened and said, 'Who are you? What do you want of me?' I kept repeating it, and I heard a voice that came from the light."

"What did you hear? Oh, tell me, please. What did it say?" Maryam said in a rush.

"It said, 'I am you, and you are me.'"

"And you were not dreaming?"

"No, it was as real as our being here is real. And after that, I was in the well."

She said, "I have had such dreams of a brilliant light, but not in a cave. I awaken as you awoke from your dreams, but not in fear. It fills me with such joy that I rush to the window and look up at the sky and say, 'O the light, O the light!'" She raised her arms as she spoke, as if reliving those moments. "Am I being silly?"

"No, no, of course not," said Ahmed.

"In these dreams, I've never heard a voice. It's a bright, warming light, and it fills me with joy."

Ahmed said, "I don't know what was meant when the voice said, 'I am you, and you are me.' What do you think it means, O daughter of Nabbash?"

Maryam was silent for a moment and shook her head. "I don't know." She turned to her cousin. "What do you think, Esther? What does it mean?"

The woman raised her hands upward and looked to the heavens. "It's a riddle. Only God knows."

"I'll make inquiries about it among the rabbis," said Maryam. "They're learned. Perhaps they'll be able to say what it means."

A week later, she returned to the palm grove, again accompanied by her cousin. Ahmed was at the top of a tree, lowering a heavy date frond to the ground when he saw them coming. The sun broke through in patches, and as they walked from shade into splashes of sunlight, the women appeared as shimmering gold. Ahmed climbed down and stood at a slave's distance from them, leaning his back against the palm trunk. As before, the women sat on the trunk of a fallen palm tree.

The daughter of Nabbash smiled and extended her hand. "There is no need for you to stand, O Ahmed. If anything, it is I who should stand in your presence."

Ahmed sat down cross-legged next to a pile of fronds and waited for her to speak.

The daughter of Nabbash said, "I have spoken with Rabbi Sallim, an elder who is very wise, about your dreams and your experience in the cave and also about the words you heard."

"I'm moved that you would do so," said Ahmed.

"The rabbi first commented on the dream of seeing a brilliant light. He told me that scholars know of these, as many of them experience such dreams. They interpret them to mean a longing for understanding, a longing for truth."

"And the fear? When one wakes up afraid? What is the explanation? Does one fear what is longed for?"

"It depends on whether what is sought confirms what is already believed, or unsettles what is believed. In the latter case, the result is fear. That's how he explained it."

"With you, it's joy."

"Yes," she said. "What I've always believed comes to me in such dreams." She was silent for a moment before saying, "When I told the rabbi that you found the cave of which you had dreamed and that the light appeared and spoke to you, he wept."

Ahmed was stirred. "Why would it cause him to weep?"

"He said, 'Only someone with an important destiny will experience the light as he has.' That's what he told me. He said he wept because we have brought a man with an important destiny among us as a slave."

"And what of the words that were spoken, the riddle?"

"It is for you to understand the words, and when you have understood, you will be on the path that God has chosen for you. That is what he told me."

Ahmed looked up at the trees and listened for a moment to the chatting of workers in nearby trees. It was a strange path, indeed, that led him here, and he again wondered if it was a dream and nothing more.

Maryam said, "What is it that you seek, O Ahmed?"

"I don't know how I got to your land, but I know that I wanted to experience true Islam, and that's what brought me here. It was my fervent desire. It was deep and sincere, so here I am, but I'm still far from the experience I seek. The true Islam is the Islam of the Messenger of God, who is the most perfect servant of God. I long to be with him."

"I want to help you. I want you to experience the true Islam of your prophet."

Her cousin became upset. "How can you say such a thing? That man is no good. A dog howling at the moon is more a servant of God than Muhammad. Look what he has done to the Jews. Look what he did to the Qaynuqas and the Nadirs. What he did to them sooner or later he will do to us."

Maryam turned to her cousin. "We each have our own path. You can't tell people what truth is, they must experience it for themselves. How else can they understand?"

She said to Ahmed. "I pledge my help. I want you to experience what you seek. I will speak to my father about you."

A week later, Ahmed was in the village delivering a cartload of dates to the sorting warehouse. As he was carrying date fronds into the building, a servant of Nabbash came to him and said, "Come with me."

Ahmed followed the servant up a dusty path that led to the home of Nabbash. They went through corridors to a large room with plastered walls decorated with tapestries. Large rugs with intricate designs covered the stone floor. Nabbash, Maryam, and an elderly man with a long beard were reclining on thick cushions and rose to greet him.

Ahmed became self-conscious in the rich surroundings. Nabbash and the elderly man were wearing fine tunics and shawls that covered their turbans and draped their shoulders, whereas he was wearing a sweaty turban, a coarse garment tightened at the waist by a grimy rope, and sandals that were covered with dust from the day's labor.

Nabbash glanced at his daughter, then at Ahmed. "I have summoned you here to inform you that it's your good fortune I have a strong-willed daughter. Because of her and the advice of Rabbi Sallim," he said, nodding in the direction of the elderly man, "I have decided to give you your freedom. You are no longer the property of Nabbash of the tribe of the Qurayzas, but are free from now on to do as you please."

Maryam smiled warmly, as did the elderly rabbi, who nodded in approval.

Nabbash continued, "It's my preference that you remain with us to learn our religion and become as we are. You have proven to be a knowledgeable and able worker, and no one has come forward with a reason to speak ill of you. I would be pleased to take you on as a foreman, but I've learned from my daughter that you want to be with the one who calls himself the Messenger of God. If that's your desire, then go your way, and may peace and prosperity be your rewards in life."

The elderly rabbi added, "We ask only one thing of you, and that is to be an ambassador of goodwill for us to Muhammad. You know from being with us that we aren't bad people. Speak well to him about us."

Maryam said, "That's what we asked of Salman, and he agreed to do so."

Ahmed felt like he had lost all of his weight, and he could now move from one place to another without even walking. It was a moment before he was able to say, "How could anyone say anything but good about you?"

"I have been in contact with Salman," Nabbash said. "He will arrive tomorrow and take you to the Najjar territory."

# Chapter 8

Salman arrived in the late morning riding high on a tawny camel with a second camel trailing on a rope.

"Mount up, O Ahmed of Golestan," he said with the hint of irony that he always used with Ahmed's place of origin.

Ahmed's meager possessions were bagged in a sheet of leather tied with a rope. With the bag slung over his shoulder, he walked up to the towering camel. He had never ridden a camel, but he had heard the words used to make them kneel. He repeated the commands, but the camel remained standing.

Salman laughed. "Didn't they teach you in Golestan about camels?"

"Horses, not camels," Ahmed said.

As if by magic, Salman brought the camel he was riding to the ground. He slid off and showed Ahmed how to kneel the other camel. After Ahmed climbed onto the saddle, Salman showed him how to tug upward on the rein and dig his heel into the camel's flank to make it get to its feet.

After they set off down the road, Salman said, "One of the companions will give you a room near the mosque. As soon as you've arranged your belongings, we'll go to the mosque."

Ahmed said, "I can't believe this is happening."

"How do you feel now that you will meet the Messenger of God?"

"Dizzy."

"That's how I felt when I first met him. Wobbly in the knees. You'll get over it. He's the most perfect man ever to exist, but he's a man, not God."

Ahmed tried to imagine how he looked. He had to be of noble bearing with compassionate eyes, but Ahmed found it impossible to visualize him. Though portraits of Imam Ali hung in homes across Iran, depictions of the Prophet were forbidden. He had seen images of Jesus and wondered whether Muhammad resembled him.

When they were beyond Nabbash's plantation, Salman whipped his camel to a fast trot, causing Ahmed's mount to do the same to keep up. Salman roared with laughter when Ahmed clung to the camel for dear life, but by the time they reached Najjar territory, Ahmed was more confident in his ability to ride the camel.

It took less than an hour to reach the sprawling village of the Najjars. Ahmed remembered from his studies why Muhammad had settled there. It was just as Abdullah said when the caravan reached the tribal territory: Muhammad's great-grandmother, Salma, was of the Najjars, so that when he emigrated from Mecca to escape the disbelievers who plotted to kill him, it was natural for him to settle in the territory of his maternal blood relatives.

Ahmed spotted the mosque from a distance. As they got closer, the call to prayer was made, something he had not heard since he was in Aliabad. A slender black man standing atop a platform was making the call in a strong voice that reached across the town. It was the same prayer call he had heard his entire life, except that it did not mention Muhammad's cousin, Imam Ali. The Shi'ite version included Imam Ali, but he understood why the call he just heard did not. The struggle for the leadership of Islam and the split into two major factions was still far in the future.

The closer they got, the louder the prayer call became. "Isn't that Bilal?" Ahmed said, referring to the famed first prayer caller.

"Yes, and we need to hurry," Salman said as he whipped his camel to a trot.

His new lodging was a room that wasn't much larger than the one at the Qurayza plantation, but it was neater and had a window. It was two hundred yards from the mosque on a narrow dirt lane that started at the marketplace. He left his belongings in a corner, and after helping Salman hobble the camels, they hurried through the market to the mosque.

They got there a minute before prayers began and joined a row far at the back of the packed courtyard. A shaded area and the platform that Ahmed had caught a glimpse of months earlier were in the front.

When they entered, everyone was standing and had assumed the initial prayer posture with arms folded across the chest. Ahmed couldn't see much through the crowd except for the back of the head of the prayer leader. He wondered if it was Muhammad himself. Whoever was leading had a strong voice that carried to the far end of the courtyard. Ahmed tried to get a better look by standing on his tiptoes, but that became useless when the kneeling and prostration phase began. He followed through, repeating verses he heard from the prayer leader. He was without a prayer rug and had to prostrate on bare ground, yet each time he touched his forehead to the ground and smelled the dust, he rejoiced that it was the soil and the dust of the very mosque of Muhammad.

When the rounds of prayers were finished, the entire assembly sat on the ground, either cross-legged or on their heels in the camel position. It was mostly men, but a section for women was off to one side, extending from the front of the prayer area. It was separated from the men's section by an open area.

The man who led the prayers climbed onto the platform and sat in an ornate chair with several steps leading up to it. He was of average build with a wide face and a full dark beard. Ahmed leaned toward Salman and whispered, "Is that the Messenger of God?"

"Yes, that's him."

Muhammad said to the congregation, "I'm detaining you today in order to repeat to you words that have been handed down to me by the angel this very morning. I had implored the Lord for guidance about this matter, and God hears us and listens to our pleas."

Muhammad recited a set of eight short verses, causing a wave of joy to pass through the assembly. Ahmed was caught up in the wave as well. God had just revealed his will to mankind through his chosen apostle, and they were honored to be the first to hear the revelation.

Ahmed was even more excited because he already knew the verses by heart, having memorized them in his youth. Muhammad asked for volunteers to test their memory by repeating the verses. Several men stood up, and one after the other recited them, making several minor omissions that Muhammad corrected. When no one else stood up, Ahmed jumped to his feet. "Will you permit me to recite them, O Messenger of God?"

Muhammad said, "I don't recognize you. Who are you?"

"I am Ahmed."

After Muhammad made a motion for him to proceed, he repeated the first seven verses without error, but when he got to the end, he realized that the words of the final verse that he had memorized when he was young were different from what had just been recited. He stopped his recital and looked at Muhammad with embarrassment.

"And the final verse?" said Muhammad.

"I don't remember how you said it, O Messenger of God."

"Repeat it how you think it is, and I'll correct you if you err."

Ahmed repeated the verse he was taught in school. Its meaning flowed from what preceded it.

Muhammad stared at him for a moment. "These are not words that were revealed by God." He repeated the correct verse.

Before Ahmed could sit down, Muhammad said, "Who knows this man?"

Salman said, "I can vouch for him. He is Ahmed of Golestan and a pious believer."

"I've never heard of Golestan," said Muhammad.

"It's in Persia, O Prophet. Ahmed is Persian, like me."

Muhammad looked over the congregation. He recited the set of verses again and repeated the final verse several more times for emphasis. "These are the words of God to his messenger. Recite them as I have recited them to you and in no other way."

He dismissed the congregation and said, "Let Ahmed the Persian come forward."

The crowd flowed around Ahmed on the way out. Some looked at him with a friendly smile, others with curiosity, while others passed him by without a glance.

As the congregation left, Muhammad descended the platform and joined several turbaned men sitting cross-legged on mats of woven palm leaves. Walking to the front, Ahmed felt weak in the knees, and his face was cold and drained of blood. He was thankful Salman was with him. When he reached the group, Muhammad looked up at him, but said nothing. He appeared neither welcoming nor unwelcoming, but Ahmed felt his gaze go right through him.

Salman had not informed him about how to act when meeting with Muhammad. Was he to remain standing, or was he to take a seat among them? He was looking down at Muhammad, who was seated cross-legged with the other men, and he thought it might be taken as rude, but as he bent to seat himself, one of the men next to Muhammad waved him off, "You have not been given permission to be seated with the Prophet. Remain standing."

Muhammad said, "Repeat the last verse the way you said it."

He repeated it the way he had memorized it in his youth.

"These are words that Satan planted on your tongue," Muhammad said. "You must repeat only what comes from God to me, and that way you will not fall into error."

Salman said, "Arabic isn't his language, O Prophet. His command of it is good, but he misses a lot. He misunderstood the recital."

"Where is this Golestan?" said Muhammad.

Ahmed said, "It's far from here, on the caravan trail to the East that ends in China. It's near the Great Wall of Alexander."

Muhammad brightened and turned to his companions. "Haven't I spoken to you of this wall? Behind the wall, the tribes of Gog and Magog are sealed up. When it's breached and the hordes of these barbarians pour through, it will be a sign that the end of time has begun."

Muhammad turned to Ahmed. "Have you seen this wall?"

"I have visited it."

"Is it a wall of ice?"

Ahmed became nervous. He had an experience of it in the future, and he was not certain of Muhammad's idea about it. In his time, the wall was eroded or covered by silt. Archeologists had uncovered a section of it twenty miles north of Aliabad, and he once visited the dig with a school group.

Choosing his words, he said, "At times, there is ice. It was built to stop invaders, that's all I know about it."

"You are far from this Golestan that is near the wall of ice," Muhammad said. "How did you get here?"

"I don't know, O Messenger of God, but I knew of you and wanted more than anything to be with you, and it's that desire that brought me here."

The man who had ordered him to remain standing said, "I remember that Salman made mention of you. You are the one they found in a well." He turned to Muhammad. "The slave trader Abdullah found him in a well and sold him to the Jews, the same Jews who gave Salman his freedom."

Ahmed had focused all his attention on Muhammad, but now he gazed at the other man. He was 30 years younger than Muhammad, though with similar features. His eyes were the most distinctive feature of his face. They were enhanced with dark eyeliner, making Ahmed think of the depictions of Imam Ali that adorned every Iranian home he had ever visited. Was this Ali, Muhammad's first cousin, the father of Hasan and Hossein? The Iranians knew them as the first three Imams, as ancestors of the Imam of Time, whom the ayatollahs believed was about to appear in Iran through the well in Jamkaran.

"They were very kind to me," Ahmed said to Muhammad, remembering the request of the elderly rabbi and Maryam that he speak well of the Qurayza Jews.

The man with the dark eye makeup spat. "They are enemies of God and His messenger."

Muhammad said, "What was your contract with them?"

Ahmed was confused. "I don't know what you mean by contract. I was a slave."

"To purchase your freedom. How much did you have to give them to free you?"

70

"Nothing. I told them that I wanted to experience true Islam, the Islam of the Messenger of God, and that the only way to have such an experience was to be with you at your mosque. Nabbash was my master, and he gave me my freedom. This happened yesterday."

"He speaks the truth," said Salman. "Nabbash contacted me to fetch him, and I did so earlier today and brought him to the mosque."

Muhammad looked around at everyone and smiled, then threw his head back in laughter. He laughed so hard that his belly shook. Everyone around him laughed, too. Wiping away tears, he turned to Salman and said in a bantering tone, "The Jews demanded gold and three hundred palm saplings to free you, and we had to plant the saplings ourselves, yet they let him go for nothing. What does that say about your negotiating skills, eh?"

Salman's face turned red. "It was God's will."

Looking at Ahmed, Muhammad said, "From now on, you are Ahmed al-Golestani. Are you prepared to pledge fealty to God and his messenger?"

"Yes," said Ahmed, his eyes brightening.

Muhammad stretched out his clenched hand. Ahmed fell to his knees and clasped his hands in both of his. He looked at Muhammad's face. Muhammad was smiling at him, and his smile made him feel like he was the most important man in the world. With all the reverence he could muster, he said, "I testify that there is but one God, and I testify that Muhammad is his Messenger, and I testify furthermore that he is the most perfect man who has ever lived."

Except for the man with the dark eye makeup, who seemed dour, the mood of the small group of bearded men became upbeat. Salman was smiling from ear to ear. "He knows how to write."

Muhammad nodded and stood up, and the other men did the same. He pointed to the mats. "Remove them." Salman and another man pulled back several of the mats to expose the bare ground. Muhammad handed Ahmed a stick. "Show me," he said.

In the dust, Ahmed traced out the words of the opening verses of the Quran, seven short verses. He knew he had the words right because Muhammad recited them during the prayer session, and they matched word for word what he had repeated ever since his youth.

Muhammad turned to the man with the eyeliner and said, "What do you say, Ali? Can you read it?"

Upon hearing the name Ali, Ahmed smiled like a man who had just spotted someone famous. So it was Muhammad's cousin, the first Imam! He hoped Ali would say something complimentary, but he shrugged and said, "I can read it. It's correct."

Without further ado, Muhammad and his entourage walked away, leaving Ahmed and Salman alone in the prayer area. As they left the mosque, Ahmed's head was spinning from the shock of speaking with Muhammad and grasping his hand to make the oath of faith.

Salman said, "I think you made a good impression. I could see he liked that you know how to write. He doesn't read or write very well, so he needs a scribe now and then. Don't be surprised if you hear from him."

As they walked through the marketplace and turned onto the alley where Ahmed had left his belongings, Salman said, "Do you know how to use a sword?"

"No, I've never had need of one."

"You will have to learn how to use a sword."

"Why?"

"The Meccans are planning another attack, and they'll be more numerous and aggressive than the last time."

He gave an account of a battle that took place eighteen months earlier at the foot of Mount Uhud at the north end of the valley. Ahmed knew that Muhammad was involved in raids and battles, but he didn't know the details. He was taught that they were necessary for the defense of Islam in the early years when the enemies of God sought to kill the Prophet. He was surprised to learn, therefore, that Muhammad had suffered serious wounds during the battle and was trapped at one point on the slope of Mount Uhud.

"It was God's will that the Meccans didn't press their advantage when he was on the mountain," Salman said. "I was still a slave, and I couldn't leave the plantation to take part in the fight, but when the Meccans come back, I will fight them. We will all have to fight them. That means you, too, Ahmed."

# Chapter 9

Two days after meeting Muhammad, Ahmed got a job as a laborer at a date plantation thanks to a recommendation from Salman. He didn't have any resources and had no choice but to work, a practical matter that he had discussed with Salman. He moved into a dirt-floor room in a village near the plantation. It was two miles from Muhammad's mosque, too far for him to attend daily prayers, but the plantation owner, a polytheist convert who was the sheikh of one of the major tribes of Yathrib, had built a small mosque in the village. A prayer caller roused the entire village at the crack of dawn. But eager to see Muhammad and hear him preach, Ahmed made the trip to his mosque each Friday on foot.

The first sermon he attended was about the importance of demonstrating faith through obedience, and he was surprised to hear Muhammad link the battle Salman had told him about to obeying God's commands. As was his custom when giving sermons, Muhammad wore a white garment and a white turban with the tail hanging down his back. After the prayers and Quran recitations, he mounted the platform and took his place in the pulpit chair. He began by chastising the archers whom he had positioned on a hilltop to repulse cavalry attacks on the flank of his battle formation. Fifty archers were to remain in place no matter what unfolded, but most of them disobeyed when the enemy panicked and ran from the battlefield. This came about when Muhammad's forces broke through the Meccan lines and attacked their camp, grabbing everything as booty. Most of the archers ran from the hill to join in the grab, which created an opening for the Meccan cavalry. The cavalry attacked the hill, killing the archers who had remained faithful to his command, and descended on Muhammad's army from behind. The result of the disobedience of the archers was defeat. "There are among us today some of those who were disobedient. God and His Messenger know who you are, and the companions know who you are, just as you yourselves know who you are."

He recited several Quran verses regarding the incident and added, "Let it be known to all that God and His Messenger have forgiven you because even though you erred through disobedience, you were on the right path. You gave proof of surrender to God by fighting in the cause of God against evil. It just was not sufficient at the moment of great testing—a lapse. God tested your firmness as believers against your thirst for spoils. You were entitled to the spoils as reward for your faithfulness, just as were the others, but you were not patient."

Muhammad stepped down from the pulpit and paced back and forth on the platform, speaking loud enough so that people in the far back of the courtyard could hear.

"You were to blame for this," he continued, "but God allowed the lapse to give some of those who disobeyed the opportunity to attain the martyrdom they desired. For those of you who survived, it serves as a lesson about the importance of obedience to God and His Messenger, and because it was intended as a lesson, God is forgiving of you for your lapse."

Muhammad recited more verses related to the battle. Ahmed was thrilled that he already knew them by heart, but he had never known their context. His religious studies with the scholars in Aliabad focused on memorizing the Quran, understanding the words, and learning how to write them in their classical form, but little attention was ever given to the events that had inspired them. Instead, he was taught the spiritual meanings contained in the verses.

He had not arrived early enough to find a place in the shaded prayer area and was in the middle of the courtyard that broiled with ferocious heat. The turban kept his head cool, but sweat rolled down his stomach and back. His legs ached, and several times he switched from sitting cross-legged to sitting on his knees, but returned to the previous position when people behind him complained that he blocked their view. He was relieved when Muhammad dismissed the assembly.

In the Friday sermon the following week, Muhammad spent two hours denouncing corrupt and unfair business practices. Ahmed was impressed but not surprised by his detailed knowledge of trade, knowing that he spent his early adulthood as a merchant in Mecca. Now, from the pulpit, he went through a list of abuses, including cheating on weights and measures and what he called the sin of the middleman. Standing at the edge of the preacher's platform, he railed against middlemen who made a business of intercepting Bedouin traders on their way to Yathrib to buy up all their goods at a price below market value, then reselling these goods for much more than their worth. Through this tactic, the middlemen ended up monopolizing certain commodities and necessities. They controlled the price.

"The Bedouins end up earning less than they deserve for their worthy efforts, and the believers end up paying more than they can often afford," Muhammad said, shaking his fist in the direction of the Najjar marketplace. He announced in a voice inflamed with indignation that from then on, the buying of merchandise from producers before they reached the market was displeasing to God and was therefore forbidden. "Fear God, and obey God and his Messenger," he concluded.

Each Friday sermon turned on a different theme, and it always began the same way. The moment Muhammad emerged from a room behind the preacher's platform, the sheikh who owned the plantation where Ahmed worked would jump to his feet and say, "People, this is the Messenger of God before you. God has given you honor and glory through him. Give him aid and support, and listen and obey." Muhammad would then step down from the platform to the prayer area to lead the congregation in rounds of prayer before returning to the platform to begin his sermon.

The signs of the end of time were the subject of the sermon on the following Friday. Muhammad began by saying that in the era leading up to the final days before resurrection and judgment before God, the world would witness the coming of the Imam of Time and the return of Jesus. Together, they would bring the peace and justice of Islam to the entire world.

These were prophecies that Ahmed was already familiar with, for he was raised in the belief that the Imam would return through the well at the Jamkaran mosque. Through him, justice would replace injustice. As Muhammad spoke, Ahmed recalled the injustices that had swept across Iran and the massive demonstrations and the brutal repression of which he had been a part. He rejoiced at hearing these same prophecies about the Imam of Time from the mouth of Muhammad himself.

Muhammad scanned the crowd from one side to the other. "If there were but one day left for the world, that day would be lengthened until a man from among my descendants, a man who will come from the people of my household, is sent by God. His name will be the same as my name, and his father's name will be the same as my father's name. He will fill the earth with justice and fairness. The world will not end, therefore, until a man of my household, whose name is the same as mine, holds sway."

The people of his household meant Ali, who married Muhammad's daughter Fatima, and they had two sons. Ahmed looked toward the women's section and wondered if Fatima was among them. She had to be. Where else but among the womenfolk would she be on Friday when her father gave the weekly sermon?

He nudged a man next to him. "Do you know if the daughter of the Messenger of God is among the women?"

The man, thin of face and swarthy of complexion, raised himself up to look. "I think she is on the other side of the women's section in the front, but I can't see her."

Like the men, most of the women were dressed in white. They wore white head coverings, but they were not veiled. When the sermon ended, Muhammad dismissed the congregation. The men and women got up to leave through the main gate, but several women walked toward the preacher's platform.

"That's Fatima," said the thin-faced man, pointing to one of the women, "the first of the three. The second woman I don't know. The third is the Prophet's wife, Aisha."

Ahmed watched Fatima glide up to Ali and a small group that gathered with him on one side of the platform.

Aisha was in her early teens. She stepped onto the platform and disappeared into the room at the back. A few minutes later, she emerged with a toddler in her arms and handed the child to Fatima. The child had to be Hasan, Ahmed thought. Who else could it be but Hasan, the first of Ali's sons? He was stirred by the scene, and his heart was filled with affection for them. It was the holy family of whom he had heard all his life. He wished he could announce himself to them as a believer from a future Persia inspired by Ali, but they would think he had lost his mind.

A month after he began working at the outlying plantation, Ahmed was summoned to the mosque. He was overseeing workers digging a ditch and was covered in dust when Anas, a servant of Muhammad, approached him. "The Messenger of God desires to speak with you," Anas said.

Ahmed brushed himself off and hastened with the servant to the mosque. Anas had come on a horse, and they rode back to the mosque together, covering the distance in the heat of the day in fifteen minutes. He followed the servant to the back of the preacher's platform to the curtain that he had seen Muhammad and others go in and out of. The servant parted it and motioned for him to enter.

Ahmed had not yet gotten over his awe of Muhammad and felt fluttering in his stomach and his knees weakening as he went in. It was a small room with an earthen floor covered by rugs. Muhammad was seated with a small group of men, and everyone looked up at Ahmed when he entered. Two of the men were seated next to Muhammad; the others were across from him.

Muhammad motioned for Ahmed to join them, and after he drew one leg under the other, Muhammad said, "The reason I have summoned you, O Ahmed al-Golestani, is that I want you to accompany these men to their territories to observe the reason for the dispute that they have brought before me."

Muhammad was hunched forward as he explained that the dispute involved water. One of the men owned barley fields and a section of date palms in the highlands. He needed water for his fields and trees, but complained that after rainfall, most of the water flowed downhill, leaving his crops and trees threatened by a lack of water. So he built a dam to retain the water. The other man was the plaintiff. He owned crop fields in the lowlands where the runoff flowed and complained that the highlander's dam deprived him of water for his crops.

Muhammad said to Ahmed, "Go with them and return to me with what you have seen."

Ahmed rode on the back of a camel with the highlander, a big man wearing a garment with vertical green stripes and a black turban, while the plaintiff, a thin man with sharp features and wearing a red turban, trailed behind on another camel. Their properties were more than a mile away, located where the highlands of the east side of the valley dropped fifty feet to the lowlands of the west side. Ahmed inspected the dam and thought it was a logical idea for retaining water. It was solidly constructed, built across a creek bed. An extensive pond had formed behind it. He saw an easy solution: A sluice like the ones on Nabbash's plantation could be built into the retaining wall in such a way that a portion of the water could be released to flow to the lowlands, while holding the rest for use by the highlander. The task then would be to determine a fair apportionment of the water.

Ahmed returned to the mosque with the men and related what he had observed to Muhammad. When the men agreed that Ahmed's solution was reasonable, Muhammad said to them, "Build the sluice." To Ahmed, he said, "Go with them and see that it's done the way you proposed, and return with them when it's finished."

Ahmed returned several days later with the men. After they were seated across from Muhammad, a servant handed Ahmed a vial of ink, a stylus, and two irregular sections of parchment.

Muhammad said, "Take down what I say, O Ahmed."

As Muhammad dictated, Ahmed wrote down the terms of the water-sharing agreement and copied it on the second parchment. Both men put their marks on them, and each man kept a copy after Muhammad put his mark on them as a witness to the agreement.

Before they parted, Muhammad said, "The best of you are the best in sharing, and among the most beloved of people to God on the Day of Resurrection will be those who shared."

Over the next month, Muhammad summoned Ahmed several more times to serve as his agent and scribe. One day, as he was leaving Muhammad's chamber and was walking through the courtyard to the main gate, Ali stopped him. His eyes half closed, his voice brusque and cold, he said, "The Messenger of God wants to have you close by from now on so that he can make greater use of your skills as a scribe. You will be given lodging, and all your needs will be taken care of."

Ali was shorter than Ahmed, with broad shoulders and a full black beard. Every time Ahmed saw him, either from a distance or up close, he felt warmth in his heart for him. He had to restrain himself from throwing his arms around his neck as one would embrace a beloved relative who has not been seen for decades. Yet if the cousin and son-in-law of Muhammad acknowledged him at all, it was with a slight nod of the head. His coolness now made Ahmed feel confused and mortified. Ali seemed displeased to tell him of his new position, as if he was following an order Muhammad had given him, nothing more.

In a humble voice, Ahmed said, "I am the servant of God and His Apostle."

He followed Ali through a door at the back of the mosque that opened on a lane. Set back across the lane was a two-story block house. Two donkeys were tethered to a pole in front, and children were at play in the shade of a palm tree. A shed and a pen with a dozen goats were next to the house.

Ali introduced Ahmed to the owner, Abu Ayyub, who showed him his new accommodations, an attached apartment on one side of the house with a separate entrance. It was modest, but with plastered walls and a stone floor, it was by far the cleanest lodging he had been given so far.

"The Messenger of God wants you to be on call to write down the inspiration that is conveyed to him by the angel," Ali said. "When you are summoned, you are to drop everything and come immediately. You will go in through that door only," he said, pointing to the mosque door they had come out of. "That way, you don't have to waste time going around to the main entrance. Is that understood?"

Ahmed nodded. "What about writing materials? I don't have anything to write with."

"That will be provided," Ali said.

# Chapter 10

After Ali left, Abu Ayyub gave Ahmed a warm smile. "Anyone whom the Messenger of God loves I love."

He was a talkative man with three wives and eleven children. He was missing an eye from a wound, he explained, that he suffered at the Battle of Uhud when a stone slung by "the enemies of God and His Messenger" hit him in the face.

"You don't need eyes to know the truth," he said with a dismissive wave of his hand. "I could do without the other one as well. All you have to do to know the truth is to listen to the words of the Messenger of God."

He boasted that after arriving in Yathrib, Muhammad had stayed at his home until the mosque was built. He scoffed when Ahmed repeated the story about how Muhammad let his camel decide where he should stay.

"It was arranged beforehand," he said as he thrust his chest out. "When his camel stopped in front, I rushed out to bring his saddle and belongings into the house. My family stayed upstairs and prepared meals for him the entire time he remained with us."

He dragged Ahmed inside the house. "This is where the Messenger of God stayed," he beamed, squeezing his blind eye shut and looking at Ahmed with his good eye. He made a sweeping gesture toward the room. "All of the sheikhs and other important people visited him here."

That same evening, just after it turned dark, Ahmed began praying at the mosque. It was always Bilal, the former black slave of one of the Meccan merchants, who made the prayer call from a platform built into a corner of the mosque courtyard with stairs going up to it. The platform was at the same level as the top of the courtyard wall, so that when Bilal stood on it, he could be seen from Abu Ayyub's house. At the evening prayer call, Ahmed, accompanied by Abu Ayyub, joined the stream of believers flowing through the front entrance.

Gripped with emotion, Ahmed said to Abu Ayyub, "This is the next best thing to being in paradise."

Bilal's voice was strong and sonorous, and Ahmed was roused by it every morning at dawn. From the first morning onward, his one-eyed landlord would wait outside for him to put on his garments and turban, and they would walk around to the front entrance and join one of the middle rows in the mosque courtyard. Without fail, it was always Muhammad who led the prayers, recited Quran verses, and spoke to the congregation from the pulpit, sometimes at great length.

Two weeks flew by before Ahmed was called to write down Quran verses. Several times before then, he was summoned to take down contracts or letters. On one occasion, Muhammad dictated a letter to Heraclius, the emperor of the Byzantines, inviting him to Islam and warning him of consequences if he ignored the invitation. Muhammad sealed his letters with a gob of melted red wax that he imprinted with a signet ring bearing his title: "Muhammad, Messenger of God." After writing down Muhammad's words to the emperor, Ahmed melted the end of a stick of red wax under the flame of an oil lamp so that it dripped onto the flap. He let the molten wax pool until it was the size of a large coin. Once the wax cooled, Muhammad held the seal between his fingers and pressed it into the wax. He handed the letter to Ali, who stood nearby, and said, "Instruct the courier to put this into the hands of the ruler of the Christians and to no one other than him, and to report back to me with his response."

Just as Salman predicted, Ahmed lost the feeling of awe that had consumed him during his first meetings with Muhammad. With frequent personal contact, he saw him now as a man among men. He now longed for the honor of taking down revelation rather than contracts and missives. Yet when a servant rushed to summon him to take down "words coming down from heaven," a shock ran through him. He felt weak in the knees once again as he followed the servant through the back entrance to the mosque and down a corridor leading to Muhammad's room. He now wondered if he was worthy enough for the role. He also worried that Muhammad would speak with feverish haste. What if he missed some of God's words?

Just before he went into the room, several of Muhammad's wives came out, their heads covered with scarves but their faces unveiled. Muhammad's youngest wife, Aisha, was still in the room, as was a man who sat in the far corner. Ahmed stood by the door, observing Muhammad. He was lying on a thin leather mattress, muttering with his eyes closed, his thick beard and trim mustache moving with his lips. He was without a turban, and his forehead glistened with sweat even though it was cool in the room.

Before leaving the room, Aisha handed Ahmed a pot of black ink, a stylus, and a long strip of parchment. Ever since he was young, he had heard of Muhammad's experiences when revelations came to him, and now he trembled at being in this small room during a moment of divine communication. He sat in the camel position, using his thigh as a writing platform, and waited. Before long, Muhammad stirred. He opened his eyes, pushed himself up until his back was against the wall. His eyes roamed the room and stopped when he saw Ahmed.

"Are you ready?" Muhammad said.

"Yes, O Messenger of God."

Muhammad began reciting verses. Ahmed wrote as fast as he could. Muhammad kept his eyes fixed on the parchment, and at times slowed until Ahmed finished writing. Ahmed had trouble holding in his joy when he recognized the verses. They were just as he had memorized them in his youth. He could have continued writing even if the dictation stopped, but he paused when he finished each set and waited for Muhammad to resume speaking. At times, Ahmed glanced at him, thinking he might see an angel hovering near him. It was said that he received his revelations from the Angel Gabriel, but Ahmed only saw that Muhammad was watching his scribe's fingers as he hastened to write down the verses.

In the opposite corner of the room, a man of strong build was seated cross-legged. He wore a turban and the usual long robe. When Ahmed entered the room, it was dark, and he couldn't see the man well enough to recognize him. After Muhammad roused and sat up, the man pulled back the curtain separating the room from the preacher's platform. As the sunlight streamed in, he recognized Umar, an important companion of Muhammad, and, as Ahmed knew, a future caliph who would one day direct the conquest of Persia and bring about its submission to Islam.

When Muhammad was finished with the dictation, he said to Ahmed, "Recite!"

Ahmed repeated what he had written, but with token glances at the parchment. He recited the verses the way he had learned them, capturing their rhythm and poetic nuances and conveying the emotion they stirred in him. When his recital was finished, Muhammad looked over at Umar. "Surely, Ahmed has been sent down to us from heaven. What do you think of his recital, Umar?"

Umar nodded, "Good."

Muhammad said, "Have Bilal call for an assembly of the faithful, and when they are gathered, have Ahmed recite God's words just as he recited them to us. Ensure that the people commit them to memory."

Muhammad lay back down on the mattress and closed his eyes. Ahmed followed Umar through the curtain to the preacher's platform. Umar sent someone to find Bilal, who ran up to them several minutes later.

Umar said, "Make the call for the believers to assemble to hear words that God has just revealed to His Messenger."

Bilal scurried up the stairs to the platform at the far end of the courtyard, cupped his hands to his mouth, and in his strong voice called out the command for the faithful to assemble, repeating it in every direction.

Twenty minutes later, the shaded prayer area and the deep courtyard were packed with people sitting cross-legged or on their knees. Muhammad's wives came out of their quarters, led by the girlish Aisha. She was the most spirited of them and walked ahead of the other wives with quick steps to the women's section.

For the first time, Ahmed saw the packed prayer area as Muhammad saw it when he preached. Hundreds of faces were uplifted toward him. He recognized many people. Salman was among them, smiling at him, as was the one-eyed Abu Ayyub, whose face beamed with delight.

Umar said, "It is by command of the Messenger of God that Ahmed al-Golestani will recite the words that God has just handed down so that you memorize them and teach them to one and all. So listen and remember, and obey God and his Messenger."

Umar stepped aside. Ahmed recited the verses the way he had recited them to Muhammad, with the same pacing and intonation he had learned as a youth. His voice was strong and carried to the back of the courtyard.

When he was done, Umar stepped forward. "Who will repeat the words of God the Almighty and Merciful that Ahmed has just recited?"

Several men jumped to their feet. Umar pointed to one of them. He repeated the first half without errors, but faltered after that. Ahmed repeated the verses. Another man volunteered and recited it, omitting several words. Ahmed corrected him. When no one else volunteered, Salman jumped to his feet and repeated the entire set of verses without a single flaw.

"Let Ahmed and Salman be your instructors," said Umar to the congregation. "Should anyone have doubts about the recital, they will guide you. Remember that there are meanings to these words that are beyond our ability to understand on our own. Learn God's words first, and soon the Messenger of God will speak to you about them."

The believers got up to leave, many repeating the verses as they headed for the main gate. A small group of men surrounded Salman and peppered him with questions about certain words.

As he stepped down from the preacher's platform to join Salman, Ahmed noticed Ali standing off to one side. Ali was glaring at him, or so it seemed to Ahmed, but before he could look again to be certain and try to figure out why he would look at him in such a way, Abu Ayyub grabbed his arm. He was all smiles. "Like I said to you before, O Ahmed, anyone the

Messenger of God loves, I love, but anyone to whom the Messenger of God has given such an honor as he has given you, I love even more."

A small group surrounded them. Several of the men shouted "Hafiz!" at him to get his attention, the honorific for someone who has memorized the Quran. Ahmed repeated several verses to them and clarified the wording of others.

As he left the mosque with Abu Ayyub, Ahmed turned to look for Ali. Muhammad's cousin was still next to the platform and was still looking at him, but he turned away when Ahmed caught his eye.

On the way back, Abu Ayyub asked him why he wasn't married. "This is something I don't understand, a young man like you being without a wife—or wives!"

"I was married once, but my wife died. It was because of an accident. I loved her very much, and I haven't wanted to get married again yet."

"Still, it's not good. You should have more than one so that if one dies, you still have others. I have three and would like to have three more, but the Messenger of God says that God will allow us only four." He offered to set Ahmed up with a wife. "I know a girl who'd be perfect for you—the daughter of a cousin of mine. She's a virgin, and what's more important, she's very pious."

At the house, they sat under the palm tree out front and continued to discuss the matter while the goats in the pen next to the shed bleated. Three tethered donkeys were grazing on weeds growing along one side of the enclosure, snorting and flicking a swarm of flies away with their tails. Children ran in and out of the house. Two of Abu Ayyub's older sons were engaged in throwing goat dung at each other.

Ahmed had given some thought to marrying again, but decided that his life was still too uncertain. He didn't know how he ended up in Yathrib or what was in store for him. If it turned out he would have to live out his life there, it would be sensible to find a wife. He shrugged. "I don't have any money for a dowry."

"Volunteer for a raid," said Abu Ayyub.

Ahmed shook his head to show he didn't understand.

"A raid, an attack on the enemies of God. If it's successful, you come back with booty."

Ahmed laughed, thinking that Abu Ayyub was joking, but before he could ask him what he meant by that, the one-eyed man said, "Do you know that the Messenger of God will take another wife soon?"

A fly alighted on Abu Ayyub's dead eye. He slapped his face with the tail of his turban to drive it away and went on, "Zaynab is the daughter of Jahsh. She was married to the Prophet's adopted son Zayd, but he divorced her when God's Apostle expressed an interest in her."

Ahmed thought of the four wives whom he had first seen in the women's section of the prayer area, and later caught glimpses of them as he went through the living quarters when Muhammad summoned him. The wives had separate rooms next to each other, accessible through a narrow corridor inside the wives' quarters. It made Ahmed think of a suite of primitive hotel rooms. He had seen enough of the wives to form a general idea about them: Sauda was a tall, ungainly woman with a silly laugh that made the other wives roll their eyes. Hafsa, the daughter of Umar, had beguiling eyes but was haughty. Ahmed liked Umm Salama because she reminded him of his mother. She had four children from previous marriages, and Muhammad allowed them to live in the compound with her. They often played in the mosque courtyard with Abu Ayyub's children and other neighborhood children. Aisha, thin and with the sweet face of a girl, appeared quiet and submissive when she brought him the writing materials, but while he went in and out of the residential quarters to carry out his duties as a scribe, he sometimes heard hot-tempered outbursts at one end of the living quarters, and he recognized the voice as Aisha's.

Ahmed didn't like to stick his nose into the private lives of other people, much less so with Muhammad. As far as he was concerned, Muhammad's private life was his business. He tried to change the subject of the coming marriage, but once Abu Ayyub started talking, it was hard to get him to stop.

Abu Ayyub went on, "If you don't include the two wives who

died, with the new marriage that will make five, yet God allows the believers no more than four. What do you think about that, Ahmed?"

Ahmed was cautious about answering questions that Abu Ayyub threw at him. He didn't know whether it was from chattiness or was a sly test of his faith.

He shrugged. "I suppose that if the Messenger of God does it, God permits it."

Abu Ayyub smiled. "You are correct. God makes exceptions for prophets, but only for the few who were also His messengers, as is our noble Prophet. You are a hafiz, so I know you already know this verse that God, in his infinite wisdom, revealed to His Messenger, allowing him to marry Zaynab."

He recited the verse: "Surely, O Prophet! We have made lawful to you your wives to whom you have paid their dowers; and those whom your right hand possesses out of the prisoners of war whom God has assigned to you; and daughters of your paternal uncles and aunts, and daughters of your maternal uncles and aunts, who migrated from Mecca with you; and any believing woman who dedicates her soul to the Prophet if the Prophet wishes to wed her—this only for you, and not for the Believers."

Ahmed knew it too, but he had never before understood that it was connected to a specific marriage. Still, he didn't think it was his business. He again tried to quiet Abu Ayyub, again without success.

"I am something of a prophet too, you know," Abu Ayyub continued. "I can make a prediction that Aisha will behave very badly about this, even though it's allowed by God. She's very naughty and disruptive." He stood up. "Follow me. I want to show you something."

They walked to the nearby adobe shed next to the goat pen. He opened the wooden door and pointed to a corner at the deepest end. "Aisha played a cruel prank on Sauda. She convinced her that the bloodthirsty barbarians of Gog and Magog had broken free and were rampaging across the land toward Yathrib. They had drunk up the water of Lake Tiberius and were on their way here to drink our blood. They were already on the other side of Mount Uhud at the Farewell Pass, and it wouldn't be but an hour before they descended on us."

He tapped his head. "Sauda's a little slow, you know. She believed every word and got so frightened that she hid in this shed. Locked it from the inside! I found out about it from my children. I went to the shed and said, 'Come out, Sauda, Aisha is playing a joke on you.' She said, 'No, they're almost here. Run, save yourself, Abu Ayyub!' I had to go fetch the Messenger of God, and he was able to coax her out."

Abu Ayyub shook his head. "I don't know why he puts up with Aisha. He's too patient with her because she's so young. I tell you, if one of my wives behaved like that, I'd do this." He made a fist and punched the shed door so hard that it rattled, causing the goats in the pen to look up. "That's what you do to women when they misbehave."

They went back to the front of the house and sat down again under the palm tree. Ahmed remembered Ali's coolness toward him. He wondered whether it would be a mistake to ask Abu Ayyub about it, but since it troubled him so much, he asked him anyway.

He explained Ali's behavior toward him. "I don't understand. I have nothing but love and admiration for him and his family. I don't know that I've done anything to offend him."

Abu Ayyub made a dismissive motion with his hand. "Pay no mind to it. It's because you, due to your merits, have gotten close to the Messenger of God. Ali becomes jealous when new people are favored by him."

# Chapter 11

Ahmed found the stylus frustrating to use. It was cut from a reed that grew along the lowland marshes. It was stiff and didn't hold much ink. It was prone to leaking ink when he pressed down on the parchment, so the writing was blotchy at times. Nobody, not even Muhammad, seemed to mind, but he was a perfectionist and took professional pride in giving the documents a neat appearance.

To remedy the problem, he fashioned several quills from vulture feathers. When he was in grade school, he used to enjoy making quills from various feathers, starting with pigeon and chicken feathers because they were easy to acquire, yet because they were so small, they were unsatisfactory. He got better results with crow and goose feathers. A visitor at his mother's cloth shop, who saw him laboring to make a quill from a goose feather, returned one day and presented him with four eagle feathers. They worked, and he was proud of the calligraphy that such large feathers enabled.

When he told Abu Ayyub about his frustration with the reed pen and that he would be of better service to the Prophet if he had a good feather pen, his one-eyed landlord came to him the next day with a set of large vulture feathers. Ahmed sliced the tips at a sharp angle using Abu Ayyub's dagger, hollowed out the shafts, and made incisions through the sharpened points, which allowed the ink held in the hollow of the shaft to draw down to the tip as with a fountain pen.

The next time he was summoned, it was to take down a contract. He pulled out one of the feathers after Aisha brought him the usual writing materials, and said, "Will the Messenger of God permit me to use this instead?"

Muhammad and the parties to the contract looked doubtful, but after Muhammad nodded for him to proceed, he wrote down what was dictated faster than with the usual writing instrument, and the writing was neater.

Muhammad smiled. "May we benefit from your cleverness for a long time to come, O Ahmed."

The calls to transcribe verses became more frequent, at all hours of the day and night. They began with a loud knock on his door, and Anas or another servant would call out, "O Ahmed, the Messenger of God summons you."

By then, he was allowed to keep writing materials. Ink, quill, and parchment in hand, he would dash through the back door of the mosque and rush down the corridors, following the quick-stepping servant to wherever Muhammad happened to be at the moment. On one occasion, it was well after midnight, and Muhammad was spending the night with Umm Salama. She left after Ahmed arrived, and in the feeble light of an oil lamp, he wrote down Muhammad's words.

The verses during this period were often legalistic, lengthy, and less poetic than in previous periods. More often than not, Muhammad would be pacing back and forth, and when Ahmed entered the room, he would say, "Take it down! Take it down!" It was all Ahmed could do to drop to his knees, pull the stop from the ink vial, dip the quill into it, and begin writing with the parchment pressed down on his thigh.

Sometimes the words flowed from Muhammad; other times, they were halting, and he would tell Ahmed to scratch out a word or an entire line. Ahmed already knew most of these verses, though not all, and at times he found himself prompting Muhammad. He had memorized it one way, but Muhammad would sometimes say it another.

In these instances, Ahmed would ask if he had heard it the way Muhammad said it, repeating his words. "Or was it this way, O Messenger of God?" He would suggest the word or words he had memorized during his youthful Quran studies at the Aliabad mosque. Without fail, Muhammad would repeat back the words Ahmed suggested. For the most part, they were minor adjustments involving rhyming or alliteration, but in other instances, the changes altered the meaning. Muhammad never batted an eye.

Other peculiarities arose. On one occasion during the early afternoon, Ahmed was taking down a "Quran," as the people called the verses, when Muhammad stopped dictating in midverse and seemed to stare at him. Ahmed waited quietly for him to resume, but Muhammad remained in the same position, staring at him in a strange way. It was unnerving because it didn't seem to Ahmed that he was looking at him. His eyes were blank. After more than a minute, Muhammad blinked several times and resumed dictating where he had left off, as if he had not stopped.

On another occasion, Muhammad dropped to the ground while dictating. They were in the room behind the preacher's platform. As he often did, Muhammad was pacing back and forth, reciting verses, when, without warning, his legs buckled under him. He toppled backward, falling on the edge of the leather mattress. His face turned red and his mouth twisted in grotesque ways, as if he was trying to speak but couldn't get the words out.

Ahmed rushed out of the room and shouted into the corridor. "O wives, hurry, something has happened to the Messenger of God. Come quickly!"

Several wives and other household members rushed out of their chambers. Led by little Aisha, the wives poured into the room and knelt beside Muhammad. Umm Salama lifted his legs, and with the help of Sauda, the strongest among them, they moved him onto the mattress.

Aisha turned to Ahmed and touched her finger to her lips. "Don't make any noise," she said in a whisper. "The Angel Gabriel is bringing a Quran to the Messenger of God. We must wait until the angel has departed."

Ahmed stood in a corner, observing Muhammad. From the way he fell to the ground, Ahmed suspected he had suffered an epileptic seizure. He couldn't think of any other explanation. Perhaps the Angel Gabriel came to him while he was in such a state, but the nature of the state was clear. He had seen his wife,

Shadi, in a similar condition many times. The doctors told him that she suffered from "atonal" epilepsy. When attacks occurred, her leg muscles weakened, and she couldn't stand up. As had just occurred to Muhammad, her legs would buckle, and she would crumple to the floor. It was always dangerous because it happened so fast that she couldn't reach out and grab onto something to keep from falling. Every time she fell, she risked hurting herself.

After a few minutes, Umar's daughter, Hafsa, entered the room and told Ahmed he had to wait outside on the preacher's platform. He went through the curtain into the bright light and sat on the edge of the platform. A hot breeze blew through the shaded prayer area. Except for children playing, the courtyard was empty.

"Epilepsy," Ahmed kept repeating to himself. "The Messenger of God has epilepsy."

An hour later, Aisha, wearing a blue scarf tied under her chin, called for him to return to the room. "The Prophet will see you again, O Ahmed."

Muhammad was stretched out on the leather mattress. He looked drained, but he told Ahmed that God had commanded him to finish what was started earlier. With his hands folded over his chest, he resumed dictating.

After finishing the task, Ahmed went back to his room. That night, he had trouble sleeping. Among other things, the goats in the nearby pen kept bleating, and he wondered if they were stirred by a loud argument that was coming from the roof of the house of Abu Ayyub, which also kept him from sleeping. His one-eyed landlord was shouting, "I will divorce you if you don't obey me." The sounds of slapping and crying reached him. It kept going on and off for more than an hour. It was a hot night, and Abu Ayyub was accustomed to sleeping with one or more of his wives on the flat roof during hot nights, making it impossible to keep an argument private.

Ahmed wrapped the full length of his turban cloth around his head to cover his ears, but he was unable to keep out the noise coming from Abu Ayyub's roof or from the nervous bleating of the goats.

Memories of his wife's illness also kept him awake. Shadi had never experienced fits before their marriage. They started months later when she collapsed in the living room of their apartment, followed by convulsions. The doctors were mystified. She didn't have a history of epilepsy in her childhood, nor was there a history of it in her family. A neurologist in Gorgan said it could be the result of a head injury from an auto accident a year before they were married. He and Shadi were in the back seat of a friend's car when they were involved in a serious collision. She hit her head, causing a concussion. "It could be a complication arising from the accident, or maybe from a brain infection of some kind. We just don't know," the neurologist said, adding that the sole recourse was for her to take anticonvulsant drugs.

In his mind, he saw Shadi as she used to be, always full of joy. The distance of fourteen centuries could not separate him from his memories of her. He recalled how she would snuggle next to him on the couch and stroke his forehead as she described what she experienced just before an attack. There was a moment of joy that was beyond all words. "It lasts for a few seconds and feels like God has wrapped his arms around me. My love for you I feel in my heart, but I feel this in my head. It's as wonderful as love, but it seems like it enters only in my head, and I feel joy beyond all words." She would look at him with her exquisite dark eyes and say, "Does that make any sense, my Ahmed?"

The neurologist told him it was from the "aura" that preceded a fit, a warning that an attack was coming. But she became convinced of a spiritual connection. Sometimes she saw humanlike shapes. "Do you think they're angels?" she asked him. She craved the experiences of supernal joy the seizures gave her, and several times she stopped taking the medicine that kept them at bay. This was against the doctor's advice and his own concerned warnings. One day, she had a fall that proved fatal.

He wondered about Muhammad. Was he being visited by a supernatural being as he believed, or did he have visions that arose from within himself while entering into an epileptic state? Did he repeat to Ahmed the words he had heard from an angel? Or did he create verses himself but believed them to be from an angel? He thought about the words he suggested to Muhammad that became part of the Quran. Because such changes were so modest, he had pushed questions about his contributions to the back of his mind, but now that he realized that Muhammad might be suffering from epileptic fits, he couldn't chase away doubts about the authenticity of the verses. He repeated to Muhammad what he had memorized in his youth, and now they became part of what his future self would memorize. Was he, therefore, the origin of some of the words that he memorized and not God? What about the authenticity of the rest of the Quran?

On one occasion, just before Muhammad dismissed him following the dictation of a number of legalistic verses, Ahmed said, "Would the Messenger of God permit his scribe to ask how revelations come to him?"

Muhammad was pacing the room. He stopped and looked at Ahmed for a moment. "Sometimes it begins like the ringing of a bell. It's most painful then. Sometimes the angel appears before me as a man who addresses me, and I'm aware of all that he is saying."

"Is the angel here even when I am with you?"

"Yes, but you cannot see him."

"Do you feel joy?"

"Yes, joy enters into me whenever God takes possession of me, and through the angel leaves me with revelations like the ones you have written down."

Days after Ahmed witnessed the seizure, Muhammad ordered him to sleep on the preacher's platform so he would be close at hand when he was needed, which had become more frequent. Until then, it took five minutes for him to appear before Muhammad after he was summoned. Now he wanted Ahmed to be available to take down revelations without any delay. After a week, he became used to sleeping on the rough boards only yards from the entrance to Muhammad's room and being awakened by the feverish command, "Come, take it down, take it down!"

It turned out that the prayer area of the mosque was not any freer from nocturnal disruptions than the room at the house of Abu Ayyub. One night, while Ahmed was asleep on the platform, he was awakened when someone shook his shoulder. Several turbaned men, one of them holding a torch, stood at the foot of the platform. The flickering amber torchlight danced on the rough features of their faces. The one who awakened him had a horse face lengthened even more by a long beard. He said, "I am Abdullah, son of Unays, and I have returned from Urana to report my success to the Messenger of God. He instructed me to inform him the moment of my return, no matter what time of the day or night, so I am doing as he asked."

Muhammad emerged from the room behind the platform. He said to Abdullah, "May you prosper, O son of Unays!"

Abdullah replied, "And may you prosper, too, O Messenger of God."

Muhammad motioned for the men to follow him, and they walked into the courtyard just beyond the prayer area. Ahmed heard them talk among themselves, but he was only able to pick up on snatches of the conversation. He gathered that Abdullah had followed Muhammad's instructions about something and came back with proof that he had carried out the mission. While one of the men held the torch close, Abdullah opened a leather saddlebag and turned it upside down. Something large and round fell to the ground with a thud, and Abdullah nudged it with his foot.

Muhammad looked pleased, and Ahmed heard him say, "You have helped the cause of God, O son of Unays. Come to me later, and God and His Messenger will reward you." As Muhammad turned away from the men and returned to his room, Ahmed watched Abdullah grab the object with one hand and shove it back into the saddlebag.

He had trouble going back to sleep. What fell from the saddlebag looked like a head, though he couldn't be sure since he was at a distance from the men. He tried to brush the thought aside. It was absurd to think that anyone would bring the Messenger of God a head, or that the Prophet would accept that someone should do so. But he was troubled because of the way Abdullah had grabbed it when he put it back in the bag. There was something for him to grab onto. Was it hair? It dangled for a moment, with features that could be mistaken for a face. He struggled with it for hours. He convinced himself it was not a head, but rather an object about the same shape and size as a head. Those were not eyes, that was not a nose, nor was that a mouth. If people stared long enough, they could see faces anywhere: in clouds, on the trunk of a palm tree, on walls, even on the surface of the moon. It was a rumpled leather saddlebag about the same size as a head, nothing more, filled with something that had to be disposed of for some reason, and whatever the reason, it was a private matter between Muhammad and Abdullah, the son of Unays. It was not Ahmed's business.

The image of the round object kept him awake and didn't leave his mind until the break of dawn, when Bilal clambered to the high platform to make the piercing call to prayer, and the faithful poured in through the main gate to form tight rows.

Ahmed joined them at the back of the courtyard, shaking obtrusive thoughts from his mind and feeling like a zombie from lack of sleep.

# Chapter 12

The memory of the round object that looked so much like a severed head would not leave Ahmed alone. No matter how hard he tried to keep it out of his mind, he was freshly reminded every night when he slept on the platform or when he went to the mosque for one of the prayer sessions. He began to fear praying there.

Muhammad soon relieved him of "platform duty," as Ahmed called his nighttime sleeping arrangement, and he returned to his room at the home of Abu Ayyub. His talkative, one-eyed landlord was now a welcome distraction. As before, he pulled Ahmed into conversations that lasted late into the night. Ahmed found it annoying because Abu Ayyub was gossipy and opinionated, but he was unable to avoid these situations without offending his host. Now these interminable conversations gave him at least a temporary distraction from the disturbing memory.

He could not escape the memory during the day, however. When he accompanied Abu Ayyub to the mosque, he again saw the preacher's platform where he slept that night. Fifteen sturdy paces away, where the shaded prayer area ended and the bare ground of the courtyard began, was the place where he had observed what he struggled not to think about. To the annoyance of Abu Ayyub, who preferred going to that side of the courtyard—almost to the exact spot where it happened— Ahmed would insist on joining a row on the opposite side and farther back. In a stern voice, Abu Ayyub would say, "Come this way, Ahmed."

Ahmed always replied, "No, it's much better over here, Abu

Ayyub. You can see and hear the Prophet so much better from this side."

Muhammad's upcoming marriage to Zaynab was also a welcome distraction. Ever since it was announced, it was the talk of the valley, particularly in the Najjar territory. Abu Ayyub was excited that the wedding was at hand. During one of his marathon conversations in front of his house, he said, "Great is the honor that comes to the Najjars because of this marriage."

He went on and on about the Najjar connection: Muhammad's great-grandfather, Hashim, was a Meccan leader who married Muhammad's great-grandmother, Salma, a comely young woman of the Najjars, while he was on a caravan trip that passed through Yathrib on the way to Syria. "He fell in love with her after he saw her at the Najjar market," Abu Ayyub said, pointing in the direction of the nearby marketplace. "So both the Prophet and Zaynab descend from my tribe, from the Najjars."

The following day, he took Ahmed to a nearby cemetery and showed him Salma's grave. With a line of white stones around the edges of the mound like a pearl necklace, it was better maintained than most of the graves.

"It's a pity she didn't know that her great-grandson would be the Last and Final Prophet of God. And what a pity she didn't know that one day God the Almighty would himself bless the union of two of her great-grandchildren."

Ahmed was always astonished at how little of Muhammad's life he had been taught in school, or even at the Aliabad mosque. All he remembered about Zaynab was that she was one of Muhammad's thirteen wives.

He strove to mind his own business about the personal affairs of Muhammad, but the gossip about the upcoming marriage swirled everywhere. Much of it was negative because Muhammad was about to marry the former wife of his adopted son Zayd. He had adopted Zayd, a slave who was given to his first wife, Khadija, as a present when he was a boy. Muhammad arranged for him to marry Zaynab, but later pressured him to divorce her so he could have her.

In the nearby marketplace, Ahmed overheard a conversation about the marriage while buying some grapes at a fruit stall. A tall man with a long beard and an oversized turban said to another man, "O son of Aktham, all this talk that Zayd was happy to give up his wife because God permitted the Prophet to marry her is nonsense. I know Zayd, and he doesn't look happy to me."

"But there is a Quran about the marriage," said the other man as he opened a small leather moneybag and pulled out some coins. "Zayd was one of the first to believe in the Messenger of God and accept the Quran as God's word and pray with the Prophet. So how can he be displeased if it comes from God? Don't be a hypocrite."

"I'm not a pretend believer," the other man replied. "What I said is that the rumors that Zayd is pleased are untrue, not that the Quran is untrue. Who would be pleased about losing his wife to his own father? This has never been permitted among the Arabs, and you know this to be the truth."

The man with the moneybag replied, "Zayd was adopted, and he divorced Zaynab, so it's different. When I saw him last, he looked cheerful enough to me."

As he was leaving the market, Ahmed bumped into Salman, who struck up a conversation about the marriage. Salman frowned as he repeated the negative comments that were circulating. "I don't care what anyone says," Salman continued. "He's God's Apostle. He's God's Chosen One, and anything he does is good and pleasing in the eyes of the Almighty."

Ahmed rubbed his forehead. His head hurt from his attempts to suppress disturbing thoughts. A stress headache was building. It began that morning at the top of his forehead, and by the time he got to the market, it had reached the back of his head. All this talk about the marriage to Zaynab was making it worse. When Salman pressed him for his thoughts, he snapped, "I don't know what to think anymore."

A week before the wedding, Abu Ayyub again predicted that Aisha would become disruptive. The following day, while Ahmed listened to his endless chatter, they heard an argument break out among the wives at the far end of the wives' quarters. Aisha's voice rose above the others. A minute later, the sound of crashing pottery reached them.

Abu Ayyub threw his head back in laughter. "What a she-devil. Do you know that when the Prophet told her that God permitted the marriage to Zaynab, she had the nerve to say, 'I see that your Lord hastens to satisfy your desires.' She refuses to accept what God has commanded and instead mocks His Prophet. Surely she's destined for hellfire."

To drive out troubling thoughts, Ahmed made himself useful by collecting bundles of palm fronds from plantations to fuel the cooking pots for the wedding feast. On the day of the marriage, he chopped the woody stems into pieces and carried them to a walled courtyard at the back of the mosque's living quarters that served as a kitchen. As he piled the sections in a corner, servants began roasting the shoulders of goats that were slaughtered that morning. They carved the rest of the meat and dropped it into large stewing pots with vegetables and herbs, stirring with long wooden paddles.

The marriage ceremony, held in the shaded prayer area of the mosque, was one of subdued festivity. The bride and groom were seated cross-legged on woven mats along with family members. Muhammad, a smile flashing through his thick beard, was dressed in his finest white garments and turban, the tail tossed jauntily over his shoulder. Zaynab, wearing a veil and a wedding gown of shimmering silk, smiled with bridal modesty and made quiet remarks to those around her. From the edge of the crowded prayer area, Ahmed witnessed the formal exchange of gifts and the dowry that Muhammad gave to Zaynab's parents.

After the ceremony, Ahmed helped supervise the flow of guests into the small banquet room, which was one of a string of rooms for the wives. Muhammad and his bride were seated cross-legged at one end. A broad leather sheet was spread on the ground, and the guests sat around it and partook of the meal. Umm Salama's children and several young servants brought in bowls of stew and plates of bread and dates. The cuts of roasted shoulder were reserved for Muhammad and the elite of his companions, who were the first to attend the banquet. After they partook of the meal and exchanged pleasantries with the newlyweds, the elite companions departed to make room for a fresh round of well-wishers and banquet guests.

Muhammad made it known that the only wedding presents he would accept were food donations for the poor, and it fell upon Ahmed to accept the gifts on Muhammad's behalf. The future caliph Umar, who organized the feast, showed him a storage area for the donations near the back entrance of the residential quarters.

"It will be your responsibility to have them brought here," Umar said. "After the wedding feast, you will supervise the distribution of the food to the poor."

Two hours after the wedding feast began, Ahmed joined the final round of guests in the banquet room. "Peace and prosperity be to you and the daughter of Jahsh," the guests said as they entered the room.

"And peace and prosperity to you, O Ahmed al-Golestani," Muhammad said after Ahmed repeated the greeting.

Ahmed had often seen Zaynab in the women's prayer section, but had never observed her up close. The wedding veil was pulled back, revealing the attractive features of her face. Ahmed remembered the wedding portraits of his wife and many of his relatives and friends. He chuckled at the absurd thought of photographers edging into the banquet room to take photos of Muhammad and Zaynab for a wedding album.

Muhammad saw him smile and said, "Share with us what it is that makes you smile so, O Ahmed."

Ahmed was caught short and struggled for words. After a moment, he said, "In truth, O Messenger of God, I've been to many wedding feasts, and this one offered on behalf of you and the daughter of Jahsh will by far be the most memorable."

Muhammad was pleased and shared the comment with people who had not heard. The bride batted her exotic eyes and gave Ahmed a gracious smile.

Other guests noticed Zaynab's beauty too, but averted their gaze to avoid offending Muhammad. Less discreet were three men on the far end of the banquet who kept gawking at her. They were chatting among themselves, disconnected from the general flow of conversation, and would glance up at her with brazen directness before resuming their conversation.

Staring at the men, Muhammad began fidgeting. When they continued gawking at her, his eyes hardened. He got to his feet and looked around the room without saying anything. It was a signal that the banquet was over. Except for the three gawkers, everyone got the hint and left.

Free of the banquet, Ahmed set about distributing the donated food, mostly dates, but there were also baskets of barley and vegetables. Word had spread that food was to be handed out to those in need. By the time Muhammad stood up to signal that the marriage feast was over, people were crowded into the mosque courtyard. Ahmed and two of the servants carried the first of the food donations to the prayer area. As soon as the baskets were brought out, men and women pushed forward, holding bowls or thrusting out cupped hands.

Ahmed was certain that none of them had ever waited in line, but he saw that getting them to form a line would make the distribution easier and fairer. He sent one of the servants to fetch a length of rope and created a barrier twenty feet in front of the piles of food.

"O people," he announced for everyone in the courtyard to hear. "Only one person at a time may approach, or a man and a woman if they are together."

Someone in the crowd shouted, "Who are you to give orders? You are not the Messenger of God."

"I have been commanded to distribute the food," Ahmed replied, "This is how it will be done to ensure that everyone gets a fair share. So get in line and wait your turn."

Servants kept the crowd from surging through the barrier, and Ahmed was delighted that the distribution proceeded in an orderly fashion. Leaving the servants to keep the crowd under control, he returned to the residential quarters several times to bring out more of the donated food. In doing so, he had to pass in front of the banquet room, and he saw the same three men in the room. Zaynab, her eyes downcast and her lips pursed, sat by herself at the opposite end.

On two of these trips to the storage area, Ahmed crossed paths with Muhammad, marching up and down the corridor, looking upset. Ahmed wondered why he didn't tell the impertinent rubes to leave. Instead, he knocked on the door of one of his wives and went in. On the final trip, as Ahmed was carrying a heavy basket of dates on his shoulder, Muhammad came out of another room and walked past the banquet room again, only to see that the men were still there. He frowned, but he didn't confront them.

About half an hour after the food distribution began, the three men emerged from the residential quarters. Still jabbering among themselves, they sauntered through the courtyard and went out the main gate.

The number of the poor dwindled, but when the donated food ran out, there were still people in the courtyard. Ahmed ordered the cooking pots brought out to serve the remaining banquet food. He allowed people to eat on the spot using the bowls and cups from the wedding feast. He fetched buckets of water to rinse bowls once they were done to use for the next person.

"The Messenger of God ate from this very bowl," Ahmed said to an elderly woman, whose eyes widened and hands trembled as she accepted it.

The criticism of Muhammad over the marriage grew following the marriage. Salman and others complained to Ahmed that even some of the sincerest believers were slamming Muhammad. Salman mimicked crocodile tears to mock their pity for Zayd. "The poor boy has been humiliated. He's been emasculated by his own father," he sniffled.

Abu Ayyub called the critics hypocrites and condemned them to hellfire, in particular the tribal chieftain who owned the plantation where Ahmed worked before he moved to Abu Ayyub's house.

"He's the chief of the hypocrites, the worst of the lot," said Abu Ayyub about the sheikh. "He is like the rest of them. They pledged belief in the Prophet as God's Messenger. They clasped his hand to make their declaration of faith, just as you and I did, but they were lying. They did so to shield themselves from God's punishment for disbelievers. Do you know what I would do to them if it were up to me?"

Ahmed shook his head.

Abu Ayyub stared at him for a moment with his good eye and drew his finger across his throat. "That's what those hypocrites deserve."

# Chapter 13

Ahmed tried not to think. He had come to the valley of the Prophet out of intense longing to experience true Islam. Now he struggled to keep anything from entering his mind that could unsettle his faith. It was all that he had to hold on to.

Following the wedding, his prayers took on greater fervency than ever before as he pleaded for God's guidance. In the evening, after Muhammad allowed him to return to his room at the house of Abu Ayyub, he imitated Muhammad by standing for a long time at night in voluntary prayer and in contemplation of God.

But even these exhausting prayers couldn't keep certain thoughts at bay. As part of his prayers, he had to repeat some of the verses containing words he had suggested. He couldn't avoid these verses, and as he recited them, they always reminded him of the day and the circumstances under which he had suggested them.

The image of a head also kept intruding on his thoughts. Every time he walked into the mosque courtyard, the memory came back of the now unambiguous nighttime scene under the flickering light of a torch. He again saw one of the men hold a round object by the hair and stuff it into a leather bag. It had eyes, a nose, a mouth, and a beard, so what else could it be but a head? He strove to chase the image out of his mind, and also the blasphemous thought that he had witnessed evidence of extreme violence that had been committed with the approval of Muhammad.

In addition to the forced nighttime prayers, he combated the intrusive images and thoughts by throwing himself into whatever duties were assigned to him, most recently the activities surrounding the wedding banquet. He was still needed as a scribe. Several days after the banquet, as he lay stretched out on the leather mattress of his room, staring at the uneven ceiling beams, a servant pounded on his door. "O Ahmed, you must hurry. The Messenger of God summons you to take down a Quran."

When Ahmed arrived with ink, quills, and parchment, Muhammad was pacing back and forth. He looked furious. Ali was sitting in a corner and glanced with indifference at Ahmed when he entered.

"Take them down, Ahmed!" Muhammad said when he entered. "Take down the words that God the Merciful has sent to his servant! The hypocrites must take heed of them, for they are warnings."

As he always did, Ahmed dropped to his knees and positioned a strip of parchment on his thigh. He dipped one of the quills into the ink and looked up at Muhammad to show he was ready. He was astounded when he heard the first set of verses. They were from the chapter that imposed the veil on women. He already knew the entire chapter by heart, but he was never taught the context. He was told they were revelations handed down to the Messenger of God, pre-existing words from the eternal tablets of God, and it was left at that. But as he hastened to transcribe Muhammad's verses, the context became clear because he had witnessed it.

He struggled to keep up with Muhammad, who spoke louder and faster than usual. Ahmed looked up several times, beseeching him with his eyes to slow down. He would slow down for a moment, but pick up speed again.

"Take it down, take it down," Muhammad snapped at one point when Ahmed asked him to repeat a verse.

Ahmed's fingers worked with feverish speed, as did his mind, as he assessed what he wrote. The verses authorized Muhammad to take the wife of his adopted son. When he wrote down the words, "Proclaim their real parentage as that will be more equitable in the sight of Allah," he grasped that it meant Zayd had never been Muhammad's son, and it was clear from the verses that followed that the practice of adoption was abolished altogether. That meant Muhammad freed himself of guilt because Zayd was now no different to him than any other man.

Ahmed suppressed the anger building in him. He knew what inspired the verses. They were related to a particular event of interest to Muhammad. They were self-serving, certainly not of any spiritual importance as he had been taught to believe.

Even the banquet was mentioned. Ahmed remembered how irritated Muhammad appeared when the three men remained behind in the banquet room, which was to become Zaynab's private room. When he mentioned the incident to Abu Ayyub, his one-eyed landlord replied that Muhammad was shy about asserting himself in such public situations, so he waited politely for the men to leave on their own. Ahmed, however, recalled that when he passed him in the corridor, Muhammad looked angry.

Ahmed almost dropped the quill as he wrote down verses where God scolds believers for the lack of etiquette at the wedding feast. Ahmed's hand trembled as he wrote, "O you who believe! Do not enter the houses of the Prophet unless permission is given to you for a meal, not waiting for its cooking to be finished, but when you are invited, enter, and when you have taken the food, then disperse, not seeking to listen to talk. Surely this gives the Prophet trouble, but he forbears from you, and Allah does not forbear from the truth."

Ahmed remembered that while in school, he had examined photographs taken by the Hubble Space Telescope that showed clouds of colorful galactic dust against a background of countless stars and galaxies suspended in infinite darkness. Other photographs showed hundreds of thousands, millions, or even billions of galaxies. Creation was so vast, and he remembered marveling at God's power to create something so immense. These images flashed through his mind in milliseconds as he wrote the words Muhammad dictated. Thinking of the immensity of it all, he wondered, "Doesn't God have anything better to do today than to hand down these words to his Messenger?"

The dictation stopped. Ahmed looked up to await further words. Muhammad was still pacing the room as if taking time to think about what came next. Ahmed wondered, "Is he waiting for the angel to reveal more to him, or is he making this up?"

He glanced at Ali. Ali was staring at him with narrowed eyes. He wondered if Ali could read his mind. He worried that his face betrayed his thoughts, that he was having doubts, that he was one of those reviled hypocrites.

He looked away from Ali and focused on the parchment and the tight script he used to cram everything onto it. His temples throbbed, and his head hurt. He wished the session were over so he could go back to his room, but Muhammad resumed dictating, his voice now spilling into fury. As he dictated, Muhammad shook his fist and raised his hands to the heavens. In one verse, God threatens punishment for those who "bothered His messenger." In another, God authorized Muhammad to kill his critics if they didn't stop: "If the hypocrites and those in whose hearts is a disease and the agitators in the city do not desist, We shall most certainly set you over them, then they shall not be your neighbors in it but for a little while. Cursed! Wherever they are found, they shall be seized and murdered, a horrible murdering."

As Ahmed penned the final words, the vision of the round object with eyes, nose, and mouth exploded into his mind. He imagined Muhammad grabbing the object, walking toward him with it, and holding it close to his face so he could get a good look. He saw the eyes closed as if in sleep, and the dried blood on the nose, and the mouth agape, and the dark beard dirtied with dust and twigs, and the severed neck with blood dripping from it.

The vision horrified him, causing him to press down so hard on the quill that the tip fractured and became useless. He snapped out of the trance enough to grab another quill. He dipped it into the inkpot, but in his haste, he tipped the pot over, and some of the ink spilled before he could right it. Muhammad had already continued with another verse, and Ahmed missed every word. He already knew the verse that followed, and if his mind had been clear, he could have caught up. But now his brain was frozen, and he couldn't remember anything.

He looked up at Muhammad and pleaded, "Forgive me, O Messenger of God. I'm not feeling well today, and I didn't get the last verse. Would you repeat the words of God so that I may take them down?"

Ali sneered, "What did I tell you about him, O Prophet. I can find you a better scribe than this al-Golestani. Arabic isn't even his language."

Muhammad stopped pacing and looked down at Ahmed. His face softened. After a brief moment, he said, "Will you be able to continue?"

"Yes," Ahmed said. "Forgive me. I had a slight lapse, but I'm better now."

Muhammad kept at it for another fifteen minutes. When it was over, Ahmed handed the parchment to Ali and went back to his room. On the way, he was dizzy and kept bumping into things. When he crossed the lane to Abu Ayyub's house, his feet dragged. He lay on the mattress and wondered if there were deeper meanings to the verses. Was he missing something?

The clerics had encouraged him to enter the seminary in Qom to study the deeper meanings of the Quran. But he wondered how there could be any deeper meaning to a verse that threatened horrible murder to Muhammad's critics. He had been present during the entire episode involving Muhammad's marriage to Zaynab. Muhammad had married Zayd's former wife. Zayd was his adopted son. His critics said it was immoral to marry the wife of one's son, even if divorced, even if the son was adopted. To counter them, Muhammad dissolved the practice of adoption so that Zayd was no longer his son. The critics, therefore, could no longer criticize him, but they continued to call him immoral, and he threatened to kill them. There was no deeper meaning to it. Muhammad invented these verses. He put words in God's mouth. He used God for his own purpose.

As he lay on the leather mattress and stared at the crude ceiling, he began to ask questions he never would have dreamed of asking before. If these verses were invented, was the entire Quran a fabrication? Was Muhammad not who he claimed to be? Was he a fraud?

The more he thought about such questions, the more pressure built up in his head, and the heaviness of depression took over his body. His fingers began to tingle, and his cheeks were like lead weights pulling his face down. He had experienced prolonged depression after the death of his wife. It was the result of profound loss. Was what he was now feeling the result of profound loss, too, the loss of faith?

He was so ill that he skipped dawn prayers. When Abu Ayyub pounded on his door after Bilal's prayer call, Ahmed forced himself to his feet. Leaning against the doorframe, he said he was not feeling well and would not be able to attend. Abu Ayyub stared at his drooping face for a moment and left without arguing. He missed the noon prayer session as well, but he forced himself to get to his feet when he remembered he had an obligation to fulfill that afternoon. A delegation from an important Bedouin tribe from a region far to the northeast of Yathrib was to arrive at the mosque in the afternoon to inquire about the new faith. Muhammad wanted him present in case an agreement came out of it, such as a nonaggression treaty similar to those he had taken down on other occasions.

With his writing materials in hand, Ahmed forced himself to trudge to the main entrance and arrived at the same time as the Bedouin delegation. Two dozen men dressed in black or dark brown robes and red or black turbans walked ahead of him through the courtyard to the prayer area. Muhammad came out and greeted the delegation. The Bedouins were tall and of dignified bearing, and after exchanging compliments and wishes for peace and prosperity, the sheikh offered Muhammad gifts of perfumes and fine Byzantine fabrics.

They sat cross-legged on the woven mats of the prayer area and were joined by a dozen of Muhammad's followers. Ali, as usual, was seated next to Muhammad. Close by were Abu Bakr, Umar, and Uthman, all of whom Ahmed knew would one day dispute the leadership of Islam with Ali.

The leader of the Bedouins was a sheikh named al-Harith, whose sharp eyes and nose were set in a face burned dark by the sun. He and other leaders asked questions about the faith and probed Muhammad about his claim to prophethood. Muhammad explained the doctrines of resurrection and judgment, the rewards of paradise, and the punishments of hell. "What I bring you is the chance to attain paradise," he said.

"We have heard these stories before," al-Harith said. "They are the stories of the Jews and Christians. If we believed them, should we not join with the Jews or the Christians? Why join with you?"

Muhammad replied, "God revealed the truth to the Jews through Moses and to Christians through Jesus, but they corrupted the truth. They changed it. God, therefore, has commissioned me, an Arab who descends from Abraham, to bring the uncorrupted truth."

"This is what you claim about yourself, but where is the proof other than your word?" the sheikh said.

Muhammad recited various Quran verses. Some were verses about Abraham and Ismael, others about the gardens of heaven, while yet others described the torments of hell. "These are the proofs. They are not from me, but are given to me as revelations by an angel."

From his position at the periphery, Ahmed had a clear view of the visitors. Their expressions were neither enthusiastic nor dismissive, but inquisitive. They were open to being persuaded. He wondered how they would react if Muhammad recited the verse from the day before that threatened to murder people who criticized him for his marriage to Zaynab.

As he observed the visitors and followed the exchange, the leaden feeling in his head and face dissipated. The discussion went on for two hours, and the longer it dragged on, the angrier Ahmed became. At first, it was because of Muhammad's descriptions of the torments of hell. It bothered him that he seemed to delight in describing sadistic torments, such as women hanging by their tongues over a fire for the sin of backbiting, or for more grievous sins, he drew word pictures of flesh roasting off the body, only to be regenerated so the suffering could be resumed, and this for all eternity.

The more Muhammad dwelt on the "punishment of the fire," as he often called the torments of hell, the more Ahmed understood that he was trying to frighten the visitors into believing.

Ahmed became even more upset when Muhammad launched into a discourse about the end of time and the Day of Judgment. He had heard him preach these ideas during the Friday sermons. Almost to the word, it wasn't any different from what the mullahs preached from the pulpit when he was growing up, that Muhammad would intercede with God on behalf of the believers to spare them the torments of hell.

He had never questioned any of this before, but now it seemed absurd. When he was growing up, Muhammad had been larger than life to him, a holy man beloved by God, but now he was merely a man like any other man sitting cross-legged twenty feet from him, someone with a thick beard, a turban, and a silken tongue. Ahmed now felt contempt. He was a con man taking advantage of the ignorance of these desert Arabs.

Ahmed couldn't contain himself any longer. He jumped to his feet, causing everyone to turn to look at him. "Will the Messenger of God permit a question about paradise?" Without waiting for an answer, he said, "Has God granted you the knowledge of where paradise and the throne of God are located? And hell, where hell is located?"

Muhammad stared at him for a moment with a hint of anger. He turned toward his visitors and pointed to the sky. "Heaven is above us. It is located above the House of God in Mecca, and the throne of God is above the seven levels of heaven. Each of the levels is the abode of the prophets and will be the abode of those who are faithful to the commands of God." He pointed to the ground. "Hell is below us," he said. He scrutinized the visitors for a moment before continuing, as if to gauge their acceptance of his words. "There are also seven levels, the lowest for those who have been the most disobedient to the commandments of God."

As he spoke, Ahmed visualized the limitless expanse of creation that he had seen in the astronomy photographs. Yet what Muhammad described sounded like the throne of God was in geosynchronous orbit around the earth, like the communication satellites of the future.

When Muhammad was finished, Ahmed said, "And there is the important question about the sun, O Messenger of God, which, as you well know, many people worship in the place of God who created the sun. Has God explained to His Messenger the mystery of where the sun goes at night, and from where it rises when we see it again in the morning?"

Muhammad looked irked, as did Ali and other men sitting near him. Muhammad answered, but again he addressed the Bedouins rather than Ahmed. "At its setting, it goes to the throne of God to ask permission to remain there in prostration, and when it is ordered to return from where it came, that is when it rises in the east."

Muhammad recited a Quran verse: "And the sun runs his course for a period determined for him: that is the decree of God, the Exalted in Might, the All-Knowing."

Ahmed knew he was being impertinent. The meeting was for the Bedouins, but he kept asking questions. The desert people glanced at one another as if trying to assess if he was someone of importance. The men around Muhammad glared at him, particularly Ali. Muhammad cut him off by addressing the visitors. "I will take questions from our guests, who have honored God and His Messenger by their presence among us."

The meeting went on for another hour. When it was over, the desert Arabs left without an agreement of any sort, saying they would meet in the tribal council to discuss what they heard. When they were gone, Muhammad and his people turned their backs on Ahmed and left.

Only Ali remained behind. He motioned for Ahmed to approach. When Ahmed stood in front of him, Ali came to within inches of his face and scolded him for "bothering the Messenger of God." He recited a verse that was among the ones that Ahmed wrote down just the day before: "Those who annoy God and His Messenger, God has cursed them in this world and in the hereafter and has prepared for them a humiliating punishment."

All that Ahmed could focus on while Ali lectured him was the mascara that highlighted his eyes. In his mind, he saw the portraits that hung in his mother's home and in the homes of everyone he knew in Aliabad. It occurred to him that the depictions of the man who was now inches from his face were accurate only in that they reproduced his habit of using eyeliner. The eyeliner and the hint of a halo in the background were intended to show him as noble and heroically spiritual. But up close, despite the angry twist of Ali's mouth as he recited the threatening Quran verse, he looked comical.

"You will not be the scribe of the Messenger of God for much longer," Ali said before he stormed away.

# Chapter 14

Grilling Muhammad in the presence of the Bedouins was an act of defiance, and it energized Ahmed. He felt challenged to investigate the claim Muhammad made to the visitors that the Jews and Christians were given the truth, but had corrupted it. In his youth, he had memorized Quran verses about the prophets: Adam, Noah, Abraham, Moses, Joseph, and many others. He no longer had confidence that they were any more authentic than the verses Muhammad dictated to him following his marriage to Zaynab.

He wondered what the scriptures of the Jews and Christians had to say about the prophets. He had no way of learning about the Christian versions, for there were no Christians he knew of in Yathrib, but the Jewish tribe of Nabbash and Maryam was nearby. They lived their lives by the Torah and kept the scrolls of their sacred texts in their place of worship. What would a comparison of their prophet stories with Muhammad's reveal?

The only way to resolve the matter was for him to visit the Jewish tribe. After leaving the mosque, he strode to the nearby marketplace to buy dates and other provisions for a trip to the Qurayza's highland territory. The next morning, he left his room before dawn to avoid Abu Ayyub and get out of Yathrib before the believers left their homes to go to the mosque for prayer. By the time he heard Bilal's call in the distance, he was already on the road to the highlands.

It took him three hours to reach the Qurayza territory. When he walked by the plantation where he used to labor, he felt invigorated. The Jews were already at work. He recognized many of the workers and waved to them. He felt like he had come home again. With a cheerful smile, he walked through the narrow lanes of Nabbash's village to the small plaza. As he went by the sorting warehouse, a woman said, "Look, there's Ahmed!" A man at the back of the shed said, "O Ahmed, come and visit with us."

Ahmed waved and pointed to the house of Nabbash and walked up the path. A servant greeted him at the door. Moments later, Nabbash, wearing a coarse work garment, appeared. He grasped Ahmed's hands. "You've come back to us, O Ahmed."

Before he could explain the reason for his visit, Maryam rushed up the path. She, too, was dressed for work, wearing a red kerchief over her dark hair. She heard in the village that he was there, and came up to greet him.

"I've known all along that we would see you again."

Ahmed was happy to see her. "I have a request to make of you. I want to know what your scriptures say about the prophets. Who can instruct me about this?"

Nabbash said, "Well, we all know about them from the Torah, but the most knowledgeable are the rabbis. They are scholars and have the deepest knowledge."

"Will they speak to someone like me?"

Maryam said, "Yes, of course. You are known to be honorable. You already know Rabbi Sallim."

"I will take you to him," said Nabbash.

He sent a servant to prepare two horses. Ahmed accompanied Nabbash to a stable behind the residence. They mounted the horses and rode deeper into Qurayza territory than Ahmed had ever gone before. They soon came to a fortress near another village and stretches of date palms. The fortress was a huge structure similar to others he had seen in the valley, thick-walled and four stories high with rounded towers at each corner. The massive entrance doors were wide open. They trotted through and rode to a stable at the far end.

"In times of trouble, the entire tribe comes here for protection," Nabbash said as they left the stable. He pointed to a storage area and a well at the far end of the enclosure. "We are well provisioned for a siege. In the hundreds of years that we've been here, the Qurayzas have survived every attack."

They went into the main structure and followed a meandering corridor to a room. Nabbash bade Ahmed to wait and went into the room. Minutes later, he came back with Rabbi Sallim. The elderly rabbi was wearing a simple tan garment and a black turban covered by a tasseled white-and-black shawl. The rabbi smiled with warmth and grasped Ahmed's hand after returning his greeting.

"Nabbash tells me that you wish to know about our prophets," the rabbi said.

"Yes," said Ahmed. "That's why I've come."

"I will be pleased to instruct you."

Nabbash left, and Ahmed followed the rabbi into the room. It was a study adjacent to the synagogue, arranged for comfort with rugs, cushions, and low reading desks. The stone walls were plastered, and throughout the room were symbols of Judaism. At one end was a rack holding thick scrolls.

After they sat cross-legged on a rug, the rabbi said, "Nabbash told me of your doubts. There is a way to determine the truth by comparing what Muhammad's Recital says about the prophets and what the Torah says about them. Let us begin with Abraham."

Ahmed recited Quran verses in which Abraham destroys wooden idols to show the idolaters that the objects they worshiped had no power. As punishment, their king throws him into a bonfire, but God allows him to walk out of it untouched.

The elderly rabbi said, "Do you know that there's nothing about this in the Torah?"

With Ahmed's help, the elderly rabbi got to his feet, and with a stoop, he walked to the scroll rack. He picked up a scroll, removed the covering, and kissed it. He carried it as in his arms as if it were a swaddled infant and brought it to a reading table.

"This is the Torah that we once used in our services, but it is many decades old and tattered. A rabbi who visited us from Syria last year brought us a new one, and it is the one kept in the synagogue, as this one used to be."

With practiced twists to the worn rollers, he scrolled the document forward. He tapped the text with a reed pointer. "This was given to Moses two thousand years ago, and what is in this scroll is the same as what was given to Moses."

Ahmed listened to every word as the rabbi translated. When he was finished, Ahmed said, "I heard nothing about the breaking of idols or that Abraham was thrown into a fire."

"There is nothing in the Torah about it, but there is something about it in the Talmud."

"I am sorry to say that I don't know what the Talmud is," said Ahmed.

The rabbi explained that a vast body of law and learned commentary had been extracted over the centuries from the Torah. "It used to be passed from generation to generation from memory, as oral tradition, but it was written down centuries ago. What is important for you is that the Talmud contains legends of the prophets, which are folk versions of the prophet stories of the Torah. From what you recited of the Quran, I am reminded of something in the legends."

With Ahmed's help, he fetched another scroll from the rack and rolled it forward. "I will translate it for you," the rabbi said.

The folk version of the Abraham story included the story of the rebellious breaking of the idols. The sentence of death by fire was similar to the one in the Quran: Abraham was condemned to die a painful death for his blasphemy, but before he could be thrown into the fire, God transformed it into a garden.

The evidence of the Jewish documents was clear. Muhammad's version of the Abraham story was inspired by a derivative Jewish folk tale that appeared in written form centuries earlier. If there was any corruption, it lay in the changes Muhammad made to the Jewish legends. It was Muhammad's altered version of the folk tale.

"Where did Muhammad learn these folk tales?" Ahmed asked.

"He knew some Jews in Mecca," the rabbi said with a dismissive wave of the hand. "They were not scholars, and they were not familiar with the Torah. They were common folk who repeated the legends they had heard all their lives. Jews who have not been given religious instruction confuse these folk tales with the Torah. And it appears these ignorant Jews were Muhammad's teachers. He nourished his Quran with Jewish folk tales."

Ahmed said, 'There are many prophets mentioned in the Quran: Adam, Noah, Joseph, Jonah, Job, Moses, and Aaron." He continued until he had named more than a dozen. "Shall we search the Talmud to find what the legends have to say about them?"

"You are our guest," the rabbi said. "You are welcome to stay with us for as long as you wish. We will share with you whatever is in our sacred books."

Ahmed ended up staying four days. They were joined by other scholars, including Kab, the tribal leader. A rich literature that Ahmed had never known existed opened to him, and he experienced the excitement of new knowledge. The wealth of it confused him at first: There was not just the Talmud, but the Babylonian Talmud and the Jerusalem Talmud, and within them there were the Mishnah, the Halakah, the Gemara, the Tosefta, and more, even divisions of the Jewish Bible: Torah, Neviim, and Ketuvim that the Jews referred to as the Tanakh. The scholars explained that the literature resulted from a gradual transition from oral tradition to written form that began after the destruction of the First Temple in Jerusalem.

As they proceeded, Ahmed wrote down verses about each prophet to make it easier to compare with the Jewish versions. At times, as many as seven scholars crowded into the study. Some were young men who listened to the discussions and fetched and returned scrolls. Most often, everyone sat cross-legged, but at other times, they were on their knees, bending over a scroll on the low reading tables.

Whenever they found folk-tale passages in the Talmudic scrolls that resembled the Quran, they broke into cheers. The discussions were spirited, sometimes heated. When they got worked up, the scholars spoke in Hebrew until Rabbi Sallim called them to order by reminding them that their guest only understood Arabic.

The more they uncovered, the more Ahmed became convinced that Muhammad had taken what was not his, that he had gotten it from the wrong source, and that he had converted it for his own use and claimed it came from God. When they exhausted all their sources, Rabbi Sallim said to Ahmed, "If it had not been for you, we would never have undertaken this study. We have all learned something from this."

Ahmed was reluctant to leave. Being among the scholars was one of the most exhilarating experiences of his life. He felt a deep respect not only for their learning, but also for what they devoted themselves to learning.

While Ahmed was taking leave of the scholars, Kab, the Qurayza leader who participated in the study, sent a servant to bring two horses from the stable. They rode out of the fortress together and trotted down the road toward Nabbash's village.

On the way, Kab said, "Have you heard yet that the Meccans are preparing another army to attack Muhammad?"

Ahmed nodded. "Salman told me about it."

"If they do attack," Kab said, "they'll come with an army many times the size of the one they came with two years ago." The Qurayzas, he said, learned of the Meccan preparations from the Jewish leaders of Khaybar. They had traveled to Mecca to talk with the leaders about the attack. "They pledged to join the coalition, but we talked them out of it. If the attack fails and Jews are a part of it, we will be vulnerable. Muhammad will attack us. Our only safety lies in remaining neutral. We've sent word to Salman to inform Muhammad that we intend to stay out of any conflict with the Meccans, but we haven't heard back from him. We don't know if Muhammad got our message."

"I will ask Salman about it," Ahmed offered. "I will make sure the message has reached Muhammad."

Kab shook his fist in the direction of the Najjar territory. "That man who calls himself the Messenger of God has brought nothing but strife ever since he came to Yathrib. He's possessed by demons. He doesn't get his so-called revelations from angels. They come from demons, and because he listens to demons, he causes strife everywhere."

They were soon in the village and happened upon Nabbash and Maryam outside the sorting warehouse. Nabbash and Kab leading the way, they walked up the narrow path together to Nabbash's house. When they were midway, Ahmed felt Maryam's hand slip into his. He glanced at her. Her head was bowed, and she seemed in quiet thought. When they reached the top, her hand slipped away.

After they were in the house, Kab said to Nabbash, "Ahmed informed me he will ensure that Muhammad knows of our intention to remain neutral if the Meccans attack."

Nabbash nodded at Ahmed. "Good. We were worried that he may not have gotten word of it. It is essential for Muhammad to know our position. If he suspects that we are a part of the Meccan coalition and the attack fails, he will banish us like he banished the other Jewish tribes."

"Or worse," Kab said.

Ahmed said, "I'm not in good standing with him any longer, so I doubt he will listen to me, but he will listen to Salman. I promise you that I will make sure that Salman has spoken to him about this."

"I fear for the future," Maryam said. "Muhammad is hostile to us because we refuse to accept him as our prophet. All that will satisfy him is that we submit to him."

Ahmed looked down at the floor, uncertain what to say. He knew she was right.

"If he attacks us, I will fight," Maryam said. "I will join with our warriors. I will fight to defend my people."

He knew they would be attacked, and he couldn't hide from himself that he knew the outcome. The outcome was recorded in history. But he wondered if the future was set in stone. Could it be altered? Could he alter it?

Nabbash offered to have one of his people accompany Ahmed on camel or horse to the Najjar territory, but Ahmed thought it best to walk. He didn't want Muhammad to find out that he had been with the Qurayzas. In parting, Nabbash gave him a water skin and a leather bag of dates for his journey.

Halfway back, he stopped and sat at the side of the road. He didn't want to go back to the Najjar territory. The mosque, the cries of Bilal for the faithful to come to prayer, the exhausting prayer rituals, and Muhammad himself had all become repugnant to him. He wondered if he should return to the Qurayzas and throw his lot in with them. He would study the Torah and accept it as his guide. If Muhammad attacked, he would fight along with them and encourage them never to surrender. If it was their destiny to be slain, he would join with them in death.

But he knew it was not his destiny. After an hour of hesitation, he got up and, with a heavy heart, continued along the road to the Najjar territory, encouraging himself with the idea that the future had not yet happened. It was not inscribed in stone.

# Chapter 15

Only the fading orange of sunset was visible when Ahmed reached the outskirts of the Najjar region. As the mud hovels of the outlying area came into view, he heard the call to prayer, but instead of going to the mosque, he went to Salman's abode and waited for him at the door.

He spotted Salman's tall, athletic frame the moment he stepped into the alley from the marketplace. When Salman reached him, he said, "Where have you been? Everybody's been looking for you."

"I was visiting friends."

Salman stroked his lengthy beard and looked at Ahmed through half-closed eyes. "I think I know who you mean."

After Salman ushered him into the room, Ahmed said, "Have the Qurayzas been in contact with you?

"Yes, a nephew of Nabbash came to me. He told me it's their intention to remain neutral if the Meccans attack and asked me to tell this to the Messenger of God."

"Did you?"

"Yes, I told him."

"What did he say?"

"He doesn't reveal what he thinks. I told him, that's all."

"Did you inform the Qurayzas that you did so?"

Salman smiled, revealing a perfect row of upper teeth through his dark beard. "So, you've been with them, and they want to know if Muhammad got the message."

Ahmed shrugged.

"I haven't sent anyone, but I will. They need to know."

"Why don't you go yourself? Nabbash and his people treated you well, just as they treated me well. They would be happy to see you."

"That's not a good idea. The Messenger of God sees them as potential allies of the Meccans. He doesn't trust them. If I went, it would raise questions about my loyalty. The last thing you want is to be branded a hypocrite."

He stared for a long moment at Ahmed. "Do you know that people are raising questions about you? Ali called you a hypocrite. You made a spectacle of yourself when the Bedouins visited. Abu Bakr, Umar, Ali, they're all pressuring the Messenger of God to drop you as his scribe, which I think he's done, given that you disappeared for so many days."

"It doesn't matter. I don't intend to be his scribe anymore."

"Do you know that you were seen on the road going to the Qurayza territory? People reported it to the Messenger of God."

"I will deal with it."

"So tell me, why did you do that? You must have known it wasn't a good idea."

"They are the People of the Book. They have their Torah and other scriptures. I wanted to know what is in their books."

"Take some good advice and be very careful. I say this to you as your friend. You're on the wrong path, and it's the path that leads to hell—here in this life and in the afterlife. If you are branded as a hypocrite, your life will become very miserable."

"Maybe you should take my advice and visit the Qurayzas to find out what is in their books. It would do you a lot of good."

"Listen to your friend and go back to the mosque for prayer as you used to do, and if it becomes necessary, ask forgiveness from God if you have offended him and his messenger in any way."

The following morning, Ahmed was awakened by Bilal's dawn prayer call, but he ignored it and lay on the thin mattress until noon. He didn't want to go to the mosque, but it was Friday, and he decided that he had better attend the weekly sermon. He still had to live in Yathrib. After pulling on his garment and wrapping his turban around his head, he sought out Abu Ayyub.

"Where have you been?" said Abu Ayyub, looking Ahmed up and down with his good eye.

Ahmed didn't like the tone of his voice. Had word gotten to him that Ali called him a hypocrite?

"I went to visit some friends," Ahmed said. "Nothing more."

"Are you sure?"

"Yes, of course."

Abu Ayyub seemed satisfied. They went to the mosque and found places in a row near the center, away from the spot where Ahmed saw the head. Muhammad came out and took his usual position in front of the congregation as the prayer leader. When the prayers were over, he mounted the platform and sat in the pulpit to begin the Friday sermon. With his eyes half closed, he surveyed the crowd for more than a minute without saying anything. Ahmed felt uncomfortable when his gaze lingered on him.

Still gazing at Ahmed, Muhammad said, "Haven't I spoken to you many times about a worm that can enter into the heart of a believer? It's like the worm that enters the trunk of a date palm and, over time, brings death to the inside of the tree so that it no longer bears fruit. It is the worm of hypocrisy, an evil disease indeed."

After a pause during which he surveyed the congregation, he continued, "Remember the words that God handed down to his servant about the hypocrites: 'Verily, those who believe, then disbelieve, then believe again, and again disbelieve, and go on increasing in disbelief; God will not forgive them, nor guide them on the right way.'"

He launched into a lengthy discourse on the manifestations of hypocrisy in the recent past, such as when a leader of one of the tribes who had pledged fidelity to God and his Messenger abandoned that pledge during the battle of Uhud two years earlier. He refused to fight the Meccans and left with three hundred warriors. And more recent, Muhammad went on, was the chorus of hypocritical voices that condemned him for his marriage to Zaynab even though it was approved by God Almighty.

Muhammad jumped to his feet and shook his fist in the air. "Didn't God then continue with the command: 'Give to the hypocrites the tidings that there is for them a painful torment?' Yes or no?"

The crowd shouted, "Yes, O Messenger of God!"

"And as for the painful torment, doesn't God mean the torment of the fire?"

The crowd again shouted, "Yes, O Messenger of God!"

"That is the warning of God for those who harbor the disease of hypocrisy," Muhammad said, shaking his fist in the direction of the crowd.

He went on, "The reason I bring this to your attention today is that we have among us someone who has given proof that he has allowed the worm of hypocrisy to enter into his heart." He looked around the assembly as if searching for the culprit. "You know who you are. I ask you, I plead with you, to stand and ask forgiveness of God and His Messenger."

Ahmed felt a shock run up and down his spine. Was he about to be singled out? He had witnessed a similar event not long after he began attending the mosque. Muhammad forced several men to stand, confess, and ask for forgiveness, which they did, tears in their eyes, amid the jeers of the crowd. It didn't make an impression on him at the time because he didn't know what had brought it about.

He glanced at the crowd. Several men near him had worried looks and stared at the ground. Others smiled and winked at one another, as if anticipating a good spectacle.

When no one got up, Muhammad, standing at the edge of the platform, growled, "He knows who he is. It is he who was seen walking toward the Qurayza territory, toward those who have rejected God and His Messenger. It is he who went in conference with those who have rejected truth and inquired about their books. Rise to your feet. Confess your hypocrisy, and ask for forgiveness from God and His Messenger."

Ahmed remained seated, his heart racing. He wished he could escape, but there was nowhere to run.

Muhammad scanned the turbaned crowd, and when he looked in Ahmed's direction, he said, "Stand up, O hypocrite. Confess, and ask forgiveness from God and His Messenger. If you don't do so voluntarily, I will declare your name. It would be better for you to declare yourself."

There was no way out. Ahmed took a deep breath to calm himself. He stood up and raised his head high. He said, "You are talking about me, and I have done nothing wrong."

"O Ahmed al-Golestani," said Muhammad, "do you deny visiting the Qurayza Jews in their fortress and speaking with their rabbis about their books?"

A sea of heads turned toward Ahmed. He glanced down at Abu Ayyub, who was seated cross-legged next to him. His mouth hung down, and his one good eye was opened so wide that Ahmed thought it was about to pop out.

Ahmed looked back at the menacing figure on the platform. He said, "They are People of the Book. I went to them to inquire about what is in their books. I see nothing wrong with that."

Muhammad's voice turned scornful. "He who seeks what is in their books seeks error, and whoever seeks error is clearly on the wrong path."

Several people in the crowd shouted, "Repent! Seek forgiveness and save yourself from the fire!"

When Ahmed said nothing, Muhammad said, "Have you forgotten what God the Almighty and Merciful has said about the Jews? Didn't he say, 'Have you not considered those to whom a portion of the Book has been given? They traffic in error and desire that you should go astray.'"

Muhammad leaned forward. He pointed at Ahmed and said, "And didn't God the Almighty also say, 'Sufficient for the Jew is the flaming fire'?"

Ahmed almost blurted out, "I know that the one who calls himself the Messenger of God has said such things."

He remained silent for a moment. It was not possible to discuss what he had discovered in the Talmud. It was not possible to show these believers that Muhammad was false, that he had based his prophet stories on Jewish folk tales and claimed they came from God. The mood of the assembly had turned ugly. He glanced at all the faces. From left to right, they were turned toward him, and the expressions ranged from contempt to rage.

If he said what he thought, he would likely be ripped to pieces right then and there.

He said, "I have no reason to ask for forgiveness from God or anyone else merely for asking the People of the Book about what is in their books."

In a cold voice, Muhammad said, "Ahmed has let the worm of hypocrisy enter into him, and there is no place for hypocrites here." After a pause, he roared, "He refuses to repent and ask for forgiveness. Remove him from this assembly!"

Ali was in the first row in front of where Muhammad stood on the platform. He jumped to his feet and turned to face the congregation. He pointed to several men sitting near Ahmed. They sprang to their feet and darted toward him. Just as they pounced on him, Abu Ayyub grabbed him by the back of his garment. People cleared a path as they pushed and dragged him through the crowd to the entrance.

Once outside, they punched him until he fell to the ground. He covered his head with his arms to keep from getting hit in the face. As the other men pummeled him, Abu Ayyub kicked him in the side. He was about to kick him again when Ahmed heard Salman's angry voice. "What do you think you're doing?" he shouted. "The Messenger of God said to remove him, not to beat him. Get away from him!"

Salman shoved the men aside. They scowled at him, but he was bigger and stronger than they were. Before going back into the mosque, one of them spat at Ahmed. "You are unclean. Don't ever come back here."

Abu Ayyub was trembling with rage. As he turned to join the others, he screamed, "I will not have a hypocrite living in my house! Remove your things from there!"

When they were gone, Salman pulled Ahmed to his feet. "You should have asked for forgiveness. Didn't I warn you?"

Ahmed felt like vomiting. One of the men had punched him in the solar plexus, and he struggled to straighten up.

"I want to get away from here," he gasped. "Far, far away."

Salman shook his head and looked at Ahmed with a mixture of reproach and sadness. "Come with me," he said. "We'll go and get your things. You can stay with me until you feel better."

"Aren't you afraid of being seen with a hypocrite?"

"No, I'll tell the truth. I'm trying to persuade you to seek forgiveness."

They went around the mosque to Abu Ayyub's house. His body still aching from all the blows, Ahmed threw his possessions into a leather bag and slung it over his shoulder. With a final glance at the corral, the bleating goats, the adobe shed, and the noisy children playing in front of the house, he followed Salman toward the marketplace, now empty because of the Friday sermon. They turned up a side alley and went to Salman's lodging.

On the way, Ahmed asked, "How did Muhammad know I went to the rabbis to find out what is in their books? Except for the Qurayzas, you were the only one who knew about it. I didn't tell anyone else."

Salman avoided Ahmed's stare. After hesitating, he said, "You can't hide anything from him. I went to him to ask permission to visit the Qurayzas so they would know I informed him of their desire for neutrality. He denied me permission, but he said he would send someone to discuss the matter with them. He kept pressuring me about you, so I ended up telling him why you went there."

"I ended up with a lot of bruises because of it."

"You brought it on yourself. All you had to do was ask for forgiveness."

"I didn't do anything that needs to be forgiven."

They went inside Salman's lodging. It was larger than Ahmed's erstwhile apartment. The mud brick walls were plastered, and the dirt floor was level and covered with a broad rug. Leather water skins hung from the wall, as did long garments and turban wraps of various colors.

"When you feel better, you can go to the plantation where you worked before the Messenger of God took you on as a scribe. I'm sure the sheikh will give you your job back. Until then, this is your home," he said with a sweep of his hand.

## Chapter 16

A few days later, as Ahmed prepared to hike to the plantation in search of work, Salman rushed in. "Forget about leaving. The Meccans are coming with a huge army. We'll all be fighting them soon, you included."

Ahmed dropped the leather sack that held his belongings. "How do you know about the Meccans?"

"An uncle of the Prophet in Mecca sent a horseman with the news that the army is on the march. We believe it will reach us in six days."

Ahmed didn't want to get mixed up in a battle, but he didn't see that he had any choice. "So what are we supposed to do about it?"

"We'll fight, but we'll fight smart." Salman thumped his chest. "I came up with a solution. I suggested to the Prophet that we do what the Persians do when faced with an invasion. They dig a defensive trench. If it's wide enough and deep enough, it will stop their cavalry and create a death trap for their soldiers if they try to cross it. So come with me. That's what we're going to do. We're going to dig a trench around Yathrib!"

The plan had already been drawn up, Salman said as they hurried toward the marketplace. Due to the rugged lava fields and mountains surrounding the valley, the only way for the Meccan force to enter was along the caravan trail at the north end of the valley. Salman made slashing motions with his finger to show that the completed trench would stretch across the north end, come down the west side, and wrap under the inhabited areas to the south.

"The Messenger of God has ordered every able-bodied man in the valley to join in the digging," said Salman. "When the Meccans get here, they'll be in for a big surprise."

The marketplace was packed solid with jabbering men carrying shovels, picks, and sturdy baskets. Ali, standing atop a cart, shouted over the murmur of voices for everyone to join work brigades. He called a dozen men forward, one of them Salman, and named them brigade commanders.

"We start now," Ali shouted, thrusting his fist in the air. "Follow your commanders to their designated site and start digging. Dig until you fall from exhaustion, and then get back on your feet and start digging again. God will reward you with paradise for aiding his religion and his Messenger, for you are their holy defenders."

Ahmed joined Salman's brigade along with dozens of other men. One of the men he recognized from the mosque handed him a shovel and said, "Redeem yourself, hypocrite. Dig until you drop dead."

Carrying an assortment of digging tools and an array of weapons, the men marched north along the caravan road until coming to a region where the inhabited areas yielded to fields and an expanse of date palms beyond them. Along the way, groups of men from outlying clans joined the march. Men on camels and horses came alongside or trotted in front of the brigades. At one point, a dozen horsemen carrying batches of small black flags galloped by and disappeared up the road in a cloud of dust. Ahmed estimated that two thousand men were in the column, a ragged army of turbaned men in long robes. He heard gossip that a thousand men were heading for the west side of the valley and another thousand were marching to the southern flank.

When they reached the dig site, half of the men split off to the right of the road while the other half marched to the left. Ahmed's group went to the left. They walked for ten minutes before Salman gave the signal to stop. The horsemen had been there before them to mark off the path of the dig with the black flags. Every hundred yards or so, one of the flags was propped up by a pile of rocks.

As other brigades continued to march farther on, Salman dug his shovel into the ground next to his brigade's flag and shouted, "Start here, O Submitters!" He pointed to another flag a hundred yards farther away, where another brigade was about to set to work. "We dig in that direction."

Several men shouted, "How wide? How deep?"

"We go down more than the height of a tall man," said Salman, "and we make it at least twice that much in width. If the enemies of God are foolish enough to try crossing, we will slaughter them in the trench."

With a shovel, he tossed dirt to one side and said, "All that you excavate gets piled along the inner rim. That will create a high rampart that we'll stay behind when the enemy comes. It will protect us from their arrows and their sling stones."

As the work progressed, more men and more digging tools arrived. Salman informed Ahmed that the Qurayzas, insisting on remaining neutral, refused to send their men to help with the digging, but as a gesture of goodwill, they sent hundreds of shovels, pickaxes, and baskets.

It was late winter and freezing, but the strenuous work kept Ahmed warm. Before it became dark, men riding camels came by to leave sacks of dates. A crew was sent out to gather firewood, and that night the workers crowded around smoking campfires to keep warm while they ate dates. After the spare meal, the men of Salman's brigade lit torches and continued digging throughout the night.

The next day, Muhammad, Ali, and other leaders rode by on horses to inspect the progress. Later in the day, Muhammad returned with two other men and joined Salman in the digging. After grabbing a shovel, he said loud enough for everyone to hear, "O Salman, you are now and always will be one of my family for proposing this ditch."

By the time Muhammad arrived at the dig, Salman's brigade had already excavated fifteen yards of the trench, and Muhammad joined them for an hour in lengthening it. He made a point of snubbing Ahmed, only looking in his direction once, and it seemed to Ahmed that he looked straight through him.

Ahmed, in turn, kept his distance. Months earlier, he would have been mortified by the snub, but now he felt only anger. He kept the anger burning by repeating in his mind one of the last verses Muhammad dictated to him: "Wherever they are found they shall be seized and murdered, a horrible murdering."

He blamed Muhammad for the powerful army on its way to wage war. It was his violence, his incessant attacks against their caravans, that brought out the fury of the Meccans. He was relieved when Muhammad mounted his horse and left.

Over the next several days, Ahmed worked to the point of exhaustion. He slept for only a few hours before Salman roused him to continue digging. Salman also sent him and others with experience climbing trees to cut fronds from the date palms of a nearby plantation. They were needed for firewood, but also as supports for low shelters built into the dirt rampart as protection against the "showering of arrows," as Salman described a tactic of shooting arrows at a steep angle so they strike people hiding behind fortifications.

On the sixth day, a horseman wearing leather body armor and a metal helmet galloped up to Salman's camp. "The Meccans and their confederates have reached the northern entrance," he announced. "They are twelve thousand strong. We are far fewer, but God and his angels are with us. So prepare to fight." Before galloping away, he shouted, "Courage, O Submitters! Paradise awaits all who defend God and His Messenger!"

Ahmed surveyed the completed trench from atop the dirt pile. It appeared as a deep gouge in the earth that stretched as far as he could see in each direction. He looked toward Mount Uhud, which marked the northern border of the valley. The sun was at its peak, brightening the slopes with the chilled sunshine of winter. The invading army was encamped at the base of the mountain. Ahmed's view of the foothills was cut off by a thick palm grove that began several hundred yards beyond the trench, but he heard the pounding of war drums, the battle cries of thousands of warriors, and the ululations and martial songs of women. Before long, Meccan cavalry and foot soldiers appeared in a thick column on the caravan road while more soldiers poured through the palm groves. The warriors stretched into a long line and advanced to the beat of war drums. It became an elongated mass of armed men that grew larger by the minute.

When the Meccans were within two hundred yards of the trench, their general, mounted on a strong horse at the front of the Meccan line, raised his hand to halt the army. He pointed to a group of cavalrymen who galloped to within fifty yards of Ahmed's position. Dodging arrows shot by Salman's brigade, the horsemen raced along the trench before returning at full gallop to report to their leader.

"Surprise, surprise!" Salman shouted to the laughter of his men, who were positioned behind the dirt rampart. "They thought they were going to trample us!"

With further signals from the Meccan leader, hundreds of bowmen moved forward and began shooting waves of arching arrows, so dense they seemed to blacken the sky.

Up and down the trench, men shouted, "Arrows!" and dove into the shelters they had built into the piled dirt. Several slammed into the ground just outside Ahmed's shelter. Down the line, someone screamed, "I'm hit!"

When the showering of arrows ceased, Ahmed peered over the rampart. Heavy pounding of hoofs shook the ground as Meccan horsemen galloped parallel to the trench. Some of them made sudden rushes toward the trench as if to gauge the defenses. Each time, they retreated when they were met with arrows and sling stones. After several hours of futile forays, the Meccans backed off and retreated to their camp.

Ahmed wished the Meccans would succeed, even at the cost of his own life, but it was clear it would turn into the exhausting standoff described in the histories. He had been swept into it by virtue of being there, but rather than a participant, he felt more like a spectator of a fated event. Salman's trench would ensure the continuation of Muhammad's religion.

Over the next day, the Meccans moved their camps forward to within shouting distance of the trench and traded insults with the defenders. From behind the dirt rampart, the defenders spent their days shooting arrows and their nights watching the Meccan campfires burn out, listening for stealth movements in the dark. Food ran short; the nights were freezing.

As the siege dragged into the third week, Salman came to Ahmed with news that the Qurayzas had abandoned their neutrality. "The Meccans have talked the Jews into attacking us from behind," Salman said. "That will create an opening for the enemy to pour across the trench and invade the valley."

Ahmed shook his head. "That's a terrible mistake. Muhammad will never forgive them."

"Your Jewish friends will soon be your Jewish enemies," said Salman.

Ahmed was saddened by the news. He sympathized with their change of heart. The invading force was powerful and determined. If the Jews attacked the trench defenders from behind, the numerical superiority of the Meccans would ensure victory. The Jews would no longer live in fear for their future. But he realized they were doomed when Salman told him of Muhammad's scheme to undermine the alliance. He sent a double agent to tell the Jews that the Meccans could not be trusted. The agent was a well-known merchant who accompanied the coalition forces, but went to Muhammad in secret to swear allegiance. The agent advised the Jews to demand hostages from the Meccans to ensure they didn't abandon the fight and leave them exposed to Muhammad's vengeance. When the Jews demanded that the Meccans turn over prominent tribal elders as hostages, the Meccans refused. The same merchant had gone to them to warn that the Jews were going to demand hostages, claiming it was necessary to keep the Meccans from leaving, but their real intention was to turn them over to Muhammad in exchange for immunity. The Jews regretted their decision to join the battle against Muhammad, and the hostages would give them bargaining power with Muhammad.

Now mistrustful of each other, the Jewish-Meccan alliance was about to fall apart.

In telling Ahmed about these developments, Salman seemed defensive and apologetic. Ahmed's stare was chillier than the air, and Salman would not look him in the eye. Salman had brought this about with his trench idea, Ahmed reminded him. Without the long trench, it would have meant the defeat of Muhammad. But now, if Muhammad's divisive tactics were successful, the Jews were certain to be in harm's way. The Meccans could not sustain the stalemate for much longer. They would give up and leave.

Ahmed struggled to shake off the fatalism that immobilized him. He couldn't bear the thought of harm coming to Nabbash and his daughter, or to Rabbi Sallim and Kab and all the other people he had come to know. He could no longer remain a passive participant, a mere spectator. He had to take action. He prepared himself to do the only thing he could think of, which was to slip away from the trench after dark and make his way to the Qurayzas to warn them of Muhammad's ploy to divide them from the Meccans. He wanted to rally them to fight. He was prepared to take up arms with them.

But that afternoon, a thunderstorm broke out. Sheets of icy rain drenched the defenders and filled the trench with a foot of water. Before nightfall, the winds turned furious. Ahmed was determined to brave the storm, but once it was dark, the storm turned into a gale. He set out for the Qurayza territory, braving the fierce winds and freezing rain that tore into him. As he trudged along, he realized he would not survive even for an hour if he kept going. With a heavy heart, he went back to the trench. He had no recourse but to bundle up inside his tiny shelter to keep from freezing to death.

He went to sleep amid the howling wind, determined to set out for the Qurayza territory in the morning even if it meant having to slip away in the full light of day.

At dawn, he was awakened by the joyful shouts and cheers of men up and down the trench line.

He crawled out of the shelter, looked over the pile of dirt, and was startled to see that the Meccan army was gone.

# Chapter 17

Ahmed followed the weary but cheerful defenders on the trudge home. Salman was nowhere to be seen, and Ahmed assumed he had gone ahead to confer with Muhammad. As the hundreds of men plodded along the road, he listened to the talk swirling among the troops, hoping to find out why the Meccans departed, but no one knew anything except that the ordeal was over and now they could all go home.

No sooner had he arrived at Salman's abode, however, than Salman came running up the alley from the direction of the mosque.

"We've been ordered to fight the Qurayzas," he said, almost out of breath. "The Prophet said that everyone who took part in the defense against the Meccans must now take up arms against the Jews."

"Why?" said Ahmed, alarmed yet knowing the answer.

"Because they broke their neutrality."

The coalition fell apart, Salman explained, because the Meccans refused to hand over hostages and instead demanded hostages from them. When they settled the matter, it was the Sabbath, and the Jews refused to fight on their Sabbath. It had to be the next day, but the Meccans were getting desperate and couldn't hold out another day. Their supplies were running low. They had little food for themselves or fodder for their animals. Some of their pack animals were dying.

"I know this because the Prophet had spies among the Meccans in their camp," Salman said. "The last straw came last night when the gale struck. It blew down their tents and overturned their cooking pots. Their leaders ordered everyone to pack up and leave. They were gone before dawn."

"I don't want harm to come to the Qurayzas," said Ahmed. "They only did what they did because they were afraid of Muhammad.

"An angel of God ordered the Prophet to make war on the Jews. He must obey God, and we must obey the Prophet."

Ahmed laughed in his face. "You can't be serious. Who told you this?"

"The Messenger of God. I was with him earlier. He said the Angel Gabriel appeared to him in the mosque courtyard and told him he must wage war on the Jews for their treachery. So he ordered the clan sheikhs to lead their warriors to the Qurayza territory and prepare to lay siege."

"How convenient. And the Angel Gabriel no less. And you believe this?"

"There's nothing that can be done about it," said Salman with a burst of irritation. "You must obey the Prophet. If you refuse to join the army and stay behind, I can't guarantee your safety. As long as you're with me, no one will touch you. You're under my protection."

Ahmed felt trapped. He had nowhere to go, but even if he had somewhere to go, he didn't have the means. He had thought about going to Persia. He possessed a handful of silver coins, but it was not enough to buy a camel and provisions. If he fled on foot, he would die in the desert.

"Is there any way to influence Muhammad so he doesn't harm the Qurayzas?"

"I don't know. He spared the other Jewish tribes. Maybe he will spare the Qurayzas."

"He didn't spare them," Ahmed said. "He drove them out and took over their lands and their homes."

"At least they left with their heads still attached."

Salman grabbed the armor and weapons hanging from pegs and handed Ahmed a sword.

Ahmed shook his head. "I will go with you, but I don't need a sword. I will not fight the Qurayzas."

"Have it your way then, but stay with me," Salman said as he rushed out the door.

On the road leading to the highlands, they joined groups of armed men as they flowed out of the Najjar territory and coalesced into irregular companies. Along the way, other men from various clans joined the march, many complaining that they had been rousted the very morning the Meccan attack ended.

Several hours later, they reached the familiar Qurayza territory. Ahmed's heart sank when he saw that Nabbash's village was emptied of its people. They had to have fled to the fortress.

Some of the warriors jeered at the sight of the outlying structures. As they marched by Nabbash's village, Ahmed felt a chill when he overheard fighters discuss the booty they had been given from previous battles and raids. A short, stocky man with a black beard and curly black hair that squeezed from under his helmet, pointed to one of the larger abodes of the village. "I'll take that one as my booty and a section of date palms."

Another man said, "Dream your dreams, O al-Khazraji. At most, you'll get a hundred dirhams and a dozen goats."

"I'll be satisfied with one of the Jewish girls," said another, a tall, humorless man who carried a spear.

The Jewish fortress was a mile farther up the road, and when its high battlements came into view, Ahmed was gripped with sadness. Only a month before, the rabbis had welcomed him and shared their knowledge with him. He remembered the warmth and conviviality of his hosts. Now he was with a force that was bent on destroying them.

By the time they arrived, two thousand warriors were already massed at a distance from the fortress. Muhammad had not yet arrived. Ali was at the front of the troops giving orders to men who were erecting a large red command tent within sight of the fortress, but out of range of arrows. Muhammad, wearing a helmet, leather armor, and a sword, soon arrived on horseback, accompanied by a guard of cavalry.

The assembled warriors hailed him and made way as he strode up to the red tent where Ali and other leaders were gathered. He conferred with Ali and stepped toward the Jewish fort. He stopped at an arrow's distance from the high walls and the massive doors of the entrance.

"O sons of monkeys and pigs," Muhammad shouted. "Ali has informed me that you insulted the Messenger of God and his wives with your taunts."

One of the Qurayzas shouted down from the top of the battlements. "O son of a polytheist, why would we want to insult someone like you?"

Muhammad shouted back, "You will soon laugh little and cry much, O enemies of God."

He turned to his troops and ordered them into prayer formation. By then, another thousand warriors had arrived. They formed huge rows and ranks and followed Muhammad in sets of prayer prostrations. At the beginning of each set, Muhammad repeated Quran verses that cursed the Jews. He recited them in a voice loud enough for the fortress defenders to hear.

Upon their arrival, Salman went forward to join the leaders at the tent, but Ahmed stayed at the back of the army where a palm grove began. He resisted the temptation to slip away through the trees and instead joined the last prayer row and went through the motions. He felt dirty as he prostrated while Muhammad repeated Quran verses in his strong voice. They were verses that incited hatred against the Jews, people he knew to be decent and good. Instead of repeating the curses against the Jews, he cursed himself for being unable to do anything to help them. He prayed that a miracle would spare them.

When the praying was over, Muhammad sent a hundred archers forward to shoot at the men atop the battlements and ordered a squad of warriors to break through the entrance with a battering ram cut from a fallen palm tree. The fighters struck several hard blows against the thick double doors, but they were soon repelled when the defenders dropped heavy rocks from the battlement.

The battering ram attack resumed the following day, but the attempt to break through the door failed again after a number of Muhammad's men were hit by arrows or crushed under large rocks dropped from high above. Ahmed was certain he saw a woman behind the battlement drop one of the rocks. He was not close enough to see if it was Maryam fulfilling her pledge to fight alongside the men, but he didn't doubt that it was her.

On the third day, after the army settled into numerous small camps, some with tents, word spread that Muhammad had called off attempts to break into the fortress. Instead of fighting, he ordered his men to wait out the Qurayzas. The Jews were surrounded. Their food stores would not last.

Ahmed heard one of the men at a nearby campfire say, "If they don't surrender, they'll starve to death." Another warrior laughed while chewing a juicy date. "They get thin, we get fat."

He kept a low profile, collecting firewood during the day by climbing date trees to sever fronds. No one took any notice of him or objected when he unloaded firewood next to campfires. At night, he stayed by a fire at the very edge of the date plantation, away from the mass of attackers. At first, he was by himself, but after a few days, several other men joined him. He sensed from the way their eyes narrowed and lips squeezed when they looked in the direction of Muhammad's warriors that they also didn't like what was being done to the Jewish tribe. They sat around the fire, and if they spoke at all, it was only to comment on the coldness of the night and the warmth of the crackling flames.

On several occasions, rumors circulated that the Jews were going to attempt a breakout at night to attack Muhammad's forces. Sentries were posted, and the warriors slept with their swords at the ready. But these turned out to be false alarms. After the third week, news spread that the Jews wanted to negotiate their surrender. Several men came out of the fortress and were escorted to Muhammad's red command tent. Ahmed spotted Nabbash among them and saw him go inside the tent. The men came out ten minutes later and went back to the fortress. Ahmed assumed they had discussed surrendering with Muhammad. He listened for rumors, but no one knew anything.

An hour later, one of Muhammad's men went into the Jewish fortress alone. Ahmed had never spoken with him, but he knew his name was Abu Lubaba and that he had been on friendly terms with the Qurayzas. He had often seen him at the mosque in the front row near Ali.

An hour after going into the fortress, Abu Lubaba rushed out and left on horseback without first reporting to Muhammad. A buzz swept through the warrior camps that he had betrayed Muhammad by revealing his intention to behead all the men. He fled on his horse out of fear for his own neck.

Two hours later, the Qurayzas began coming out of the fortress, first the men, then the women and children. With their eyes downcast, they crowded into the open area on both sides of the entrance. Standing in front of his tent, Muhammad shouted, "Keep the men and women separate."

The men were forced to one side, while the women and children were pushed to the other. After the Qurayzas stopped coming out, Muhammad sent squads of fighters into the fortress. They came out shoving a dozen men and women ahead of them. Two of the men threw punches, but they were beaten and kicked, and forced to join the other men.

Not long after, a tall, portly man riding a donkey arrived from the Najjar territory, accompanied by a dozen warriors. The man needed help to dismount. Ahmed recognized him as the leader of a clan that had once been an ally of the Jews. His name was Sa'd Muadh. He had been hit in the forearm by an arrow during the Meccan attack, and it was rumored he was dying from an infection. The crowd of warriors opened a path for him, and he walked with difficulty up to Muhammad. They disappeared into the tent. A rumor spread that Muhammad was going to leave the decision about the fate of the Jews to the wounded leader.

They came out of the tent fifteen minutes later, accompanied by Bilal, who stepped out in front of them. In a powerful voice, he cried out, "It is the judgment of Sa'd Muadh, and with the assent of God and his Messenger, that all the men of the Qurayzas are to be executed, and it is his judgment that all the women and children are to be sold into slavery."

Ahmed felt like the wind had been knocked out of him, and he braced himself against a palm tree to keep from falling. He slid to the ground with his knees pulled up and leaned his forehead against them. He was in too much shock even to weep. He only looked up again when horsemen snapped whips and shouted at the captive men to go out to the road.

There were eight or nine hundred men, young and old. They were at a distance from Ahmed, but he recognized Nabbash, Kab, and men he had known when he worked on the plantation. Many walked with shoulders slumped and heads bowed, but others held their heads upright and their shoulders thrown back.

Among the last of the column was Rabbi Sallim. He was with a small group of elderly men who walked leaning on canes. One of the riders cracked his whip to make them walk faster. With the elders in the rear, the captives disappeared down the road flanked by dozens of horsemen.

The women and children were kept in front of the fortress for another hour. Throngs of warriors were crowded up toward Muhammad's tent, making it impossible for Ahmed to see what was happening. One of the burly men at a campsite near Ahmed lifted a smaller man on his shoulders to see over the crowd.

"Speak to us, O al-Khazraji," said the burly man to the man on his shoulders. "What are they doing?"

"I see a lot of young women lined up in front of the Messenger of God's tent. He's talking to one of them. I think he's going to claim the prettiest for himself."

"That's his reward for being the Messenger of God," said a warrior standing next to them. "He gets the first pick of the booty."

After a few minutes, the man who was sitting on the burly man's shoulders shouted, "He's made his choice! He's sending them all back except for one. Hurry, carry me up closer so I can get a better look at her."

When the warriors around Muhammad's tent dispersed, horsemen crowded behind the women and children to force them to the road. Some of the children began wailing, but became quiet when the riders shouted at them and snapped their whips. The women, holding children by the hand or carrying them in their arms, walked in clusters. Ahmed was crushed when he saw Maryam, her head held high, at the front of the column.

Salman was among the horsemen. He spotted Ahmed and halted. After they stared at each other for a long moment, Salman whipped the flank of his horse and galloped down the road, leaving a trail of dust.

As soon as the captives were gone, warriors who remained behind rushed into the fortress. Shouting *"Allahu Akbar,"* they carried out everything that was movable. Fearing he would be ordered to join the plundering, Ahmed slipped into the date plantation and ran between the trees until he reached a field on the other side. He wandered through various fields and date groves until he came to Nabbash's village. It was also being pillaged by men who chattered and laughed as they piled the wealth of the village onto the road. He made a long detour through more palm groves and stopped when he came to the field of saplings that had been planted the year before to obtain Salman's freedom.

He cursed Salman. He had sealed the fate of the Qurayzas. No one would have thought of digging a trench if he had not come up with the idea. Without the trench, the overwhelming force of the Meccans would have put an end to Muhammad, sparing the Qurayzas from this injustice.

Ahmed had no choice but to leave Yathrib. His meager belongings and the modest sum of money he had accumulated were still at Salman's lodging. He had to get there, gather everything, and somehow get away. He prayed that Salman would help him obtain a mount.

It was getting dark, and it was impossible to continue without walking along the road. He spent the night at the edge of the plantation, protecting himself from the cold by burrowing under a pile of palm fronds. In the late morning, warmed by the sun and nourished by dates overlooked from the harvest, he made the long walk back to the Najjar territory.

Once in town, he went through a maze of alleys to avoid the mosque, but he couldn't skirt the marketplace. It was thick with people standing shoulder to shoulder. Every few minutes, a roar of *"Allahu Akbar!"* arose from the crowd. Ahmed tried to go around, but everywhere he went, he ran into a mass of people pushing forward. Even the alley leading to Salman's lodging was jammed. He tried to edge through to get into the alley, but the crush of people swept him back into the marketplace.

As he looked for a way out, he caught sight of an open area at the center of the marketplace. An enormous trench had been dug. The excavated dirt was piled along one side, just as it had been done with the defensive trench. He had to stand on his tiptoes to see over the many turbans. On one side of the trench, five men were on their knees, one of them a teenager who had often helped him carry loads of dates into the sorting warehouse. Ali and Zubayr, another of Muhammad's first cousins, stood next to them. Ali was holding a sword raised high.

Ahmed was jostled by people who pushed from behind to get a look. All he was able to see was Ali's swords slashing downward. The crowd roared, *"Allahu Akbar,"* repeating it four more times in quick succession. He forced his way forward, earning seething curses and sharp jabs from people he displaced. One of the men in the crowd recognized him and said, "It's the hypocrite Ahmed. You should be among the Jews, O hypocrite."

Ahmed ignored him and peered between the people in front of him. Muhammad was seated a short distance from the trench. Another group of Jews was brought forward, among them Nabbash. He was without a turban, and his gray hair was tousled. His arms were tied behind his back in such a way that it forced him to bend forward. As he approached the trench, he struggled with the guards gripping his arms. He head-butted one of them and struggled to free himself, but the guards beat him to the ground.

"You are less than animals," he spat out. "Not even jackals would behave like you are behaving."

Muhammad motioned for his men to bring Nabbash to him. When Nabbash stood before him, Muhammad said, "You could have spared yourselves God's punishment by accepting that I am the Messenger of God. But now it's too late."

"I don't regret opposing you, Muhammad. You are false, you are evil, and it is you who will face the punishment of God."

Muhammad motioned to his men and roared, "Take him to the trench!"

Ahmed felt his legs weakening. His head began to spin, and

he feared he would collapse. He was about to push through the people in front of him and shout, "Leave them alone!" when he felt a powerful grip on his arm. It was Salman. He pulled Ahmed close and said, "Don't do anything stupid or you'll end up in the trench with them."

It took Ahmed a few seconds to realize that Salman had spoken to him in modern Persian. Ever since he had known him, they had always spoken in Arabic. Ahmed looked at him in astonishment.

"I don't want anything to happen to you," Salman said, again in the modern Persian as he gripped Ahmed's arm with steely firmness.

They were interrupted by more cheers of *"Allahu Akbar,"* repeated in quick succession. Ahmed looked back at the trench. While Ali and Zubayr stood to one side, other men threw the torsos into the trench, followed by the severed heads.

A herald stepped from behind Muhammad. He cried out, "Bring the daughter of Nabbash forward. It is she who dropped the millstone on a believer during the siege of the Qurayza fortress and killed him. God has ruled that the penalty for killing a believer is death!"

Maryam was brought forward by two strong men, each gripping her by an arm. Her long hair was uncovered and tied at the nape of her neck. Muhammad, his eyes narrowing at the sight of her, said nothing when she was dragged before him. He stared at her for a moment and signaled to the guards to take her to the trench. At the edge of the trench, she stretched out her arms. Tears streaming down her face, she cried out, "O my father, O my people."

Ali growled at her to get on her knees, but she remained standing. He pushed down on her shoulders to force her to kneel. When she was on her knees, she raised her arms to the sky and cried, "O the light! O the light!"

Just as Ali raised his sword over his head, Ahmed ripped himself away from Salman. He shouted, "This is evil! This cannot be allowed! Stop this atrocity!"

He struggled to break through the crowd. The moment Ali slashed down with the sword, he felt a powerful punch to the back of his head. He dropped to his knees. Another powerful blow just above his neck caused him to fall on his side.

All he remembered before blacking out were dirty sandals and dusty toes that almost touched his nose and the strong hands that gripped him under his arms.

# Chapter 18

Ahmed awoke with a painful neck and a raging headache. Without moving his head, he glanced to the right and left and saw he was in Salman's room. No one answered when he said, "Are you there, Salman?"

He had no idea what time it was, but light was streaming in through the small window. He listened for cries of *"Allahu Akbar"* from the marketplace, only a stone's throw away, but all was quiet.

He groaned and felt tears welling up. He wept as the scenes of death filled his mind. Again and again, he heard Maryam's cry before she was killed. He felt sickened at the memory of Ali's brutality. He was raised to believe in Muhammad's cousin as a sacred vessel who carried the light of truth that Muhammad brought to the world. Ali, the beheader of the Qurayzas, the "guardian of God" in the Shi'ite call to prayer; Ali, who begot Hasan and Hossein, and Hossein, who begot Ali Zayn al-Abidin, who begot Muhammad al-Baqir, who begot Jafar al-Sidiq, and on and on until Imam Mahdi, the hidden Imam of Time whom they await to appear from the well of the mosque of Jamkaran to bring the light of truth to the entire world.

He said words that he never imagined he could ever say. "You are a thug, Ali. And you, Muhammad, are the inspirer of thugs and the creator of a thug religion."

He wondered if the Shi'as and the Sunnis and the members of the other sects of Islam became aware of the heinous crimes of their founders, that they would remain believers. They should all go back in time as he did. They should become scribes and take down Muhammad's verses and suggest words to him that their future selves would memorize as words of God. They should stand in the marketplace and witness their holy Imam Ali cut off heads—the same Ali of the depictions they hung in their homes with the hint of a halo around his head and the mascara that gave him the look of virile spirituality.

He wanted to experience true Islam, and now that he had experienced it, he wanted to get as far away from it as he could. But he had to have a camel. Without a camel, there was no way for him to leave. Salman was his only hope. Where was Salman? He had to talk to Salman.

After an hour of lying on his back, he forced himself to get up. He massaged his neck and the back of his head. When he felt better, he went into the alley and walked to the marketplace with the vain hope that he'd had a nightmare, that what happened had not happened.

His hope was shattered when he got there. Men were shoveling dirt over the trench. The dirt was piled more than a foot above the level of the market grounds, like a mound over a fresh grave in a cemetery. Vendors were at their stalls, but except for the men shoveling dirt, the marketplace was nearly empty. Ahmed went to the edge of the mound and stood where Nabbash and Maryam were forced to their knees before they were killed. He raised his arms to the heavens just as Maryam had done and said a prayer for the Qurayzas to be with the light.

The workers stopped the shoveling to watch him. One of them said, "That's the hypocrite Ahmed." Another said, "I regret that we're not shoveling dirt over you, too, O hypocrite!"

He returned to Salman's lodging. While waiting for Salman, he stuffed his possessions into the leather bag. He loosened the string of his money purse and counted the silver coins. It was not much, but if he could get a camel, he would go far away. He would find work. He knew all about date farming now. Surely he could make himself useful on a date plantation somewhere. He heard of Jewish plantations in Khaybar, Fadak, Wadi al-Qura, and other oases far north of Yathrib.

Salman came an hour later. He leaned against the wall, his

arms folded, and stared at Ahmed for a moment. "How do you feel?"

"How do you think I feel after what they did?"

"I mean your head."

"It hurts."

"I'm sorry. I had to do that to you. You would have been killed if I hadn't stopped you."

"I want to leave. I don't want any part of this anymore. I need a camel. Can you help me?"

"Yes. In fact, that's what I've been doing all morning. You'll have a camel tonight. I've made arrangements. You'll meet me on the caravan trail outside the Najjar territory. It's important that nobody sees you leave, so it has to be late."

"Won't that cause you trouble with your 'Messenger of God'?"

Salman shrugged. "All I know is that you left for the plantation of the hypocrite sheikh Abdullah to look for work."

"I'm thankful for your help."

"I don't want anything to happen to you, Ahmed."

Salman said the latter sentence in modern Persian, just as he had done the day before. Ahmed had forgotten about it. He looked at Salman in confusion. "How can it be that you speak Persian the same way that I speak it?"

"What do you think?" Salman said, smiling. "It's because I'm like you, but from Isfahan."

"You mean . . ."

"You're not the only one. There are others besides you and me. But you're the only one I'm sure about."

"I'm not going to deny it, but how did you know about me? I told no one about this. Who would have believed me?"

Salman laughed. "You gave yourself away that very first day when you told Nabbash you were from the Land of Roses. Golestan is the name for the region that came into use much, much later. At this time, it's known as the Land of the Wolves—Varkana, or Hyrcania as the Greeks call it."

"How did you get here?"

"I didn't end up drowning in a well like you. My father is a prominent businessman in Isfahan. You would recognize his name if I told you. I saw the injustices of our society under the mullahs. I didn't think it was true Islam. I wished I could experience the pure Islam of Muhammad and Ali, just like you. Then one day I woke up outside a monastery in Ninevah. A monk shook my shoulder to wake me up. As for how I got to Yathrib, it's close to what is said in the history books."

"Did you have a dream of light?"

"Yes, many times."

"You saw the truth about pure Islam yesterday in the market-place," said Ahmed.

Salman lowered his head and looked away. "I didn't like what happened. I argued against it after the Qurayzas surrendered, but no one listened to me."

Ahmed snapped at him. "You could have prevented it. All you had to do was not give them the idea of the trench. The Meccans would have swept over the entire valley. They would have destroyed Islam once and for all. Muhammad would not have survived, nor any of his people. Think about it, Salman. Iran would be a different place. The entire world would be different."

"If there hadn't been a trench, you and I would have been killed."

Ahmed shrugged. "What difference would that make? That's not important."

"I fulfilled my destiny," Salman said. "Do you know that when I was young, I visited the Mausoleum of Salman in Iraq and various shrines to Salman in Iran? I had no idea they were dedicated to me, Salman al-Farisi! How can what exists be changed?"

Ahmed said between clenched teeth, "If you had not told them about the trench, those shrines would never have come into existence."

Salman shook his head. "You're deluded if you think you can change the past. You can't. All you can do is experience it. You were just like me. You wanted to experience pure Islam. Now you've experienced it. Be satisfied with that."

Ahmed was furious that Salman was right. He had not been able to do anything to change the outcome. If he had been killed along with the Qurayzas because of his outburst, would he even have a future existence? He wondered if someone born in the future could die in the past, if they would negate each other. It was a conundrum, and his head already hurt too much to think about it. Now all that was important was to get away, the farther the better.

Salman told him where they were to meet: on the caravan road where it cut through a date plantation just outside the Najjar territory. He would wait for Ahmed near a small village that was on the other side of the last grove.

"The moon will be nearly full, so you'll have enough light to guide you. Just follow the road."

At the appointed hour, Ahmed, his possessions slung over his shoulder, left Salman's lodging and hiked along the caravan trail, guided by moonlight. After trudging for nearly an hour, he found Salman where he said he would be. He was standing at the side of the road holding the reins of two camels, one with provisions in bulky saddle bags. Ahmed rode the latter, and they followed the trail for two hours to a mountain pass at the north end of the valley. It was known as the Farewell Pass, and it marked the beginning of the caravan trail to Gaza and Damascus, a more than a month-long journey.

When they were at the top of the pass, Salman pointed north. "Travel by night and find secure places to sleep by day. That way, you'll avoid brigands."

He handed Ahmed a sword, a dagger, a bow, and a quiver of arrows. "I know you don't like such things, but having them with you will give you a feeling of security, and they'll make people think twice about bothering you."

Ahmed looked back at the valley of Yathrib, visible in the moonlight.

"Where will you go?" Salman asked.

"I don't know. I want to find true religion, a religion that is worthy of my humanity, so that's where I'll go. Where there is true religion."

He told Salman about the cave and the experience of the light. "It said to me, 'I am you, and you are me.' What do you think that means?"

"It means we've both had this experience of finding ourselves where we never imagined we would be."

After they stared in silence into the darkness for a long while, Ahmed said, "Why don't you come with me? We'll go to Persia—to Isfahan and to the Land of the Wolves. We'll see the Persia of the Zoroastrians."

Salman shook his head. "I will stay."

"Why? You know that Muhammad is a fraud. You know that what he created is evil. You've been a witness to his evil."

Salman remained silent for a long time, looking into the distance. "I'll tell you why I'm staying. It's because it's exciting to be around him. I've never known anyone like him."

Ahmed felt a burst of anger. It took him a moment to calm down. "So be it then, Salman. I bid you farewell."

He nudged his camel forward, and it plodded down the trail. When he had descended the mountain and was already at a distance, Salman cried out from the top of the pass in a voice so loud it rolled down into the desert like the rumbling that precedes thunder. "I hope you find what you are looking for! Can you hear me, Ahmed? I hope you find what you are looking for!"

# Chapter 19

He wandered for days and nights, not knowing where he was, but he was certain from the stars at night and the sun by day that he was going north. He came to the Red Sea and followed the trail, sleeping in safe places during the day as Salman advised and traveling only after it was dark.

He felt heavier than he had ever felt before, so much so that he was often unable to sit upright in the saddle. As the sturdy camel plodded along, he lay forward and let his arms dangle.

One night, his camel wandered into a Bedouin camp that consisted of several tents and a herd of goats bleating nearby. As he drew near, a dozen men sitting around a campfire jumped to their feet and put their hands on the hilt of their swords. Women and children fled to the tents.

"Who are you?" their sheikh demanded.

They were turbaned desert people, and the light of the fire danced on their rough features. Several of them disappeared into the darkness behind Ahmed and soon shouted from a distance, "He's alone!"

"Who are you?" the sheikh demanded again. "If you are one of those Muhammadans, you are not welcome here."

"I want to know about God," Ahmed said from atop the high saddle. "Can you tell me about God?"

The sheikh stepped up to the camel and peered at him in the feeble light of the campfire. "Come, join us then. You are welcome among us."

Ahmed spent the night around the fire with them, and they shared the meat of a large lizard they had caught that day. They told him of their reverence for everything: the moon, the stars, the mountains. But most important to them were the three daughters of God, in particular the goddess Manat. The sheikh took his name from Manat. He was known as Abdul Manat, the servant of Manat.

"We've made the pilgrimage to Mecca to perform the circum-ambulations of the temple in honor of the gods of the temple," he said, "but mostly we perform the pilgrimage only to the temple of Manat. It's two days from Yathrib near the sea, and it's a place of beauty that is worthy of our beloved goddess."

Ahmed leaned forward. "You believe in a supreme God. Why then don't you pray to him?"

The servant of Manat smiled and looked around at the other men. Some of them broke out in laughter. He pointed to the blaze of the Milky Way.

"Where is God?" he said. "God caused all of this, but can you see God?"

"No," Ahmed conceded. "Only His creation."

"But you can see Manat," the sheikh said. "She's in the temple. We can visit her at her temple, and we can make sacrifices before her altar and pray for her to intercede with God so that the rainfall is sufficient to give our herds generous forage. She is our intercessor with God."

Ahmed spent two days with them, talking more about the gods, but they also questioned him about Muhammad. They were disturbed by the news of the massacre of the Jews.

"We do not accept what he has to offer," said Abdul Manat. "We have our beliefs, and they are good enough for us. We don't try to make others believe as we do."

When Ahmed prepared to leave, the Bedouins offered him a guide to take him north to Ayla, a town on the Red Sea, "a Christian town," said the sheikh. "What they believe is superior to what Muhammad believes."

Ahmed and the guide traveled by day for a week through barren regions far from the caravan trail. The brief time Ahmed spent in the Bedouin camp had lifted his mood, but the heaviness he experienced after leaving Yathrib returned as they progressed north. He again lay forward on the saddle and let his arms dangle. The Bedouin guide, a slender man who spoke little, observed him but said nothing. In the late afternoon of the seventh day, they reached the crest of a mountain pass. In the distance was the blue expanse of the Red Sea, and nestled against the foothills below was a port town.

"Ayla," said the guide, pointing to the town. "You will be safe from here on."

He turned his camel to leave, but Ahmed said, "Wait!" He handed the Bedouin the bow, the quiver of arrows, the sword, and the dagger that Salman gave him.

"This is to thank you and your people. Tell your sheikh that I will remember all that he told me."

The Bedouin touched his heart in acknowledgement of the gift. He secured the weapons to his saddle, prodded the camel forward, and soon disappeared in the distance.

It was not long before Ahmed was in the busy town. He hobbled his camel in front of a small church and went in. The scent of votive candles was in the air. Rows of benches divided the room. A half-dozen women were praying in front of a statue of a beautiful woman with a serene smile.

Ahmed sat in the back, staring at the cross above the altar and frescos on the walls depicting events he knew nothing about. He knew little about Christianity, only a version of it coming from Muhammad, but someone once told him the words of Jesus before he died on the cross: "Father, forgive them for they know not what they do." He also remembered that the mother of Jesus was at the foot of the cross: Maryam, the mother of Jesus. He whispered the name, and the image of the daughter of Nabbash broke into his mind. He saw her hands raised to the heavens before she was killed, and he began to weep. He tried to suppress it, but he could not.

At some point, a young priest entered from a side room, knelt for a moment before the altar, head bowed, and set about tidying the church and straightening the benches.

When the priest came near him, Ahmed stood up and said, "I want to know about Jesus. Please, tell me about Jesus."

The priest looked at Ahmed's reddened eyes and glanced over at the praying women. "Come with me then, so that we don't interfere with their devotions."

Ahmed followed him to a room where they sat on a thick rug and leaned against cushions placed against the wall. The priest, reserved at first but soon cheerful and animated, went over the tenets of the faith, that Jesus was the son of God, sent as Redeemer to reveal God as a loving Father and to take upon himself the burden of the sins of mankind through his death on the cross. He told him about the major events in the life of Jesus.

The conversation, however, turned away from Jesus when the priest asked him about his origins. Ahmed limited his reply to saying that he had been a follower of Muhammad, who claimed to be a messenger of God, but that he had abandoned the faith only two weeks earlier. "I was close to Muhammad in Yathrib. At one point, I was his scribe, and so I came to understand that everything he claims about himself is false. Now I am seeking true religion."

The priest said, "You were in Yathrib? Do you know that just three days ago, merchants coming from that region told us about rumors of a great massacre of Jews in Yathrib? Is there any truth to that?"

"I witnessed those crimes. That's why I left."

The priest jumped to his feet. "Come with me. I want you to meet our bishop."

Leading his camel by a rope, Ahmed followed the priest to a large church in the center of town. The bishop was a robust man in black clerical garments with a jeweled cross dangling from his neck. He listened to Ahmed's account of the slaughter, shaking his head.

"I would like to instruct you more about Christianity," the bishop said, "but first, I want to invite you to speak to a group of us about Muhammad and his Recital, as he calls it."

That evening, Ahmed was in a room with two dozen people: the priests and deacons of Ayla, monks from a monastery, and several prominent laymen. He summarized what Muhammad claimed about himself, and related what he and the rabbis uncovered in the Talmud about Muhammad's prophet stories. He spoke about his experiences as Muhammad's scribe, which led him to doubt the authenticity of the Recital.

The clerics peppered him with questions about Jesus. "What about the divinity of Jesus?" the bishop asked. "What does Muhammad preach about it?"

"Jesus was born of a virgin," Ahmed said, "but he was a man favored by God, not divine."

"What about the Passion of the Christ?" the bishop asked. "We have heard that Muhammad denies it."

Ahmed replied, "He claims it was a substitute who was crucified, a disciple who volunteered to die in the place of Jesus. God made him look like Jesus, and it was the volunteer who was tortured and died on the cross. Jesus was taken up into heaven at the time of the Last Supper. God put him to sleep, opened a hole in the roof where the Last Supper took place, and Jesus was raised up into heaven through the hole."

Many in the audience laughed. One of the priests cried, "That's ridiculous!"

The young priest who had introduced Ahmed to the bishop asked, "What does Muhammad have to say about the Trinity?"

"He accuses Christians of polytheism for believing that God had a son, and therefore also a spouse. To him, Maryam was the spouse of God. His understanding of the Trinity is that it consists of God, Jesus, and Maryam."

The bishop was fuming. "He understands nothing. There is one God who manifests in three persons, the Father, the Son, and the Holy Spirit. This Muhammad is an ignoramus."

At the prompting of the bishop, Ahmed gave a chilling account of the beheading of the Jews. He talked about the failed Meccan invasion, the digging of the defensive trench, the siege of the Qurayza fortress, the surrender of the Jews, and the trench that was dug in the marketplace. His voice faltered when he told them about the beheading of the men of the tribe and their burial in the mass grave.

"Surely, he is the anti-Christ," shouted one of the deacons.

"Pray that God will protect us from his evil," the bishop said.

When it was over, the bishop arranged for Ahmed to stay at the monastery, where he remained throughout the summer. He prayed when the monks prayed, facing an altar with a crucifix above it. He labored with the monks in their fields, orchards, and olive groves. The monastery library abounded in sacred literature in Greek, Latin, and Aramaic, and Ahmed observed that the monks spent hours every day copying texts in exquisite calligraphy that they framed with pleasing designs.

When Ahmed entered the study for the first time and saw the books and scrolls, he felt the same thrill of new knowledge that he had experienced when he was with the rabbis poring over the Torah and Talmud. The monks instructed him about the life of Jesus, the doctrines of the Church, and translated passages of the Gospels for him. Over time, he became so moved that he stood up in an assembly and declared, "Truly, you have given your hearts to what is worthy of your love and devotion, and I now share your love and devotion."

Ahmed learned shortly after his arrival that Ayla was the terminus for caravans originating in Egypt and was the starting point of the caravan route going east as far as China and India. Caravans were always going in and out. One of the most important of the caravan centers was near the monastery. Ahmed often chatted with the merchants and camel drivers, who told him of their travels to Persia, Bactria, Sogdiana, China, Tibet, and India, and to the great cities of Ctesiphon, Ecbatana, Balkh, Samarkand, Chang'an, Mathura, Benares, and more. There were so many names that his head spun. The travelers told him of the Zoroastrians, the Manichaeans, the Taoists, the Buddhists, and the Hindus; they spoke of sadhus, sunyatsins, and the liberation of the soul from the cycles of rebirth.

He became filled with the desire to join a caravan heading east. More than anything, he longed to see the Persia of his ancestors and, if possible, to travel to his own land, to the eventual Golestan. Thinking about home kept him awake at night. Would he be able to recognize anything? Would Aliabad exist as a village, or would the region be a forested and wild land of wolves? He wanted to learn as much as he could about the religion of

Zarathustra. The mullahs belittled it as fire worship, a form of idolatry. Yet it was the religion of the Persian Empire for more than a thousand years before the invasion of the Muslims, who imposed Muhammad's religion. He wondered what Iran would be like if Muhammad and his religion had died in Yathrib and the faith of Zarathustra had continued to inspire Iranians. He had no answer because he knew little about the religion. That would be his priority in traveling to Persia: to learn about the religion of his ancestors.

When he announced his decision to leave, the monks were saddened but cheerfully helped him gather provisions. When the bishop learned he was joining a caravan, he held a drive to raise money for bolts of Ayla fabrics and flasks of perfume for Ahmed to bring with him.

"You will need to become a trader to finance your trip," the bishop said when he presented the gifts to him.

He loaded everything onto the camel Salman had given him and named it Seeker. The caravan was enormous, a string of five hundred camels accompanied by a squadron of armed guards on horseback. Ahmed felt a tug in his heart when his friends, who came out to bid him farewell, faded in the distance.

Along the trail, groups of merchants with their strings of camels joined the caravan at various stages. By the time it reached Palmyra, the caravan had doubled in size. It was the talk among the merchants that the region was in upheaval due to war between the Byzantine and Persian empires, but the caravan master assured them that commerce into Persia continued despite ferocious battles raging to the north.

Once inside the Persian Empire, which began on the banks of the Tigris River at the Persian summer capital of Ctesiphon, the caravan grew or shrank as it reached various branches of caravan roads. Along the way, Ahmed made brief visits to various fire temples, but because the visits occurred during one-night stopovers at caravan facilities and the temples were at a distance from the trail, he was unable to learn what he wanted.

He also became frustrated by the difficulty he found in understanding the Persian of the era, which was similar yet distant from his native Persian. It turned out there were a number of Zoroastrian merchants in the convoy. He befriended them and spent his time learning the language and listening to them speak about Zartosht, as they called Zarathustra. "It's called the good religion," said one of his caravan friends. "It creates upright character in people by encouraging the practice of good thoughts, good words, and good deeds."

When he heard this, Ahmed was reminded of his mother. Throughout his childhood and youth, she repeated those same words to tell him how he should conduct himself in life. "This is what our ancestors taught, and it is good," she would say. The caravan master was Persian and told him that in the city of Rey, still weeks away, there were several fire temples and a thriving community of the religion of Zartosht.

"Seek out the high priest Shapur," the caravan master advised him. "He will instruct you in what you want to know."

Ahmed wondered if it was the same Rey that would become a suburb of Tehran, Shahr-e Rey. If so, a day or two before the caravan arrived, he would see the snowy volcanic peak of Mount Damavand that rose above the Alborz Mountains and provided a backdrop to Tehran. When the white peak came into view, Ahmed thrust his fist into the air and let out a loud cry. "Home! At last, I'm coming home!"

Two days later, the caravan entered the gates of the fortified town. As Ahmed breathed in the cool air blowing down from the mountains, he sprinted to the top of one of the defensive towers and surveyed the fields and forests that extended north to the foothills of the mountain range. Barely twenty miles north would be the eventual location of the boulevard where he had witnessed the violent repression of the people.

He quit the caravan, sold the Ayla textiles and perfumes at the merchant market, and obtained a room at an inn that had a stable for camels. After leaving the inn, he inquired among the people about the fire temple of the chief priest Shapur. He was soon on his way to the temple in the company of a young man who offered to take him there.

The temple courtyard was packed with people praying in front of the fire temple, an open structure with huge arches on each side that gave a view of a fire rising from a wide urn in the center. Priests dressed in white robes, white caps, and with a white covering over their mouths were reciting prayers. As a priest sprinkled incense into the fire, the faithful repeated prayers. Ahmed did not understand the meaning of the rituals or the words of the prayers, but he felt in his heart the fervor of the devotees.

"The fire symbolizes the essence of the Wise Lord," the young man said when Ahmed told him he was there to learn about the religion. "To pray to the fire is to pray to the Wise Lord."

Following the ceremony, Ahmed sought out the high priest Shapur, a stocky man with a brown beard, round face, and cheerful eyes. "I want to know about the Wise Lord," Ahmed said. "Will you teach me about your religion?"

He was soon part of a group of initiates who met daily to memorize the psalms of Zartosht, discuss their meanings, and participate in the rituals of the religion around the sacred fire.

Because of Ahmed's enthusiasm, Shapur took a personal interest in him, and before long, they engaged in lengthy discussions about the religion of Zartosht and other religions. Just as when he was with the rabbis, and later with the monks, Ahmed was again immersed in a world of thought. It was another philosophy, another way of looking at the world. Within the temple complex was a library of ancient texts and their learned commentaries. He wished to acquire the ability to read and study them, but Shapur cautioned him to temper his enthusiasm with the understanding that the pursuit of knowledge was worthwhile only if it led to wisdom and wise living. They were followers of the Wise Lord, and their religion was one of seeking wisdom.

Part of its wisdom lay in its emphasis on freedom to choose, including one's religion, Shapur told him. This idea was unique in Zartosht's time because he lived in a tribal society, and the tribe dictated what people believed. "Zartosht changed that with his teaching that people should choose their own religion, but carefully and thoughtfully," Shapur said.

In part because of language difficulties, Ahmed struggled to follow the complexities of the thought behind the teachings, but he grasped the outcome in the people around him. The priests and the people who came to the temple displayed a pleasing buoyancy of spirit and attitude. They were farmers, merchants, artisans, tradesmen, and soldiers. Ahmed found them to be cheerful and helpful. They delighted in the comical but frowned on humor that wounded. He observed how they cultivated in their children the practice of good thinking, good speaking, and good action, and when the children were older, taught them the reasons for these virtues in preparation for the rites of initiation into the religion.

"We push back the darkness by practicing goodness," Shapur said to Ahmed on one occasion. "We do it for the sake of goodness, for it is the way to take power away from all that is the opposite of goodness. In doing this, we are allies of the Wise Lord."

The discussions with Shapur and other priests sometimes triggered painful memories that Ahmed strove to suppress, memories of the furious darkness of Yathrib. The excitement of the new that he experienced upon arriving in Rey helped him keep such memories at bay, but he couldn't keep them out of his head for long. He came close to disclosing his experiences to Shapur several times, but he held back.

He was troubled by his foreknowledge. In Yathrib, he had denied his knowledge of what would happen to the Qurayza Jews. It was established in history, but he pretended to himself that it was not so. He hid the outcome from himself, believing the past was malleable and could be changed. But it happened anyway. And now he had foreknowledge of what would soon become of Persia. What was done to the Qurayzas would be done to the Persians. The people he loved in Yathrib were slaughtered, and many of the people he now loved and admired in Rey would also be slaughtered, and the rest forced into a religion that was not theirs. He knew it, and it kept him awake at night.

As the weeks and months went on, his foreknowledge became unbearable. A part of him wanted to tell Shapur everything; another part of him didn't want to cause a disturbance to the serene world that had taken him in.

He kept quiet. But one day, while he was conversing with Shapur, he had a terrifying vision of destruction. He saw hordes of warriors laying siege to Rey, sacking the town. He saw swarms of ferocious men overwhelming the temple, where people were fleeing for refuge. He saw the fierce ones killing people with swords, spears, and arrows. He saw Shapur pushed to his knees and his head cut off. He saw the library and the sacred literature in flames. The vision came to him even though his eyes were wide open. He was so shaken that he trembled.

The priest became concerned. "Something troubles you, Ahmed. What is it?"

Ahmed shook his head to chase away the awful vision. "I have reason to fear for Persia," he said, still trembling. "A great darkness will soon descend upon it."

He told Shapur everything he had witnessed in Yathrib. "You must preserve your sacred works for the benefit of the future. Copy them and hide them where future generations can restore the good that was lost. You must begin this immediately."

"How can you know this?" the priest said.

"What is coming is what I witnessed in Arabia. This darkness will not be confined to Arabia for long."

Several weeks later, he announced his departure. The visions of destruction kept assaulting him, and it became too painful to remain in the very place that inspired them. He was impelled to continue his journey even though his formal initiation into the religion of Zartosht was not far off. He had to move on.

In parting, he said to Shapur, "You have awakened me to the fact that in my soul I have always been Zarathustrian."

Prior to his departure, he rode Seeker to a stretch of farmland twenty miles north of Rey where the future boulevard would exist. Instead of wheat fields, he saw enormous crowds of protesters and relived the moment squadrons of motorcycles attacked them. He heard the gunshot again, and he saw the young woman crumple to the ground.

He prayed that Iran would return to its true spirit. "If you do, you will become a missionary of good to the world rather than an agent of darkness."

# Chapter 20

Eager to go east, Ahmed joined a caravan that set out along the foothills of the Alborz Mountains in the direction of Balkh. In addition to the usual provisions, he loaded Seeker with one hundred pounds of red brass ingots he had purchased from a local refiner after learning of a huge demand for the unusual alloy in the East.

Three days after leaving Rey, the caravan came to a stage stop near the mountain pass leading to the north side of the Alborz Mountains, the same pass that would eventually become the route of the railroad and highway connecting Tehran with Gorgan. He learned that a small caravan of four dozen camels was about to head for the pass. He was torn between joining the merchants, hoping to see the land of his birth and perhaps finding the cave, or continuing the journey east. Hardly a day went by since the time Abdullah pulled him out of the well and sold him into slavery that he didn't think about the cave and the cryptic words he heard from the brilliant light, but he was still as perplexed as ever about their meaning. "I am you, and you are me." Would he be any closer to grasping the meaning even if he were able to find the cave?

He decided to continue east and threw himself into it with enthusiasm. He was eager to learn about the ideas people had about God. To his caravan companions, he said, "I want to know about God, so tell me about God!"

With the merchants, the usual talk was about the selling price of their wares, the dangers and hardships of the road, and memories of exotic places. But with Ahmed's cheerful prodding, the talk turned to their personal beliefs. While walking in front of their camels, sitting around sparking campfires, or seated in the noisy taverns and dining halls of the stage stops, the talk was of the divine.

From Manichaeans, Ahmed learned about the religion of Mani; from soldiers, about the Mithraic cult; from Chinese traders, about Taoism, Confucianism, and Buddhism. The talks were spirited and often turned on banter and polylingual puns as they drew in ever more diverse people. Ahmed soon acquired a nickname: He Who Asks About God. His reputation went ahead of him with other travelers, and at the next caravan stop, people would often inquire in various languages about He Who Asks About God.

"Most people will tell you about God," said one of the camel drivers, "but you are one of the few to ask about Him."

After a month on the road, the caravan reached the sprawling trading town of Balkh, where the trail branched into routes leading to China, Tibet, and India. During the journey, Ahmed heard of numerous Buddhist monasteries outside of Balkh. An enormous statue of Buddha was said to exist there, and he was eager to see it. He thought about remaining behind to devote time to the study of Buddhism, but he changed his mind after a young Indian merchant named Ganid approached him.

"If you want to know about God," Ganid said. "Come with me to India. India is the Land of God."

When Ahmed told him of his desire to stay in Balkh to learn about Buddhism, the young merchant said, "My destination is Kashi, the holiest city of India. The Buddha gave his first sermon and acquired his first disciples near Kashi at the famous Deer Park. So come with me to Kashi. You will be my guest, and I will tell you all about the one God and the many gods of the Indians. I will even take you to the Buddhist monastery at the Deer Park so you can speak with the monks."

"So it will be then!" said Ahmed, cheered by the enthusiasm of the young Indian.

His new traveling companion was the son of a wealthy Kashi merchant. He was in command of a convoy returning from the

Levant carrying cargoes of Damascus-steel swords and daggers, and other merchandise prized in India. Three weeks after leaving Balkh, Ganid's caravan descended a mountain pass into the vast Indus Valley. As they crested the pass, Ganid said, "Say farewell to the land of the religions of the end of time, Ahmed. We will soon be in the land of the cycles of time."

During the journey, often while walking in front of their camels, they had discussed the differences in religious philosophies between the West and the East. With Zoroastrianism, Judaism, and Christianity, Ganid observed, the human trajectory was like an arrow that shoots straight to the target: birth, death, resurrection, judgment before God, followed by reward or punishment, with the world ending at that time. "What a burden to place on people to say they must attain perfection in a single lifetime," he said. "In the Land of God, we believe we are born and reborn many times until we are spiritually advanced enough to break free once and for all from the bonds of mortal life."

They crossed the many rivers of the Punjab and went through cities with opulent temples. Some cities had thriving commercial markets where Ganid stopped to allow caravan merchants to do business. He advised Ahmed not to part with his brass ingots. "Wait until we get to Kashi. I'll get you the best prices there. They'll love you for what you bring them."

The journey took them along the Yamuna River, which flowed eastward until it merged with the Ganges. When they reached the banks of the Ganges, Ahmed was surprised to see the merchants and camel drivers rush to the river. To Ahmed's astonishment, they waded into the water fully clothed, laughing and splashing each other until they were soaking wet.

"Come on," Ganid cried out to Ahmed. "The holy water of Mother Ganga will cleanse you of your sins."

Ahmed waded into the flowing water and imitated the purification rituals. Laughing, he said, "What if you commit more sins later in the day?"

"Why then," Ganid said, pouring water onto Ahmed's head, "you go back to Mother Ganga the next day to purify yourself all over again!"

After the caravan crossed to the north side of the Ganges on wide ferryboats, Ganid led the merchant convoy downstream. A week later, they entered Kashi.

Throughout the journey into India, Ahmed was amazed by the numerous temples and shrines, some elaborate with multiple ornate spires, others smaller, with walls embellished with intricate carvings of the many gods. Before they reached Kashi, Ganid listed more than three hundred gods and goddesses and explained why people became their devotees.

"It is said there are as many gods as there are Indians, but to worship any one god is to worship the supreme God. There is only one God, Brahman; all the others represent facets of the one God."

Kashi was dense with temples, more than Ahmed had ever seen anywhere. After accompanying him to the merchant market to sell the ingots, Ganid took him on a tour of the narrow streets and squares next to temples built on the banks of the Ganges. One was a temple of Vishnu, the Upholder, erected atop huge pillars that were sunk into the river. The streets were thick with people in colorful dress, navigating around rattling pushcarts and docile white cows. Everywhere they went, Ahmed breathed in air scented with incense, wood smoke, and spicy food.

Ahmed at first felt overwhelmed by the Indian pantheon. During the journey, he had spent many evenings with Ganid and other merchants talking about the many gods. Despite his fluency in Persian, Ganid used religious terms that were at times difficult to translate. But amid the freewheeling conversations, Ahmed grasped the fundamental idea that Brahman was impersonal and inscrutable, impossible to describe since any attempt to describe ultimate reality stripped it of its absoluteness.

"Nevertheless," Ganid said, "Brahman becomes personal in Ishvara, who is the creator, upholder, and destroyer of the world. When he is the creator, Ishvara is Brahma. When the upholder, he is Vishnu, and when the destroyer, he is Shiva." The merchants shared with him what they knew of the rituals and hymns of the Vedas, the wisdom of the Upanishads, and the struggles of the gods in the epic tales of the Mahabharata and the Ramayana.

"What you believe is good and beautiful," Ahmed said to his companions.

Ganid lived with his numerous extended family in a mansion on the hill above the soaring temple of Vishnu. He gave Ahmed use of a private apartment on the upper floor with a balcony over-looking the Ganges. As an honored guest, Ahmed joined Ganid's wife and children, his mother and father, his younger brothers and sisters, and his grandmother and grandfather in daily ritu-als before a shrine of the four-armed Vishnu in the main room of the home. The ritual included chanting prayers and offering flowers. One of the children would lay the flowers in front of the statue, and the family would chant, "We are your flowering, and we offer ourselves in service to you, O Lord."

To Ganid's family and friends, Ahmed was known as Ahmed the Persian, but to ascetics and holy men, Ganid introduced him as He Who Asks About God. Wearing only loincloths, the ascetics often gathered beneath an ancient tree near the temple of Vishnu. Ahmed spent many afternoons with them, probing ever further into the religious philosophy.

As his understanding grew, he became intrigued by the idea of the indwelling eternal soul, the God within. It was particular to each person, and it was the soul essence, yet from what he had gathered, it was the same as Brahman. God within was the same as God without. The goal of spiritual discipline was to experience what that meant. One of his questions caused a discussion that lasted several days. "Does the soul that has achieved liberation from the cycles of rebirth then merge with the unqualified abso-lute of Brahman, thereby losing its identity, or is the individuality of the soul preserved?"

The sages were divided on the matter. Some said that the soul at some point was absorbed into the ultimate, whereas others argued that the soul was imperishable, and once liberated, it was raised up into the "highest home."

In their answers to Ahmed's questions, they cited scriptural authority, but the meaning was often contained in hymns, apho-risms, or legends that were impossible for Ganid to translate. At his frequent moments of incomprehension, Ahmed enjoyed watching the animation of the ascetics, mostly wrinkled old men with white beards, as they discussed his questions among themselves.

A year went by in a flash. During those quick months, Ahmed visited more than a hundred temples in and around Kashi. At one point, Ganid took him to the deer preserve where the Buddha gave his first sermon. He ended up spending a week conversing with the monks at the monastery.

One of the Kashi ascetics was a swami who became his guru and taught him to meditate in the lotus position, saying, "Thus you will find the God within, thus you will become enlightened." In the late evening, Ahmed often sat on his balcony meditating as he had been taught. With closed eyes, he would attempt the challenge of clearing his mind of thought. At other times, he would gaze at the sparkling Ganges. On clear nights, the golden moon glistened on the river, creating millions of lights dancing on the dark water.

He would often abandon meditation and let his mind drift to the dark cave above Zarringol, so distant in time yet so close in memory. He would shut his eyes and see Baba Koushiyar leaning against the boulder, motioning for him to go back into the cave despite the fear the brilliant light caused him. There on the balcony, he imagined himself being enveloped again by the light, and he felt joy when he heard the voice again saying, "I am you, and you are me."

Was this what the ascetics and sages meant when they said that God is within us, he wondered? God is within, God is without? He spent many evenings on the balcony, pondering the words of the cave. At times, he would repeat them like a mantra; at other times, he would empty his mind, using the methods he learned from the ascetics, hoping that a cleared mind would open the way to unambiguous understanding.

One night when the moon was at its fullest, the light on the water sparkled in a way he had never seen before. Countless lights underwent fleeting changes in form, like the flames of a fire. At times silvery, at times golden, they appeared at first as bright patches, but then they flared upward. He imagined they were arms reaching upward, toward the moonlight that gave them life. All along the river, the lights performed the same movement.

He spent many nights on the balcony, absorbed by the dancing light. He began to think of the sparkles as the stream of people he had known since fleeing Yathrib. They were the polytheist Bedouins of the desert, the Christians of Ayla, the Zoroastrians of Rey, his numerous caravan companions on the road to the East, and the endless peoples of the Land of God. They all, in their own way, raised their arms toward the Creator.

On another night, as he watched the brilliant water from the balcony, it occurred to him that in his eagerness to find a religion worthy of his humanity, he had missed what was important. It was not so much the particular ideas that people formed about God or the rituals they created to express them. What was important was the very fact that they formed ideas about God. "Is this not evidence of a drive in all people to know God and to reach out to Him, each in his own way?" he wondered.

The words "God longing" came into his mind. Everywhere he had traveled, he found it. Like the surging lights on the river, people reached upward to the source that gave them life. Was that what the light of the cave wanted him to understand?

"I am you, and you are me."

He imagined the Creator reaching down to His creation with this sublime gift, a spark that He implants in all people, and he imagined creation reaching up to Him in a multitude of expressions: countless faces, countless arms, countless hearts lifted upward. Surely it was a divine endowment, he thought, a gift that was the same within all people.

As he contemplated the dancing lights of the Ganges, words came into his mind that were as clear as the voice of the cave: "To love and honor the flame of God longing in all people is to love and honor the Creator who is the source of the flame."

He was stunned. It was a simple truth that had been denied to him all his life. He had been told from his earliest days that only one expression of the longing for God had validity; all others were false and their adherents condemned. Now he realized that through his miraculous journey, he had been given the experience of witnessing the origin of the violence that plagued his own time. And now at last he understood that it came from a rigid and unyielding expression of the longing for God created by a man who was blind to this simple truth.

He became so filled with joy that he couldn't contain himself. He jumped to his feet, and like the lights on the river surging upward, he lifted his arms to the heavens. He cried out again and again, each time louder than before, "I am your flowering, O Light, and I offer myself in service to the sublime gift that you have given to all people."

As he gazed at the stars, tears streaming down his face, several hesitant knocks sounded on the door. He rushed to open it. Ganid was standing there.

"Forgive me for intruding on you, my dear friend, but I became concerned about you when I heard you shouting. Is everything alright?"

Ahmed laughed. "Yes, yes, more than alright!"

He invited Ganid into the room. They spent hours immersed in conversation about what Ahmed had come to understand. He told Ganid about his experience of the cave, leaving out the facts of his origin. He had not spoken to Ganid about it before, but now he poured out his experiences in Yathrib. "All expressions of our longing for God owe their origin to the sublime gift, but how can their validity be measured except through their acceptance of the validity of other forms of its expression?" Ahmed asked.

"This is what we understand in our own manner," said Ganid. "You have said it in a way that I have never heard before, but it is why we are so tolerant. Stay in Kashi, my friend. We will build a temple to God longing."

He had long given up hope of ever going home, but now that he understood what he had been tasked with understanding, he wondered if he could now return to his own time. He shook his head to show regret. "I can't remain, Ganid. I must return to where I came from."

For the remainder of the night, all he could think of was to go to Varkana-Golestan and search for the cave. It was through the cave that he came into the past, so would it be through the same cave that he returned to his own time? The cave was formed in solid rock, so surely it had to be there. If he were able to find the cave, perhaps the light would allow him to go home.

In the morning, Ganid had Ahmed's camel brought from a family farm outside of Kashi, where it had been left to graze. Ahmed was so eager to leave that he didn't bother to buy merchandise to resell later. He had a tidy profit in gold and silver from the sale of the red brass ingots, so he had more than enough money to travel on. He loaded Seeker with the usual provisions. Ganid assigned him two tall guards to accompany him as far as Persia. After taking leave of the ascetics and Ganid and his family, he set out with a caravan bound for Balkh.

On the way out of Kashi, Ahmed chanted, "I am your flowering, O Light, and I offer myself in service to your gift."

As the caravan passed through towns and villages, Ahmed saw people differently than before. It was as if he could now see beyond the often-worn exteriors. The people he encountered were all so different in height, weight, age, and features, yet within all was the same flame, the flame of longing to know their Creator.

He smiled at everyone he came across and touched his heart even when they didn't return the smile. At one of the caravan stops, someone recognized him and said, "Aren't you the one who is called He Who Asks About God? Now you are telling people about God."

"You are mistaken, my brother," Ahmed said. "I don't tell people about God. I tell them about God longing. What drives people to form an idea of God? It is the spark within that pulls everyone toward Him, each in his own way. It is common to everyone, and if they would only realize the truth that the light within themselves is the same within everyone, it would bring about the brotherhood of all people."

In Balkh, Ahmed learned of a caravan going through a mountain pass at the edge of the Alborz Mountains. He joined the convoy after the caravan master told him they would go through Hyrcania, a Persian military town next to the Great Wall of Alexander. When the mountain pass at last came into view, Ahmed was overjoyed. He rubbed his camel's neck and said, "We're almost home, Seeker. It won't be long now!"

The Great Wall began on the other side of the mountain pass. Soldiers were stationed at forts every five miles along the caravan trail, which ran parallel to the wall. After several days, the caravan came within view of the fortified town of Hyrcania, the gateway for merchant convoys heading north into Turkmen territories or west into the Persian provinces along the Caspian Sea.

Ahmed was certain Hyrcania was the same city that would become known as Gonbad-e Kavus—the City of Kavus Tower—for the distinctive tower built centuries later. He had visited it several times in his youth. If it was the same location, the site of the future Aliabad was about 20 miles south. Rather than entering Hyrcania, he parted company with the caravan and followed dirt roads and trails south, using the Alborz Mountains as his guide. The closer he got to the foothills, the happier he felt, yet the more apprehensive. What if he couldn't find the cave?

He rode through numerous villages surrounded by broad fields and patches of trees. Along the way, he asked villagers about settlements in the folds of the foothills, but they told him only forests lay ahead. He kept going until reaching the foothills and was dismayed to see that they were indeed thickly wooded.

"Which way now, Seeker?" Ahmed said.

When the camel swung his head to the right, he prodded it forward and followed the tree line along the foothills, going in and out of canyons. The future village of Zarringol was half a mile up a narrow valley where a river flowed from the mountains and meandered into the plains below. He found a number of such valleys along the way and explored each, but without finding any landmarks that showed he was in the right valley.

After days of searching, he began to despair. His food supplies were running low. If he didn't find the cave soon, he would have to go to Hyrcania for provisions. When he was about to give up, he came to a wide opening in the trees created by a river that stretched far into the mountains. Apart from the dense trees that flanked the river, the scene had the look of the valley just east of Aliabad. If it was the same valley, then the area occupied by the future Zarringol had to be nearby. The clue to finding it would be a creek that carved a rocky path down the canyon above Zarringol and continued as a tributary of the river. It was the creek that he and Baba Koushiyar followed to find the cave.

Leading Seeker by the bridle, Ahmed walked along the river in search of the creek. Half a mile up the valley, he came to a dry creek bed where it merged with the river. He became excited when he explored and found that it contuned along a canyon several hundred yards farther up.

"This has to be it!" he said to Seeker. "This is where Zarringol will be in the future!"

Careful to walk along the grassy sides of the creek so the camel would not stumble on the rocks, Ahmed followed the creek bed to the base of the canyon. If it was the right canyon, the cave would be farther up the mountainside, amid the trees.

He searched for half an hour before coming across a familiar sight—a slide of broken rocks that had fallen from the soaring cliff above. He couldn't see the cave because of a thicket of trees, but he was certain he had found it because of a boulder at the base of the rock slide. It was the same boulder Baba Koushiyar was leaning against when he climbed up to the cave.

Ahmed hobbled Seeker next to the boulder and scrambled up the sharp rocks. At the top of the rock slide, he spotted the cave entrance behind a line of bushes. It was the same opening, low and narrow. His heart pounding, he was about to edge through the entrance when he thought of his camel. What if, by a miracle, he entered the cave and found himself home again? Seeker would be left to die of thirst, or worse, would be set upon by wolves.

He went back down and released the camel. "If I don't come back, you will be on your own, O Seeker."

But what if nothing happened and Seeker was gone when he came back? The camel had a curiosity streak and was always on the lookout for forage. He thought about stashing the saddlebag with his gold and silver next to the boulder. If he couldn't find Seeker again, at least he would have something to survive on. But he decided against it. It would show a lack of trust in God. He left the saddlebag along with all his possessions strapped to

Seeker. "If I don't come back, go and find a new master, someone who will treat you well."

He climbed back to the cave. As he had done years before, he squeezed through the narrow entrance into the darkness and breathed in the odor of dust and stone. It was darker than before because of the shade from trees and bushes that blocked much of the light from entering. He went deeper into the darkness, guiding himself by touching the cold wall. When he was as far in as he had been when he was enveloped by the light, he stopped. He leaned his back against the stone wall. His heart racing, he said, "O Light, I understand now what you meant when you said, 'I am you, and you are me.'"

From the depths of the cave came the squealing and scampering of small animals frightened by his voice. He continued, "What am I to do with this understanding now that I have it? It has a purpose, and its purpose is my purpose."

When nothing happened, he sank to the ground and assumed a meditative position. His eyes closed, he kept repeating, "I am your flowering, O Light, and I offer myself in service to your gift."

A feeling of homesickness overwhelmed him. He prayed that he could now go outside the cave, and Baba Koushiyar would be waiting for him down below. Several hours went by, and the only light he could see was the dimming glow at the entrance. He became concerned that if he stayed too long, it would become dark outside.

He said, "If it's your purpose that I remain, then so be it. Whatever your purpose, it is my purpose."

As he sat in the darkness, wondering what to do, an image of a temple came to him. It was a temple on a hill with stairs leading up to it. It was like nothing he had ever seen before. At the top of the hill was a mount with a dome thrusting up in the center, upheld by pillars. It was an open building. As in a fire temple, a flame arose from a large urn mounted on a pedestal. Surrounding the domed structure was a circular colonnade. The more he imagined it, the more it grew in detail, but after half an hour, he could no longer sustain the vision. It faded, and he wondered whether he had been shown something he must bring about.

"It will be called the Temple of God Longing," he said out loud. "It will be your temple, O Light."

He became aware again that it was getting dark outside. With a heavy heart, he got up and made his way to the entrance. He still harbored the hope that when he stepped out of the cave, the world he used to know would be there. But after sliding sideways through the opening, he found the same uninhabited valley.

The sun had just gone down. He had to find Seeker before it got dark. He scrambled down the slope and called out for the camel, but he didn't hear the familiar deep grumble when he called his name. He searched the woods along the river. As darkness closed in, he made hasty plans. He would have to find a secure place to stay for the night and make the trek to Hyrcania on foot to find work.

Just as he was about to give up, he yelled "Seeker!" one more time as loud as he could. Off to the side, behind a thicket of bushes, he heard a lazy moan. He went around the bushes and found Seeker at rest in a patch of grass.

He rubbed the camel's neck. "Am I ever happy to see you!"

He led the camel to a sandy area at the foot of a cliff and, after removing the bundles and the saddle, he hobbled him for the night. He warmed himself at a fire he started with flints and dry grass. As he ate the last scraps of bread, he pondered what to do. After fleeing Yathrib, he had ceased praying in the manner of the followers of Muhammad, but he had learned the practices of the religions he encountered on the caravan trail. The one he found most conducive to relaxation and clear thinking was the lotus position. Thus, with his feet tucked on his thighs, his back arched, and his upturned hands resting on his knees, he asked the Light for guidance. After a while, the word "warner" entered his mind. He was unable to drive it out: "Warner! You are a warner!"

There was indeed something to warn about. He knew what was soon to come. Savage armies would burst out of Arabia, swords held high, and destroy the good religions in their path. He would warn of what was in store so that people could prepare to defend what was true and good. Salman told him he could only experience the past, not change it, but he wondered how that could be so. "The past is my present, so why can't I have an impact on the future just like everyone else?"

In the morning, after strapping the saddle on his camel and reloading his baggage, he headed for Hyrcania.

"I am a warner now, O Seeker. I will warn the world of what is to come!"

# Chapter 21

In Hyrcania, Ahmed joined a caravan bound for Damascus, following the trade route that went through Rey. Along the way, he preached about the inner light and the gift of God longing, but also about betrayals of the light by those who refused to honor it in others.

"It is the desire of our Creator that we honor and respect and love the God longing of others," he told everyone, "for it is His gift to everyone."

During the stopover in Rey, he visited the chief priest Shapur and warned him once again to prepare. He repeated to him the source of the threat and what awaited Persia if it allowed itself to be overrun. The fire temples would be destroyed, the priests and the faithful slaughtered, and the sacred literature torched. He stressed the importance of hiding copies of the sacred texts to preserve them for the future in the event the followers of the religion of Muhammad prevailed.

"If they have these sacred documents, people of the future will be able to re-ignite the flame of wisdom that Zartosht brought," Ahmed said. He donated most of his trade profits to support the scribes needed to produce a copy of the primary literature, promising to return for the documents. He intended to bury them in the cave above Zarringol in a manner that assured their preservation far into the future.

Before leaving, he asked to be initiated into the religion. Shapur conducted the ceremony in front of the temple fire, attended by other priests and men and women who had befriended him during his earlier stay. The high priest guided him through the pledges to live his life in accordance with the faith's virtues.

With his right hand raised, Ahmed repeated after Shapur: "O Wise Lord, in your thoughts you created our form, our wisdom, and our conscience. You breathed life into us and gave us the gift of words and deeds. You intended that we choose our faith and our doctrine as we see fit. Thus, at this great moment of choice, I wish to choose, with full freedom and knowledge, my own way of life, and it is to you that I turn."

Shapur gave him a slender white cord with which to tie three knots, one for each vow to live a life devoted to righteousness in thought, in word, and in deed. As he made the vows, he tied the knots and wrapped the cord around his waist. The ceremony concluded when he repeated the words, "May all my actions be attuned with wisdom and good thought and in harmony with the law of righteousness that I may please you and bring happiness to the soul of the Earth."

In order to take the initiation vows, he had to overstay in Rey. It took him several days to catch up to the caravan. For the first time, the slowness of a camel caravan became unbearable. He burned with impatience to reach Ctesiphon in the hope of obtaining an audience with the emperor. He carried with him a letter from Shapur urging the emperor to "give attention to this worthy subject of our beloved King of Kings and to hear his message."

But to Ahmed's dismay, the Persian Empire was in a state of disarray. It had been weakened by a string of coups and countercoups. Not long after he joined the caravan at Ayla two years earlier, the powerful emperor Khosrow, who had ruled for three decades, was overthrown by his son Kavadh, who slew many of his half-brothers and anyone who might aspire to the throne. Six months later, Kavadh died from the plague. This came about not long after he made peace with the Byzantines and returned relics that his father had taken as booty when he conquered Jerusalem fifteen years earlier, including the revered fragments of the True Cross of Jesus.

The quick succession of rulers that came after Kavadh was

the talk of the caravan trail. While Ahmed was in India, a series of pretenders and usurpers had taken the Persian throne by force, only to be deposed weeks or months later. On the way to Ctesiphon, rumors circulated among the merchants and camel drivers that yet another coup had taken place. A day before the caravan arrived in the Persian capital, Ahmed learned that the latest emperor had been deposed and was about to be executed. He despaired that his warning would be useless to people who were slaying one another over power.

He didn't linger in Ctesiphon, but continued with the caravan across the Tigris into the land of the Byzantines. He was now determined to seek an audience with Heraclius, the emperor of Byzantium, to warn him of what was to come out of Arabia. Now, only the Byzantines had the power to stop the Arab invaders. At various stage stops, he heard that Heraclius was taking the relics of the True Cross to Jerusalem. After Kavadh returned them as a gesture of peace, Heraclius had them taken to Constantinople for display in the Hagia Sophia. Now he was on his way to Jerusalem to restore the relics to the Church of the Holy Sepulchre, where they had been kept until Khosrow sacked Jerusalem and took them to Ctesiphon.

When Ahmed's caravan reached Damascus, he learned that the Byzantine emperor and a vast entourage of courtiers, soldiers, and priests had gone through Damascus two days before. He visited several caravan stops before finding a merchant group about to leave for Jerusalem, and he set off with it. He arrived in Jerusalem the day after Heraclius entered the city.

Jerusalem was festive. People everywhere were celebrating the return of the sacred relics of the cross. They overflowed with praise that the emperor himself had carried the heavy silver reliquary containing the fragments of the True Cross on his shoulder along the Via Dolorosa all the way to the Church of the Holy Sepulchre.

After finding lodging for himself and a stable for Seeker, he set out for a fortress near the Temple Mount where Heraclius was holding court. He was brought before a magistrate who screened those seeking an audience with the emperor.

Ahmed said, "I come with a warning of a danger emerging from Arabia that will threaten not only the Byzantine Empire, but Christianity itself."

Though Shapur's letter of recommendation was intended for the Persian emperor, Ahmed gave it to the magistrate and translated it for him. After writing down where Ahmed was lodged, the magistrate said with a dismissive wave of his hand, "You will be summoned if your request for an audience is accepted."

One of the men staying at Ahmed's lodging was a Persian Christian who offered to show him the path Jesus was forced to take to his crucifixion. They started at the Antonia fortress and went uphill along narrow lanes. As they walked along the path, the Persian gave him an account of memorable locations: "Here is where Jesus fell under the weight of the cross. Here is where he met his mother, Maryam. Here is where he was helped by Simon of Cyrene."

When they reached an open area in front of a church near the top of the hill, the Persian pointed to the ground. "This is where Roman soldiers nailed the hands and feet of Jesus to the cross." He pointed to a nearby stone church. "The church was built over the site where the cross was erected and where Jesus died."

Along the route, Ahmed imagined himself in the place of Jesus. He felt the pain of scourging, the weight of the cross on his shoulder, and the suffering of nails being driven into his hands and feet. While he and his Persian companion stood in front of the church, he saw in his mind the cross with Jesus slumped on it. Tears streaming down his face, he said, "And this is where the dying Jesus said, 'Father, forgive them, for they know not what they do.'"

While awaiting word from the court of Heraclius, Ahmed toured Jerusalem, calling it the City of God Longing for all of the churches and pilgrims. The city teemed with people seeking to connect with God through their love for Jesus.

Three days after he appeared before the magistrate, an officer came to his lodging and told him to be at the court the following morning. Ahmed purchased Byzantine clothes and went to a barber to have his thick beard and long hair trimmed. He felt presentable when he entered the imperial court. A court official instructed him about how to approach Heraclius once he was called.

"When you approach the Emperor, go as far as the rope. Kneel on your right knee and bow your head. Do not look up or stand until you are told to do so."

When his name was called, Ahmed walked up an aisle flanked by other petitioners. Heraclius was a robust man of middle age, wearing a jeweled crown and a flowing brown tunic with a cross hanging from a gold chain around his neck. He sat on a throne on a dais with royal curtains as a backdrop. Two dozen officials and soldiers of rank stood to the sides of the throne. Ahmed knelt where a rope crossed the aisle, and he bowed as he had been instructed.

"You may rise," said a courtier standing near the throne.

Heraclius stared at Ahmed for a moment as if assessing him and said, "So, I am told you come to me with a warning."

Ahmed said, "Yes, but first I wish to express my love for you, O Emperor, for your love of Jesus who is so worthy of your love and devotion."

Heraclius nodded. "And now, what is your warning?"

"It is only a matter of a few years before the followers of a false prophet will come out of Arabia in great numbers and at great speed. My warning is for you to prepare, for if you don't, you will be overwhelmed by a savagery that you've never seen before or even imagined possible."

One of the men to the right of the emperor handed him a document. Heraclius looked at it and said, "This is a letter from a priest named Shapur recommending you to the Persian Emperor. Have you given him this same warning?"

"It was my intention to do so, but the day before I reached Ctesiphon, the emperor was deposed. The Persian Empire is in turmoil, so there is no one to whom to give the warning. Persia has been weakened by struggles over power and will not be able to defend itself against what is to come. You are the only hope."

"How do you know what is to come? Are you a seer?"

"No, but I have knowledge that most people do not possess. I lived with the false prophet and know what he is like."

"I've heard of this man. His name is Muhammad."

"Yes, Muhammad. I was raised to believe in him as the Messenger of God and that he conveyed God's will to mankind through verses that came from God. But I lived with his household for a year and served as his scribe. I myself suggested words to him that he claimed God had given him. He calls his verses the Recital, but it and everything about him is false."

Ahmed went on to describe how Muhammad altered the folk versions of the prophet stories for his Recital, citing the example of Abraham. He spoke of his studies with the rabbis and of comparisons with the Torah and Jewish prophet legends, which showed that Muhammad's versions were often inspired by mere folk tales. With an occasional pause to contain his emotions, Ahmed spoke of the butchering of the Qurayza Jews.

"I was a witness to this atrocity, O Emperor. What Muhammad did to them, his followers will do to Christians, Jews, Zoroastrians, Buddhists, Hindus, and all who refuse to accept him as their prophet."

"I received a letter from Muhammad more than two years ago inviting me to his religion if I desired security. After it was read to me, I had Arab merchants brought before me to tell me about him."

He turned to his aides. "What was the name of their leader, a merchant from Mecca? The name escapes me."

"Abu Sufyan, my Lord," said one of the aides.

"Yes, Abu Sufyan. What he had to say about Muhammad was not as harsh as what you say."

"The Meccans are afraid of him," said Ahmed, "so that is why Abu Sufyan said what he said to you. If he had spoken truthfully, he would have been severe. As for the letter, I'm familiar with it because I was the scribe who wrote down Muhammad's words. It contained a threat if you didn't comply with him."

The emperor shrugged. "We had a clash with him in a region known as Mutah, a three-day journey south of Jerusalem. This happened several months ago. He sent a force of three thousand. We killed many of them, and the rest went scurrying like lizards. My commanders still laugh about it. We can deal with any threat coming from this false prophet."

The emperor raised his hand, and without turning, he signaled with two fingers for someone to come forward. An aide stepped up to Ahmed and handed him a leather purse full of silver coins.

Ahmed looked at the purse with surprise. "O Emperor," he said, "I didn't come here with the idea of seeking a reward, but to warn you of things to come."

"It is to thank you for your trouble."

"Would it be an offense if I were to ask that this money be distributed instead as alms to the poor?"

Heraclius stared at him for a long moment and said, "So shall it be."

Feeling saddened and discouraged, Ahmed left the court. The Byzantines couldn't imagine their world any other way than it was, and would make a fatal mistake if they didn't take defensive action. The only people he could warn now were the Meccans. Muhammad would soon invade Mecca. If they could organize a defense in time, perhaps they would be able to repel the invaders.

While he stood outside the fortress immersed in thought, a centurion accompanied by a detachment of soldiers came up to him. Thumping his chest in a stiff salute, the centurion said, "I have been commanded to assure your security while you are in Byzantium."

The centurion assigned a personal guard of six Christian Arab soldiers who, riding powerful war horses, accompanied him to Gaza. Prior to his audience with the emperor, Ahmed learned of a Meccan caravan in Gaza that was preparing to journey south. It was a major caravan of more than a thousand camels laden with merchandise that was returning to Mecca along the coastal route by the Red Sea. The soldiers remained with him even after he set out with the Meccans from Gaza and stayed with him until the caravan reached Ayla, which marked the southernmost reach of the empire.

He took advantage of the stopover to meet with the bishop and priests to give them the same warning he had given to Heraclius. He prayed with the monks at the monastery before rejoining the caravan for the trek south.

# Chapter 22

The fact that he had been accompanied as far as Ayla by a guard of soldiers assigned to him by the mighty emperor of the Byzantines gave Ahmed status among the caravan merchants, and the leaders were eager to befriend him.

During the journey to Mecca, he told them about his experiences with Muhammad. The merchants, in turn, told him what had transpired since he fled Yathrib. The caravan leader was Safwan, a short, round-faced man whose father and brother were slain during the first major battle between the Meccans and Muhammad. He told Ahmed about dozens of raids Muhammad had carried out against tribes up and down Arabia since the massacre of the Jews.

The most chilling was the attack on the Jewish agricultural oasis of Khaybar, ninety miles north of Yathrib. After a long siege, Muhammad conquered the oasis and killed many of the noblemen. Among the many atrocities was his beheading of the leader of one of the Khaybar clans for hiding tribal treasures from him. He forced the nobleman's young widow to marry him, and he divided the date plantations, crop fields, and herds among himself and his followers.

"No one feels safe from him any longer, not even we who have a truce with him," said Safwan.

As the caravan continued its long journey south, Safwan told him the Meccans had worked out a truce allowing them to resume trade with Syria. Such trade, vital for their survival, had been cut off by Muhammad's incessant attacks on their caravans. In exchange for safe passage, they had agreed to allow him to seek alliances wherever he pleased. And they also had to allow him to make a pilgrimage to Mecca.

"To see him enter Mecca with his followers was the most difficult part," said Safwan. "He had slaughtered many of our leaders during the first battle with him, some of them his very own uncles and cousins. We had to allow that despicable killer to perform the orbits around our beloved temple."

It was always difficult for Ahmed to orient himself in time, but he knew enough of the sequence of the events of Muhammad's life to know what was to come next. "He will soon break his truce with you," he said to Safwan. "He will find a pretext and will march on Mecca with a large army, as big as the army you led to Yathrib. You must prepare to defend yourselves. This is the warning I've come to give you."

"Everything you've told me, I want you to repeat to Abu Sufyan and the other leaders as soon as we get to Mecca," said Safwan.

When the caravan crested a low mountain pass and descended into the narrow valley of Mecca, Ahmed was filled with joy. Standing in the center next to a dry riverbed was the cubic temple, covered on all sides with ornate, full-length drapes, just as it would be in the distant future.

All his life, he had longed to perform the pilgrimage to Mecca as a part of his religious duty. It so happened that the Meccan caravan left Gaza at the start of the pilgrimage season, and the merchants arrived in Mecca only days ahead of the first wave of pilgrims. As he gazed at the temple, he smiled at the thought that he would now be able to perform the pilgrimage, not with believers in Muhammad's religion, but with the very polytheists whom Muhammad condemned to hellfire.

The Meccan leaders greeted him from a stone platform extending from one side of the temple, used for meetings and speechmaking. Abu Sufyan, the Meccan leader who had commanded the army against Muhammad in Yathrib, said, "We have heard of you, O Ahmed. We have heard that you were a scribe for Muhammad and that you suggested words to him that he used in his Recital. You must speak to us about this."

Ahmed formed a bond with the Meccan leader when they discussed the Battle of the Trench, as the failed Meccan attack on Yathrib was now known. It turned out that Abu Sufyan, a short, overweight man with a piercing glare and an air of authority, was only a hundred yards away from his position behind the trench. Ahmed explained the stratagems Muhammad used to divide the coalition, preventing the Meccans from achieving victory.

"He caused you to demand hostages from your allies and they from you," Ahmed said. "He caused you to mistrust one another. The coalition fell apart at that point. I abandoned the trench to go and warn the Qurayzas, but I was blocked by the storm."

"I've heard the same from several sources, so I know what you say is true. Now we can only regret that the Qurayzas didn't do as we requested. If they had attacked Muhammad from behind the trench line, we would have rid ourselves of him once and for all," said Abu Sufyan as the other nobles nodded their agreement. "You would not be here among us with warnings that he's about to invade."

Ahmed was certain the attack was imminent when he learned that Abu Sufyan had just returned from a visit to Muhammad in Yathrib to smooth over a fight that occurred near Mecca, resulting in a number of deaths among Muhammad's followers. Some Meccans were implicated in the deaths.

"He will use the incident as an excuse to attack you," Ahmed declared. "He will claim you violated the truce you had with him. I gave this warning to Safwan during our journey from Gaza, and it needs to be repeated to you: You must prepare to defend yourselves and your beliefs. Even as we speak, I can assure you that Muhammad is preparing an army as big as the one you led against him two years ago."

"We will need more to go on," said one of the merchants. "Abu Sufyan didn't return from his trip with evidence that Muhammad intends to invade us. You must provide us with proof that he has ill intentions."

"If you wait for proof, it will be too late," Ahmed replied. He pointed to the northern pass of the valley. "Your proof will be his army up there."

"It will take a lot to rouse us," said another merchant. "We are exhausted by all the wars with that man. Many of our nobles and the best of our youth are dead. We have spent much of our wealth, all to no avail."

The pilgrims were about to arrive in large numbers, and the leaders used this to argue against Ahmed's warnings. "He will not violate the holy months," said Abu Sufyan.

Frustrated by his lack of success, Ahmed took his mind off what he knew was coming by volunteering to assist with the pilgrimage preparations. Among other tasks, he helped erect a network of leather cisterns to supply water to pilgrims and their mounts, and assisted with installing a new set of Yemeni drapes on the exterior of the temple. He was allowed to go inside and was astounded by the numerous idols. The most prominent was a large onyx statue of the moon god Hubal, the temple's titular god, mounted on a pedestal. He was surprised to see depictions of Jesus, Maryam, and Abraham painted on one wall.

When the beginning of the sun pilgrimage was announced, Ahmed donned the white garments of the pilgrim. Riding Seeker, he was happy to join the dignitaries on the journey to Mount Arafat, fifteen miles outside Mecca, the starting point for the sun-worship rituals.

In the entourage was Muawiya, a son of Abu Sufyan who was about Ahmed's age. As they rode to Arafat, Ahmed couldn't help but observe him. If Muhammad succeeded in conquering Mecca, the son of Abu Sufyan would be destined to become the founder of a Muslim dynasty three decades later, following the assassination of Ali. Thereafter, the rulers descending from Muawiya would slay the descendants of Ali because of their claim to leadership of Islam based on their blood link to Muhammad through his daughter Fatima, whom Ali married and had two male offspring. One after another, they would be poisoned until the twelfth and final descendant with a blood claim to the title of leader of Islam, the Imam of Time, would be sent into hiding to protect him from assassination. It was he whom Ahmed once believed would emerge from hiding through the well in the mosque of Jamkaran. It was to the awaited Imam that Ahmed, while visiting the Jamkaran mosque with a group of schoolchildren, dropped a petition through a narrow opening at the top of the well. It was there that he prayed for the Imam to return as foretold so that he would bring the peace and justice of Islam to the entire world. Now he laughed at the absurdity of the belief.

Ahmed hoped he would still be able to keep the attack on Mecca from succeeding. He struck up friendships with Muawiya and other noblemen in the entourage. He repeated his warning to all of them, but he was always greeted with the same negative response.

It became clear that the Meccans, ground down financially and psychologically by the incessant conflicts with Muhammad, had turned fatalistic. They believed their way of life was about to end, and they undertook the pilgrimage in honor of their gods, knowing in their hearts it would be the last. In despair, Ahmed acknowledged that Salman was right. It was not possible to change the past. All he could do was experience it.

With the rest of the pilgrims, he waited on the slopes of Mount Arafat for the sun to drop below the horizon, and rushed with them in the darkness west toward an enormous bonfire on the mount of Muzdalifah. There, the pilgrims waited overnight and cheered when the sun reappeared. Ahmed celebrated the returning sun with cheers, too, and followed the pilgrims to Mina, where he threw stones at the three pillars of the devils.

He could not bring himself to participate in the mass slaughter of the sacrificial animals. Instead, he joined other pilgrims who continued on to Mecca to take part in the temple's moon-worship rituals. He walked with them around it seven times, touching the Black Stone at each turn. He imitated the other pilgrims in the quick walk between the nearby mounts of Safa and Marwa, which was also done seven times.

Thus, the pilgrims expressed their longing for God, and Ahmed saw it as good. They were moved by the same longing for the Creator that he had seen everywhere. He saw the light within them in their devotional concentration as they performed the temple orbits and in the fervent way they kissed or touched the Black Stone. It was their way of connecting to the divine.

When the pilgrimage was over, Ahmed wondered what he should do. The invasion was imminent. If Muhammad captured him, he would be killed as an apostate. He bought provisions, thinking of saddling Seeker and heading south. But he became paralyzed by indecision. Even if he went as far as Yemen, he would be within reach of Muhammad. He became gripped by the same fatalism as the Meccans.

Two weeks after the pilgrims dispersed, a rumor shot through the valley that Muhammad was at the head of a huge army camped less than a day away from Mecca. Abu Sufyan and two other men left on horseback to investigate. That night, Ahmed joined people carrying torches in front of the temple to hear the latest rumors.

The following morning, Abu Sufyan galloped into Mecca, waving his hand and shouting for everyone to assemble at the temple. "You must listen to what I have to say!"

From the steps of the temple, he announced that Muhammad and his army would arrive in less than an hour. He had met with him and secured a promise that as long as people stayed in their homes and offered no resistance, they would not be harmed. When they heard that, the townspeople ran off into the surrounding neighborhoods shouting, "Muhammad is coming! Lock yourselves in your homes, and you will be safe!"

After the people dispersed, Abu Sufyan signaled to Ahmed that it was urgent they talk. "I have bad news for you. Muhammad has somehow learned of your presence here, and he has included you on a list of people who are to be killed on sight. You are at the top of the list. We can't harbor you without risk to ourselves. You must leave right away."

The Meccan leader sent someone to fetch Ahmed's camel from a grazing area, and when Seeker was brought out, the Meccan leader helped him saddle it and strap on provisions.

Ahmed felt panicky, but got a grip on himself. "What should I do? Where should I go?"

"Go through the South Pass and keep going until you reach Yemen. You can find a merchant vessel at one of the ports that will take you to India." He handed Ahmed a small leather bag containing gold coins. "This will help you. We should have listened to you, my friend."

Riding Seeker at a fast trot, Ahmed neared the pass, eager to get through it and head south, but before he reached it, a dark mass of warriors mounted on horses and camels appeared at the top. They raced down with the speed of a flash flood and split into two branches. Just as Ahmed turned his camel around, one of the divisions attacked a small group of Meccan cavalry that had rallied to defend the valley. As sword blades clanged and warriors shouted battle cries and curses, Ahmed raced in the opposite direction, back in the direction of the temple. As he neared it, the main force of Muhammad's army poured into the valley from the northern pass amid the fierce beat of war drums and shrill war cries.

He stopped in front of the temple, his heart pounding even harder than the approaching drums. He looked in every direction. The streets and lanes were empty of people. Not even stray animals were to be seen. He was certain there was no escape when a group of cavalrymen detached from the main force and raced toward him, waving swords and shouting *"Allahu Akbar!"*

He jumped off Seeker and scrambled up the temple stairs. He pushed the door, but it held firm. He panicked and shoved against it with his shoulder until it opened. He rushed inside just as a dozen horsemen galloped up. He grabbed a thick board and wedged it against the door to block it. Men pounded on the door, shouting, "Come out of there, Ahmed! You can't escape us."

The pounding soon stopped, and he heard a crowd of voices outside. After several minutes, the pounding began again, but now it was the ferocious hammering of a battering ram. The board that he had shoved against the door clattered to the floor, and the door flung open. As he stepped back behind a pillar, several men rushed into the dark interior.

Ahmed's eyes were adjusted to the darkness, but the men were still blinded. Ali was in front of the others, his sword held upward. Umar was next to him, his sword drawn as well. Muhammad and Bilal came in behind them. Ahmed backed up to the farthest corner, next to the statue of Hubal. As he took the last step, he bumped against something.

Ali pointed with his sword. "He's over there!"

Muhammad shouted, "Kill him!"

Ali rushed toward Ahmed and slashed the sword downward, missing him by a few inches. Ahmed fell back against the wall and slid down to the stone floor, his heart racing so fast it felt like it was about to explode.

Ali's face was twisted with rage, but just as he raised the sword above his head for the death blow, Ahmed lost all his fear. It happened so fast that he was surprised. He had been terrified from the moment he realized he was trapped, but now the fear was gone, and he felt calm, as if accepting his end.

He stared at the angry face, studying the black eyeliner that made Ali's future portraits stand out so much. It seemed so strange that Ali, the First Imam, whose descendant was awaited in Iran at the well in Jamkaran, wanted to kill him. He felt pity for this poor, misguided soul. He extended his hand in a gesture of goodwill and said, "Would you slay people because their longing for God isn't expressed the way you express it? Don't you know, O forefather of a distant future, that I am you, and you are me? Don't you know that what burns in your heart burns in mine and that what is in you and me is in all people?"

The sword seemed to linger in the air. Ali gripped the hilt with both hands, but he was slow in bringing the sword down. Did his words make Ali pause?

From behind Ali, Muhammad roared, "Slay the apostate!"

It was strange that Muhammad's voice now sounded different. His words seemed garbled and hollow, like a recording device playing back at slow speed.

Upon Muhammad's slurred command, Ali's eyes became even more inflamed, but the widening of his furious eyes seemed to happen in even slower motion, as did the blade when it started its downward slash. It was as if time had slowed down. If death was coming, it was still far away.

Ahmed stared at the slowing sword with curiosity and wondered if Ali had changed his mind about killing him and was struggling to stop the blade before it reached him. When the sharp edge was within inches of his head, Ahmed was astonished that it stopped and began to expand on both sides. It became translucent, and he was sure he could pass his hand through it without harm. Ali's face expanded as well, as if the molecules of his eyes, nose, and beard were flying apart.

Ahmed reached out to touch the dissolving blade, but as he did, everything became dark around him. The floor, the walls, the statues, the temple pillars, all seemed to fling away until there was nothing but blackness. His body began to spin, and he felt he had lost all weight. Had the sword cut through him? He wondered if he was dead yet still aware. He was in darkness, but he didn't feel fear, only curiosity about the colorful lights that appeared as flashes and disappeared just as quickly, and the roars and whistles and grinding sounds that assailed him from every direction. He wondered whether he was in the tunnel that people go through after death. But if he was in the tunnel, where was the brilliant, streaming light that was supposed to be at the top? Where was the joyful welcoming by people he knew and loved who had already crossed over? Would his father be there?

It seemed it would go on forever, but the dizzy spinning of his body stopped, and the flashing lights and grinding sounds were gone.

All that remained was darkness except for a shaft of light beaming down on him from above.

*PART II*

# THE WELL
# OF
# THE MAHDI

# Chapter 23

Ahmed was lying on his back, and he didn't know what to make of it. He touched his face and beard and turban and chest. He felt the white cord with its three knots that he kept tied under his garment. He was all in one piece, but he wondered where he was. Above him, light streamed through a set of slits. He wondered if they had knocked him out and thrown him into a dungeon. He was lying on something soft and uneven. He ran his fingers over it, and it felt like paper. A dungeon with a bed of paper?

He heard voices, and it sounded like people praying. Was Muhammad leading his warriors in prayer outside the temple? But it didn't sound like Arabic. The more he listened, the more he heard snatches of Persian. As he lay there wondering where he was, the slits of light above him darkened for a moment. Something fluttered down and fell on his chest. He grabbed it and was astonished that it was a piece of paper.

He rolled over and got to his knees. He was in a box of some sort, so low he wasn't able to stand. He peered through the slits and saw the sky and puffy clouds. The voices became louder. It sounded like they were speaking Persian, the Persian of his own day and age, not the Persian of the Zoroastrians. He tried to push the frame where the slits were. It didn't budge, but it seemed like it could be opened and closed. He felt around underneath and found hinges on one side and two clasps on the other. He released the clasps and pushed up. He kept pushing until the cover fell to one side with a metallic clang, leaving an opening wide enough for him to climb through.

He hesitated before climbing out. What if it was a cage that Muhammad and his people put him into? If he were spotted trying to get out, he would be attacked and perhaps killed instead of being forced back into the cage. He thought he should be cautious, but the moment the cover fell to one side, the voices outside stopped. They were already alerted. He had no choice now but to climb out. Squeezing his shoulders through the opening, he placed his hands on the sides. With a powerful thrust, he pushed himself out of the box and stood straight up on top of it.

He almost fell off when he saw an enormous crowd in front of him. Their mouths dropped, and their eyes stretched wide open. He looked around. He was in a huge courtyard outside an ornate building that looked familiar. He felt shock at the realization that he was at the mosque of Jamkaran, standing atop the very well where he, as a boy, had dropped a petition praying for the Imam of Time to come into the world.

Someone cried, "It's the Imam of Time. Our Mahdi has come! Rejoice!"

Hundreds of people, men in various types of clothing on one side and black-shrouded women on the other side, stretched their arms toward him. People throughout the crowd cried, "Speak to us, our beloved Imam!"

People from other parts of the complex pushed into the courtyard, straining over the growing crowd to see him. Men held up children so they could see him, too. A number of people, both men and women, fainted. Others wept.

An elderly cleric wearing a white turban stepped forward. In a trembling voice, he said, "O Imam, our beloved Savior. It was foretold that you would lead everyone in prayer after making your appearance. May I invite you to lead us now in prayer?"

Ahmed got down from the well and stood before the cleric. He was confused, alarmed, and above all, ashamed. How could he tell these people that he was not the Imam of Time? He was just Ahmed, the son of Abdollah from the town of Aliabad in the province of Golestan. He couldn't even explain to himself why he was there, let alone to the people. One minute, Ali was about to slice his head in two inside the cubic temple of Mecca, the next minute, he was in the Jamkaran mosque, and people were taking him to be their long-awaited Imam. If he told them the truth, they would think he was a madman. Even worse, they would have him arrested for hiding in the sacred well and impersonating the Awaited One. He would be condemned to death for blasphemy.

The elderly cleric made an inviting gesture towards a niche on one side of the enormous courtyard, indicating the direction to Mecca for prayer. Ahmed followed him to the niche, trying to disguise the trembling he felt throughout his body.

The call to prayer was heard, and men and women assembled in separate prayer formations. It would have been the practice for him to turn his back to them to lead them in the prayer rituals and recitals from the Quran, but instead, he faced the people and said, "Rather than praying with you, I wish to speak to you. Please sit down."

After hesitating for a moment and glancing at one another, the people sat down, either cross-legged or on their knees.

Ahmed closed his eyes to calm himself and gather his thoughts. He felt as trapped as he had been in Mecca. He had to say something to all these people. He breathed deep to calm himself. After a long silence, he said to the adoring crowd, "You, the faithful, you said when I appeared before you, 'The Imam of Time is with us.' And it seems to be the truth that I am he of whom you speak because this very day, and indeed only minutes ago, I was with Ali, the son of Abu Talib, whom you know and love as the First Imam and the father of Hasan and Hossein, the second and third Imams, whose stories you know so well. In parting with the son of Abu Talib before coming here to you, I said to him, 'Don't you know, O forefather of a distant future, that I am you, and you are me? Don't you know that what burns in your heart burns in mine, and that what is in you and me is in all people?'"

He surveyed the assembly. Many of the faces showed awe, others reverence, and yet others seemed reflective, as if trying to grasp the meaning of his words. He continued by repeating the words he had repeated to many people since leaving Kashi: "What I meant when I spoke with the son of Abu Talib is that there is a spark of longing in all people everywhere, longing for God. It is the gift of the Creator to each and every one of us. He reaches down to us with this sublime gift so that we may reach up to Him. It manifests itself in a multitude of religions. I have come to tell you that to love and respect and honor the flowering of God longing in all people is one of the best forms of worship, surely the most pleasing to our Creator."

He went on for another ten minutes, elaborating on the theme of God longing as the common denominator that unites all people. He didn't know where the words came from, but they came to him within a flow of deep feeling. Before he finished, a wave of weeping broke out in the women's area and spread to the men's section. A man jumped to his feet and cried, "The Imam has come to us with truth! God wants us to love all people!"

The entire assembly was on its feet. People surged toward him, pushing him back against the wall. Men and women tried to hug him, kiss him, touch him. A burly man lifted him up onto his shoulders and carried him through the adoring crowd out to the plaza in front of the mosque, where the crowd was even denser than inside. The burly man carried him through the thick of it to the road, where a joyous procession formed.

Ahmed feared it was not going to end well. He would be found out, and very soon. He became alarmed when two black limousines with dark windows pushed through the crowd and stopped the procession. Men in black suits, wearing dark glasses, jumped out, flashing badges.

One of them said for everyone to hear, "We have been ordered to bring the Imam to the White Palace, where the president and our Supreme Leader wait to give him a formal reception."

Ahmed was lowered to the ground. The man in the black suit who had spoken to the crowd approached him. With a warm smile, he said, "Please, come this way, Imam. You are awaited."

Ahmed had no choice but to comply. He slid into the back seat of the first limousine. Through the tinted window, he observed people crying and holding their arms out to him as the sleek limo pushed through the crowd and accelerated up the road, followed by the second limo.

The man who asked him to get into the vehicle was in the passenger seat. He turned to Ahmed. "I'm Reza, Imam, and this is Maziar," he said, pointing to the driver.

Maziar glanced at Ahmed in the rearview mirror and gave him a reassuring smile. "You don't have to be concerned, Imam," he said. "You are safe with us."

The limo sped along the highway toward Qom, followed by the second black vehicle. To go to the presidential palace in Tehran, they would have to drive through Qom and take the main highway north. Ahmed wanted to tell them to take him somewhere else. He was disoriented and struggled against rising panic. If he were brought to the president and the Supreme Leader, it would be a death sentence.

When they reached the last neighborhoods of Jamkaran, the driver turned onto a street lined with block apartments and turned again down a narrow lane of modest houses. The other limo followed close behind.

Maziar pressed the button of a two-way radio. "Stop midway and stay there until I call you again. If anyone has followed, they won't get through."

A crackling voice replied, "So far, so good. No one has been following."

Ahmed was confused. Maybe it was never their intention to take him to the presidential palace. Something else was going on, but what? He was in the same quandary as at the mosque. He wanted to explain that he was not who they thought he was, but he didn't know anything about these people. He couldn't tell them the truth without running a risk.

The limo made several more turns before stopping in front of a warehouse with a roll-up door. Maziar pressed the button of a small device, and the door went up. He drove inside and parked next to a pale yellow delivery van.

With a hint of exasperation, Ahmed said, "Would someone explain what is going on?"

"You have nothing to fear, Imam," Maziar said. "We couldn't allow you to fall into the hands of the clerics. They would use you, or they would destroy you if you refused to cooperate with them."

"I'm still confused. What's the date?"

He was shocked to learn that only six weeks had gone by since he entered the cave above the village of Zarringol, yet he had been gone for more than four years.

The driver got out and rushed to open the door for him. He had an appealing smile that made Ahmed want to trust him. There was something about him that looked familiar, but he couldn't place him.

"Please follow us, Imam," Maziar said. He pointed to a staircase that led to the landing of a modest apartment.

Once inside, Maziar pressed the button of the two-way radio. "We're safe. Dispose of the limo and return to base."

He said to Ahmed, "If you would like to freshen up, Imam, there's a bathroom with a shower and plenty of hot water. But if you'll permit me to make a recommendation, I don't think it would be a good idea for you to shave or even trim your beard should you have a desire to do so."

Not even two hours before, he was soaked with the sweat of fear as he strove to keep from being slain. His garments and black turban were thick with dust. Yet somehow in the dizzying return to the present, his garments became as clean as if they had just been laundered, and his body felt cleansed as well. Nevertheless, he couldn't turn down the idea of a hot shower. For four years, he had to bathe in rivers and creeks or make do with pouring lukewarm or cold water on himself while sitting in a shallow bronze or wooden basin.

He stood under the steady stream, letting the jets of hot water fall onto his head and shoulders and his back. It felt so good that he stayed in the shower until the water got cold. He rubbed himself down and wiped the fogged mirror, but turned his gaze away when he didn't recognize himself. He dressed in modern clothes and shoes left for him and placed the turban, the long garment, and the sandals into a carrying bag intended for him.

While he was showering, the two men had prepared a simple meal of rice and lamb. They partook of the meal and a pot of rose tea with sugar cubes in a bowl. During the meal, Maziar said that they had listened in on his sermon. "One of the disciples, that is to say, one of our friends, was in the mosque and held up his cell phone for us to hear you speak. What you said was beautiful and true and moving, Imam. It's what people need to understand. That and so much more."

When they were done, Maziar took a cell phone out of the inner pocket of his black suit and handed it to Ahmed. "If there's someone you wish to contact, Imam, this phone is secure. We can step outside so you'll have privacy."

Ahmed nodded. When the men left, he stared at the phone and realized they knew more about him than they were letting on, but he had no reason to suspect any ill intent. Their attitude toward him was more than polite. It was reverent.

He thought about calling his mother, but decided against it because it might be too much of a shock for her to hear from him suddenly. Better to call Behrouz first.

It took him a minute to remember Behrouz's number. He pressed the numbers, and after a few rings, he heard the gruff friendliness of Behrouz's voice.

"Who's calling? I don't recognize the number."

"This is Ahmed."

A few seconds went by before Behrouz bellowed, "Ahmed! I can't believe it! Where have you been?"

"It's too complicated to explain right now, but I'm safe and in good health."

"Your mother has been worried sick. Baba Koushiyar told her you went on a journey, but neither he nor anyone else heard anything from you."

"Tell her I'm fine and that I'll see her soon."

"Where are you?"

"In Jamkaran."

"Really? Then did you hear that the Imam of Time, or someone claiming to be him, appeared out of the well? It's all over the news."

Ahmed smiled. "I heard something about it."

"Someone is playing a joke."

"I think so too. Can you pick me up? I think I can arrange to meet you in Tehran, on that street corner where you saved me from the militia. Do you think you could find it?"

"I know where it is, but Tehran isn't safe. It's still crawling with guardsmen and *basijis*. I hear there's a warrant out for you for desertion, so somewhere outside of Tehran would be the safest."

Ahmed thought for a moment. He remembered when the train slowed into Pishva after he fled Tehran, battered and bruised, and the dome of the shrine of Imam Zadeh Jafar came into view. It was a half-hour drive east of Tehran. "How about in Pishva, outside the shrine of Imam Zadeh?"

He opened the door to the landing and motioned for the two men to come back in. He explained the conversation he was having with Behrouz. They were eager to take Ahmed anywhere he desired, but Maziar said it was not a good idea to drive through Tehran. He looked up secondary roads to Pishva on the Internet and said he was certain they could be there by midnight. They thought the Pishva train station was a much safer place to meet than the shrine.

When they said they would go in the van parked in the warehouse, Ahmed said to Behrouz, "Look for a yellow cargo van in the parking lot of the train station in Pishva."

Ahmed felt a bond of trust with the two men, yet they were strangers. He knew nothing about them or their motives. They were younger than him by a few years, and they wore the trim Shi'ite beard. After the arrangements with Behrouz were made, he said, "I don't know who you are, or why you're helping me."

"How I wish we could answer your questions, Imam," said Maziar. "But we're not permitted to speak about anything at this time except to assure you that you're among friends. There is still something important that needs to happen before it can all be made clear to you."

# Chapter 24

They arrived at the train station early and parked in the main lot. Ahmed's rescuers had changed out of their black suits and ties into casual clothes. Ahmed remained in the back of the van for the entire trip. It was windowless, with a thick rug covering the cargo area floor and large cushions for him to lean against.

He felt strange wearing a shirt, trousers, a belt, and stiff shoes with laces. For the entire time he was gone, he had worn nothing but long flowing garments, sandals, and a variety of black turbans, including the turban he fashioned out of the black cloth his mother had wrapped around his chest after he returned, bruised and sore, from the streets of Tehran.

He brought the Arab garments with him in the carrying bag, if for no other reason than to have proof of his strange journey. Abu Sufyan's gold coins were also there, still in the leather moneybag. He forgot that he had stuffed it into an inner pocket of the garment after the Meccan leader gave him the coins, and he only remembered he still had them when he was putting the robe into the carrying bag and felt the hard bulge of the moneybag.

The train station turned out to be a poor choice for a meeting site. It was patrolled by revolutionary guardsmen in green uniforms. They wore side arms and carried rifles. At one point, two of them tapped on the driver's window and asked Maziar what they were doing there.

"My brothers," said Maziar with a disarming smile, "we're waiting for the next train to arrive with our uncles and cousins from Tehran."

The guardsmen grunted and sauntered away. Not long after, Behrouz arrived in a beat-up Paykan and parked next to the yellow van. Maziar jumped out and slid the cargo door open. As Ahmed got out, Maziar said, "We or others like us will always be close by, Imam. Think of us as your guardian angels."

When Ahmed slid into the passenger seat, Behrouz's eyes opened wide, and his mouth dropped. "Ahmed? Is that really you? I can't believe my eyes. What happened to you?"

"Drive, and I'll tell you."

Behrouz was incredulous and mocking as Ahmed gave him an overview of his experiences.

"What am I getting myself into?" he said. "What if you're not Ahmed, but an agent of the Revolutionary Guard posing as Ahmed, and you want to trap me into saying bad things about the Islamic system?"

Ahmed said, "Tell me, Behrouz. What were you doing yesterday morning?"

"I was getting ready to go out to the airfield. I had some fields to spray."

"Well, as for me, yesterday I was in Mecca and Muhammad's army was invading. I was on his list of people to be killed. I tried to flee on a camel through the pass to the south, hoping to reach Yemen, but his army came in from all directions. I ended up trapped inside the Kabah. I blocked the door, but they broke it down with a battering ram, and Ali, Muhammad, Umar, and Bilal rushed in. Ali was just about to cut my head in two with a sword when I returned to our time through the well in Jamkaran, and because of that, I was taken to be the Imam of Time. But I'm just Ahmed, the Ahmed you've always known. I don't understand how this came about. I only know that it happened."

Behrouz laughed and slapped the steering wheel. "This is insane! If I didn't know you, I'd think you were crazy."

"Look at me. I'm wearing the evidence. Do you think I could grow a beard like this in six weeks?"

He reached into the carrying bag and retrieved the leather purse. He tossed it up and down so that the coins jingled. He opened it and counted. There were thirty-seven coins, all bearing the likeness of Heraclius. "These are the gold coins Abu Sufyan gave me just minutes before Muhammad attacked. For me, this happened not even twelve hours ago. So, if you still don't want to believe me, here's more evidence," he said, displaying the coins.

They drove all night, traveling first through the pass of the Alborz Mountains that Ahmed crossed with the caravan that he had joined in Hyrcania. He told Behrouz everything, starting with the cave of light above Zarringol.

Behrouz shook his head. "Okay, I believe you, but it's going to take me a while to absorb all of this. You've overloaded my poor brain."

After they went through Gorgan and were on the road to Aliabad, Ahmed asked him what happened after the brutal attack on the protesters in Tehran.

"The regime kept showing its true colors. A lot more people were killed in the streets, and a lot more were arrested, and not just in Tehran but in other cities. Even in Gorgan. Some people are still unaccounted for. We hear a lot of rumors about serious abuses and torture in the prisons."

"Khomeini's revolution promised heaven," said Ahmed, "but it delivered just the opposite."

"It's going to get worse," said Behrouz. "We've been hearing of forced confessions, which means people were tortured. Just two days ago, a show trial began in Tehran against a hundred well-known people, and I mean politicians, journalists, even some top clerics. They're accused of making war against God and other strange things. This is being shown on television, Ahmed. You should see their faces. They looked destroyed."

"What was your role in this?" said Ahmed. "You were still in the militia when I disappeared."

"I called Omid the day after I left you at the train station. I told him I wasn't going to be a part of it anymore. I resigned. He got angry. I was an enemy of the Islamic revolution. I was taking the side of those who wage war against God. He said there were going to be repercussions."

"Have they done anything to you?"

"Not yet. They've got bigger fish to fry."

He added that both men and women were being brutalized into signing false confessions that they had conspired to overthrow the Islamic system and that they were agents of foreign powers. He heard that some were hanged based on forced confessions. The Supreme Leader even placed the reformist candidates under house arrest and jailed many of their prominent supporters.

"Demonstrations are still taking place," Behrouz went on, "but the number of people willing to take part in them has dropped. If those bastards intended to create fear, they succeeded."

It was light out when they reached Aliabad. Behrouz drove to Ahmed's mother's apartment above the cloth shop and parked behind the building.

Ahmed said, "I think it would be best for you to go up first and tell her that I look different so that she won't be so shocked when she sees me."

Before getting out of the car, Behrouz said, "I believe that everything you said is the truth, Ahmed. I want you to know that you can count on me for anything, beginning with keeping my mouth shut."

A few minutes after going up to the apartment, Behrouz signaled from the landing for Ahmed to come up. Even though prepared, his mother was shaken when he entered.

"It's me, Mother," Ahmed said as he put his arms around her shoulders.

Tears were rolling down her face. "I've been worried sick about you. Baba Koushiyar said you went on a journey, but he wouldn't say anything more about it. Why didn't you contact me? And look at you. You look older, and you didn't have such a beard when I last saw you. How has this come about?"

"We have a lot to talk about," Ahmed said. "I'll tell you everything."

After Behrouz left, he gave her a short version of what he went through. When he told her that Ali came within inches of splitting his head in two with a sword, she became so upset that she removed the portrait of him from the prominent place it had always occupied on the living room wall. She marched into the kitchen with it, and Ahmed heard the sound of ripping. Amineh marched back into the living room and said, "From the moment we're born, we're lied to about this religion. I won't have anything more to do with it."

He was weary. He slept on the living room sofa for a few hours and awoke. He couldn't go back to sleep and stared at the ceiling. He tried to convince himself he had been dreaming. Now that he was back in familiar surroundings, it seemed like a dream, but try as he might, he couldn't dismiss it as a dream. His thick beard and Abu Sufyan's coins were proof that it happened. He had poured out the coins to show his mother and unfolded the ancient, flowing garment and the black turban he had fashioned from the cloth she had wrapped around his bruised ribs. He had shown her the white cord Shapur had given him at the time of his initiation into the religion of Zartosht.

Nor could he dismiss his experience in Jamkaran as a dream. His mother saw cell phone recordings of his sermon that were broadcast on television. She didn't recognize him, but the fact that she saw it confirmed that it really happened. But how could he be the Imam of Time? He was Ahmed, son of Abdollah and Amineh, born in Aliabad. He was from the present, not the past.

After he awoke, his mother turned on the television. News of the Imam of Time's appearance was everywhere. A speech by the Supreme Leader confirming that the Imam's arrival was real was carried on every channel. The Supreme Leader pointed out that thousands of people pray at the well in Jamkaran every day, and at night, security guards and cameras keep it under constant surveillance, so it was impossible for anyone to enter the well with the intention of posing as the holy Imam. He would have been caught. Moreover, people reported a glow that emanated from the well before the Imam's emergence. The Guardian Council had examined video evidence confirming it. "So it is with the greatest enthusiasm and joy that I welcome our beloved and glorious Messiah," the Supreme Leader concluded.

The president, meanwhile, said in a separate televised address that the fervent prayers of the believers in the end of time and of resurrection and judgment before God had hastened the Imam's arrival. "Did I not tell you that his appearance was imminent?"

he said. He denied sending anyone to bring the Imam to Tehran, noting that his office was looking into reports that people claiming to be government agents took him away in a limousine. He invited the Imam to visit him at the presidential palace. "We will give you a glorious procession through the streets of Tehran, a welcome befitting our beloved Imam."

Ahmed groaned. With all its intelligence resources, the government would eventually discover his identity. He would be ripped to pieces. His mother's life would be turned upside down. He looked at her with sadness. "I'm sorry that you've been dragged into this, Mother."

The more he thought about it, the more he became convinced that Baba Koushiyar knew what was in store for him when he went into the cave. If not, why would he tell his mother that he had gone on a journey? Under normal circumstances, Baba Koushiyar would have climbed up to the cave to search for him when he didn't come out. So what did it mean when he told her that he had gone on a journey? What explanation could there be other than he knew what was going to happen to him?

He called the mosque on the cell phone that Maziar gave him and asked to speak with Baba Koushiyar. When the cleric answered, Ahmed identified himself. He detected defensiveness when Baba Koushiyar said, "I was expecting to hear from you."

"I have a lot of questions," said Ahmed with a hint of coldness.

After a brief silence, Baba Koushiyar said, "I know. I want to meet with you. Where are you?"

Ahmed feared being recognized. If the townspeople knew it was he who came out of the well, they would denounce him as a fraud and a blasphemer, just a local boy playing an unholy game. They would turn him over to the paramilitaries.

"I'm with my mother at her home. Can you come here?"

"Wait for me. I'm on my way."

When he knocked on the door twenty minutes later, Amineh answered and withdrew to her bedroom, but Ahmed said, "Mother, please stay. I want you to hear everything."

Baba Koushiyar was dressed in the usual clerical garb. After Amineh brought out a pot of tea and a bowl of sugar cubes, Ahmed told him what happened after he went back into the cave and about his experiences in the past. He gave him a more detailed account than he had given his mother.

"You knew about the cave because you brought me there, and you told my mother I went on a journey. How could you know that I went on a journey?"

It took Baba Koushiyar a moment to reply. "You're not the only one to have this experience," he began. "I had a similar experience, though not in the same time period as you, but like you, it was motivated by a desire to experience true Islam. There are many others who have also had this experience, more than seventy that I know of. But it's different for everyone, both in the manner of going and in the manner of coming back."

"The men who came in the limousines, are they among them?"

"Yes, Maziar, Reza, and the others who were helping them are also disciples, as we call ourselves. We are more than seventy."

"Disciples of whom?"

The mullah looked at Ahmed with deep affection. "We are your disciples, my beloved Imam. You are the Imam of Time. You are he, for it is you who came back in the manner that was prophesied for him. It is you who returned through the well in Jamkaran, not anyone else."

Ahmed shook his head. "How can it be? I'm Ahmed, a student at the Agricultural University. This is my mother, Amineh. I was born in Aliabad. The traditions say the Imam will come out of Khorasan, but we're in Golestan."

The mullah laughed. "You know how prophecies are. They may predict something that comes about, but the details and the timing are usually off."

"This isn't something I asked for."

"Oh? Who came to me with questions about good and evil? You had many more troubling questions on your mind than just that, questions about what you were raised to believe. You wanted to experience true Islam. It was your longing for such an experience that set you on this path."

"I'm just Ahmed. I'm a humble man."

"If you wanted this, you would be a man of ambition. That

would mean you weren't right for it. We were confident it was going to be you who came back in the manner prophesied because the light spoke to you. That hasn't happened with anyone else. And after you went back into the cave, you didn't come out. I went looking for you, and you weren't there. No one else has gone into the past through a cave but you."

Ahmed pressed on. "Maziar, Reza, and several others were at the Jamkaran mosque after I came out of the well. How could they have known beforehand when it would happen? They were there when I was carried out of the mosque."

"All of us spent years in the past," said Baba Koushiyar, "but when we returned, only weeks had gone by in our own time. That was the pattern. So we knew it was just a matter of weeks before your return. We worked out a plan to get you away before the authorities could intervene. We couldn't let you fall into the hands of the clerics."

Ahmed fell silent. He still didn't know what to think. He glanced at his mother, hoping to get her opinion. She sat with her eyes closed, as if praying.

He said, "I told Maziar and Reza that I didn't know who they were or why they were helping me. Maziar said they weren't permitted to speak about it, that there was still something important that needed to happen before it could all be made clear to me. What did he mean by that?"

"What he meant is that you must accept who you are. That's the important step that must be taken. Once you accept who you are, the disciples of time, as we call ourselves, will become known to you and will coalesce around your leadership. That's what we all understand and accept."

"To lead is to have something to lead about. What do I have to lead about?"

"Allow me to quote your words, Imam: 'God longing is the glue that binds all people together. It is the gift of the Creator to his creatures, planted deep within them, so that they may seek Him. To love and honor the God longing of all people is to love and honor the Creator who gave this gift to all people. It is the best form of worship, surely the most pleasing to our Creator.'"

Ahmed glanced at his mother, who remained silent.

Baba Koushiyar continued, "That was the message you gave in your sermon in the mosque in Jamkaran. You should listen to yourself. I heard it on television and was moved to tears. All of the disciples of time have come to a similar understanding, but you have articulated it in a way that no one else has. You now wear the mantle of the Imam of Time. We know who you are, and now it is for you to accept who you are."

Tears were running down Amineh's face. "I didn't know that it was you giving that sermon, my son, but this is the effect it had on me," she said, as she wiped away tears. "It was true, beautiful, and good, and it's what people need to understand in this time of such turmoil."

"I have only one reason for caution," said Baba Koushiyar. "If you accept, it must be done without any illusions about the dangers that you—and your disciples—will face. There are very dark forces that will seek to destroy us."

Ahmed stood up. "I need time to think about it. I can't just rush into this."

"I understand," said Baba Koushiyar.

Ahmed said he wanted to go for a long walk to clear his mind and think things over, but he was still concerned about being recognized. After Baba Koushiyar left, he slicked back his hair and donned the long-beaked military cap his father had worn. He went to the cemetery and sat next to Shadi's grave for an hour. After praying for her, he bent forward in prostration to kiss the grave and hiked to the foothills above Aliabad. He followed a rugged trail along the hillside in the direction of the valley of Zarringol. In the distant past, when he went in search of the cave, hoping to return home, the valley was uninhabited and forested. Now it was the developed agricultural zone that he had always known, with cropland instead of trees. The only similarity was the river that flowed through the valley.

He crossed the river on the bridge to Zarringol, but skirted the village by going into the hills above it. He found the creek that led to the cave. After a fifteen-minute hike, he came to the familiar rock slide and the boulder that Baba Koushiyar had leaned against when he went into the cave. He stared up at the cave entrance and wondered if the light would appear to him again. He felt so alone and vulnerable. More than anything, he needed not so much guidance as reassurance. He feared he was not capable of bearing the weight that had been placed on him.

He felt the knotted cord under his shirt. He untied it from his waist, wrapped it around his neck like a necklace, and proceeded to climb the fragmented rocks to the cave entrance. He entered into the darkness, now without fear, and made his way to the place where the light had enveloped him. He sat on the ground in a meditative posture. He removed the cord from his neck and wound it around his hand. As he held the cord, it occurred to him that Zartosht understood the divine spark millennia ago and knew it was the possession of all. It was as if his descendants had to rediscover the truths he revealed and discard the false ideas imposed on them.

He closed his eyes and reflected on his bewilderment when he came out of the well in Jamkaran. He had not chosen it, but if he was the one who was chosen, then so be it.

"Your will is my will," he whispered. "Your purpose, O Light, is my purpose. I accept what you have brought about. Give me the strength to bear the responsibility of spreading your light."

He felt a glowing presence and opened his eyes. The cave was filled with the same brilliant light as before. It was a luminance that didn't blind. It enveloped him and filled him with certainty that all that had occurred and all that would come was good and purposeful.

As he sat in contemplation, the image of a temple came to him, just as it had when he was in the cave so long ago. He saw it as before: a temple on a hill, beautiful and beckoning. He wondered if it was his purpose to build a temple. Why else would an image form in his mind like this, persisting like the dreams he used to have of the cave? Perhaps a temple was in the future, but he decided his purpose had to be more than that. He had a message, and messages needed to be delivered. He must speak to people in groups, the bigger the better. But how could such meetings be arranged? He had years of experience organizing rallies for annual celebratory events. These were always held in sports stadiums. Now that they believed him to be the Imam of Time, could he draw large numbers of people to stadiums to hear words they had never anticipated would come from their long-awaited Imam?

After the luminance dissipated, he got up and squeezed through the narrow entrance. He looked down the slope. Baba Koushiyar was at the bottom, leaning against the boulder, waving to him.

When he got to the bottom, Baba Koushiyar said, "I knew you would be here."

Ahmed said, "I want to meet the disciples of time.

# Chapter 25

They left Zarringol in Baba Koushiyar's car and drove to a small farm outside of Aliabad, where one of the disciples was waiting for them. On the way, Ahmed was refreshed by the sight of the expanses of croplands that had meant so much to him in his youth.

As he drove, Baba Koushiyar kept glancing in the rearview mirror to see if they were being followed. "I was certain you were going to decide to go forward with this, Imam, so I invited Koroush to my farm. He drove here overnight from Tehran. He's the one who organized the rescue operation. I can tell you for a fact that he's the first disciple, so he's very eager to meet you. After his return from his journey, he located people with the experience of time, including me, and brought us together to await your coming. We've set up networks of supporters throughout the country who will assist us in spreading your message."

"I'm eager to meet him," Ahmed said.

"He wanted me to tell you before the meeting that he was one of the intellectuals who helped shape the Islamic Republic. He was an advocate of a republican form of government under the guidance of Islamic scholars, which he believed was a workable theocratic system. He was even consulted during the drafting of the Constitution. But over time, he saw the oppressiveness of the regime he helped create, and that's what eventually led to his own journey. He wants to tell you about it."

Ahmed tried to form a mental image of Koroush, but could only think of the arrogant regime intellectuals he had seen on television.

"What about your journey, Baba? I want to hear about it."

Baba Koushiyar glanced at Ahmed. "Do you remember when you came to me at the mosque with your questions about good and evil?"

Ahmed nodded.

"It was like listening to myself many years earlier. I realized that our religious leaders were willing to destroy the world with the idea of bringing what was left under Islam. They're very dangerous, and I was just like you in thinking that this was not true Islam. Like you, I wished I could experience the Islam of Muhammad and Ali, and one day I found myself in Mecca. This was several years before Muhammad declared himself a prophet, and I got to know him well during those years."

"What was your impression of him?"

He shrugged. "My first impression was that there was something wrong with him. I found myself in Mecca during the reconstruction of the temple. The old temple didn't have a roof. It wasn't at all like they want you to believe. It was just four walls of stacked rocks, a little more than my height. It had been damaged by a flash flood, so the Meccans decided to replace it. I had managed to secure protection from one of the clan leaders, which I needed to avoid being taken as a slave, and so I showed my gratitude by volunteering to help. I ended up on the construction crew with Muhammad. It was during this hard work that I witnessed him drop like a rock. That's the only way to describe it, like a rock. It was the custom for workers to strip off their garments and fold them to use as shoulder cushions for carrying rocks down from the hills. Those rocks were heavy and cut into your shoulder if you didn't have thick padding. Even though it was embarrassing, I stripped down too. But Muhammad refused until the pressure from his clansmen became so great that he ended up doing what everyone did. As soon as he removed his waistcloth, his legs buckled, and he fell unconscious on his back. He was choking on his tongue, and I remember seeing saliva dripping from his mouth. Some of the workers said he was devil-possessed, but I understood what happened. When he came out of it, he cried out for his waistcloth and hurried to put his clothes back on. He was very weak at that point, and his uncles helped him return home."

"That was an epileptic seizure," said Ahmed. "It was the same while I was with him. I knew what it was because my wife used to suffer from seizures."

"I know you're right because I've since studied the matter."

"That's where Islam comes from, Baba, from the epileptic visions he had. He thought his visions came from God, but they came from his illness."

The car soon turned onto a graveled lane that led to a stone farmhouse shaded by trees. It was a modest farm ten miles outside Aliabad that had belonged to the Koushiyar family for generations. Baba Koushiyar and his wife, Soraya, often stayed there. Two nephews and their families lived in separate houses behind the main farmhouse and worked the fields and raised animals.

"No one knows who you are except for our friend Koroush. I haven't told anyone else about you, not even my wife."

Several young men standing in front of a shed waved to them. When Baba Koushiyar stopped next to a car parked in front of the house and got out, a gaggle of his young nieces and nephews ran up to him, and he gave them a hug before sending them off to play.

Just as Ahmed stepped into the front room, an older man who was sitting on a sofa jumped to his feet. He was in his sixties, tall, with thinning hair, a prominent forehead, and a penetrating gaze. He grasped Ahmed's hands. "Imam, there aren't words to express how much I've waited for this moment."

"We have a lot to talk about," said Ahmed.

A young woman whom Baba Koushiyar introduced as his niece entered the room carrying a tea service that she placed on a low table before withdrawing.

When she was gone, Koroush said, "I asked Baba to tell you something about my background, and that's because I wanted to make a confession up front that some of the weight of what has happened to our country is on my shoulders." With a dismissive wave of his hand, he said, "It's the role of intellectuals to have ideas, and it's the role of everyone else to suffer the consequences of them."

"It has taken all of us time to become free of our false ideas," said Ahmed.

"Baba told me about your hesitation to accept who you are and shoulder such an important responsibility, but in this regard, I want to assure you that we are here for you. We are here to support you in whatever manner the spirit inspires you."

Ahmed said, "Baba told me there are more than seventy people with the experience of time. I want to know about them."

"They're anything but average. Some are, in fact, quite accomplished or hold important positions. One is a gifted computer programmer, another a talented social media expert, while another is a senior analyst with the Ministry of Intelligence."

"He's been particularly valuable," said Baba Koushiyar. "He has important connections high up in the government, so we learn a lot from him about the thinking of the ayatollahs and the direction of regime policy."

"Among the disciples, we also have some doctors, lawyers, engineers, artists, and musicians," Koroush continued. "All but three are men. They've all had the experience of time, and for all of them, it began when they started questioning what they were raised to believe, just as it happened with us."

"I'm eager to know them," Ahmed said. "When can this be arranged?"

"We've set it up so that you will meet most of them tomorrow in Gorgan," said Koroush. "About sixty of them will be there. The rest are living abroad, some in Frankfurt, others in the Los Angeles area."

Koroush added, "As for how the disciples came in contact with one another, it always started during their experience of time. At some point, they heard their own language being spoken, the Persian of this day and age. That's what occurred between Baba and me just after I found myself in Mecca."

Baba Koushiyar laughed. "I saw him in front of the Kabah. He was being auctioned as a slave and was swearing in Persian at people who were making bids, so I knew where he came from. I intervened and told them he was of my tribe and was under my protection."

"I was able to become established with the Meccans thanks to Baba," Koroush said. "He had accumulated some money as a merchant and shared it with me. Over the next four years, I got the experience of true Islam I had longed for. I also learned about making a living by wheeling and dealing, something very much outside of my experience until then."

"My return happened six months later," said Baba Koushiyar. "This was ten years ago in current time, and even though our distinguished friend stayed in Mecca another four years, it wasn't but six weeks after I came back that he contacted me from Tehran. Over the years, we were able to identify people who, in turn, knew of others."

Koroush nodded. "As our numbers grew, we understood that something of great importance was coming into being. We came to believe the prediction of the appearance of the Imam of Time was somehow connected to our experiences, so we anticipated that someone with the same experience would return in the manner foretold. Because of what we learned about you and what happened to you in the cave, we were confident that you would be the one to return through the well in Jamkaran, so we organized the rescue operation. Please accept my apologies that Maziar and Reza couldn't clarify the situation for you at that time. That had to depend on you realizing and accepting who you truly are."

"I was fortunate you arranged it. If I had been brought to the presidential palace, I would have been placed in the middle of their delusional beliefs at a time when I didn't understand what had happened to me."

"They're very cynical," said Koroush. "They would have used you to further their own ends, and if you refused to cooperate with them, I can assure you they wouldn't hesitate to kill you."

Baba Koushiyar broke into a smile. "Do you know that rumors are spreading that you were kidnapped by the Zionists and the Americans? The Supreme Leader and the president deny sending anyone to pick you up in Jamkaran. Since no one has heard from you, it has to be that you were kidnapped by the enemies of the revolution. They kidnapped you because they fear you will destroy them."

"We don't think it would be good for you to remain out of sight for long," added Koroush. "We have to dispel these rumors. Our leaders are sure to use them to start trouble."

"Do you think that a speaking tour could be set up for me at sports stadiums?" said Ahmed. "The more people who hear my message, the better, so big facilities would be the best. Who wouldn't come to hear the Imam of Time?"

"I've been thinking along those lines," said Koroush. "In fact, I've made inquiries about a stadium in Mashhad because of its symbolic importance, so what better place for you to begin? I think it can be done on short notice. We have a lot of friends everywhere. They've been awaiting your arrival and are eager to help in any way they can."

Ahmed said, "When can we set it up?"

"Tomorrow you'll meet with the disciples in Gorgan," Koroush said. "We can see about arranging for you to speak the day after."

"Is Salman among the people I will meet? Is he one of the disciples?" Ahmed said.

"Salman?" said Koroush.

"I'm referring to Salman al-Farisi, the Salman we all know about from the histories. I knew him well, but I only learned before I fled Yathrib that he was from our time. He said his father is a prominent merchant in Isfahan."

"If he has returned, we haven't heard from him," said Koroush. "After your ministry begins, maybe he will step forward."

They stayed up until late into the night. Koroush and Baba Koushiyar told Ahmed more about their experiences. They were both keen observers, and Ahmed was impressed by how detailed and insightful their memories were.

"All of this represents an enormous wealth of experience," Ahmed said. "Has anyone made a record of it?"

"I have," said Koroush, "and so has Baba. I've completed a memoir in three volumes, very exhaustive. Everything I can re-member is there. Every encounter with Muhammad is recorded. Everyone I knew, every conversation, every thought I had while in Mecca, it's all there. Of course, none of this is publishable at this time. I would be signing my own death warrant if I came out with it. But it is written down."

"My account isn't as detailed," said Baba Koushiyar. "But everything essential is there. We've encouraged other disciples to record their experiences as well."

"We can't allow any of this to be forgotten," said Ahmed.

# Chapter 26

Behrouz came to the farm the following morning to take Ahmed in the back of an airport van to the meeting with the disciples while Baba Koushiyar, now wearing normal clothes, drove there with Koroush.

Ahmed had Behrouz drive him first to his mother's apartment in Aliabad to pick up the "garments of time," as he now called them. His mother grew sad when he told her about their plan to go to Mashhad, the first stop on a speaking tour of unpredictable duration.

"But you've only just returned," she said.

"I promise you, at some point you'll be able to join us."

As he folded the ancient garments into a carrying bag, he came across Abu Sufyan's gold coins. He handed the leather moneybag to her. "Keep these in a safe place. We don't know what the future holds. If there's ever a need for money, you can sell some of the coins. They'll have a great value with collectors."

Now that he could be recognized, he had to stay out of sight. He was tempted to trim his beard and hair, but he refrained from doing so. He would have to appear in Mashhad just as he looked when he came out of the well in Jamkaran. He would have to dress in the ancient flowing garb and wear the black turban. But there was no need to wear such garments for his meeting with the disciples. Instead, he wore a trim blazer borrowed from one of Baba Koushiyar's nephews.

As they sped out of Aliabad, Ahmed in the back of the van, Behrouz said, "I don't know what to call you anymore. I've always known you as Ahmed, but now everyone calls you Imam."

"I'm not comfortable with it either. In private, you can still call me Ahmed, but when there are others present, you should call me Imam because that's what is expected now that I'm taken to be the Imam of Time."

Behrouz asked, "Tell me what I have to do to become a disciple, Ahmed. Do I have to go back in time like you and the others?"

Ahmed shook his head and repeated what he had been saying to everyone: "Love God and love the flame of God longing that he has placed in all of us. Love and honor it in yourself and in all people. That's all that's needed to become a disciple. And not my disciple, but a disciple of the Light."

"You and I experienced evil first-hand in Tehran," Behrouz continued. "How do you explain this evil when God longing is the gift of the Creator to everyone?"

"Not everyone acknowledges the flame within them. Or if they do, they only accept it in people who express it the way they do. That was the fatal error of Muhammad. He only accepted people who adopted his way of expressing it, and he terrorized those who didn't. That put him in contempt of the Creator, and he led others into his error. That's what we witnessed in the streets of Tehran. Contempt for our Creator."

"I want to go with you wherever you go. I heard what you said after you came out of the well, and I accept it as the truth."

"There's going to be a lot of travel. Don't you have steady work spraying fields?"

Behrouz smiled. "You know that sometimes I fly upside down and do loops and other crazy stunts. I'm not trying to show off. It's because I'm bored out of my mind. I want to do something important, like helping you. I have some savings. I'll quit."

"Come with us to Mashhad. You can take turns driving."

An hour after leaving the farm, they arrived at an older hotel in Gorgan, where a conference room had been reserved under the name of a technical society. When Ahmed entered, the disciples erupted into cheers. With broad smiles and glowing eyes, they crowded around him, eager to grasp his hand. One man was about to kiss Ahmed's hand, but he drew it away. "Rather, it is I who should kiss your hand." When someone shouted, "Imam, you are our prophet!" Ahmed shook his head. "No, I'm not a prophet. The world doesn't need any more prophets. What it needs is common sense. Our message is one of common sense."

Maziar and Reza, his rescuers in Jamkaran, stepped forward. "We're so happy you made the decision we were praying you would make, Imam," Maziar said.

Ahmed was pleased to see them again. "I understand now why you had to keep me in the dark."

As he worked his way through the group, shaking hands and exchanging greetings, he came to three women without headscarves. They also grasped his hand, their eyes bright. One of the women, the youngest of the three, said her name: Rayhaneh. She introduced the other women, Laleh and Nousha.

"I'm very happy to know you," Ahmed said, "but I'm disappointed there aren't more women."

Koroush extended his hand toward Rayhaneh. "Rayhaneh is the daughter of a close cousin of mine. She returned from her journey only a month ago and came to me about it. She and Laleh and Nousha all had important experiences, and they're eager to speak to you about them, Imam."

Ahmed said, "We will make time to talk as soon as possible. I want to hear about your experiences."

His attention lingered on Rayhaneh. She seemed familiar to him, but before he could think about it, Koroush and Baba Koushiyar ushered him to the podium. The microphone was gone, removed as a security measure. A wave of laughter rippled through the room when Ahmed said, "I can't tell you how happy I am to be with the Zionists and the Americans who kidnapped me."

He praised Baba Koushiyar and Koroush for their efforts in seeking out and bringing together people who had also gone on the journey. "My only regret is that I didn't know you when we were in the past."

The disciples were seated in rows of conference chairs. Maziar was in front. He stood up. "That isn't entirely so, Imam. I'm no longer wearing a turban or a long beard, so you don't recognize me, but we did meet in Yathrib."

Ahmed stared at him for a moment and remembered thinking there was something familiar about him when he and Reza drove him away from the Jamkaran mosque. "I had a feeling I knew you from somewhere. Where was it that we met?"

"It was during the siege of the Qurayza fortress. There were some of us who wanted to stay as far away from it as we could, and so we gathered around a campfire at night at the edge of the plantation. When I saw you in Jamkaran, I knew that you were among those at the campfire."

Ahmed brightened. "I recognize you now."

Reza stood up. "I was there too. Do you recall how quiet we were? None of us dared to speak about what was being done to the Qurayzas, so we sat around the fire without revealing our thoughts. We were mistrustful."

"Yes, that's true," said Ahmed. "We were uncertain of one another, but now there's no longer any reason for mistrust."

A tall, slender man seated in the middle got to his feet. "Like Maziar and Reza, Imam, I no longer wear a full beard or a turban, so perhaps you don't recognize me either, but we crossed paths in Rey. My name is Mirza. You were among the acolytes studying at the fire temple, as I was. I remember you were there only for a few months. You left for Balkh with a caravan. I know you came back more than a year later because I was among those who witnessed the High Priest Shapur initiate you into the Good Religion."

Ahmed's eyes glowed at the memories of Rey. "I recognize you now, Mirza, but you look older."

"That's because I remained for eight years. I returned only a year ago."

Ahmed loosened the triple-knotted cord, hidden by his shirt, that Shapur gave him as part of the initiation ritual. He wrapped the cord around his hand. "I told Shapur that I wanted my identity back, and he gave it back to me. This is my identity." He held the cord up for everyone to see, eliciting nods and murmurs of approval.

Mirza continued, "You gave Shapur a warning of what was to come, and you asked to have a copy of the sacred texts prepared for you. As the various scriptures were duly copied, they were stored in the library to await your return. I also knew what was in store for the future, so when years went by, and you didn't return, I made the decision to hide them in a safe place, but before I could do so, I found myself back here."

Ahmed said, "I intended to hide them in a cave outside of Aliabad to safeguard them for the future. I regret I wasn't able to return for them."

Mirza said, "I want to introduce you to a disciple who appeared in Rey years later and was there during the final days." He turned to a man seated next to him. "I'm speaking about my good and dear friend Yari."

Yari, a short man with broad shoulders and a trim black beard, stood up. "I want to share my story with you, Imam, if you will allow me."

When Ahmed nodded, the man continued, "It befell me to appear in Rey rather than in Arabia as happened to you and most of the disciples. Like Mirza, I undertook the study of the sacred texts of the religion of Zartosht. I was there for a total of six years, and my days there ended when the invaders reached Rey. They slaughtered, they pillaged, and they raped. I was present during this. We tried to defend the temple, but their numbers overwhelmed us."

Ahmed remembered his vision while he was with Shapur, and he began to tremble at what Yari was about to say. "They killed everyone at the temple, men and women, young and old, it didn't matter. They rounded up the priests. Shapur, the high priest whom you knew, was by then in his seventies. He was the last of the priests they killed. They forced him to watch the beheadings. When they were done with the other priests, they pushed him to his knees and cut off his head."

Ahmed groaned and closed his eyes when he felt tears welling up. After a moment, he said, "How were you able to survive, Yari?"

"I hid in the library with some others. It was a place I loved. As you know, it held one of the most complete collections of Avestan texts anywhere, as well as sacred writings and commentaries on Hinduism and Buddhism. I thought if I was going to die, at least I would die surrounded by truth. After they broke into the library, they forced us to remove the entire contents and pile everything outside in the courtyard. They laughed when one of them threw a torch onto the pile and said, "You worship fire, so here's a fire for you." After the fire died down, they killed the others. With each killing, they shouted *"Allahu Akbar."* I was about to be beheaded when I vanished and found myself back in the present."

A disciple at the back of the room shouted, "Evil conquered good. And the evil remains. How are we going to rid ourselves of this evil, Imam?"

Ahmed was still holding the podium to steady himself from the shock of hearing that his vision had come about. After getting a grip on his emotions, he said, "I will tell you what the high priest Shapur told me when I asked him a similar question. He said the light will defeat the darkness, provided we choose to make it so. Haven't we made our choice? Wasn't it our desire to experience the truth that sent us on our journeys? Now that we have found what we sought, it's for us to go forward with the truth of our experiences. We must share them. In this way, we will bring an end to the darkness and bring back the light."

Another man stood up. "How do we do this, Imam? No one who hasn't experienced what we've experienced would believe us. I've tried speaking about this, but people think I'm crazy."

"Follow the lead of Koroush and Baba Koushiyar. They've written down their experiences. There's no need to use your real name. These can be published as books and put into circulation on the Internet. That will lay the foundation for the future. But you must protect yourselves. The time isn't yet ripe for you to go public. It's still too dangerous."

"When will that be, Imam?" one of the disciples said.

"I don't know, but tomorrow my public work begins in Mashhad, for it was I who was thrust to the forefront. Koroush, Baba Koushiyar, and some of the disciples will assist in this. Pray for our success and our safety."

He spent two hours mingling with the disciples and listening to brief accounts of their experiences. He was amazed by the range. Much of it overlapped and interlocked, and it covered a period of fifty years that ended with the sacking of Rey. To everyone, he said, "Write down your experiences. They were miraculous. They were God's gift to you, so now you must make them your gift to the world."

One of the older disciples, a middle-aged man named Bahram, introduced himself as a political analyst with the Intelligence Ministry. He said his entry into his experience of time was in Mecca just prior to Muhammad's flight to Yathrib. He returned to the present while in the midst of the hand-to-hand combat of the Battle of Uhud, fighting on the side of the Meccan army. He had rough features, with a nose that had been broken more than once. He had a long scar on the ridge of his jaw that showed through a trim beard. He pointed to his nose and the long scar. "Just so you'll know, these were from fights growing up in a rough neighborhood in Tehran, not from Uhud."

"When was your return?"

"A little more than three years ago, Imam."

"And you're still with the Intelligence Ministry?"

"Yes. At first, I wanted to resign. I didn't want anything more to do with those people. But I decided to stay after I met Koroush. He convinced me to stay so that when you emerged, we would be able to know what the government knows and thinks."

"What do they know and think about the Imam?"

Bahram told him of the ministry's efforts to ensure that the man who emerged from the well in Jamkaran was not a fraud. "They sent me at the head of two dozen agents to interview witnesses and acquire surveillance videos and cell phone recordings. We also inspected the well and found that no one could enter from the outside. There's an entrance underground that only the mullahs know about. It's used to clean out all the petitions dropped into the well, then it's closed and sealed again. The seal was untouched. What convinced them that you are indeed the Imam of Time was video evidence of a glow that surrounded the well just before your emergence. I saw it myself on the videos we brought back to Tehran. There was a flash followed by a steady glow."

Ahmed said, "There's not enough time right now, but I'm eager to know more about your experiences." Before he left Bahram to talk to other disciples, he repeated what he said to everyone: "Love our Creator and love the flame of God longing that he has placed in all of us. That's what unites us all."

He wanted to speak more with Rayhaneh and twice caught her eye, but before he had the opportunity, Koroush reminded him it was time to prepare for the trip to Mashhad. Koroush and other disciples were going to drive ahead to Mashhad to begin making arrangements for his appearance, whereas he, Baba Koushiyar, Maziar, and Behrouz would follow later, traveling along the same route over the mountains in the yellow cargo van.

As Ahmed was about to leave, Rayhaneh rushed up and presented him with a pendant depicting the winged symbol of Zoroastrianism. He bowed when she offered to place it around his neck.

"May our past be our future," she said with a timid smile once the pendant dangled from his neck.

Ahmed looked at her warm and expressive eyes, again thinking he knew her from somewhere, or that she resembled someone he had known. She seemed flustered and looked down. After a moment, she looked at him again. "Imam, I can't bring myself to agree with your dissatisfaction that there are so few women among the disciples. I can affirm from my experience and that of my friends Laleh and Nousha that it was the mercy of our Creator that only a few of us were sent back. I haven't told Koroush about my experience because I doubt even he would believe me."

"I will believe you," Ahmed said. "When there's an opportunity, I want to hear about it."

# Chapter 27

The small group arrived in Mashhad early the next day. The only danger they encountered during the overnight trip occurred when they drove into a checkpoint manned by the Revolutionary Guards. As Ahmed, Baba Koushiyar, and Behrouz tensed up in the back of the cargo van, Maziar flashed an identity card that Bahram had gotten him from the Intelligence Ministry. The guardsmen waved the van through, no questions asked.

Less than an hour later, they arrived at a safe house in Mashhad that Koroush had set up, an impressive home with high walls separating the house from neighboring residences. Two black limousines like the ones that showed up at the Jamkaran mosque were parked in a circular driveway.

"We have your sermon arranged for this afternoon, Imam," Koroush said as he helped carry travel bags into the house. "Word is already spreading throughout Mashhad that you'll make your first public appearance at the stadium, so you can anticipate it will be full to overflowing. Our greatest priority is to get you into the stadium and out of it without any interference from the clerics."

Several hours later, Ahmed was on his way to the stadium in a limousine driven by Maziar. He had changed out of his travel clothes and now wore the flowing Arab garment and the black turban. On the way, he dwelt not so much on what he wanted to say, but rather on the spirit he prayed would flow through him so that he would say what needed to be said in the way that it had to be said.

Koroush had arranged so that the leading ayatollah from the

major shrine of Mashhad would announce Ahmed's presence before he entered the stadium. As he went up the stairs from the parking garage to the stadium, he heard the ayatollah on the stadium loudspeakers:

"O ye faithful who are gathered here today, O ye who believe in Allah and his Prophet, may peace be upon him, I have been given the privilege far beyond my merit to present to you our long-awaited and most beloved Imam, he who has come to us through the sacred well of Jamkaran in fulfillment of prophecy. Listen to his words and obey."

Ahmed went through the door accompanied by Koroush, Baba Koushiyar, and other disciples who wore long beaked caps and wrap-around sunglasses, making them hard to recognize. They escorted Ahmed along a short walk to a podium set up next to an area reserved for religious dignitaries. To one side, cut off by a rail, were dozens of clerics of high rank, most wearing white turbans, while others wore black. They stood up when Ahmed came through the door. Many appeared stunned; some seemed close to fainting; others were filled with rapturous joy and stretched out their arms toward Ahmed, crying, "O Imam, our prayers have been answered."

Ahmed acknowledged them by touching his heart and bowing slightly. He stepped up to the podium and faced the immense crowd. The entire stadium erupted with chants of "Imam" and "Mahdi."

The playing field was thick with clerics and seminarians in their distinctive garments and turbans. A soccer match had been scheduled, but the players agreed to postpone the game, asking only to be permitted on the field for the appearance of the Imam. They were crowded to the sidelines by a battalion of clerics, who had arranged themselves from the top to bottom of the playing field in ranks and rows in anticipation of ritual prayers led by the Imam of Time.

As the thunderous welcome continued, Ahmed thought how strange it was that in conventional time, only six weeks had gone by since that brutal day in the streets of Tehran, yet that brief span encompassed the four years of his miraculous journey. He was still in awe that the journey had ended just as miraculously only three days before. He gazed down at the rows and ranks of the clerics and seminarians and knew their thoughts. They were steeped in the belief that his return signaled the beginning of Islam's supremacy in the world. They were present for this grand moment, believing they would be part of the bright and glorious future that awaited Islam. He was their Messiah and leader, and they were certain Jesus would also soon return to fulfill prophecy. Jesus would break the cross to show his contempt for the Christian belief that he was crucified. He would declare Muhammad's religion of submission to be the true and only faith. Together, the Imam of Time and Jesus would lead the armies of God to reclaim Jerusalem and destroy the Jews. They would inspire the conquest of the world so that it would be illuminated by God's light. They would cleanse the entire world of its impurities and corruption, and when their mission was completed, there would be no other but the religion of God. The world would be a place of universal peace and justice. And this would all come about in preparation for the end of days, for the final hour that signals the time of resurrection and judgment is at hand.

As Ahmed adjusted the microphone to give himself time to let the spirit bubble up in him, he felt saddened that the entire edifice of the belief of the people jamming the stadium, the belief that he himself had been raised with, was based on the rejection of simple truth. It had resulted in so much cruel destruction through the centuries. Yet he was not there to denounce the error or its originator, but to announce the simple truth that had been denied to them. He imagined he was not in a stadium standing before tens of thousands of people, but on the balcony overlooking the Ganges, marveling at the countless sparkles on the river that were like arms reaching up in joy to the source of the light that shone down upon them.

"O people of Mashhad," Ahmed began in a firm and confident voice. "Do you believe that you have come here because of the Imam of Time?"

He let the question hang a moment before continuing: "I say to you that you have not come here because of the Imam of

Time. Rather, you have come here because of the spirit that we all share. This is the spirit that is our endowment from our Creator. It is the spirit of God longing. It is his gift to his creation—to us. What you seek from me, a connection with our Creator, is already within you, just as it is within all people."

For nearly an hour, he elaborated on the simple truth that the longing for God was universal and found expression in the numerous religions of the world. Among the many analogies he offered, he compared these expressions to a bouquet of beautiful flowers of different colors and shapes that the world offers to the Creator. "So I say to you, love the flowering of God longing in all people, even though it may not be expressed the same way you express yours. That is the best way to honor your Creator. That is the best form of worship."

As had happened in Jamkaran, his words stirred emotions. Many people wept. When he finished speaking, thousands of people jumped to their feet and cheered wildly, shouting, "The Imam has come to us with truth! He speaks the truth!"

The ayatollah who introduced him, an elderly man shrunken by age, stood up among the clerical dignitaries, and, in a reluctant voice, said, "Will the Imam now lead us in prayer?"

During the sermon, Ahmed avoided looking at the distinguished clerics, for their reaction to his words could not have been any different from that of the mass of mullahs and seminarians on the playing field. Their expressions had changed from open-mouthed awe at the beginning to confusion and consternation by the end. When the ayatollah asked if he would lead them in prayer, Ahmed looked at the distinguished clerics for the first time and saw what he had seen on the playing field: mouths hanging open, whispering behind hands, pursed lips, and with some, closed-eye reflection.

Ahmed touched his heart and bowed once more to the ayatollah. He turned again to face the stadium. "I will now lead you in prayer," he began.

He asked everyone to stand. In an instant, the people in the bleachers were on their feet. The clerics and seminarians who had been seated cross-legged on the ground or on their haunches hesitated, but they arose after the tens of thousands of people in the stadium stood up.

"By giving us the gift of life, our Creator has shared his universe with us," Ahmed continued. "So I ask you, what is said to someone of a generous heart who gives you something? We all know the answer to that. All that is necessary are simple words spoken with warmth and sincerity, and those words are, 'Thank you.'"

He asked the crowd to repeat after him: "Thank you, our Creator and Lord, for giving us the gift of life. Thank you for sharing your universe with us."

After the crowd repeated his words, Ahmed said, "If you were the Creator, wouldn't you be pleased with that?"

When he was done with the prayer, thunderous cries of "Imam!" broke out across the stadium. The aging ayatollah and the other leading clerics jostled one another as they hurriedly stepped down from the dignitary section in an effort to greet him. But before they could reach him, they were blocked by a group made up of disciples and friends of the disciples, all of them dressed in black. They formed a tight line that kept people from surging forward along the short walkway that Ahmed had taken when he entered the stadium.

Baba Koushiyar said, "Leave this way, Imam. Come this way, hurry."

Before he reached the exit, he heard religious dignitaries pleading. "O Imam, won't you meet with us, we who are your devoted servants? Please don't bring us humiliation by turning your back on us!"

After he went through the door leading to the parking garage, the disciples in black followed. When they were inside, Behrouz slid a thick dead bolt forward to secure the door, a locking mechanism installed the night before in secret. They went down the stairs to the parking area. Koroush had arranged for several black limousines to be stationed in the garage to serve as decoy vehicles.

While the disciples jumped into the various limousines, slamming the heavy doors, Behrouz guided Ahmed, Koroush, and Baba Koushiyar to a white cargo van parked next to a wall.

Behrouz pushed the side door open and motioned for them to get in the back. He slid into the driver's seat and watched the sleek limousines speed out of the parking garage with tires squealing.

A few minutes after the last of the decoy vehicles exited into the street, Behrouz followed. He gave a pre-arranged signal to the attendant, who raised the security gate, and he drove out of the stadium. They were soon lost in heavy traffic.

"That was a diversionary tactic to throw them off if they tried to follow," said Behrouz as he maneuvered through the thick of vehicles.

Ahmed sighed that such tactics were necessary. It would be so much better if he could move around freely. But the truth of his origin was like a sword hanging over his head. It could be used to destroy him.

"The clerics are dangerous, Imam," Koroush said, "and they'll get more dangerous as time goes on. We can't let you fall into their hands."

After they were clear of the stadium, Koroush got a call on his cell phone, and when the call ended, he turned to Ahmed: "We've just gotten word from Bahram. He picked it up at the Intelligence Ministry that the Supreme Leader and the president were about to fly to Mashhad this morning in the hope of meeting you, but they changed their minds at the last minute out of fear of being snubbed."

"Their world has been turned upside down," said Ahmed.

Behrouz drove into a high-rise residential neighborhood and made a series of left and right turns down various side streets until arriving at an underground garage.

The yellow cargo van was parked inside. They got into the van, and Behrouz drove through Mashhad until they arrived at the high-walled safe house.

# Chapter 28

In less than an hour, all the men in black arrived as well, now in nondescript vehicles and wearing normal clothes.

They gathered around a long table and watched various television broadcasts about the sermon. All the reports omitted the crowd's enthusiastic reaction. The channels also carried brief messages from both the Supreme Leader and the president complimenting the Imam on his "impactful" sermon and asked him to honor them with a formal meeting.

Ahmed didn't recognize himself on television. It still seemed so strange that only six weeks before, when he was fleeing the boulevard of death, such words could never have come from him, yet now he had just stood before tens of thousands of people to utter them. He felt humbled that the words didn't come from him, but through him.

Koroush had stocked the kitchen with food, and they spent several hours preparing favorite dishes that they shared around the long table. Before they ate, Ahmed said a prayer of thankfulness to the Creator for "the gift of conviviality with friends who have embraced your purpose for them."

When supper was over, Ahmed spoke to them about his experiences on the Silk Road and on the balcony overlooking the Ganges, which led him to the understanding he spoke about in his sermon.

"It took more than three years for me to grasp what was meant when I heard the voice in the cave. It's the truth of the spark that resides in all people and pushes us toward God. That was the message of the light, a simple, true, and beautiful message."

"Shouldn't we denounce Islam?" said one of the disciples. "It will never accept the truth. The ayatollahs want to impose their beliefs on the entire world through *jihad*. They're pushing to build nuclear weapons to advance their goal."

Baba Koushiyar shook his head. "For us to attack it would be suicidal. We've seen what they're capable of in how they've been dealing with the demonstrators. And look at their history of brutality going back to the Revolution."

"It's for us to preach the truth of God longing," said Koroush. "It's as the Imam says. God longing is the common denominator among all people. When people are brought to recognize they are brothers and sisters in spirit, regardless of their different ideas of God, they will judge what they've been raised with. It's like a measuring stick that will allow people to determine the validity of what was taught to them as truth."

Ahmed said, "It's also crucial to share the truth of your experiences. They were given to us for a purpose. It's not necessary to denounce our former belief. I agree it would be a mistake. But the experiences of seventy-five people—seventy-six if you include me—represent a powerful repudiation."

"We'll make sure this gets done as quickly as possible, Imam," said Koroush. "We can call them Testimonies of Time, and when they are all compiled and disseminated, they will help to bring an end to the fatal error, as you call it."

"I will also prepare my testimony," said Ahmed. "It will begin with what happened in the streets of Tehran, and it will end at the mosque in Jamkaran."

One by one, the disciples expressed their eagerness to begin, but several worried they didn't have the necessary writing background. They would not know where to begin.

"It's easy," said Koroush. "Talk into a recording device. Start where your experience began and keep going until you get to the end. These recordings can be transcribed and edited."

Baba Koushiyar added, "It's helpful to have someone with you to ask for clarifications or details, or to prod you if it becomes too painful to talk about certain things. It will be difficult because so many of our experiences were embarrassing or traumatic. Talking about them to someone who is sympathetic will be therapeutic."

"Rayhaneh, Laleh, Nousha, and several others have volunteered to help with the editing," Koroush said. "It doesn't have to be the full story with everything in it on the first effort. What's important is to get the essential experience down in writing so it can be published. The sooner, the better. A more detailed and expanded version can be published later."

After several of the disciples offered to help as listeners and interviewers, Koroush asked, "What do you wish to do after Mashhad, Imam?"

"It's important not to lose momentum," said Ahmed. "So what do you recommend, Koroush?"

"With your permission, I can set up another event in Birjand for the day after tomorrow. Friends have assured us the use of a private home there, and we've already had people visit the sports stadium, so we know the layout." He pointed to the men seated around the table. "We will carry this out in the same manner as we did in Mashhad by announcing your appearance and assuring your security while going into the stadium and exiting."

Ahmed nodded his approval. "And then?"

Koroush smiled. "And then more appearances in the provinces. People in big cities are better educated. They're more likely to despise the mullahs and are more open to your message, whereas rural people tend to be conservative. Win them over, and you win the entire country."

Ahmed looked around the table at the disciples, most of whom wore short dark beards to appear like religious conservatives. When they nodded in agreement, he said, "Very good. We'll begin with Birjand."

The next morning, Koroush left for Birjand with the disciples, leaving Baba Koushiyar, Maziar, Behrouz, and Ebrahim, one of the disciples who was on the security detail at the Mashhad stadium. Ahmed asked him to stay behind. During his conversations with the disciples the evening before, he learned that Ebrahim had appeared in the Jewish oasis of Khaybar, and his entire experience, lasting five years, occurred there. He witnessed

Muhammad's attack on the oasis, and his return occurred at the very moment he was about to be killed.

"Let's begin recording the testimonies with your experience, Ebrahim," Ahmed said.

Behrouz drove to Mashhad to buy a recording device and returned with a compact digital recorder, raving that the audio files could be downloaded to a flash drive for later transcription. After they figured out how to work the device, Ahmed sat with Ebrahim in the living room. Ebrahim was nervous. His return had occurred three years before, yet he still felt traumatized by an experience he likened to a terrifying dream. He didn't understand why such an experience had been given to him until he was put in contact with Koroush, and he joined the disciples in anticipation of the return of the Imam of Time.

Ahmed knew about the Khaybar attack from the histories and from what the Meccans had told him about it. It occurred a year and several months after the massacre of the Jews in Yathrib. He calculated that the Khaybar Jews were being slaughtered about the same time he reached the Ganges and entered Kashi.

"We'll start from the beginning, and we'll keep going until we get to the end, my dear friend," Ahmed said in an encouraging voice. "The beginning is where you were in the present time when you vanished and where you found yourself in the past. Tell me about it, Ebrahim!"

Ebrahim allowed Baba Koushiyar, Maziar, and Behrouz to sit in. They gave him encouragement and asked questions to push him deeper into his memories. Ebrahim had a memory for detail and described the people he had known in a way that brought them to life. He was from a Shiraz merchant family and was successful in his own right. When he appeared in the past, dazed and disoriented in one of the Khaybar villages, he was first given work as a laborer on a date plantation, but he soon showed his merchant savvy and was taken in by a noble family. He became close to their leaders and was privy to their fear of Muhammad, particularly after Muhammad sent a team of assassins to murder one of the most important of the Khaybar leaders. When the attack on Khaybar began, Ebrahim joined in the defense, shooting arrows from the battlements and falling back as the strongholds were conquered one by one.

"Everyone knew about the massacre of the Qurayzas, so we were certain that would be our fate if we didn't die fighting. Many brave men were killed in the fighting."

To spare themselves, the defenders of the remaining fortresses worked out a deal for Muhammad to allow them to leave Khaybar if they surrendered, but it fell through when the nobleman who had taken Ebrahim into his family hid a small fortune of gold, silver, and jewelry from Muhammad and was tortured and beheaded after he refused to reveal the location.

Ebrahim's voice rose to trembling fury when he said, "I was present when his wife Safiya was dragged before Muhammad. They brought her to his tent along a path where they had dumped her husband's body so she would see it. She was a beautiful young woman, and Muhammad claimed her as part of his booty. After that, all of the male members of the nobleman's household were put to death. I was among those to be killed."

Just as he was pushed to his knees and the executioner raised his sword, he reappeared in the familiar world of the present, as if awakening from a nightmare. "But it wasn't a nightmare, as all of you know from your own experiences."

The recording session lasted late into the night. Ebrahim ended up sweaty and exhausted, as if from a strenuous workout. He managed a weak smile when Ahmed and the others thanked him for his courage by revealing such painful experiences. More than ten hours in all were recorded.

Behrouz downloaded the audio files onto a laptop and copied them to a flash drive that he handed to Baba Koushiyar. As he gave him the flash drive, Behrouz said, "I've said to some of you that I wished I'd had the experience of going into the past. I take it back. The present time is bad enough."

Early the next day, they left in the yellow cargo van for Birjand, a six-hour journey along a two-lane highway with traffic slowing in small towns along the way. In Birjand, Maziar drove to another walled home where they waited until it was time for Ahmed to speak at the stadium. It was smaller than the one in Mashhad, but it held a sizeable crowd. The crowd broke out into wild cheers and chants of "Imam!" when he stepped up to the podium dressed in the garments of time.

As they cheered, many with arms outstretched to him and tears in their eyes, Ahmed scanned the contingent of turbaned clerics on the playing field. Many were stroking their beards or leaning to speak to the person next to them. Others had pursed lips and crossed arms. A much smaller number had rounded smiles and seemed eager to hear him speak.

He raised his arms to quiet the crowd and invited everyone to take their seats. His sermon was the same as in Mashhad. It centered on the singular truth revealed to him through his experience of time. He expanded on it, offering fresh images and analogies to convey its meaning. He spoke of Kashi and the balcony and the lights that danced on the water, of glittering hands raised upward, of God longing as a divine gift shared by all of humanity.

When it was over and prayers were expected, one of the clerics shouted from the playing field, "Will you lead us now in prayer, Imam, but in the manner to which we are accustomed?"

"I will lead you in the best prayer and in the best manner possible," Ahmed replied. "The best prayer is the prayer of thankfulness to our Creator for giving us the gift of life in His universe and for implanting in us the longing to know Him. The best way to say this prayer is while standing on your feet—proudly. What is there not to be proud of when you are a child of God?"

He looked at the thick crowds in the stands and saw many nodding. He noted the reaction of the clerics, most with looks of disapproval. He went on, "So many of us have been raised with the habit of dropping to our knees and falling forward in prostration as the required form of prayer. Do you know where this practice came from?"

One of the clerics shouted, "It was taught to us by our Prophet Muhammad, may an eternity of blessings be upon him. We follow his example."

Ahmed had been thinking about the practice of ritual prostration the entire morning. He recalled that when he was on his way to Ctesiphon with the High Priest Shapur's letter recommending him to the Persian emperor, his caravan companions told him of the manner in which people were required to use in approaching the emperor. They had to enter the throne room with their heads bowed, looking only at the floor, and they were made to lie face down in full prostration with their arms stretched forward. They could not rise or look to one side without permission; otherwise, they risked being put to death. Even in the court of Heraclius, Ahmed recalled having to kneel and bow his head in recognition of the might of the imperial throne.

"In olden days, people had no choice but to bow down or prostrate themselves before their rulers," Ahmed continued. "That was because their rulers had such power over them, so it was natural to fear the rulers, particularly the despotic ones. We have continued this practice when it is not needed. Do you truly think you should fear your Creator?"

From the playing field, a cleric shouted a Quran verse, which ended with, "And fear Allah that ye may prosper!"

Ahmed replied, "Do you fear the good parents who have brought you into the world out of their love? Do you bow down before them? Or, if people give you a gift, do you drop to your knees and throw yourselves down before them? Can you imagine how they would be embarrassed if you did so? Let us not embarrass our Creator. Let us stand on our feet and declare our thankfulness for his loving gift to us, his children."

Ahmed made a motion for everyone to stand, and the crowd in the stands stood up. Some of the clerics on the playing field jumped to their feet as well, but as happened in Mashhad, most remained seated, glancing at one another in confusion. They didn't get to their feet until a chorus of voices from the stands chanted, "On your feet! On your feet!"

When the clerics were standing, Ahmed asked the crowd to repeat the same words he had used in Mashhad: "Thank you, our Creator and Lord, for giving us the gift of life. Thank you for sharing your universe with us. Thank you for implanting in us the longing to know you. Thank you for giving us a mind that allows us to recognize that what you have implanted in us, you have implanted in all people. And we affirm this and give praise to you when we say to one another and to all people, 'I am you, and you are me!"

When it was over, the disciples, now aided by many dozens of volunteers, formed a tight cordon to protect Ahmed from the crush of the crowd pressing forward to touch him and from the clerics clamoring to meet with him.

He was soon out of the stadium, hidden in the back of a cargo van while a half-dozen black sedans fanned out into the street to create a diversion.

# Chapter 29

Ahmed spent nearly a month on the road, giving sermons in more than a dozen provincial towns. He expanded on the sermons of Mashhad and Birjand, using new analogies and fresh images that touched on the daily lives of his listeners. He did not know where the words came from. They were unrehearsed and seemed to flow through him.

He was not concerned when the government-controlled media stopped broadcasting the events, as the turnout remained overwhelming. Uproarious chants of "Imam!" and "Mahdi!" always greeted him, and the crowds ended with arms outstretched, crying out, "The Imam of Time has brought truth to us! You are God's blessing to us!"

At the end of the swing through the southeastern cities, he and the dozen disciples who accompanied him made a secret trip to Yazd, where a Zoroastrian community preserved their beliefs and practices. He met with the priests and attended ceremonies at one of the few remaining fire temples. The group spent an entire week with the priests, discussing the religion with its practitioners. Koroush and Baba Koushiyar were eager questioners, as were the disciples whose knowledge of the religion of their ancestors was limited.

Mirza and Yari, the disciples whose experience of time took place in Rey, arranged the stay. They had become part of the Yazd community, but had not yet spoken to the elders about their experiences. Who would believe them? Ahmed decided to reveal the truth during a confidential meeting with the priests that included the two Rey disciples. He spoke about his experiences in Yathrib and dwelt on his time with the High Priest Shapur. He removed the knotted cord from under his shirt and held it up. "Shapur gave this cord to me at the time of my initiation. These are the knots I made with each vow to live by the virtues preached by Zartosht, and I have been faithful to my vows."

After Ahmed's revelation, Mirza and Yari also revealed their experiences. The priests, dressed in the white garments and white cap of the priesthood, wept at Yari's account of the sacking of Rey, the massacre of the faithful, the murder of Shapur and the other priests, and the torching of all that was in the library.

"It is our struggle to preserve what is left of our sacred works," the chief priest said.

Ahmed spoke to them of the cave and the visions he had of a temple inspired by the fire temples. "Zartosht chose fire as the symbol of the divine fire of creation and the righteous order that the Wise Lord desires for creation. The fire is also the best symbol for the longing for God that burns in all people. I swear to you that the day will come when I will build a temple to honor the spirit of God longing, and the central feature will be fire. In this manner, we will honor what is true, good, and beautiful."

While on the road, the disciples accompanying Ahmed recorded their testimonies, assisting one another as sympathetic listeners and probing interviewers. In all, they accumulated more than 300 hours of oral testimony. Other disciples, scattered around Iran or living abroad, were also working on their testimonies, either as voice recordings or in writing. Most had gotten word to Koroush about their progress, and he expected to hear from the rest.

It was clear to everyone that an enormous amount of work lay ahead in transcribing and editing the testimonies. Ahmed eventually agreed with Baba Koushiyar that his farm was the ideal location for the work. "It's in the countryside, far from prying eyes. The farmhouse has many rooms so people can stay for as long as necessary, and the farm's produce and poultry will provide the food we'll need."

From Yazd, the group traveled to the farm. With Behrouz's help, Koroush set up a bank of computers in one of the rooms and recruited volunteers from among the disciples for transcription and editing duties. The farm was soon abuzz with activity. A dozen disciples, including Laleh and Nousha, busied themselves in "the office of time," as they tagged the computer room. Koroush knew of a program that transcribed voice to type and acquired a copy in Gorgan. Though it was prone to numerous errors, the program sped up the transcription process.

The volunteers included Ahmed's mother and Baba Koushiyar's wife, Soraya. Both women came to the farm the day after Ahmed arrived from Yazd. They were dressed in black chadors for the trip to the farm, but threw them off once indoors.

Soraya was taller than Baba Koushiyar, slender and gracious. Ahmed spent an afternoon getting to know her and appreciated her sense of humor. She described herself as a former pious woman who lost her faith after her husband convinced her that his experiences were real.

"I couldn't deny that he had aged during the weeks he was gone, and I've never known him to tell a lie." Both of them became crypto-apostates, going through the motions of the faith in order not to draw attention to themselves.

Baba Koushiyar said, "I've never told you about this, Imam, but I decided to stay on at the mosque to use the pulpit to preach better things. I found a few innocuous verses in the Quran and used them as the basis for sermons on the virtues practiced by our ancestors, particularly in performing good deeds. And behind that cover, Soraya and I awaited your coming."

Ahmed was happy when Rayhaneh arrived to help with the work. He had been thinking about her and wondered about her experience. Koroush made a special trip to Tehran to pick her up from the home of her parents. When she arrived, she was wearing the stylish clothes and sunglasses of a well-to-do Tehran woman and wore a loose scarf over her abundant brown hair.

Koroush took Ahmed to one side after Rayhaneh joined the transcribers and editors, telling him that it had been two months since her return, yet she still avoided talking about her experience. "I don't know what happened to her, but I suspect it must have been shattering. She's the only one who hasn't wanted to talk to me about her experiences, but I think she's ready to talk to you. Just give her time."

From the front room where he worked on the testimonies, Ahmed sometimes heard Rayhaneh join in the bantering of the volunteers. He had assigned himself editorial duties and spent his time on the long sofa of the front room with printouts stacked next to him. Red pen in hand, he marked up the copy with editorial symbols, comments, and requests for clarification.

On the third day after her arrival, Rayhaneh tapped on the door and asked him if he had a moment to speak with her. He invited her in and pulled an armchair up near the sofa. He was wearing the Zoroastrian pendant she had given him at the meeting of the disciples in Gorgan, and as he bent to pull the armchair forward, it dangled from his neck.

"You honor me by wearing the pendant, Imam," she said.

"I wear it as a reminder of our meeting," he said in a calming voice, realizing that she was nervous.

She got comfortable in the armchair and said, "You told us at the meeting that our experiences wouldn't have any value unless we shared them, so I've made up my mind to talk about what I experienced."

Ahmed nodded. "Whatever you say, I will believe you."

She was twisting her fingers and looking down at her hands. After hesitating, she said, "You know, of course, that Muhammad had many wives, thirteen in all."

Ahmed nodded.

"You know then that one of them had my name."

Ahmed again nodded.

She looked at him for a long moment and said, "Imam, I am that Rayhaneh."

Ahmed was stunned. It was the last thing he would have expected. It took him a moment to get over the shock.

"How did this come about?"

"It started three months ago. It was the day after the protesters in Tehran were attacked by the police and the paramilitaries. There were shootings. People were killed. I was there, and I witnessed it. The next day, I was in my apartment in Tehran. My parents were upset with me for putting myself in danger, and I was debating whether I should risk going out to join another protest. Another had been organized over the shootings. All of a sudden, I was in the midst of hundreds of women and children who were holding each other and crying. Hundreds of men were there too, with their arms around the women and children. Their dress was different than what we see in Iran. They looked like a mass of refugees. We were inside some kind of fortress, and they were speaking Arabic. This happened in an instant, Imam, in the time it takes to blink."

With all the disciples, it was instantaneous like that, Ahmed thought. One second here, the next second there. His transition seemed to have been a dizzying exception.

"Do you think I'm making this up?" said Rayhaneh, concern edging into her voice when he didn't say anything.

Ahmed shook his head. "Not at all. I believe you. It happens that way. In the blink of an eye. Please go on."

She continued, saying that she became confused and frightened. People were staring at her because of her clothes. In a panicky voice, she asked the people around her, "Who are you? Where am I?" She said it first in Persian and then in Arabic. She was proficient enough in the classical Arabic she studied in school to understand and make herself understood, and she soon realized her plight. She was caught up in a battle, and the people in the fortress were about to surrender.

Ahmed's heart raced when she said, "Imam, can you imagine my shock when I heard the name Muhammad? These were Jews. They were surrendering to him after a long siege. Their food had run out. If they didn't surrender, they were going to starve to death, yet if they gave up, they were certain the men were going to be slaughtered. I didn't know how I got there, but I knew I was in a time and place that weren't my own."

Ahmed began to feel weak. He knew without her saying another word that she had appeared among the Qurayzas. He was outside the fortress while she was inside.

"A young woman took pity on my fear and confusion. She

came up to me. She took my hand and said comforting words. I remember her name, Maryam."

Ahmed felt like a knife had been thrust into his heart. He tried to control his reactions, but his head felt like it was about to explode from the rush of memories. He closed his eyes and rubbed his forehead. Tears began welling in his eyes.

Rayhaneh became alarmed. "Is something wrong, Imam? Maybe I should stop."

He stood up and paced back and forth until he felt better. He wanted to tell her that he was there, too, and about Maryam and Nabbash and his experiences with them on their plantation and in their village, but he held back. It was her testimony. She needed to get it out. He could tell her about his involvement later.

"I'm sorry," he said. "Don't let me interrupt you. Everything you have to say is too important."

She agreed to have the interview recorded. Ahmed clipped a small microphone to her blouse. She repeated what she had told Ahmed and went on to describe how the huge gate was pushed open, and hundreds of men armed with swords and spears poured in. They separated the men from the women and children and forced the men to go outside the fortress first. The women and children were made to go out after them, but they were kept to one side, separate from the men. She remained with Maryam the whole time.

Her memory coincided with what Ahmed remembered. Rayhaneh didn't know, however, that Muhammad had brought a wounded clan leader to his tent to make the decision about the fate of the Jews. She only knew that the men, women, and children were forced to stand for hours. But she heard the announcement: All of the men were to be executed, the women and children sold into slavery, and the possessions of the Jews turned over to "God and his messenger."

She remembered not believing her ears and was shattered when the women and children began wailing. The men were forced to march off in a long column. After the men were gone, a dozen young women, including her and Maryam, were selected from among the captives and brought to Muhammad. "We were made to stand before him one at a time. Maryam and I were the last. When it came to her turn, someone whispered something to Muhammad, and he became furious and ordered her taken away."

As she continued telling Ahmed about it, Rayhaneh's eyes flashed with anger. Until the moment she was made to stand before Muhammad, she tried to believe that what was happening was only a very bad dream, the worst she had ever experienced. Only hours before, she was in her apartment in Tehran. Now she was in an alien and primitive place. Tough-looking men with ragged beards and dirty turbans and garments flanked Muhammad, while a crowd of greasy, sweaty men pressed in from the sides. The smell of people who had not washed in a long time was overpowering. Muhammad was seated cross-legged on a rug in front of the entrance to a red tent. After all the other young women were sent away, Muhammad motioned for her to come forward. When she didn't budge, she was pushed from behind.

"He asked my name with an exaggerated sweetness. Instead of telling him, I said, 'Who are you?' That startled him. Everyone was supposed to know who he was. He turned to some men standing next to him and said something I couldn't hear, but it made them laugh. He turned back to me and said, 'I am the Messenger of God.' I felt an intense dislike for him, such as I've never felt for anyone before. I wanted to say, 'I'm so relieved to hear that you're God's messenger. For a moment, I thought you were just some arrogant warlord thug.' But I didn't know the words for 'warlord' and 'thug' in Arabic."

Before she could say anything, Muhammad got to his feet. He was fascinated by her unusual garments and by the scent of perfume, a light French fragrance she had sprayed on that morning in Tehran. He touched the fabric of her blouse and head scarf. He put a loose end of her scarf to his nose and sniffed it before stepping back and taking her in from head to toe.

Ahmed's head began to hurt. He couldn't have been more than a hundred yards away when this was occurring. He remembered the thick crowd of warriors up near the tent. They cut off his view, and he only heard someone commenting that Muhammad was selecting a woman from among the Jews as his booty.

Rayhaneh continued, "He sat down again and said, 'Now, tell me your name,' and so I told him."

She looked at Ahmed for a long moment. "Imam, I was raised in the faith, but as I grew older and attended the university, the religion lost its hold on me. What was left was hanging by a thread, and the thread snapped when he said, 'Do you know that you are now my possession, Rayhaneh?' He offered me freedom in exchange for marrying him and adopting his religion. He assumed I was Jewish since I came out of the fortress with the Jews. I told him there was nothing I could do regarding his control over me, but I said I knew about his religion and didn't want any part of it. He replied, 'It matters not. God allows His Messenger whatever women his right hand possesses.' I remembered those words from the Quran. They mean 'slave.' From then on, I was his slave, his concubine."

Her words brought back the leaden heaviness that had gripped him after he fled Yathrib. He felt his body sinking deep into the armchair. To pull himself out of it, he said, "Will you permit me to interrupt you for a moment?"

"Yes, of course, Imam."

"I can't hold it back from you any longer. I was present during all of this."

It was Rayhaneh's turn to be stunned. She had heard fragments of Ahmed's experience from Koroush and other disciples, and at the meeting of the disciples at Gorgan, she remembered that two of them spoke about being around a campfire with him, but she didn't hear everything they said. "Where were you, Imam? I didn't see you among those men."

"I kept far in the back, at the edge of the date plantation. I didn't want to be there. I was considered an apostate and could be killed, but I was under the protection of Salman al-Farisi, and he was part of the army that laid siege to the Jewish fortress. So I had no choice but to be there. "

When he told Rayhaneh about Maryam and her father, Nabbash, and his deep affection for them, she began to weep. "I know they were killed. I was taken to Muhammad's mosque and put in one of those filthy rooms they lived in. The next day, I heard that all the men were being executed, and also one of the women, and that it was Maryam. Every few minutes, I could hear people shouting *'Allahu Akbar,'* and I knew it signaled that people were being killed."

Ahmed stood up and paced back and forth. He felt a powerful desire to be alone. He thought about going outside for a walk to clear his mind.

"You'll have to excuse me, Rayhaneh. We can continue later, or if you like, we can have one of the disciples help you record your experiences."

"I can see that you're troubled by this," she said. "But I don't think I could talk to anyone else. These events connect us, Imam. You've said that you want to make a record of your experiences as well. When I'm done with my testimony, I would be the happiest woman on earth to be your sympathetic listener and probing questioner."

"Let me think about it," Ahmed said.

.

# Chapter 30

Ahmed went for a solitary walk and ended up sitting under the shade of a tree. He closed his eyes to let his mind envision the light and soon regained composure and resolve. He was an agent of the light, he reminded himself. He was the servant of its purpose. As long as he kept the awareness of this purpose superimposed in his mind, ever present despite the swirl of life around him with its distractions and burdens, he would never fail to move forward.

That evening, he resumed the role as Rayhaneh's interviewer. Ahmed liked that she was intelligent and articulate and that she possessed a phenomenal memory. By the end of the evening, it was clear that it would take a week, if not longer, to do justice to all that she had experienced. Over the following days, he became the perfect listener, the ideal questioner. At times, he prodded her to loosen memories; at other times, when she curled up on the sofa, clutching her abdomen or weeping, his probing was gentle, aimed at weakening her defenses and countering the embarrassment that locked many of her memories.

After two days of recordings, he turned the first batch over to the transcribers. Before the day was out, Soraya knocked on the door to ask permission to enter the interview room, which was still the front room. She came in, followed by Nousha and Laleh. They had begun work on the recordings and wanted to thank Rayhaneh for her bravery in revealing the truth and to encourage her to continue.

"I think your testimony will turn out to be the most powerful of them all," said Soraya, "and they're all very powerful."

At times, Ahmed and Rayhaneh went for a long walk to take a break from the grueling process. Their conversations turned to this and that: the birds fluttering away at their approach, the rustling of leaves in the breeze, the warmth of the bright sun, the snow atop the distant mountains. He brought the recorder with him just in case a blocked memory surfaced.

Upon returning to the farmhouse, they sometimes stood in the workroom doorway to watch the activity and chat with the volunteers. Nine computers were in use, half desktops and the others laptops. The disciples wore headphones and were focused on their monitors. Koroush ran the makeshift office like the editorial room of a newspaper or magazine, organizing the workflow and channeling audio files to transcribers and the finished work to editors. The disciples were mostly needed to transcribe the audio files. Baba Koushiyar and Soraya were responsible for deep editing, contacting disciples on secure cell phones or encrypted email for clarifications, and undertaking the final line-by-line copy editing. Koroush wrote prefaces and formatted the testimonies into books.

"With all this talent, we could open a publishing house," he said to Ahmed.

Ahmed and Rayhaneh helped Ahmed's mother, who had taken up the duties of preparing food for the numerous visitors and carrying out household tasks. Along with an endless supply of tea, she delighted in preparing pastries and honey-glazed sweets that she brought to the workroom and left on trays.

The interviews with Rayhaneh lasted another week. As the memories of the end of her experience approached, she said, "You know from the history books that Rayhaneh died after four years. This, of course, was not so. I vanished."

She went on to describe the last moments in Yathrib. She was in the adobe room of the wives' quarters, where she had lived since the day of the Qurayza massacre. It was her night with Muhammad, and she lay on her mattress wishing it would all end. She had fallen into a prolonged depression and fantasized about hanging herself or throwing herself off a cliff. Then, "in the blink of an eye," she was in a park with green grass and beautiful flowers and a thicket of trees. People in modern dress were staring at her. She was barefoot and was wearing ancient garments. She realized she must look like a beggar. She asked in Arabic where she was, but heard Persian in response. "So I asked everyone in Persian, 'Where am I? What year is this?'"

She was told she was in Tehran, about a month after she disappeared. An older couple took pity on her when she begged them to take her to her parents' home in north Tehran. Her parents almost died of shock when they opened the door and saw their daughter with tears streaming down her face, crying, "Mother! Father!" They fell into each other's arms in tears. Her parents had been in despair over her disappearance. They believed she had been arrested during the demonstrations and taken to a prison somewhere. They visited all the jails where they heard people were being held, including the notorious Evin Prison, but no one could provide them with any information. Everyone knew many people, young and old, men and women, were being tortured and killed in the prisons, and they feared their daughter had met such a fate.

Rayhaneh tried to explain what happened to her, but her parents were convinced she had been abducted and beaten by hooligans, maybe even drugged. She imagined what she was telling them in order to deal with trauma. However, they couldn't deny that she appeared older. Her father told her that his cousin Koroush had once spoken to him of the theoretical possibility of traveling through time and that he was investigating alleged instances of it.

A month later, she accompanied Koroush, Laleh, and Nousha to Gorgan for the meeting of the disciples with the Imam of Time.

It took Ahmed a while to absorb it all. Hardly an hour had gone by listening to Rayhaneh that he didn't feel his head spinning. After she told him about her return, he shook his head and said, "It's one miracle after another!"

She told him about the difficulties integrating back into the contemporary world, and her pain upon discovering what had happened to many of the demonstrators.

"Did you participate in many of the protests?" Ahmed asked.

"I was in all of them, right from the first day. The election was an obvious sham. I was a university student studying architecture and, like everyone else, was furious about the abuses of the system. I wanted to be in the streets to show my solidarity with the people. I was there when it turned violent, when they started beating and shooting people."

"Has Koroush told you about my involvement?"

"No, I don't know anything about that, Imam. So you were there too?"

Ahmed had not wanted to intrude on her memories, but he now told her about his membership in the Aliabad militia. He had been mobilized a few days after the protests started and was sent to Tehran. "I didn't want to go, but I was too much of a coward to refuse."

"It was terrifying," Rayhaneh said. "I was there when a young woman was shot. The militiamen attacked on motorcycles, but others were on foot. One of them had a gun. He pointed it in my direction, and I thought I was about to be killed, but the bullet hit a woman standing next to a parked car. She died right there. It was cold-blooded murder."

Ahmed was stunned. The memories of that day rushed at him, making him tremble. "I was there. I saw it happen."

It dawned on him where he had seen Rayhaneh before. It was on the boulevard, just after the shooting, when protesters surrounded him and began shoving him. She was the young woman who said, "Leave him alone. He's not the one who did it."

Rayhaneh scrutinized Ahmed's face. "There was a militiaman who threw down his helmet and truncheon and kept shouting to the people around him, 'This is not Islam!'"

"That was me."

Rayhaneh stared at him for a moment and began laughing so hard she fell to one side on the sofa. It was a lovely laugh, Ahmed thought, mirthful and endearing. It sounded like the most beautiful music. It made him laugh, too.

After getting hold of herself, she sat up and wiped tears from her eyes. She said with excitement, "So that was you! Yes, I recognize you now. If you take away the beard and a few years, there's no question it was you."

Ahmed said, "I didn't want to be a part of it. I fled down a side street and ended up getting beaten by a group of militiamen. Behrouz rescued me. I should ask him to tell you about it."

She was sitting on the edge of the sofa, leaning forward. "This is so delicious, so delicious! The militiaman was the awaited Imam of Time. Truly, our Creator is the God of humor."

"And of multiple realities," Ahmed said. "The day I was getting pulled out of a well by slave traders somewhere in Arabia, that same day you were inside the Jewish fortress, and at the same time I was outside of it."

"You have my testimony, Imam. We must get started on yours now. I want to know everything that the God of humor and multiple realities brought about with you."

She could hardly contain her joy when Ahmed handed her the recording device and said, "Then let's begin."

As she clipped the small black microphone to his shirt, she kept repeating, "This is so marvelous, Imam, so absolutely, so totally marvelous. I want to hear everything."

Ahmed leaned back on the sofa and, after gathering his thoughts, he spoke for an hour about his anger at the obvious fraudulence of the election and of his regrets at being a member of the militia mobilized against the demonstrators. He went on about his role in the attacks on the protesters, his flight from Tehran and return to Aliabad, his recurring dream of the light in the cave, his meeting with Baba Koushiyar, and finding the cave and hearing the words that came from the light.

"Tell me more about the light," Rayhaneh said. "It's all about the light."

Ahmed found it a joy to be with Rayhaneh. Hers was an effervescent personality, and she possessed an engaging sense of humor. As an interviewer, she did for him what he had done for her: She listened with undivided attention, asked probing questions, and prodded him when the memories became too painful. When they felt drained, they took long walks, during which the conversations turned personal. At first, they sat apart, he on the sofa and she on the armchair, but soon they sat next to one another, often sharing little jokes.

It took twelve days and one additional morning to complete his testimony, resulting in more than a hundred hours of recordings that were turned over to the disciples for transcription.

The interviews were woven into the day-to-day activities at the farmhouse. These included the noontime and evening meals the disciples shared around a makeshift table long enough to accommodate everyone. Ahmed sat in the center with Rayhaneh at his side, and everyone else took a seat without a prearranged order, though Baba Koushiyar and Soraya always sat at one end and Koroush at the other.

"These moments of conviviality are the best part of the day," Ahmed would remark before saying a prayer of thankfulness for the food and the company of friends.

The meal times turned into spirited discussions of the most recent transcripts, in which the disciples analyzed and compared the perspectives of the same incidents experienced by different disciples. The gatherings were also a time when they celebrated the arrival of volunteers who brought more audio recordings or manuscripts, and they became going-away events for those who were obligated to return to the duties of their daily lives.

Behrouz had too much nervous energy to remain in front of a computer monitor for long. Ahmed, therefore, gave him the responsibility of picking up or dropping off disciples at the train station in Gorgan and purchasing bulk supplies needed to keep the farmhouse operation going. He also gave him the task of monitoring broadcasts for news of disappearances, deaths, and forced confessions of the political opponents of the system.

He also tasked him with monitoring the news for anything related to the Imam of Time, but the reports became so frequent that Behrouz ended up giving him briefings several times a day. On one occasion, while Rayhaneh was recording his testimony, Behrouz interrupted them so they could listen to a startling broadcast in which the Supreme Leader came to his defense against foreign detractors. This happened after the muftis of Egypt and Saudi Arabia, both important Sunni religious leaders, denounced him as a fraud, part of a ploy by Tehran to expand its hegemony in the Middle East. The Supreme Leader replied, "We have examined the appearance of the Imam in Jamkaran from every angle, and we reject any imputation of fraud. He is, in fact, the Imam of Time. Thus far, he has chosen to speak in generalities, but we are confident that he will soon take concrete actions in fulfillment of prophecy."

As the work progressed, Koroush worried that Ahmed had been out of the public eye for too long, yet it was not possible to organize any further public appearances because of the intensive labor required to prepare the testimonies for publication.

"It's gotten to the point that some people are speculating that you've gone back into hiding," he said to Ahmed. "And some people are spreading rumors again that the Zionists and Americans have kidnapped you."

Ahmed agreed that the testimonies had to be completed before he made any more public appearances. Koroush estimated it would take at least three more months. Instead of traveling, Koroush proposed they create podcasts for global distribution. One of the recent arrivals was the disciple Arash, who worked for a tech firm in Tehran and was a social media expert. Koroush invited him to the farmhouse to advise them on the most secure way to circulate the testimonies via social media.

With Behrouz's help, Arash set up a makeshift studio with a pale green curtain as the backdrop and a camera mounted on a tripod. Ahmed wore the familiar garments of time for the productions, which became weekly events. In each, he repeated his fundamental message of the unifying bond of God longing in all people. Alluding to the testimonies of time, he gave notice that a period of great revelation was fast approaching "when light will at last replace darkness."

# Chapter 31

While on a walk with Rayhaneh, Ahmed spoke of recurring visions and dreams of a temple. "This came to me first in the cave above Zarringol after I made it back to Persia with a caravan. And it came again when I went into the cave after my return. And also it has been coming to me in dreams."

He described his vision: a temple atop a hill, with stairs leading up to it on all sides. "I see a circular colonnade. In the center of the colonnade is a dome, and beneath the dome is a large fire urn, as in a Zoroastrian temple. The fire has a new meaning: the flames shooting upward symbolize the longing for God. They are like hands lifted upward to the heavens; thus, the temple would be known as the Temple of God Longing."

He saw the temple as golden in the rising and setting sun, but splendidly white in the full light of day. The stairs symbolized the effort required to rid oneself of false or narrow ideas in order to reach the pinnacle of understanding.

"There are stations on the way up with benches for people to sit and reflect and discard what hinders understanding," he continued. "Those who enter the temple will do so with clear eyes and open hearts and minds."

When they were back at the farmhouse, Rayhaneh found some large sheets of paper and sketched an architectural concept inspired by his dreams and visions.

"Yes, that's what I saw," Ahmed said when she showed him the drawing.

The sketch became the topic of conversation throughout the evening, beginning with the communal dinner until late at night. Pointing to the sketch, Ahmed said, "In my dreams, I see it somewhere near Yazd. There's a beautiful hill that extends from a mountain, and everywhere else it's flat desert."

"How could it be built?" said Baba Koushiyar. "It would be very expensive."

"We have many wealthy friends living abroad," Koroush said. "They've already been very generous with funds. I'll ensure they know of the Imam's vision, and we'll see what comes of it."

Ahmed held up Rayhaneh's sketch. "Here is my vision. Can you send them this?"

"Yes, I can scan it and send it securely to the disciples in Hamburg and Los Angeles."

"I can make additional drawings from different perspectives," Rayhaneh offered.

Ahmed felt a burst of optimism. He looked around the long dinner table and said in an upbeat voice, "We can offer prayers of thankfulness for this right now because I know, as if I'm seeing the future, that it will come about."

Koroush scanned the sketches and sent them out that same night. While they waited to hear from abroad, Ahmed and the disciples continued their work on the testimonies. Red pen in hand, he, Rayhaneh, Baba Koushiyar, and Soraya read the ones Koroush had not yet had time to review. While the other disciples continued the labor of transcription, they edited the texts for readability and ensured the anonymity of the authors by striking out identifying information. Only common first names would be used as author names.

Ahmed had a general idea of each disciple's experiences, but he was always astonished and often shaken by the details revealed in the narratives. Taken together, they formed a vast and disturbing panorama. "When these are published, what was hidden will now become known to everyone," he said.

Baba Koushiyar cautioned about the reaction. "I think we should anticipate outrage and that vicious attacks will be made on the credibility of the testimonies. We also have to anticipate that the clerics will do everything possible to find out who's behind them. We have to be realistic about the dangers."

Ahmed shrugged. "Whatever the reaction, it will draw attention to the testimonies. Everyone will want to read them. Their reaction will be the best publicity."

A week after Koroush sent the sketches abroad, word came back that wealthy supporters in Europe and the United States had discussed Ahmed's vision and pledged funds for the temple. A cousin of one of the disciples who lived in Los Angeles offered to arrange for a large tract of land in the desert region north of Yazd to be donated. The property included a hill at the foot of a mountain, within half a mile of a two-lane road linking several remote towns and villages with Yazd. The hill had a shape that would make it work as a temple mount, Koroush was told. The property was located within 30 miles of Yazd and near several historical Zoroastrian shrines and temples.

A few days after word of financial backing reached them, Koroush got a call from the owner of an architectural firm in Tehran, inviting him to meet "to discuss a project of mutual interest." With Ahmed's blessing, he left the following day, accompanied by Rayhaneh.

Koroush came back four days later, brimming with excitement. "This is moving at the speed of light," he said to Ahmed. "The architects have already received funds to undertake the surveying work and begin preliminary architectural drawings. They've taken on Rayhaneh as an advisor, and she'll keep us up to date. Tomorrow, she leaves with a senior architect and a group of engineers to survey the property. I can't describe how happy she is. It's like her feet aren't even touching the ground."

Ahmed was thrilled the project was moving forward at such speed and was happy that Rayhaneh had just taken her first step into professional life, but he couldn't hide from himself his regret that she would no longer be at the farm. "When will we see her again?" he asked Koroush.

"She'll come after getting back from Yazd, Imam. She'll bring a ton of photos of the site and also preliminary designs for you to look at."

Thrilled that the temple project was underway, Ahmed threw himself into editing the testimonies. The security of the disciples and their families was of utmost importance, he told everyone, so they continued through multiple readings to keep out identifying information. There were only two problematic testimonies: his and Rayhaneh's. Everything pertinent about him had to be there, including his role with the paramilitary, and it would not take much analysis to identify him. His testimony would also be an acknowledgement of his contemporary origin. The clerics would jump on it to undermine his message and destroy his credibility.

As for Rayhaneh, her name among Muhammad's wives was recorded in numerous historical accounts. The records of history could not be altered, nor could she change her name in the present. She could be identified because her name was uncommon, and someone with the same name could be wrongly blamed for her testimony.

"Her testimony must be withheld until such time that its release will not bring harm to anyone," Ahmed said. "As for my testimony, it should only be released in the event I'm assassinated or if I'm facing execution. That's when the truth must be revealed."

By then, the transcription work was entering its third month, yet only half of the testimonies were ready for release. Ahmed was happy with the progress, but was eager for it to be done. Between editing, he continued producing podcasts, taking up new themes. He kept clear of politics. It grieved him to learn of what was being done to protesters and critics of the system. It was barbaric, but he realized it was more of a spiritual than a political problem. It was a problem of false belief.

Two weeks after she left, Rayhaneh returned with Koroush. He made a trip to Tehran to meet with the architects and brought her back with him. Ahmed was eager to see her again. When they arrived, she gave him the traditional kiss on both cheeks and said, "You're going to be very pleased with what we've brought to show you, Imam."

She laid out photos and professional drawings on the long dining room table. Everyone in the household crowded to get a look. She handed photos around showing the hill from various angles. The peak was a hundred feet above the desert floor with gentle slopes on three sides, a perfect angle for creating the wide stairways up to the temple that Ahmed saw in his visions and dreams.

"What the engineers suggest is to build a rectangular stone retaining wall." She pointed to an architectural drawing showing a rock wall built into the upper part of the hill, giving it the appearance of a medieval fortress. "Once the retaining wall is built, it will be filled in by leveling the top of the hill. The leveling will create a flat area where the temple will be built. Reinforced concrete will be the primary building material for the mount's floor, stairways, colonnade, and dome. When finished, it will be a real jewel to behold."

Ahmed examined the photos and pored over the architectural drawings. It was exactly as he had envisioned. The colonnade formed a circle around the central feature, a high dome that sheltered a large fire urn between the columns holding up the dome; a wide circular open area separated the colonnade and the dome; the fire urn stood on a raised platform with several low steps leading up to it, as in the ancient Zoroastrian fire temples. The entire architectural composition emphasized the idea of the temple: the centrality of God longing in human experience.

With a burst of warmth, Ahmed thanked Rayhaneh. "This is the temple I saw in my dreams and visions."

Rayhaneh related how impressed she was by the work the engineers carried out at the site. In addition to surveying, they conducted numerous tests using electronic equipment to assess the hill's stability and found it to be solid rock with a loose overlay of sand and stones.

Koroush added, "In terms of construction, it's a pretty straightforward project. I'm told the only real challenge will be the installation of the dome."

Rayhaneh continued, "After a budget is developed and the funds arrive, the next step is to hire people for the work. We intend to hire Zoroastrians from the region."

"How long will it take to build?" Ahmed asked.

"From what I've heard," Koroush said, "I can make a prediction that nine months from now you will be presiding over the dedication of the temple."

During the communal dinner that night, Rayhaneh raved about the Zoroastrian pilgrimage sites outside of Yazd. She and the engineers were able to visit most of them.

"They were close by, and no one wanted to go back to Tehran without seeing them."

She became animated, describing the Grotto of the Weeping Lady, as it was called. It was a deep cave in the side of a mountain north of Yazd that had been transformed centuries before into a fire temple. A small Zoroastrian community living at the site maintained the grotto.

"It's so serene and inspiring," she said.

She retrieved photos from her traveling bag and handed them around the table. "It's believed that the grotto originated as a shrine to the youngest daughter of Yazdegerd, the last ruler of the Persian Empire. When the Muslim army attacked the capital city, she fled with a sister and a brother, hoping to reach safety in the eastern part of the empire, but they ended up trapped in the mountains north of Yazd. In the historical account, the daughters committed suicide rather than fall into the hands of the invaders, but according to the legend of the grotto, when the emperor's youngest daughter saw there was no escape, she prayed for divine help. Her prayers were answered when the mountain opened up and wrapped around her just before she could be captured. And there she remains. Water seeps through the mountain and drips into a pool inside the grotto, keeping it fresh. According to the legend, these are the tears of the daughter of Yazdegerd over the destruction of the Persian Empire.

She pointed to a photo showing the pool of water inside the grotto. "Here are her tears for what was taken from us. They are my tears as well."

She showed several dozen more photos of the grotto and the Zoroastrian hamlet outside. One of them was a group photo of Rayhaneh and the engineers standing at the top of the stairway leading to the grotto entrance.

"I was so moved by the legend that as we were leaving,

I turned to the mountain, and I shouted, "O daughter of Yazdegerd, weep no more! Your grotto will be the womb of our future!"

Ahmed smiled as he imagined her crying out the emotion the grotto inspired. "I can't tell you how happy I am that the temple will be close to her grotto, Rayhaneh. I can't think of a better place for it."

There were a half-dozen other Zoroastrian pilgrimage sites in the region, each with a compelling legend. Rayhaneh knew them all. One that caused a great stir among the disciples was a similar legend about the son of Yazdegerd. The invaders had trapped him at the foot of another mountain, and, like his sister, he prayed for divine help.

"According to the legend, he was about to be slain when he vanished into thin air," Rayhaneh said.

Koroush and Baba Koushiyar exchanged quick glances and looked at Ahmed. "What do you make of that, Imam?" Baba Koushiyar asked.

"That's amazing," Ahmed said. "It's like my experience and that of some of the disciples, such as Bahram. He was about to be slain during the Uhud battle when he vanished. And Yari also vanished in Rey just before he was to be killed. The same happened to Ebrahim at Khaybar. So maybe the son of Yazdegerd is someone from our time."

"I've often wondered if there are people we don't know about," said Baba Koushiyar.

"We know about Salman, but if he's returned, he has chosen not to make himself known," said Ahmed.

Koroush added, "Allow me to make another prediction, Imam. When the testimonies are published, the people we don't know about are going to come forward, maybe Salman as well."

# Chapter 32

A month later, just as they were nearing completion of the testimonies, Bahram made a hurried, unannounced visit to the farm. He had picked up on important information at the Intelligence Ministry and asked for a private meeting with Ahmed and Koroush. "I've come to warn you that they've discovered your identity, Imam."

Ahmed felt a momentary shock. He knew it was inevitable, but not even six months had gone by since his return. "How were they able to identify me?"

"There were several things that made them wonder about you. For one, you have a hint of a Golestan accent. Why would the Imam of Time sound like someone from Golestan of all places? They've also gotten their hands on sophisticated facial recognition technology. It's not precise because their databases are incomplete, but they narrowed it down that way. They did a forensic analysis of videos from Mashhad, Birjand, and other cities where you gave sermons. They had agents filming each event. First, they identified Behrouz. He didn't always pull his cap low, and his sunglasses weren't always the wraparounds that the disciples wear. They linked you and Behrouz through the ID photos they have in their system for the Aliabad paramilitary."

"That means they have doubts about my appearance through the well in Jamkaran. Do they think it was some kind of magician's trick?"

Bahram shook his head. "They don't doubt it at all. They're stumped. They can't deny the miracle of the well. The Supreme Leader himself, along with a group of top intelligence officials from the Revolutionary Guard, traveled to Jamkaran to examine the well. This was a month after I went there with a ministry intelligence team. They analyzed the videos that show the glow and you coming out of the well. It was all recorded on multiple surveillance cameras inside the mosque. They went down into the maintenance room underneath the well and examined the custodial seal on the door that's used to clear out the petitions. They didn't find any evidence of tampering. So they don't believe that you somehow got inside the well from that room and faked coming out of the petition box. They also found it curious that the names of your parents are the same as those of Muhammad's parents, as foretold. And your name is the root of the name Muhammad, so it all fits with prophecy. Because of that, they ordered a study of your ancestry, which found that you are, in fact, a descendant of the family of Ali and Fatima, and therefore of Muhammad, also as foretold. But they're unable to fathom how you can be Ahmed of Aliabad, the son of a martyr of the Sacred Defense, and also the awaited Imam of Time. One of them advanced the theory that the spirit of the Imam entered into you when you were born so that the Mahdi would be familiar with the language and customs of our time."

Ahmed laughed. "That's ridiculous."

Bahram shrugged. "I'm just telling you what's been going on in their meetings. The idea was dismissed as fanciful because there is no support for it in the Quran or in any of the traditions about the Mahdi. It was also rejected because it didn't explain how you came to be in the well. You had to enter it somehow. They're unable to explain it, so they haven't decided how to deal with you yet."

"I suppose that's the good news," Koroush sighed.

"Here's something else you need to know, Imam," Bahram continued. "I suspect that people close to the Supreme Leader have had the experience of time—three of the members of the Guardian Council. If I'm not mistaken, and I don't think I am, then they understand why you can be both Ahmed of Aliabad and the Imam of Time."

Koroush said, "That's not so surprising. We suspect there

are many others who've made the journey that we don't know about."

More curious than alarmed, Ahmed said, "Who are they? What makes you think they've had the experience of time?"

Bahram gave the names of ayatollahs. "I studied the photographs of the Supreme Leader's entourage and the members of the Guardian Council that we have in the ministry files because some of them looked familiar, and the more I examined the photos, the more I realized that I had crossed paths with three of them while I was in the past. One was the man who was about to kill me just before I returned to the present."

"That makes them a danger," said Koroush.

"Yes, but not in the way you may think," Bahram said. "They're not going to risk ridicule by claiming such an experience. Who would believe them?" He turned to Ahmed. "They will be advocates of harsh measures against you, Imam. You hold up a mirror to them, and I don't believe they like what they see. You followed the light of truth, and they didn't. They went after power, prestige, and money. They're the ones to be the most concerned about. The clerics who don't know the truth about you fear you, but the ones who know the truth hate you."

"It changes nothing," said Ahmed. "If anything, it makes me more determined."

"There's something else that's important for you to know," Bahram said. "I'm in a privileged position, and it allows me to learn things most people can never know about the people in power. Everyone suspects they're corrupt, but I don't think many people have any idea about the extent of it. I know for a fact that our Supreme Leader and his Revolutionary Guard have taken over financial control of a number of state enterprises in areas such as oil, mining, shipping, and arms manufacturing. They get rich off of this. Our own Supreme Leader makes a show of humility. You can see how pious he looks when he leads the Friday prayers. But he's become very wealthy, and he's gotten that way by skimming money from these industries."

Koroush became angry. "And people wonder why our country keeps getting poorer."

Bahram nodded. "It can only get worse, Koroush. The revenues from these industries are misused in other ways. That is where the money comes from to finance their secret nuclear and missile programs and to fund the terror networks they've set up abroad. The mullahs are counting on using nuclear terror to bring the world to submit to them."

"They proclaim belief in the Imam and in the end of time and judgment before God," said Ahmed. "Are they just cynical liars? Is power all they want?"

Bahram shook his head. "Maybe with the exception of the three ayatollahs I told you about, these people believe in their own fairy tales. They're confused about you, but they do believe that you're the Awaited One. They believe you should lead them in imposing Islam around the world. But so far, you've refused to even talk to them. You've treated them like they don't exist. But they do exist, and they're getting more dangerous the more you ignore them. In fact, I think that you and all of the disciples should have a contingency plan to flee abroad. Sooner or later, it may become necessary for you to get out of the country."

"The disciples are free to do as they think best, and I wouldn't object to any of them leaving," said Ahmed. "But I must remain no matter what."

"I understand, Imam," said Bahram. "But you must be careful. I don't think they're ready to make a move on you yet, but if you resume your public work, I urge you to be aware of your surroundings at all times. The mullahs have everything to lose. That makes them very dangerous."

After Bahram left, Ahmed repeated to Behrouz what Bahram told him. "I'm sorry I dragged you into this. If it hadn't been for me, you wouldn't be in this situation."

Behrouz shrugged. "I'm not going to worry about it. I believe in your message. I want to help you carry out your work."

"We have powerful enemies. I wouldn't hold it against you if you decide to leave the country."

"I'll stay. If I end up dying, at least I'll die for something worth dying for."

By the time of Bahram's visit, the editing labor was close to the finish line. Ahmed threw himself into completing the testimonies. The more exhausted he became, the more he pushed himself, setting the pace for the volunteers. When the last testimony was ready, Ahmed brought Arash, the social media expert, to the farm. While the testimonies were being prepared, Arash collaborated with disciples in Los Angeles to set up a website that would serve as the primary repository for the testimonies and as the official site for posting commentaries and comparative studies of the experiences of time. Everyone at the farm agreed it was safest to circulate the testimonies abroad first. They would soon manage to get through government filters and circulate inside Iran as well, but they had to have secure hosting abroad.

"The testimonies are at last complete," Ahmed said when he invited Arash to come to the farm. "Now is the time to send them to the disciples in Los Angeles. Because of all of the work you've done to help set up the website, I want you to have the honor of carrying out that task. So come and join us here."

A tall, personable man who wore glasses, Arash was one of the eleven disciples who had submitted their experiences of time in written form. His treatment was thorough and didn't need much editing. Ahmed felt close to him because his journey in time unfolded among the Christian communities and caravan towns in northern Arabia. His entry was in the Red Sea town of Ayla, where Ahmed stayed for three months at the monastery. Arash knew people Ahmed knew, and he was witness to their subjugation only a few years after Ahmed returned to the present time.

All of the volunteers gathered in a hush around Arash when he sat down at a computer and began sending the testimonies. As he worked, he explained the government's methods of censoring the Internet, particularly through blocking proxy servers, but he knew how to get around such filters.

Ahmed's mother brought in tea and pastries for everyone. Ahmed stood quietly, sipping tea, while Arash worked. He felt thrilling tension as Arash peered at the computer screen and clicked away on the keyboard. The equivalent of several hundred years of their combined experiences was now maneuvering through invisible electronic channels to avoid interception by an equally invisible enemy. After half an hour, a disciple in Los Angeles sent an email through the same encrypted channel. The room burst into cheers and applause when Arash read the message: "Imam: We got them all! Now our work begins!"

Ahmed called for a celebration with a feast and the joy of music, and song, and dance. One of the newly arrived disciples showed his skill on the sitar; Nousha had a voice most professional performers could only dream of. When Behrouz put on popular Iranian music from his collection, everyone jumped to their feet and danced the way Iranians dance. Ahmed's mother, who had worked so hard to keep everyone fed and maintain the busy farmhouse, danced with everyone. Even Ahmed broke out of the stiffness that his role as Imam imposed and joined in.

Before the celebration began, he said to the assembled group, "We were given extraordinary experiences, and now they will carry out their purpose. Now people everywhere will be able to judge the truth of what they were raised to believe, and not just here, but everywhere, for the testimonies will circulate around the globe."

# Chapter 33

Now that the testimonies were published, Ahmed decided it was time to move to a safe house in Tehran and resume his public ministry. Before leaving, he spent an hour in the cave above Zarringol, engrossed in prayers of thankfulness. He couldn't see it, but he felt the warming presence of the light.

He listed the things for which he was thankful: for his extraordinary experience, for the miraculous journeys of the disciples, for the testimonies that were now completed, and for the joy of the camaraderie at the farm. He thanked the light for the vision of the temple and for the gift of knowing Rayhaneh, who was now guiding the temple work. Surely with her involvement, it would become the splendid temple of his vision.

When he finished praying, he left the cave and went back down the craggy rocks to the boulder where Baba Koushiyar, Maziar, and Behrouz were waiting. "Thank you for being so patient," he said when he reached them. "I had to visit it before we leave because I may never have the opportunity again."

Everyone laughed when Baba Koushiyar said, "We're so relieved that you finally came out of the cave, Imam. We were getting worried we might have to rescue you in Jamkaran again!"

A cargo van was parked where the creek bed came out of the ravine, out of sight of the village of Zarringol. Ahmed and Baba Koushiyar got in the back while Maziar and Behrouz went up front. Soon they were on the highway, heading for a walled residence in the foothills of north Tehran that Koroush had secured. On the way, they discussed ideas for a series of sermons in the cities of the northwestern provinces, ending in Tabriz.

Koroush was at the residence when they arrived. The property was secluded, with high privacy walls, beautiful gardens, and tall trees. The house was large enough to accommodate as many people as Baba Koushiyar's farm.

While Koroush busied himself with sending advance teams of disciples to scout stadiums and make arrangements with supporters for safe houses and vehicles, Ahmed kept abreast of the progress of the temple construction. The highlight of his day was always when he talked with Rayhaneh by phone. She was at the construction site, making only rare visits to the architectural firm's Tehran offices. She was the guest of a Zoroastrian family in Yazd, who drove her to and from the temple. Work had already begun on the retaining walls and the staircases leading up to the temple mount. A road had been graded through the desert linking the site to the two-lane road leading to Yazd. Concrete columns, entablatures, and other building elements were now being cast in Yazd in molds that replicated ancient Persian architectural features. By the time the temple platform was finished, the building elements would already be at the construction site.

"They've coordinated this so the temple will be completed ahead of schedule," Rayhaneh told him.

When the temple was ready, Ahmed envisioned a formal dedication ceremony during which representatives of various religions would together light the fire, symbolic of the flame of God longing. He would ensure the ceremony had a global audience by inviting international media. At that point, the temple would become known to the entire world. Any harm done to it would result in universal condemnation.

While waiting for the speaking tour to begin, Ahmed wondered what the reaction would be to the publication of the testimonies. Surely they would not be ignored for long, given the touchiness of the believers. He imagined it would be limited to Iran since the testimonies were published in Persian. It would take several years for them to be translated into other languages. He was therefore surprised when influential Arab Sunni clerics railed against them. This happened during the Friday sermon in important Middle Eastern mosques two weeks after Arash sent the testimonies to the disciples in Los Angeles. The most furious reaction came from Cairo, where the Grand Mufti of the Egyptians wagged his finger at the camera and warned, "The authors of these ugly fictions are playing with fire. When they are found out, they will be given the punishment demanded by God for blasphemy against his religion and his holy prophet."

A few days later, Iranian TV carried a denunciation by Pakistan's ambassador to the United Nations. Before a meeting of the UN General Assembly, the ambassador fumed about the testimonies. He demanded that blasphemy laws be applied worldwide "to punish anyone, anywhere, who dares insult Islam and our revered holy Prophet."

Given these outbursts, Ahmed thought it odd that Iran's reaction was muted. One of the broadcasts carried a formal statement by a prominent ayatollah: "We are aware of these outrages and are investigating their origin." In another, a leading cleric said the religious authorities found it lamentable that Iranians were the authors of such "vile rubbish."

Koroush rubbed his hands together. "They've swallowed the bait. Now everyone will want to read the testimonies."

Ahmed sent a long message to the Los Angeles disciples, thanking them for their diligent work and encouraging them to post videos of the outrage on the website.

A few days later, Ahmed was on the road again, leaning against cushions in the back of the cargo van as they headed to the first stop of the new tour, the Caspian city of Rasht. He was pleased when the Rasht event went well. He had not made any public appearances in more than four months, but his absence had not dampened enthusiasm. He entered the packed stadium to wild chants of "Imam!" and "Mahdi!" He spoke about what he always spoke about with fresh words that he knew did not come from him, but through him.

At the end of the sermon, he launched an oblique attack on the intolerance of the theocratic system and its religious controllers. "Those who seek to divide and cause strife begin at the spiritual level," he said. "They will tell you, 'Not this, not that, only what we believe is true.' But they are in grievous error."

He knew it was going well when the people jumped to their feet, shouting, "You speak the truth! The Imam has come to us with the truth!"

In all of the cities and towns he visited, he was given an enthusiastic welcome. But mindful of Bahram's warning, he kept alert to anything unusual occurring in the stadiums. During the last three appearances, he noticed small groups of rough-looking men pushing through the crowds to get close to the podium. Their sloppy civilian dress, Shi'ite beards, and surly air gave them away as paramilitaries.

He wondered if the intimidation meant they were going to make a move to corner him and take him away, but he dismissed the idea. The mullahs would face an insurrection. He concluded they were there to show him the mullahs were watching.

Koroush was more concerned about their vulnerability while on the road. With Ahmed's approval, the small convoy zigzagged from province to province to create an unpredictable pattern of movement. One day Ahmed was in Urmia, not far from Turkey; three days later, he appeared more than a hundred miles to the northeast in Ardabil, near the border with Azerbaijan. Two days after that, the sermon was in a city south of Urmia. As an added security measure, Koroush arranged for the disciples to change vehicles frequently, including the cargo van.

Koroush, as concerned as Ahmed about the paramilitary threat, sent observers with binoculars to various points in the stadiums to monitor the crowds. The observers blended in and provided a flow of information via phones to him and other disciples. He stationed other observers outside the stadium to monitor the exits and the parking area where the decoy vehicles were placed in strategic locations.

Ahmed thought it all seemed too easy. The government was biding its time, waiting for a decision from the Supreme Leader to take action against him. Until that happened, he would continue his mission of truth.

The tour ended in Tabriz, leaving Ahmed to believe that a move against him could be in the offing. He gave his sermon in the huge modern sports stadium in Tabriz, which was filled to overflowing. Even the playing field was covered with people. A large screen at one end of the stadium showed him at the podium in enormous size. It bothered him because it was his message that was enormous, not himself.

Midway through the sermon, he spotted the same suspicious movement of rough men pushing through the crowd, but there were more of them than before, and they were coming from two directions. Below him, dozens edged through the crowd while another group muscled through from the stands off to one side. It was clear they were militiamen.

In response, the disciples organized a thick cordon of supporters, saying to everyone, "Bad people are trying to get close to harm our Imam. Hurry! We must protect him!"

Hundreds of people rushed to form a human chain, five people thick, below Ahmed, behind him, and on each side, blocking the militiamen from getting close to the podium. From their blocked positions, they glared at Ahmed with undisguised anger. Ahmed ignored them and continued his sermon without missing a beat.

When they were clear of the stadium and on the way to the safe house, Behrouz said, "What I don't get is that if they wanted to get their hands on you, Imam, you'd expect them to take over the parking area and block the exits. But just like at the other stadiums, they were only inside."

"It's an intimidation tactic," said Ahmed. "It means they're not ready to make a move."

# Chapter 34

A hmed returned to the high-walled residence in Tehran amid news that dozens of people claiming to have the experience of time were now coming forward, fulfilling Koroush's prediction. The Los Angeles disciples notified Ahmed that people from numerous countries had emailed them through the contact form on the website where the testimonies were posted.

"We're getting two or three such contacts every day now, Imam," the administrator enthused in an email. "And it's no longer just Iranians."

They sent Ahmed copies of the emails. They had the ring of authenticity, but Ahmed became concerned about the possibility of infiltration, a problem they had not considered.

"The Revolutionary Guard has agents in Europe, the United States, and many other places, even in Latin America," Ahmed said to Koroush. "What's to keep them from having their agents pose as people with the experience of time? What's to keep them from seeking to arrange a personal meeting with the disciples involved with the website? The Revolutionary Guard has a history of kidnapping, interrogating, and killing dissidents, even in foreign countries."

They decided on a rigorous screening procedure. People claiming the experience of time who asked to meet with disciples had to provide a synopsis of their experience, giving the time frame and location of their stay in the past, the significant events they witnessed, and descriptions of notable people they encountered. They would have to provide a precise account of the time and place they were when they vanished into the past. They would also have to reveal the time and place of their return, their thoughts about why they were sent into the past, and how they were changed by it. Before personal contact could be allowed, they had to provide proof of identity via the contact form and provide the names and contact information of people who could vouch for them, as well as other details that would allow the disciples to conduct a background check.

Everyone nodded when Ahmed said, "This is of the greatest concern for the ones who say they're in Iran. If they can't agree to provide proof of identity, we can't agree to a meeting, no matter how important the experiences they claim."

Ahmed wanted to embark on another speaking tour, but he couldn't shake the feeling that something was in preparation against him. The presence of paramilitaries at the stadiums was a reminder that the more he traveled, the more he was exposed to danger. Though certain he faced physical danger, he feared more than anything that the unifying message of his primary truth could be undermined by the malicious exposure of his secondary truth. The regime was aware of his dual reality. He was he who emerged from the well in fulfillment of prophecy, but he was also Ahmed of Aliabad, an AWOL *basiji*.

He wondered how the clerics would use their knowledge. His testimony would reveal the truth in great detail, but to be released, it would require either his assassination or a death sentence in a sham trial. He wanted to delay that moment as long as possible so he could continue bringing his message to the people.

Rather than dwell on potential threats, he planned another speaking tour with Koroush and Baba Koushiyar. He wanted to go to cities in the south and southwestern provinces. Baba Koushiyar favored beginning in Hamadan and ending in Isfahan, whereas Koroush argued it was better to begin with the largest city of the region, which was Isfahan.

Ahmed wondered if they could combine the tour with a trip to the temple site. In every phone call, Rayhaneh encouraged him to see the progress for himself.

"The photographs don't do it justice," she said in their last phone conversation. "The only way to appreciate the beauty of it is for you to see it in person."

Yazd was closest to Isfahan, Koroush noted, so they could make a detour to visit the site, but he pointed out that it would add 200 miles to the journey. They would have to drive south through Qom and Jamkaran to reach Yazd.

Baba Koushiyar worried about security. How could the visit be kept secret? Would they draw attention to the site? To date, the project had remained under the government's radar, but would it remain so if they visited the temple?

Ahmed decided on a visit after Rayhaneh informed him that the construction crew and engineering staff had the day off every Friday. If they came on a Friday, they would have the temple to themselves. The only other person present would be the project manager, a man loyal to Ahmed's message and the temple's purpose.

They spent two weeks planning the trip, sending disciples to arrange secure lodgings and visit stadiums in each city to determine the safest way for Ahmed to enter and exit.

With the preparations in place, Ahmed was eager to start the tour, beginning with a stopover at the temple site. The day before they were to leave, however, Bahram arrived at the safe house without having made any advance arrangements. He was carrying a bulky package and looked worried.

"I dislike coming here without notice and in my own car," he said to Ahmed, "but I took precautions, so there's no cause for alarm. What I have to tell you is urgent."

They were in the living room with Koroush, Baba Koushiyar, Maziar, and Behrouz. Bahram looked at everyone in turn and finally at Ahmed. "I rushed here to warn you of a great danger, Imam. I've just learned the Guardian Council has decided the only way to deal with you is to kill you. They'll look for an opportunity to have you assassinated. They'll use a fall guy, someone they can pin the blame on to hide their involvement."

Ahmed was shaken, but not surprised. "How did you learn of this, Bahram?"

"You know that the problem of how to deal with you has been under discussion for a while now. Some of the leaders hoped you could be co-opted, but they're a minority. Others argued that belief in you could be destroyed by exposing your contemporary origin and branding you a false Imam. The third group is led by the three clerics, who, I'm now certain, had the experience of time. They're the chief advocates of assassination, and they just won out."

"They would turn me into a martyr," said Ahmed.

"I think that's their intention," Bahram said. "They'll suppress what they know of your origin. They'll cast you as a victim of injustice, just like the previous Imams who were murdered. They'll mourn in public but rejoice in private that you're no longer a problem for them."

Baba Koushiyar scoffed. "We won't let them get close enough to the Imam to cause him harm."

"Looking at it objectively," Koroush said, "it's clever of them. It would give the people who believe in their nonsense one more reason to flagellate themselves."

Ahmed imagined the ludicrous scenario of his body being carried through the streets of Qom or Jamkaran, followed by men whipping their bare backs until they were covered in blood. It had always been a spectacle that nauseated him, particularly when the zealots cut the heads of their children with razor-sharp knives to make them bleed.

He refused to be intimidated by the prospect of death. "We've all been given the experience of time for a purpose, and I intend to go forward with my purpose no matter what."

"I know you will do what the spirit prompts you to do, Imam," said Bahram, "so I decided to bring you this."

He unwrapped the package that he had with him. Inside was a black garment similar to a shirt, but it was sleeveless and bulkier. He handed it to Ahmed.

"What is it?"

"A bulletproof vest. If you continue with public sermons, you need to have body protection. You can wear it hidden under your garments. If they shoot at you, they will aim for your chest rather than your head because the upper body offers a bigger target."

"We are his bodyguards," Behrouz fumed. "Not one of us would hesitate to die in the place of the Imam."

"These things can happen at lightning speed," said Bahram. "What if you can't react fast enough?"

"I don't want harm to come to anyone," said Ahmed. "Can you get more of these for the disciples?"

"This is the only one I have. It was issued to me last year, but I'll see about getting more of them."

"Can you find out about the specifics of their plans?" said Koroush.

"I doubt it. What I pick up are policy decisions, not much on the planning. But I'll see if I can find out more. I'll certainly let you know."

Baba Koushiyar said, "At least you've warned us. That gives us an advantage."

"Please be careful, Imam," said Bahram. "These are premeditated killers, the worst kind of people."

# Chapter 35

It was a five-hour drive to Yazd in the afternoon heat. Riding in the back of the cargo van, Ahmed and Baba Koushiyar bore the stuffy air with patience.

On the way, they talked about the assassination threat. They doubted an attempt could be made while they were on the road. Their travel arrangements were secretive, making Ahmed invisible. It would have to happen while he was giving a sermon.

When they were going through Qom and Jamkaran, Maziar, who was driving, recalled the rescue outside the mosque. He confessed that he was jittery when he drove into the huge crowd to stop the procession carrying Ahmed through the street.

"We practiced for a number of contingencies and rehearsed what we were going to say," Maziar said, glancing at Ahmed and Baba Koushiyar in the rearview mirror. "The limos and the black suits and sunglasses were important, but I think the badges Bahram got us from the Intelligence Ministry made us credible. After we got out of the limos, we flashed the badges and spoke with an authoritative voice. I can't tell you how relieved we were when the crowd didn't think twice about letting you come with us."

"You had me convinced," Ahmed said. "I thought I was on my way to Tehran."

For most of the trip, Koroush and Behrouz drove far ahead in the advance vehicle. When they reached the desert location and turned onto the graded road leading to the construction site, Maziar pulled up close behind them.

Ahmed was as eager to see Rayhaneh as he was to see the temple. When he stepped out of the van, she was standing outside an office trailer with the project manager. He felt inhibited about making an overt display of affection, and he sensed she felt the same; they exchanged only the traditional greeting with a light kiss on the cheek.

Sagdeh, the project manager, was a courteous middle-aged man with dark hair combed back. He wore thick-rimmed glasses and a white shirt and blue tie despite the desert heat. He appeared nervous meeting the famed Imam, but Ahmed's warm greeting put him at ease, as did Rayhaneh when she introduced Sagdeh as "my boss."

"I'm the project manager in name only, Imam," Sagdeh said. "Rayhaneh is the one in charge around here."

In a cheerful voice, she said, "Then, everyone, please follow me."

At the base of the temple hill was a huge truck crane, and behind it, stacked on their sides on wood separators, were prefabricated columns, entablatures, sections of dome, and other temple components. Rayhaneh pointed to them. "When they're lifted to the temple mount, the workers guide them into place. The assembly work has been going so well that we're now two weeks ahead of schedule."

As they went up the steps, Sagdeh said, "Unless we encounter some unforeseen problems, Imam, the temple should be ready in two months."

The stairways were steeper than they appeared in the photos. Two wide rest areas divided the stairs into sections. It was as Ahmed had envisioned: a long climb to the temple, symbolizing the effort needed to discard false or narrow ideas and achieve an understanding of the temple's unifying message.

Ahmed was moved by the austere beauty of the temple. Though incomplete, it was already coming to life. Half of the columns of the circular colonnade were installed along with the entablatures and roof beams. In the center, the raised platform for the fire urn was completed. The dome columns were in place around it, awaiting the installation of the dome sections.

Construction materials were lying about. It made Ahmed think of an ancient ruin being restored.

He couldn't part from his role of Imam of Time. He stood on the platform where the fire urn would be placed and said a prayer of thankfulness. He finished by pointing to the heavens. "The inspiration for the temple came from up there. It passed through my head and became Rayhaneh's sketches, and from there it has become a reality thanks to the labor of our beloved friend," he said, looking with warmth at the project manager.

The tour continued under Rayhaneh's guidance. She explained the ins and outs of the construction challenges as they walked through different areas of the mount. The hardest work was already done. That involved constructing the retaining wall and the three staircases, grading and filling in the mount once the retaining wall was in place, and finally pouring concrete for the reinforced floor. Now it was a matter of assembling the remaining temple pieces.

Ahmed admired Rayhaneh's poise and self-assurance. She had been crushed during her experience of time, so recent yet so long ago, but she was of an optimistic nature, and now her true self was unfolding as she took on the numerous challenges of the temple construction.

He wished they had a moment to themselves. When the group wandered off to a far corner of the mount so that Sagdeh could point out the location of the Grotto of the Weeping Lady in the distance, he took Rayhaneh's hand and led her to the retaining wall at another part of the mount where there was a view of the quiet expanse of desert and mountains.

He had not wanted to say anything to her about Bahram's warning, but the thought that he could soon be assassinated preoccupied him. He didn't want to alarm her, but he needed to prepare her for that possibility.

They were facing each other, her head tilted up. He took both her hands into his. "You know there's a danger when I speak in public," he said, almost whispering.

"I'm always concerned for you," she said. "I pray for your safety."

Koroush and the others were walking back from the far corner. They stopped at a distance, pretending not to notice Ahmed and Rayhaneh together. Ahmed saw them over her shoulder. It was a reminder that they soon had to leave.

"If anything were to happen to me, I want you to do everything in your power to ensure the temple is completed and turned over to the Zoroastrians as an endowment so they'll take care of it as they do the grotto and the other pilgrimage sites. With them as stewards, it will become a protected site like all their shrines."

"Is there something you know that I don't know?" she said, a worried look on her face.

"There's a danger, that's all I know."

"You must be very careful."

"I have to leave now. Before I go, there is something important I need to say to you."

"Yes?" she said in a soft voice.

He raised her hands to his lips. "I want you to know that I love you, Rayhaneh, with my whole heart, my whole mind, and my whole soul."

"And I have something important I need to say to you. I love you, my Imam."

"I'm Ahmed, your Ahmed."

"My Ahmed," she said, her eyes brightening.

Late that night, Koroush's vehicle, followed by Maziar's cargo van, reached a secure house outside of Isfahan, where they joined the advance team of disciples.

Ahmed had hoped to secure the big general-purpose arena in Isfahan, but it turned out that it was undergoing reconstruction, so the first sermon of the tour had to be given at the much smaller stadium of a nearby industrial town.

The next day, after Ahmed's appearance was announced, the roads leading to the town were jammed. By the time he stepped up to the podium, the bleachers were overflowing. Even the playing field was packed.

Koroush had again taken the precaution of planting

observers in the stands with binoculars. They soon reported the presence of a contingent of plain-clothed militia. They were weaving through the crowd from three directions, one above the podium area. To counter them, Koroush had the disciples organize thick knots of supporters to protect Ahmed on all sides.

With the bulletproof vest under his garment, Ahmed felt confident he would survive an attempt on his life. He kept an eye on the paramilitaries while he gave the same message as before. But he alluded to the menacing presence of the militia by speaking about the presence of "hardened hearts" in the stadium and asked the people to pray for them.

"Praying for the benefit of someone other than oneself is second only to the prayer of thankfulness. So pray for those with hardened hearts that they come to an understanding of the true meaning of the God longing that they have within them, but which they deny in others."

The same scenario of surging *basijis* unfolded in Khorram-abad, Ahvaz, and Kermanshah, but not at the stadium in Arak, where he appeared two weeks after the tour began. Ahmed was surprised. The clerics had as much time to mobilize the para-militaries there as they had in the other cities. He wondered if they had given up on their intimidation tactics.

As they returned to the safe house in Arak, Koroush said, "Maybe they want us to drop our guard."

"I have a bad feeling they're going to make a move soon," said Baba Koushiyar. "Maybe we should think about going back to making podcasts."

Ahmed shook his head. "The people want to see the Imam of Time. I can't hide behind a camera."

"How about a thick Plexiglas screen around you at the po-dium?" suggested Baba Koushiyar. "We could have that made so that it folds in sections and bring it with us everywhere. I bet we could find someone here in Arak with Plexiglas. A screen like that will keep you safe."

Ahmed shook his head again. "That would send the wrong message. The clerics would believe I'm afraid of them, and the people would think I don't have trust in them or in God. The bulletproof vest will have to do."

The next sermon was set up at the sports arena in Hamadan. It was a smaller arena with packed low stands, as was the playing field. Koroush was in constant contact with observers in the stands with binoculars and cell phones. As a precaution, he organized a thick cordon of people around the podium area.

While he spoke, Ahmed scanned the stadium for signs of trouble. Midway through the sermon, a group of men began pushing through the crowd on one side of him. He couldn't see them without turning, but he knew what was happening from a signal Koroush gave him. Koroush sent groups of supporters to thicken the cordon. When the paramilitaries reached the human shield, they began to shout obscenities and throw punches at people in the front line of the barrier.

Ahmed glanced in the direction of the ruckus. Just as he did, Behrouz spotted a gun being raised in front of the knot of supporters forming a barrier below Ahmed, on the side opposite the disturbance in the stands above. Behrouz shouted, "Imam, watch out!" He lunged for the gun, grabbing the hand that held it, but not before a shot was fired.

The bullet struck Ahmed in the vest just below his heart, causing him to stumble backward. He struggled to regain his balance by grabbing onto the pulpit.

A gasp went up from the crowd. "They've shot the Imam! They've killed our Imam!"

The vest stopped the bullet, but the impact caused Ahmed such pain that he thought he was going to black out. He held onto the pulpit with both hands. With an effort of will, he forced himself to stand up straight. He grabbed the microphone from its holder and waved it in the air before bringing it to his mouth.

"I'm not hurt," he said. "Please remain calm."

Behrouz, Maziar, and several other men held the shooter by the arms. He struggled to free himself. He was short and wiry, with pale skin, a short, unkempt black beard, and the glassy eyes of a fanatic. Ahmed sized him up in an instant. He was typical of many of the men recruited into the urban paramilitary units: poor, uneducated young men, pious believers, but often with a background of petty crime.

"Bring him here," Ahmed said to Behrouz and Maziar.

They pushed the shooter forward until he was face-to-face with Ahmed. He continued to struggle, but his arms were locked behind him, and he was unable to move. Behrouz handed Ahmed the gun. It was a semiautomatic, the same kind that some of the militiamen wore the day the protesters were attacked in Tehran, very likely the same kind of weapon used to shoot the young woman on the boulevard near Niloufar Square.

"Why did you try to kill me?" Ahmed asked.

He held the microphone close to the man's mouth, like a journalist doing a street interview. The man struggled to turn his face away.

Ahmed held the gun up high for everyone in the stadium to see. "Speak! You tried to kill me with this gun in front of all these good people. They deserve an explanation."

"You are evil," the man spat out.

"What makes you say I'm evil?"

"You speak words that Satan puts in your mouth."

"Which words?"

"All of them."

"You were here from the beginning, so you heard everything I said. Tell me what I said that came from Satan."

The man turned his head away from the microphone, as if trying to avoid a foul smell. Ahmed felt sorry for him. He was brainwashed. Someone manipulated him and took advantage of his ignorance. It was clear that the ruckus of the paramilitaries in the stands behind him was a diversion to draw attention away from the assassin so he could get close enough for a clear shot. Ahmed was certain the shooter didn't know he was being used.

Behrouz handed Ahmed the shooter's identity card. It was a *basiji* ID with a photo, date of birth, address, and the name of his paramilitary unit.

"You are a member of the Basij. Your commanders told you my words come from Satan, isn't that so?"

"Yes."

"What else did they tell you?"

"That you are a false prophet. You came out of the well in Jamkaran using a magic trick to fool everyone."

"Do you believe them?"

"Yes."

"Did your commanders send you to kill me?"

"No."

"Who sent you?"

"No one. I planned it on my own."

"What keeps you from thinking for yourself, Jabbar?" Ahmed said, repeating the name on the ID card. "If you listened to my words with an open mind and heart, you would know that none of them are evil."

Ahmed saw it was useless to question him any further. "I want to let you go, Jabbar. If I let you go, will you try to shoot me again?"

The man looked surprised, but he didn't say anything.

"Release him," Ahmed said to the men holding him.

They relaxed their grip. Jabbar pulled away and, without looking at Ahmed, turned and pushed into the crowd. People cleared a path for him.

Ahmed handed the gun to Behrouz and turned to the people in the stadium. Forcing himself to stand erect despite the pain, he said, "Let no harm come to the man. I ask you to pray for him. He is misguided. Pray that he will see the light within himself. Pray that he will understand that it is the same light within all people. Pray that the light will guide him to love all people, for we all share the same gift from God."

## Chapter 36

Ahmed was in too much pain from the bullet impact to continue the tour. During the return trip, he lay on his back and tried to hide the throbbing soreness by bantering with his van companions.

Rayhaneh rushed to Tehran after learning of the shooting, arriving only hours after Ahmed got to the residence. She cried when she saw the bruise.

"We need to take you to a doctor for X-rays, my Ahmed. What if your ribs are fractured? We have to know for sure."

He pointed to the other side of his chest where the *basijis* had once kicked him with their heavy boots, and again when he was thrown out of Muhammad's mosque. "This has happened before. More likely, it's only bruising. It hurts, but I think it will heal on its own."

His mother arrived the next day with Soraya. "I don't understand why they want to harm you, my son," she said when she saw his chest. "You're a good person, and everything you preach is good and true."

"That's why they want to harm him," said Soraya.

Nousha and Laleh came, too. Ahmed liked that so many women were fussing over him, particularly Rayhaneh. Her voice was soothing, her smile warming, her touch tender.

Koroush knew a retired physician whom he deemed trustworthy. He went with Maziar to fetch him in the van. After examining Ahmed, the doctor agreed that a fracture was unlikely. Even with a fracture, the treatment was the same. He gave Ahmed some painkillers and told him the best cure was to stay in bed for a week and apply ice packs. "Expect to feel sore for a month or two," he said.

While he recuperated, Rayhaneh updated Ahmed daily on the temple's progress. Almost all of the columns of the colonnade were in place. Half the dome was now installed. The fire urn, made of brass, had been delivered to the site. Before the other half of the dome was put into place, the urn would be lifted to the mount and placed on the pedestal.

"Sagdeh assures me we're far ahead of schedule," she said. "Very soon, you will be able to hold the dedication ceremony."

Ahmed wanted to begin planning for it. He conceived of it as a universal temple. He reiterated his hope of bringing religious representatives from all faiths to participate in the ceremony, culminating in the symbolic lighting of the fire. "Christians, Buddhists, Hindus, Jews, Zoroastrians, Sikhs, Baha'is," he said. "Who am I leaving out?"

"Yazidis," Baba Koushiyar suggested. "They're very accepting of other faiths."

Ahmed wanted to meet with religious representatives to explain the meaning of the temple and the importance of their endorsement through their participation in the dedication.

"Here is what I will tell everyone: 'Let us never allow the differences in our ideas about our Creator to divide us. Let us rejoice in the beautiful expressions of God longing that have been brought into the world.'"

It was impossible for the government-controlled media to avoid reporting the assassination attempt. Reports appeared everywhere on television, in newspapers, and on the Internet. It even made the international news. Grainy cell phone videos were aired that showed Ahmed, wearing the garments of time, reeling from the impact of the bullet, and they recorded him questioning the shooter.

Knowing the clerics were behind the attempt on his life, Ahmed found it unsurprising, yet still unsettling, when the Supreme Leader came out on television in vigorous condemnation. "We will exhaust every possibility to find out who was behind this hateful act," he said in a broadcast carried by all the state media.

"We have reason to believe there were more people involved than just the one who pulled the trigger. They will be identified, and they will be given the punishment that is due to those who wage war against God and his holy representative on earth."

"Liars and hypocrites," Baba Koushiyar fumed. "They are the ones who are waging war against God."

Bahram came to the residence two days after Ahmed's return, this time in the back of the cargo van instead of his own vehicle. He shook his head when Ahmed showed him the bruises. "I wish I had a better vest to give you, Imam, but the one I gave you was supposed to be the best."

"It worked," Ahmed said with a cheerful smile. "I'm still alive."

Ahmed showed him the pistol confiscated from the shooter. Bahram examined it and scoffed. "It's a cheap Iranian knockoff of a Makarov. This is what they issue to some of the militia when they're ordered out into the streets. They're numbered and have to be returned, so if this Jabbar had one, it means he was allowed to have it."

"He denied anyone put him up to it," said Ahmed.

"I know they've got him in one of their secret Intelligence Ministry prisons. Before long, I think we'll see him on TV making a forced confession. Maybe they'll even have him implicate some people they want to get rid of."

"Do you think they will try again?" said Baba Koushiyar.

Bahram shook his head. "It's unlikely, but that doesn't mean you shouldn't continue wearing the vest and taking other precautions," he said to Ahmed.

"Our Imam has them running scared," said Koroush. "They thought their problem was going to be solved, but it's blown up in their faces. If not another attempt on his life, what do you think they'll do now?"

Bahram shrugged. "I wish I knew. Right now, they're busy trying to cover their backs and come up with an official story."

"You informed us weeks ago that the Guardian Council has debated ways to deal with the Imam," said Koroush. "One of them is to expose his contemporary origin. Could they try that now?"

"No, that will be a last resort. I think they'll try to co-opt the Imam before they do that."

"How am I to be co-opted?" said Ahmed.

"They'll offer you money and power. They'll offer you leadership in the conquest of Jerusalem, Mecca, and Medina. For them, the role of the Mahdi is to spearhead the takeover of the Middle East and, after that, the entire world."

"They are foolish if they think I would go along with them," said Ahmed.

"Then they'll find a way to expose your background. They'll try to destroy belief in you and your message."

"I'm prepared," Ahmed said. "For the time being, I want to move ahead with my message. I want the next sermon to be at the stadium in central Tehran, right under their noses. Do you think they'll try to block me from entering, Bahram?"

"They haven't blocked you yet, and your fame has grown since the assassination attempt. If you walked into the Parliament and asked to speak, I'm sure they would drop everything to accommodate you."

"It's the people I want to speak to. In the stadium."

"Right in the belly of the beast," said Koroush. "When do you want to do it? We can begin making preparations."

"First, I want to meet with religious representatives to get commitments for the temple dedication. After that, we can hold the sermon at the stadium."

Koroush and Baba Koushiyar went to fetch a list of individuals and groups they had already contacted and went over it with Ahmed. Inside Iran, Koroush noted, rabbis from Shiraz and Isfahan, Zoroastrian priests from Yazd and Kerman, Baha'i leaders from the Caspian region, and Assyrian Christians from the border region near Azerbaijan had sent back emails. They were eager to meet Ahmed about the temple. Except for the Zoroastrians of Yazd, it was the first time any of them had heard about the temple, but they had listened to Ahmed's numerous sermons. They found the idea of the temple "bold and inspiring," as one of the Baha'is wrote, but they wanted to know more before committing themselves.

Outside of Iran, the religious representatives who had responded so far were more cautious. Many had questions about Ahmed and what was said about him. Koroush hastened to reply that the Imam had never made any claims about himself. He was given an experience he had not sought, and to his astonishment, he was taken to be the Imam of Time. Koroush also emphasized that the Shi'ite religious leaders who investigated using forensic methods confirmed that his emergence from the well was authentic. "Even though they have rejected his message, their investigations have confirmed the event was not faked," he wrote to the foreign religious leaders.

Ahmed said, "If I must, I'll tell them the whole truth about my experience so they'll understand."

Two weeks later, Ahmed was in a conference room in Isfahan with six dozen religious representatives. It was similar to the meeting when he first met the disciples in Gorgan. A small conference room in an older hotel was reserved, and Ahmed made a discreet entrance after he, Koroush, and Baba Koushiyar arrived in Maziar's cargo van.

Isfahan was chosen as the meeting site because Bahram was able to secure tourist visas for people with passports from banned countries, provided they flew to Isfahan. Koroush organized it so they assembled in Athens and flew together to Iran. "We have friends in the immigration service in Isfahan, and it's all arranged," Bahram told Ahmed. "Everyone will be given 30-day tourist visas upon arrival, no questions asked."

The religious leaders were enthusiastic when Ahmed mingled among them to greet them. None wore traditional religious garments; all were dressed as travelers, but Ahmed could guess their religions from appearances and mannerisms. Many brought interpreters with them. As they took his hand, they gave him their names, their religion, and the groups and organizations they belonged to. They represented a wide spectrum of beliefs: Christians, Jews, Hindus, Sikhs, Jains, Buddhists, and others. A quarter of the people were from various Christian sects, including pastors from an African evangelical movement. A number of them were women, as were many of the interpreters. A dozen of the representatives were Iranians belonging to religious minorities with legal status in Iran, among them two Zoroastrian priests from Yazd, whom Ahmed already knew.

Rayhaneh was present. After caring for Ahmed, she resumed her duties at the temple site and attended the Isfahan meeting accompanied by Zoroastrian priests, the disciples Mirza and Yari, and the project manager Sagdeh. She and Ahmed exchanged warm smiles, but he avoided an open display of his feelings for her. His love for her was a private matter, folded within a sacred place in his heart.

When he stood at the podium, he smiled and said, "I don't think there is a single person among you who doesn't have this question in mind: 'Just who are you?'"

Ahmed was pleased when laughter and smiles spread through the audience. "The answer is simple," he said. "I am you, and you are me."

He had decided to hold nothing back. He had to be truthful with the religious representatives, no matter what. They had to understand; they had to see and feel what he had experienced in order to understand what he understood. He first told them of the violent happenings, now more than a year before, in the streets of Tehran and of his questions and doubts. He told them about the cave and the brilliant light that spoke to him. He described finding himself in a strange land in a distant time and spoke of his experiences in Yathrib, his stay in a monastery, and the love he came to have for Jesus. He told them of his travels along the caravan trail and the endless conversations with his caravan companions about their ideas of God. He described his journey to India that ended on a balcony overlooking the Ganges and the simple truth that came to him as he watched the moonlight dance on the sacred river.

"There is a spark of the divine within all people," Ahmed said, "It is as if our Creator reaches down to present us with this gift from His loving hands, and through this gift we reach upward to Him with loving hearts. That is what the temple of God longing is devoted to. It is to give honor to the gift, to the flame of God longing that burns within us, and to recognize it as the common denominator among all people, for it is this flame that gives rise to all religion."

Ahmed opened up the meeting for questions. A Jesuit priest, scholarly in appearance, stood up. "It's clear that you can't accept the theological meaning that is attributed to the well of Jamkaran, yet you returned from your journey through it. What are your thoughts about that?"

Many in the audience laughed when Ahmed said, "I can only guess that our Creator has a sense of humor. It was unnerving to find myself in that situation. But I believe it was purposeful. It forced me to speak about the simple truth of God longing. It gave me a ready-made audience."

A short, thin man wearing round wire-rimmed glasses identified himself as a Hindu priest from Benares. He asked if Ahmed knew of accounts that were beginning to circulate on the Internet from people who claimed similar experiences. "They are called Testimonies of Time. Do you know about them?"

Ahmed nodded. "They are statements from the disciples of time, as they call themselves. We learned about one another through networks of people who also had the experience of time. Since it was I who returned through the well in Jamkaran, they looked to me for leadership. They agreed with me about the importance of sharing their experiences with the world, and that is what they have done."

An African man, short, round-faced, and with a cheerful disposition, stood up and identified himself as the bishop of an evangelical ministry in central Africa. He said he had heard talk of others with such experiences. "But their accounts don't appear to be among the testimonials noted on the website. Do you have an explanation for this?"

Ahmed replied, "There are many we didn't know about. But as a result of the publication of our testimonies, many people have been contacting the website administrators. The administrators are Iranians who have also had the experience of time and are now living in the United States."

He looked toward Koroush, Baba Koushiyar, Maziar, and the

Zoroastrian disciples in the front row with Rayhaneh and the project manager. "What is the latest number?"

Koroush pointed to Baba Koushiyar, who stood up and said. "As of yesterday, 371 people have claimed the experience of time, Imam."

Ahmed motioned for him to step up to the podium. He walked to the front of the room with an air of authority. He had not worn a turban or clerical garments since Ahmed's return, and Ahmed thought how much better he looked in normal clothes, pleasingly rotund and with distinguished gray hair combed back.

Ahmed smiled with warmth at him. "Please break it down for us, Baba."

Baba Koushiyar took out a folded sheet of paper from the inner pocket of his tweed blazer. He slipped on his glasses to peer down at the sheet and looked up at the audience. "It's been quite a shock to find out that most of them aren't from Iran. Everyone we first knew about was Iranian. But of these, only one in ten is Iranian. More than half are from Arabic-speaking countries, primarily Saudi Arabia, where 179 people are claiming the experience of time, all of them Sunnis!"

He read the numbers: India, 27; Indonesia, 13; Pakistan, 36. He went through a list of a dozen more countries with smaller numbers. "There are even six Uyghurs," he added.

A tall, bearded man who identified himself as a Sikh leader from Punjab asked, "How can you be certain they're genuine?"

"There are procedures in place," Baba Koushiyar replied. "It's true that people can invent stories, but their authenticity can be established through a number of tests. It's something we take very seriously because, among other concerns, we have to be careful about infiltration by those with bad intentions."

A man with a shaved head who identified himself as the chief monk of a Buddhist monastery in Thailand asked Baba Koushiyar, "Your presence at the podium and your words suggest you are one of the disciples of time. Is that so?"

Baba Koushiyar glanced at Ahmed, as if ceding the response to him. Ahmed stepped up to the podium. After looking toward Koroush, Rayhaneh, Maziar, Mirza, and Yari, he said, "I can affirm that, apart from me, there are several people with the experience of time among you today."

He paused when a murmur arose, and people glanced around the room, whispering to one another. After a moment, Ahmed continued, "It will be up to them if they wish to speak to you in private about their experiences. If they do, confidentiality is a must."

A rabbi from Frankfurt stood up next. "We do have serious concerns about security if we attend the dedication ceremony, some of us more than others. What's to prevent the government from detaining us, or even imprisoning us? This government isn't known for religious tolerance. Especially for Jews."

Ahmed was silent for a moment as if thinking about what to say. "We can assure your safe entry and safe exit at the Isfahan airport. Apart from that, I can't give an ironclad guarantee that nothing will happen. I can only pray there won't be any trouble. However, if this government takes any such action, it will face international censure to a degree it has never experienced before."

An Iranian Assyrian Christian rose to his feet. His voice was passionate. "Everything that is true and good in our world has been brought about by people of courage," he said, looking around at the audience. "The Imam has bravely brought forth a clear truth that is unifying and healing. So let us show the world our courage by standing with him for the temple dedication."

The questions, answers, and discussions continued for another two hours. The delegates agreed that freedom of religion was essential for people to live in peace and that it required respect for the expressions of God longing in others. The Sikh delegate expressed the consensus when he stood up and said, "It is as the Imam states, that practicing love for the flame of God longing in all people is the best form of worship of the Creator, for it is He who has endowed each of us with it."

The meeting ended after the delegates pledged their presence. A tour of the temple site was set for the following day. Ahmed introduced Rayhaneh and Sagdeh as the tour guides, calling them "beloved friends who took up the idea of the temple and brought it to life."

# Chapter 37

A week later, Ahmed made his entrance into the Tehran stadium amid thunderous applause and wild cries of "Imam!" It was just after sunset, and the stands and the playing field were packed. Leery of government agents, Ahmed scanned the crowds, but he couldn't detect anything but joyful enthusiasm. He was moved to tears.

The words came to him without effort, as if all he had to do was to begin speaking, and thoughts and images that could only come by inspiration would flow through him. He felt humbled by his own words. He spoke of the truth of the cave of light and the stirrings of the flame within that urges people to sally forth in confidence that their lives are part of a grand purpose.

"God has given us the privilege of being a self-aware part of His vast enterprise of creation, so rejoice and offer prayers of gratitude to the Giver of Life for His gift of life to us."

At one point, the sermon was interrupted by two military helicopters that circled less than five hundred feet above the stadium, drowning out Ahmed's voice. It was obvious that it was intended to be disruptive. Thousands of people jumped to their feet, shaking their fists at the helicopters. They shouted, "Go away! You're not wanted!" When the helicopters finally left, Ahmed resumed speaking as if nothing had occurred.

He spoke of Zartosht, who came into the world at a time of oppressive tribal religion. "What the tribe believed, everyone believed," said Ahmed. "Zartosht was bold and revolutionary. He preached that religion was a personal matter. He preached that people have been endowed with free will, one of their most precious possessions, and that they must exercise it in choosing their religion. But they must choose thoughtfully and wisely."

He paused for a moment. He knew he had entered dangerous territory, but he continued on when the huge crowd remained silent, as if holding its collective breath in anticipation of his next words. "Have we returned to the tribalism of yore where the tribe tells us what to think?" he asked. "Have we surrendered our free will? Can we no longer think for ourselves?"

He continued speaking for another hour, pausing several times when the disruptive helicopters returned. Although it had not been his intention when he entered the stadium, he kept returning to Zoroastrian themes. The inner prompting of the light and the flow of inspiration led him in that direction, and he followed their lead.

When it was over, the stadium erupted in electric enthusiasm. People alternated between shouting "Zartosht" and "Imam." It seemed the chants would never end, but they came to an end after Ahmed thanked the people for their inspiring enthusiasm, and said, "Let the flame of God longing be your guide. It will take you where you desire to go."

Koroush had arranged for the usual decoy vehicles, but their exit was blocked by joyful crowds that packed the streets, hoping to get close to the Imam of Time. It took the decoys fifteen minutes to get out of the parking garage. Maziar's van remained hidden in the parking area, waiting for an opportune time to exit.

When Ahmed got into the van, he was surprised and delighted to see Rayhaneh. He thought she was still at the temple site helping oversee the final stage of the project, which was now two weeks from completion. Baba Koushiyar was also there, as was Behrouz. They smiled when Ahmed sat against the cushions next to Rayhaneh at the back of the van, and leaned over to kiss her hand, saying, "An angel has come down from heaven."

Rayhaneh said, "We've prepared a beautiful surprise for you, my Ahmed."

When the exit was clear, Maziar drove into the street, thick with nighttime traffic. He drove in and out of residential areas with tall apartment buildings, his usual tactic to avoid being followed.

After a number of right and left turns, he stopped in front of a tall apartment building somewhere in central Tehran. The door to the underground garage opened. After finding a place to park deep inside, he turned to Ahmed. "You will like this, Imam."

Rayhaneh led Ahmed by the hand to the elevator, and everyone piled in when the door slid open. The elevator shot up to the top floor. They followed a corridor to a door that said "Roof Entrance."

When he went up a flight of stairs and stepped through another door, Ahmed was surprised by a burst of cheers from a huge crowd that filled the rooftop. Koroush was there, along with the disciples who had undertaken security roles at the stadium, and many dozens of others. They pushed up close to him to embrace him and shake his hand, telling him how much his words meant to them.

Rayhaneh said to him, "We're not the only building with people on the rooftops. Look!" She pointed to adjacent rooftops.

Ahmed looked over the parapet. He was on the roof of one of the tallest buildings, with a clear view of the buildings nearby. People were crowded on the roofs of all of them. He was wearing the garments of time and was hard to miss. Hundreds of people waved and called out to him.

Someone standing next to Koroush shouted to the people on a nearby rooftop. "The Imam is with us. Are you ready?"

"Yes," numerous people shouted back.

The cry "Imam, Imam!" went up. It started on Ahmed's rooftop and was picked up by other rooftops. The chant kept jumping from rooftop to rooftop until thousands of voices joined together.

Someone with a pair of binoculars standing near Ahmed said, "Imam, I see people coming out onto the rooftops everywhere. They're going to join in."

Rayhaneh was an energetic part of the chorus, pumping her fist in the air with each syllable. "We're not loud enough," she said to the people around her. "We need to let the universe hear us."

She climbed a metal ladder to the top of the roof entrance. It was a small, cubic structure with the roof entrance door on one side and a flagpole on the other. Ahmed shouted to her, "Have them chant 'Zartosht,' and 'Jesus,' and 'Buddha.'"

Holding on to the flagpole with one hand, Rayhaneh shouted down to the people, "Zar-tosht! Zar-tosht!" while thrusting her fist in the air. She kept repeating it until the chant was picked up by everyone and spread to other rooftops.

The chanting became thunderous when numerous rooftops also shouted "Zar-tosht, Zar-tosht," at first discordantly, then in synchrony. It soon was heard on distant rooftops to the north and south. It made the rounds of the city several times until a rooftop to the east began chanting, "Je-sus, Je-sus," and it was picked up and repeated everywhere.

Down on the boulevards and side streets, drivers joined in by honking their horns. It became a tremendous roar coming from every end of the city, competing with the chants. As at the stadium, military helicopters circled the city, sometimes flying over Ahmed's building, but the noise of their powerful engines and rotors was drowned out by the joyous rooftop chanting and the blare of horns down on the streets.

It made Ahmed think of the rooftop chants after the disputed election the year before. People had taken to the roofs and shouted *"Allahu Akbar"* in mockery of the religious establishment after the brutal attacks on the people when they came out into the streets in protest of their stolen election.

The cries of "Imam" and "Zartosht" circulated again and were replaced by "Buddha" and "Jesus." Five minutes later, it was the turn of Krishna. The cry of "Jesus" made the rounds once again.

Rayhaneh shouted down to Ahmed, "Who are we forgetting, my Imam?"

Ahmed shouted back, "Nanak."

She didn't hear him at first and put her hand to her ear to get him to repeat the name. She brightened when she understood and shouted down to the people, "Na-nak, Na-nak." It was picked up and quickly spread throughout the city.

Koroush squeezed through the crowd. Ahmed had never seen him so happy. His eyes aglow, Koroush said, "What do you think about all of this, Imam?"

Ahmed felt a tightening in his throat, making it difficult to speak. "I've never been happier in my life, Koroush. Thank you for this beautiful gift."

"The people have heard your message, Imam, and this is their answer."

Ahmed could not take his eyes off Rayhaneh. She was a powerful and inspiring presence. She held onto the flagpole with one hand to keep her balance while pumping her fist in the air to mark the syllables of each name that came up. Leaning forward, she joked and laughed with everyone as the chants made the rounds. "Baba, Maziar, Behrouz," she cried out when the chant of "Zartosht" reached their rooftop again. "Louder! Tehran can't hear you! Anosha, where's your voice? Did you leave it at home? Radin, Yazan, inspire us with the power of your lungs!"

Ahmed felt a tremendous burst of love for her. When it was over, she came up to him, exhausted but with happiness in her eyes. "This was for you, my Ahmed. It was to thank you for all you have brought forth."

He had something important to ask her, but not in public, not surrounded by so many people. Later, when they had a moment away from everyone, he drew her close to him. "Show me your hands like this," he said, holding his palms out. When she held out her hands that way, he pressed his hands against hers and let his fingers lace around hers.

Looking into her deep brown eyes, he said, "I want you to be with me, and me with you. I want you to be my wife. Will you marry me, Rayhaneh?"

She pulled closer to him. "I want to be your wife, my Ahmed. I want to marry you."

# Chapter 38

They were married in a Zoroastrian ceremony at the Grotto of the Weeping Lady. Rayhaneh wanted the wedding to be held there so "the daughter of Yazdegerd will smile upon us and give us her blessing."

Days before the wedding, she underwent the initiation rites to become a Zoroastrian, pledging as she tied knots in the ritual cord to live her life guided by the virtues of good thoughts, good words, and good deeds.

The Zoroastrian priests of Yazd, attended by Mirza and Yari, performed the wedding ceremony on the steps of the grotto entrance, with a large group of disciples, family members, and well-wishers in attendance.

Ahmed wanted the marriage to follow custom, but given the circumstances, the drawn-out betrothal traditions had to be shortened to less than a week. Among other considerations, both he and Rayhaneh wanted their union to take place before the dedication of the temple out of concern for the possibility of disruptive repercussions.

Ahmed was attentive to obtaining the consent of their parents. At a minimum, Rayhaneh's parents, both educated professionals with modern ideas, would have to meet Ahmed's mother, and together they would have to give their blessings to the union. A complication arose because Rayhaneh's parents did not know about her involvement with him, and Ahmed worried about the shock it would cause them.

Her parents lived only a few miles from the Tehran safe house. To prepare her parents, Rayhaneh first brought Koroush and

Baba Koushiyar to their home, and they spent an entire afternoon explaining the truth to them. When her parents got over their shock, Ahmed's mother spent a day with them, and Ahmed was pleased when they gave their formal blessings to the marriage.

The parents were nervous when Rayhaneh introduced them to him. "Our daughter told us about her experiences, Imam," said Rayhaneh's father, a thin man with dark wavy hair. "We believed she had suffered a traumatic experience during the protests and had imagined it all, but after listening to Koroush and Baba Koushiyar about you and the disciples, we now accept that what she told us is the truth. And we also accept that what you have brought forth is the truth."

Rayhaneh's mother, a trim woman who resembled her daughter, added, "I don't know why such an experience happened to her, but it happened. Now she will be with a man who cherishes her."

Following the marriage, Ahmed and Rayhaneh spent the days leading up to the temple dedication at the grotto in one of the pavilion apartments used to lodge pilgrims. The Zoroastrians who lived at the mountainside retreat and maintained it prepared traditional meals for them, and Ahmed and Rayhaneh dined with them and joined them in prayers led by a priest in front of the sacred flame inside the grotto. In their quiet moments, they lounged for many hours together on the apartment patio, chatting and enjoying the view of the pale desert that stretched far into the distance.

Koroush and Baba Koushiyar, meanwhile, made the final preparations for the temple dedication and kept Ahmed up to date via cell phone. Before giving him the update, Koroush—or if it was Baba Koushiyar making the call—always began by apologizing for "intruding on the Imam and his bride."

Ahmed wanted the dedication to be an inspiring event that would attract international attention. The temple was a religious statement, but it couldn't be separated from its political implications. The presence of the international media was therefore essential to ensure that any attempts at repression would draw the censure of the international community, at least in the West, where religious freedom was championed. "The main thing is to get the media here without alerting the religious establishment beforehand," he said to everyone.

In his latest update, Koroush informed Ahmed that the number of religious delegates would be triple the number of people he had met with a month earlier. As before, they would assemble in Athens and fly together to Isfahan the day before the dedication. Bahram assured Koroush that he had set it up with "our secret friends" in the immigration service so the standard 30-day tourist visas would be issued to everyone debarking from that particular flight. Hotel reservations and transportation were already arranged in Isfahan and Yazd.

Koroush also arranged for filmmakers to be present. "News reports are brief and incomplete," he said to Ahmed. "With videographers present, we can be assured the entire dedication will be documented."

Ahmed was certain there would be repercussions. The clerical establishment would see the temple as a challenge to their exclusivity. He didn't fear for himself, but he feared for Rayhaneh. If he became a target again, she would become a target as well.

He looked at Rayhaneh with a mixture of joy and sadness, joy because of their marriage, but sadness because he didn't think their bliss would last much longer. In the distant past, he had foreknowledge of the fate of the Qurayzas, and he knew what awaited the empire of the Persians. These were recorded in history, stamped forever as facts of time. Though he had tried, he was unable to alter them. Now he had a foreboding of his own end. It couldn't be changed unless he became someone other than who he was. It was as if his future was already a fact of time.

As the day of the temple dedication approached, Ahmed said to Rayhaneh, "I fear the system is about to unleash its fury. I don't want you to be touched by it. Maybe it would be best for you not to be at the dedication. There will be cameras. You will be filmed and photographed."

"I'm not afraid," Rayhaneh said.

"If harm comes to me, that's one thing, but if harm comes to you because of me, that's another. You're the vehicle of a different truth than mine. The day will come when it will be for you to declare your experience of time to the world. That's your purpose, and your life must be preserved in order for you to fulfill your purpose."

"I've never heard you speak like this before."

"We mustn't hide it from ourselves that difficult times are ahead."

Rayhaneh had with her large, stylish sunglasses against the desert sun. She put them on and wrapped a headscarf, covering her hair and ears.

Ahmed smiled at the severe Shi'ite appearance she had given herself. She said, "What do you think? Am I me, or am I not me?"

They agreed to go to the temple in separate vehicles and to keep apart in public. The morning of the dedication, she rode with a group of Zoroastrians in one car, while Ahmed arrived later in another vehicle driven by one of the priests.

Ahmed had not seen the temple since his visit months earlier, and he caught his breath when he beheld it in the distance. It was a work of elegant simplicity that gleamed like a jewel in the desert sun. The dome was now in place, the encircling colonnade was complete, and finishing touches had been added, including benches at the rest stops built into the stairways. There was neither electricity nor plumbing, only stone and concrete and the thick wood that formed the roof of the colonnade. It was just as he had first imagined it in the cave above Zarringol after his return from India, beautiful and meaningful to all who grasped the truth of the flame within.

An enormous crowd had assembled near the base of the hill. Vehicles of all sorts were parked in the surrounding desert. When he arrived, his vehicle was encircled by the cheering throngs who recognized him from his garments of time. Koroush and other disciples ushered him to the foot of the hill, where a section was cordoned off for the religious dignitaries. They stood smiling as he walked among them, extending their hands to grasp his and congratulate him on completing the temple.

Another section was roped off for the media. Ahmed had never seen so many journalists and cameras before. Men predominated.

They were from Iranian and international media outlets, all vying to catch his attention with their questions. Koroush and Baba Koushiyar busied themselves informing them that the Imam would be available following the ceremony.

A microphone awaited Ahmed at the first rest area of the staircase, about thirty feet above the desert floor. The sound system was powered by batteries connected by cable to a vehicle parked off to one side with its motor running.

Ahmed walked up the stairs to the microphone, followed by twelve religious leaders selected from the group as speakers. Standing in front of the microphone, he looked over the mass of people. They were under the hot sun, shading themselves as best they could, and he didn't want to subject them to a long talk. He spoke for less than two minutes, and as always, the words seemed to flow through him.

He said in conclusion, "We are here to dedicate the temple to our shared gift of God longing. We will light the symbolic fire in its honor and in thankfulness to the Creator who has so endowed us."

Ahmed stepped aside to let the religious leaders speak. They identified their religious affiliation before making a brief statement. A Catholic bishop from Africa said, "The temple celebrates a fundamental truth of human experience. Therefore, let us dedicate the temple to this truth and pray together." A monk from an international Buddhist association remarked, "We accept that we are all brothers and sisters in our quest for enlightenment." A Sikh leader from India said, "The temple is a place of gathering for people of all religions to honor the universal drive to seek God. We are proud to be a part of this dedication."

Following the brief speeches, Ahmed and the twelve dignitaries were given flaming torches. Carrying them high, the small group fell in behind Ahmed as he went up the stairs to the temple mount, followed by the rest of the religious representatives and the media.

Chiseled into the entablature of the colonnade above the entrance were the words "I am you, and you are me" in Persian, English, and Arabic. Ahmed noticed the inscription when he reached the entrance. He smiled when he remembered that Koroush had told him a surprise awaited him there.

The procession of torches first went through the section of the colonnade facing the multitudes below and veered toward the brass urn beneath the dome. The solemn torchbearers followed Ahmed up the several steps to the wide platform where the urn, chest high and a yard wide at the top, was mounted. Sticking out near the edges was tinder, while in the center, cedar and other aromatic wood were stacked in a pyramidal form.

A microphone was set up next to the urn on a side visible to the crowds below. With his torch held high, Ahmed stood in front of the microphone and said, "Together, we now consecrate the truth of the temple by the lighting of the sacred fire. It is the fire that is within all people. It is the fire that prompts all people to seek He who caused them to be."

When he lowered his torch, the twelve religious representatives, standing in a circle around the urn, did the same. The tinder caught fire and spread to the firewood. When flames shot high, wild cheering broke out from the thousands of people at the base of the hill.

Addressing the multitudes, Ahmed said, "Let the temple become a place of pilgrimage, a place of contemplation to reflect upon the great gift within each of us. Now that the temple is dedicated, I invite you to come up as pilgrims. Come and offer prayers before the sacred fire. Give thanks to our Creator for giving you life and for implanting in you the spark of longing to know Him."

Just as he completed the invitation for the people to ascend to the temple mount, a string of military helicopters appeared in the distance and were soon overhead. Ahmed counted six in all. Four of them circled two thousand feet above the desert, while the other two descended to five hundred feet and hovered over the temple. It was the same as had occurred at the Tehran stadium, intended to disrupt and intimidate. Ahmed prayed that the men in the helicopters would one day be among those to come to the temple in joyful recognition of its truth.

He peered into the distance at the two-lane road that led to

Yazd. If there was going to be trouble on the ground, it would come in the form of a convoy of revolutionary guardsmen and *basijis* in transport trucks, but he was relieved to see the traffic on the road was sparse.

"Don't be concerned," he said to the religious delegates about the helicopters. "They are demonstrating that they fear the meaning of the temple. They will make noise and nothing more."

Ignoring the helicopters, people formed long lines to take turns ascending to the temple. The disciples guided them when they reached the top, giving tours and leading others to the central urn. Ahmed and the religious leaders remained near the leaping fire to greet people and join them in prayer. When the pilgrims completed their visit, the disciples guided them to the other staircases so they could return to the base of the hill to make way for more people.

Ahmed kept glancing at the distant road but didn't see any unusual movement of vehicles. The helicopters finally left, prompting cheers and laughter from the crowd.

The pilgrims kept streaming up to the temple until sunset, but by the time it was dark, almost everyone was gone. Ahmed and Rayhaneh left together in a vehicle driven by Zoroastrian priests, intending to return to the grotto for a few more days.

Before they reached the main road, he asked the priests to stop. Everyone got out to gaze at the temple, now a half mile in the distance. The fire continued to blaze, parting the darkness with an orange glow that illuminated the dome and the colonnade.

When the fire died down, Ahmed and Rayhaneh were again snug in the back seat. As the priests drove back to the grotto, they leaned against each other, holding hands.

# Chapter 39

They spent a week at the grotto, during which they met with the Zoroastrians to discuss the temple's future.

Ahmed asked their leaders to take charge of it and administer it as they did the grotto and other pilgrimage sites. He envisioned a future hamlet built around the mount, with its inhabitants dedicated to maintaining the temple and receiving and guiding pilgrims. The Zoroastrians pledged to discuss the matter in the Yazd community. Ahmed, in turn, promised to seek funding from foreign donors to bring electricity and water to the site, and to build a center explaining the meaning of the temple.

"The temple is a prototype," he said. "People will come to it and be inspired to replicate it elsewhere. So we must make it a welcoming place, with lodging and conveniences for travelers like you have at the grotto and other sites."

The official reaction to the temple ceremony was not what Ahmed anticipated. It was ignored as if it never happened, as if no such temple existed. Behrouz and others monitored broadcasts and print media, but found nothing about the temple or the dedication ceremony. They were, however, confident that stories and videos about the dedication made the news around the world and could not be completely blocked. By the time Ahmed and Rayhaneh returned to Tehran, reports and videos were beginning to filter in from abroad.

Ahmed worried about the disruptions caused by the helicopters. Were they harbingers of harsh things to come? "I can hear the ripping of their patience," he confided to Koroush and Baba Koushiyar when they met to discuss the next step.

They spent a week planning another appearance in Tehran. Ahmed wanted to hold it in the same stadium as before as a bold statement. They planned similar security procedures as before, both in entering the stadium and exiting.

When the event began, the stadium was even more packed than before. The stands were filled to capacity, and the playing field carpeted with supporters. He was greeted with the same enthusiasm as before. Helicopters were absent this time, leading Ahmed to wonder if the religious establishment had given up on harassment.

Yet it all seemed too easy. After the event, as Ahmed got into the back of the cargo van to leave the stadium, he had a powerful foreboding that he, Maziar, and Behrouz would not make it out of the parking garage.

"Be on the alert. Something is going to happen," he said as they waited for a call from a spotter outside the stadium that is was safe to leave.

Just as the call came, two black Mercedes with tinted windows screeched to a stop in front of the van, blocking it. Men in immaculate white uniforms, high peak white caps, and the golden epaulets of the presidential guard jumped out and surrounded the van. One of them pointed a handgun at Maziar and Behrouz and ordered them out of the van.

Another guardsman, tall and wearing the same trim Shi'ite beard as the other men, slid open the cargo door. "Come with me, Imam," he said to Ahmed with stiff politeness. "You are awaited."

While guardsmen shoved Maziar and Behrouz into one of the black vehicles, the tall guardsman opened the rear door of the other vehicle and, with a gesture, invited Ahmed to get in. After slamming the door shut and tugging the handle to make sure it was locked, the guardsman got into the passenger seat and signaled for the driver to leave. The vehicle had small flags bearing the presidential logo sticking up from the sides of the hood.

They were soon in heavy traffic. The driver turned onto the central boulevard of Tehran, going north. Ahmed understood they wanted him to be seen with them because all the windows rolled down the moment they turned onto the boulevard. His beard and black turban made him easy to spot. People in other vehicles or on the sidewalks pointed with excitement and waved or shouted, "Imam!" He worried about Maziar and Behrouz. Where were they taking them? Had they arrested other people as well?

Twenty minutes later, they drove through the gate to the White Palace complex. Ahmed had never visited the enormous park that housed the president's offices and official residence, but he recognized landmarks from photographs and television. He looked out of the rear window, hoping to see the other black vehicle, but it was not there.

The driver stopped in front of the entrance to the White Palace. Three dozen presidential guardsmen carrying ceremonial rifles with slim bayonets stood at attention. They were in rows, creating a wide pathway leading to the palace stairs. Television crews were positioned at the top with their cameras pointed at the vehicle.

The tall guardsman got out and opened the door for Ahmed. "The president awaits you," he said.

Just as Ahmed exited the limousine, the president appeared at the top of the stairs, smiling from ear to ear.

Ahmed glanced around. He was trapped. The guardsmen were on both sides, forming a corridor for him, while the tall guardsman from the vehicle fell in behind him and followed him up the steps.

"Welcome, welcome," the president said with showy enthusiasm when Ahmed reached the top. "We have waited so long for your visit, Imam."

When he extended his arms for an embrace, Ahmed frowned and didn't return the gesture.

Still with a smile, the president grabbed Ahmed by the arm, digging his fingers in hard as he guided him into the building. They walked side by side along a wide, ornate corridor. More cameras were positioned at one end of the corridor. The walk ended at the gilded room reserved for the official reception of foreign dignitaries. The president stood behind a luxurious chair to indicate where Ahmed was to sit.

Ahmed glared at him and sat down. The president seated himself in an identical chair next to him.

Everything in the room was ornate, from the massive crystal chandelier hanging from the high ceiling to the golden frames of paintings adorning the walls. Journalists were ushered in and allowed to take photographs, but not to ask questions. Ahmed was about to say, "I'm here against my will," but held back when he thought about Maziar and Behrouz. He worried it could have consequences for them and anyone else who had been arrested.

When the media left, the only other person in the room besides Ahmed and the president was a cleric, one of high rank, judging from his age and appearance. He sat on an ornate sofa positioned at an angle so he could observe them without having to turn his head. The president didn't introduce him.

"I must apologize for the manner of bringing you here, Imam," the president said. "But you ignored our pleas to meet with us. Yet more than anyone, we are the servants of the Imam."

Ahmed wondered what he intended to accomplish. He knew they had identified him a long time ago, but they didn't know that he knew.

Ahmed said, "What I have to say is for people who are eager to hear it. I've gone to them."

The president smiled. "And we are not eager to hear it?"

Ahmed glared at him. He had never liked his looks. His face was narrow and his eyes set close together. He looked crafty; his voice was grating; his smile insincere. It was he, along with other leaders, who sent the police and paramilitaries to crush the opposition that arose following the fraudulent election. If it had been clean and honest, someone else would be seated in that chair. Ahmed's eyes drilled into him. The man calling himself president was sitting atop the bodies of possibly hundreds of people killed outright or tortured to death in prisons after false confessions were coerced from them.

"Why have you brought me here?" Ahmed demanded.

The president touched his heart and gave him a sorrowful look. "You've caused me so much distress, Imam. You travel around in a lowly van in the company of lowly people whom you call your 'disciples.' You spend your energy building a temple far out in the desert that few people will ever visit. This is all beneath the dignity of the Imam of Time."

Ahmed remained silent, astonished by the smooth insincerity of a man who knew of his contemporary origin.

"If you had come to us in the beginning," the president continued, "how different it would have been. We would have arranged a state welcome for you. You would have been taken through the boulevards of Tehran amid a grand display of public joy worthy of our beloved Imam." He was silent for a moment, raising his eyebrows as if preparing to make an important point. "This can still be arranged."

Ahmed remembered Bahram's warning about the three members of the Guardian Council with the experience of time who wanted him assassinated. That was attempted, and it failed. Another group sought to co-opt him with the lure of wealth and power, while another faction hoped to undermine him by exposing his contemporary origins. It was clear the co-option faction was now in charge. It was plan number two.

"What has become of the people you took into custody?" Ahmed demanded.

The president laughed. "You needn't worry about your 'disciples.' They're safe." His eyes half closed, he added, "But their future is in your hands."

Ahmed glanced at the cleric. He had to be an observer who reported to the Supreme Leader and the Guardian Council, the real powers of the revolutionary system. Ahmed assumed he was present to ensure there was no misunderstanding about what was said during the meeting. He nodded from time to time, as if to show he agreed with the president.

"We are going to give you the opportunity to think over your relationship with us, Imam," the president continued. "You will be our guest here at the White Palace tonight, and tomorrow you will meet with our Supreme Leader and clerical authorities."

The president looked at the cleric, as if to pass the floor to him. He introduced him as Ayatollah Sohrabi, the Supreme Leader's personal secretary.

The cleric had a friendly look about him. His smile was polite. "We shared the same desire to meet you as the president, and we are happy that it will take place. The Supreme Leader and all twelve members of the Guardian Council will assemble here tomorrow. The reason for my presence is to convey to you their hope that you will listen to what is said about the role of the Imam of Time, and that you will understand that it is to be in fulfillment of prophecy."

When Ahmed said nothing, they stood up to signal the meeting was over. The president gripped him by the arm again. "Come, we'll show you to your accommodations."

They went up a wide staircase to the next floor and through an elegant corridor, stopping in front of a door with a polished lever handle that appeared to be of solid gold. The president pushed down on it and opened the door. He made a sweeping gesture with his hand for Ahmed to enter.

The room was as ornate as the rest of the building, with regal furnishings that included an even more regal bed with elaborate drapes as the backdrop.

"The last person to sleep in this room was the Shah. We are honored to have you stay here as our guest, Imam." The president looked around the room and said, "Good things come to people who do what is expected of them."

After saying that dinner would be brought to him, the president and the cleric left Ahmed standing in the middle of the room. The apartment included a large bathroom with solid-gold fixtures and a wide balcony overlooking a vast garden. He tried to open the double doors to the balcony, but they were locked. He tested the door to the corridor and discovered it was locked from the outside. The only furnishing that was out of place was a flat screen television sitting on a table that did not match the room.

An hour later, a military officer pushed a cart into the room with an ample dinner laid out. He saluted and left. Ahmed had not eaten since the morning. He sampled the food and poured tea, but ceased eating when he thought of Maziar and Behrouz. They must have been taken to Evin Prison. Were they being kept in a cold cell and deprived of food? How could he eat if they were being mistreated? He worried that other disciples had also been arrested and taken to prison.

Two hours later, the television turned on by itself. It was tuned to a news program announcing the arrival of the Imam of Time at the White Palace and his reception by the president. Ahmed watched himself get out of the black limousine and walk between the presidential guards. The video showed him going up the stairs to where the president stood. The broadcast cut to show them walking together through a long corridor, and seated near one another in the diplomatic reception room, the president with a smile, he with a frown. The report was edited to make it seem he was there of his own free will. It was cold and calculated, and the malevolence of it shook him.

He worried about hidden cameras and stripped down in the bathroom, hoping they would not see him remove the bullet-proof vest. He had worn it again as a precaution for the stadium appearance. Night garments were left for him on the marble sink, but instead of getting into the bed of the Shah, he wrapped himself in a blanket and slept on the floor. He couldn't justify sleeping in luxury when his friends and companions were likely being mistreated in prison. In the morning, he dressed again in the garments of time and wore the bulletproof vest underneath, along with the knotted Zoroastrian cord. He wished he could get rid of the vest, but there was no way to dispose of it without it being found. He wondered if it could be traced to Bahram.

A military officer soon wheeled in breakfast. Ahmed nibbled at it while sitting on an elegant sofa near the balcony doors. He wondered how to deal with the Supreme Leader and the guardians. The Supreme Leader always publicly proclaimed himself to be the vicegerent of the awaited Imam, a stand-in who would be glad to relinquish his leadership once the Imam returned to the world. That meant the Supreme Leader was to answer to him, their captive.

He reflected on the role of the guardians, who saw themselves as the final arbiters of a legal system based entirely on what was false and dangerous. He wondered if they truly believed that what was found in their books was a revelation of God's will.

Certainly, the three guardians with the experience of time were only in it for the power and prestige. Should he tell them about his experience of time? Or should he only reaffirm what he had come to understand as truth through his experience of time?

The president, cheerful and energetic, came for him at mid-morning. He escorted Ahmed to the ground floor and through a wing of the palace with meeting rooms. They arrived at a large double door where two Revolutionary Guard officers stood at attention. One of the officers opened the doors for them, and they went in. It was a large room as ornate as all the other rooms. The Supreme Leader and the twelve guardians were seated in a curved row of chairs, with the Supreme Leader in the center in a regal chair larger than the others. They remained seated as the president escorted Ahmed to the middle of the room and stopped at a point twenty feet in front of the group.

"Stand here," the president said. He walked to one end of the row and took a seat next to a guardian.

Ahmed looked at them with the same coldness that they looked at him, sizing them up. To the left of the Supreme Leader were six jurists, prominent legal scholars appointed by Parliament. They were dressed in expensive suits but without ties, each with a trim Shi'ite beard of varying degrees of grey. On the other side were six ayatollahs wearing turbans, clerical garbs, and beards, all of them appointees of the Supreme Leader. Ahmed recognized two of the three ayatollahs whom Bahram believed had the experience of time. He could only guess at the third.

The Supreme Leader looked little different from how he appeared on television and in the ever-present propaganda photos: an elderly man with a long white beard, thick glasses, and an oversized black turban denoting his descent from Muhammad's bloodline. His right hand, partly covered by his sleeve, was withered from a wound he had suffered in an assassination attempt two decades earlier. He looked oddly inoffensive, even though it was known he had a role in the horrific terror that followed the revolution and that his approval was always behind the brutal repression that had occurred ever since he became Supreme Leader.

The room was silent for more than a minute, only ending when the Supreme Leader said, "We welcome you, but we are saddened it has taken such a long time for us to meet."

Ahmed said, "I have not chosen to be here."

He noted narrowed eyes and smirks among the guardians. He looked at them one after the other, lingering on the ayatollahs with the experience of time.

The Supreme Leader said, "Do you know why you are standing before us and not the other way around?" When Ahmed didn't reply, he continued, "It is because we are not convinced you are who you claim to be."

"I've never made any claim about myself."

"People call you the Imam of Time."

"They choose to call me that."

"You emerged from the well in Jamkaran. Doesn't that make you the Imam of Time?"

"It makes me the one who came out of the well. I make no other claim about myself."

The Supreme Leader smiled for the first time and extended his good hand toward Ahmed. "We know who you are. We know you are Ahmed, son of Abdollah from the town of Aliabad. Your father is honored as a martyr of the Sacred Defense. We know that you were invited to enroll in the seminary, but you chose instead to study agronomy at the Agricultural University in Gorgan, where you were distinguished as a graduate student. We know that you were a member of the Aliabad militia. We know that your life was exemplary in every respect until you were sent with your militia unit to Tehran to help deal with the enemies of God. But there, you abandoned your duty. You disappeared, and six weeks later, you came out of the well in Jamkaran. Is this an accurate summary of your life up until that day in the Jamkaran mosque?"

Ahmed looked at the Supreme Leader and at each of the guardians in turn, but remained silent.

The Supreme Leader said, "Do you know that you committed an unpardonable blasphemy by hiding in the sacred well and pretending to be the promised Messiah?"

"I cannot explain how I came to be in the well."

"Do you know that the punishment for such blasphemy is death by hanging?"

"You have the power to do whatever you wish," Ahmed said. "But you know that nothing about it was false. You examined the well yourselves. You reviewed the videos that showed a glow prior to my emergence. So you know the truth about it." He looked at the ayatollahs with the experience of time. "Some of you know the truth about it better than others."

The two clerics averted their gaze, as did the ayatollah seated next to them, leading Ahmed to believe he was the third guardian with the experience of time.

The Supreme Leader lifted his withered hand onto his lap and folded his other hand over it. He gazed at his hands for a long moment before looking up at Ahmed. "Do you know what the role of the Imam of Time is supposed to be?"

"If it is the Imam of the books, it is to bring peace and justice to the world after he leads all people to Islam."

"And what have you brought?"

Ahmed replied with warmth, "A simple truth, that of God longing, that it is the endowment of our Creator to all people, that this gift unites all people rather than divides them."

The Supreme Leader made a dismissive gesture. "No one here would dispute that all people desire God. It is the path they take that is important. The only true path is the one shown to us by our Holy Prophet, may peace be upon him."

Ahmed replied, "People who believe there is only one way to express their longing for God believe falsely."

The Supreme Leader became heated, his voice menacing. He leaned forward and said, "It is the purpose of the Imam to lead the disbelieving world onto this true path. He will be the inspiration for armies of conquest if such armies become necessary. When the entire world submits to God's religion, then and only then will there be universal peace and justice. To bring this about is the role of the Imam of Time."

Ahmed didn't like to argue with people about their beliefs. He said what he had to say, and it was up to people to accept or reject. He especially did not want to get into a theological argument with a roomful of people committed to believing what they believed. How could he convince them that theirs was an absurd idea? How could he convince them it was false, that it could only be imposed with the extremes of terror that they were already bringing about wherever they could? They had been conditioned to believe they were right, and no amount of reasoning could ever change their thinking. All he could tell them was that it was not something he could ever become a part of.

The Supreme Leader was noted for learned speeches delivered in a soft voice, but when Ahmed remained silent, he launched into an angry exposition about the Imam of Time. His face turned red, his eyes narrowed. He kept thrusting his forefinger in the air or wagging it at Ahmed. He recited word for word the endless literature about the Imam of Time, tradition after tradition, authority after authority. Such was the role, such was the purpose of the last of the Imams.

Ahmed was unable to listen. He slipped into memories of his experiences of time. Lucid images of the violence he witnessed filled his mind, memories that he always tried hard to suppress to keep them from whipping him with their fury. As he watched the Supreme Leader's mouth form words, he relived the long, painful journey that led him to lose his faith and seek truth elsewhere.

When the Supreme Leader, almost pleading, kept at his learned exposition, it occurred to Ahmed that he must truly believe his appearance from the well was miraculous. The evidence was in the videos and the testimony of witnesses. If Ahmed was indeed the awaited Imam of Time, he must fulfill the prophecies that were made about him. It could not be otherwise, because if the man who was standing before him, wearing the very garments he wore when he came out of the sacred well, rejected the role of the Imam of Time, it would destroy everything he believed in. His long lifetime of praying and studying and preaching and killing would have been for nothing.

As a final argument, the Supreme Leader said, "Didn't God reveal to our Holy Prophet these words: 'Whoever accepts a religion other than Islam will never have it accepted of him and he will be of those who truly feel the fire in the hereafter.' And didn't God also reveal to him these words, 'So fight them until there is no more disbelief and all people submit to the religion of Allah alone.'"

With the memories of the massacre of the Qurayza Jews stirred, Ahmed bristled. "I once lived with the man who claimed God told him such things."

Murmurs arose among the guardians. With a dark look on his face, one of the ayatollahs with the experience of time leaned toward the cleric next to him and whispered something. The other man nodded before looking at Ahmed with coldness.

The Supreme Leader glanced at the six ayatollahs and at the six jurists. After a moment of reflection, he said, "I am going to give you the opportunity to accept what is ordained as your destiny. Then we will know you are truly the Messiah. If you do this, we will join with you. All it will take is for you to say, 'I accept my sacred role,' and we will place ourselves under your authority. It shall then be we who stand before you rather than you who stand before us. We will pledge ourselves to serve you. We will gladly seek martyrdom under your banner."

Ahmed shook his head. "I cannot be part of what is false."

The ayatollahs with the experience of time exploded. One of them shouted, "There is nothing but blasphemy coming from his mouth. The punishment for blasphemers is death."

The cleric next to him said, "Let us not waste any more of our time with this impostor."

The Supreme Leader motioned for them to be silent. To Ahmed, he said, "I am saddened by your words. However, I do not see them as final. I am going to give you time to reflect on everything we have discussed. And I will give you incentives to help you bring your thinking into alignment with prophecy."

He pushed the button on a small device. The Revolutionary Guard officers stationed in the corridor entered and saluted.

The Supreme Leader pointed to Ahmed. "Take him away!"

# Chapter 40

Ahmed was handcuffed, blindfolded, and shoved into a vehicle. The vehicle accelerated and, twenty minutes later, came to a stop. He wondered if he was being taken to Evin Prison.

He was pulled from the vehicle and forced to walk blindfolded up a series of stairs. He could see a sliver of ground from under the blindfold so that he was able to follow the feet of whoever was leading the way. When he fell back several times, someone pushed him from behind.

He was led to a room where the handcuffs and the blindfold were removed. His eyes stung under the harshness of fluorescent ceiling lights. He squeezed his eyes together several times and looked around. An older man of official appearance was seated behind a desk. He had a square face, close-cropped gray hair, and a trim Shi'ite beard. Two guards stood nearby.

The official said, "Remove your clothes, and put them in that bag." He pointed to a large plastic bag that one of the guards was holding.

Ahmed looked around the room. It was windowless, painted in light green. "Where am I?"

"You are where no one who is in his right mind wants to end up," the official said in a gruff voice. "Remove your clothes."

Ahmed placed the black turban in the bag first. He pulled off the flowing garment of time, revealing the bulletproof vest and the knotted Zoroastrian cord.

The official smirked. "Give me those."

He put on a pale blue jail shirt without a collar, baggy trousers with a tight elastic band at the waist, and oversized sandals.

The official shoved a paper and a pen forward on the desk. "Sign here to acknowledge you've handed your personal belongings over to us."

It was a government form. The official had written down everything taken from him, including the bulletproof vest and the knotted cord. Ahmed's true name was typed in at the bottom. It meant they anticipated he would be taken there and had already prepared the form. If he signed, it would provide them with documentary proof that he acknowledged his contemporary identity. He made a squiggly line at the bottom and pushed it back across the desk.

The official smirked again when he saw the squiggle, but said nothing. He signaled to one of the guards to put the blindfold back on. Ahmed was led from the room and marched through several corridors until he was told to stop. He heard the sound of a key jiggling into a lock and a heavy door squeaking open. He was pushed from behind through the door.

"You may take the blindfold off now," a guard said.

Ahmed pulled it off and looked at the guard. He was young, and his voice and mannerisms were neither friendly nor unfriendly.

"You are to keep the blindfold with you. Any time you are taken out of the cell, you must put it back on. Is that understood?"

After the guard shut the heavy door, Ahmed looked around the small cell. It was six feet wide and eight deep and appeared to be of recent construction. He had heard that the conditions at Evin Prison were deplorable, but the cell was clean with walls painted white. In a corner, a stainless-steel toilet without a seat jutted from the wall. In another corner was a stainless steel sink with hot and cold faucets. The floor was covered with a thin carpet. Three coarse military blankets were folded in a corner.

He sat on the floor and thought about Maziar and Behrouz. Had others been arrested as well? If they knew of the cargo van, surely they would have known about the decoy vehicles. Were Koroush and Baba Koushiyar now in jail as well?

He spent hours praying for them, only stopping when he became sleepy. The fluorescent light, built into the ceiling and covered by a grate, was always on. He spread out one of the blankets as a mattress and used the others as a cover against the cold.

He wondered what was to come next. It was known that political prisoners were mistreated, often subjected to torture to extract false confessions. He imagined that at any moment the cell door would soon swing open, and he would be taken to an interrogation room and beaten and threatened. But nothing happened. Days went by without any contact with anyone, not even with the guards. Occasionally, he heard footsteps in the corridor, but never voices. Meals were pushed in silence through a rectangular opening near the bottom of the door, usually a thin stew of lentils with some vegetables and occasionally small chunks of lamb mixed in. When he was done with the meal, he slid the tray back through the opening into the corridor. He called out several times when the food tray was being pushed into his cell, but no one answered.

After several days without any human contact, it became clear they hoped to disorient him through the stress of solitary confinement. Koroush once told him that isolating people from all human contact was a technique the system used to break political prisoners psychologically. Few people, particularly the sensitives who were drawn to political activity because of their outrage over injustice, could stand total isolation for long.

He soon lost track of the days, but he learned to tell the time from the recorded prayer calls broadcast over loudspeakers. He now hated the sound and loathed the words, but they served as clocks.

He fought the isolation through meditation and prayer. Sitting in the lotus position, he emptied his mind to allow the light to enter him. He imagined he was back in the cave, welcoming the light when it rushed toward him and enveloped him. He relived the moment he heard the words, "I am you, and you are me." It became as easy as breathing to imagine himself back on the balcony in Kashi, once again contemplating the lights on the Ganges surging upward like arms reaching toward the source of the light.

When he was not in contemplation, he prayed for his friends that they would be spared harm. Rayhaneh was always uppermost in his thoughts. He prayed for her safety. He wished he could communicate with her to urge her to leave the country.

It seemed that ten days or possibly even two weeks had gone by before a guard opened the cell door and announced he had a visitor. When the guard stepped aside, Ayatollah Sohrabi was standing at the door.

"May I enter?"

Ahmed almost burst out laughing. He made a motion for the cleric to come into the cell. "I don't know if both of us will fit in this closet, but you're welcome to come in."

The ayatollah glanced around the cell and frowned. "Even if you're a prisoner, you do deserve better than this."

He was wearing clerical garments of expensive fabric, but he sat down on the carpet as if in the cleanest of mosques. He invited Ahmed to join him.

When Ahmed was seated cross-legged, the cleric said, "I, of course, have been thinking about you and wondering how you're being treated. No one has laid a finger on you, I trust."

Ahmed shook his head.

"Good," the cleric said. "Those people can get out of control."

It sounded like an implied threat. "Where am I?" Ahmed asked, "Evin?"

"No, no, no," the ayatollah said, waving his hand. "This is a private facility run by the Revolutionary Guard. While you're reconsidering your rejection of the role that is expected of you, it must remain a secret that you're in detention. That wouldn't be possible at Evin. People would recognize you, and word would get out. For the time being, the public is being told that you're in consultation with the Supreme Leader and members of the Guardian Council."

"You lie for your own sake, not mine."

He smiled. "It's a good lie for a good cause."

Ahmed liked his face. It was a cheerful, friendly face, one that invited trust, but he hesitated to give him trust. He knew why the ayatollah came. It was to find out if he had had a change of heart. If he continued to refuse to collaborate with them, the friendliness would surely cease.

"You have some of my friends in custody. What has become of them?"

"You needn't worry. They're not being mistreated." He looked around the cell for a moment. "You know, I've been wondering about your physical transformation in such a short period of time. I've studied photographs of you. You had a trim beard when you were with the paramilitaries in Tehran, but six weeks later, your beard was very long, like it is now. It would take a year to grow a beard that long. How do you explain this?"

"I went on a journey, a very long journey."

"Oh? Tell me about it."

"I don't think it's something you would be able to understand."

The ayatollah laughed. "I'm not made of stone. I'm capable of understanding more than you imagine."

Ahmed thought about it. He had nothing to lose by telling him the truth. Sooner or later, his testimony would be published, very likely soon now that he was imprisoned. He gave the cleric an overview, beginning with the cave experience. Though it was a simplified account, it took him an hour to cover all the significant events and the people he had known, including Ali, Umar, the wives of Muhammad, and Muhammad himself. As he spoke, he noticed involuntary facial reactions around the ayatollah's eyes and mouth. The more he spoke about his experiences, the more the ticks occurred, and it seemed to him the cleric was struggling to suppress whatever emotions the account of his experiences of time was causing him. He seemed particularly disturbed when he talked about Salman and described parting with him following the massacre of the Qurayza Jews.

"You don't flatter our Prophet by what you say."

"I've only told you what I witnessed and what I experienced," Ahmed said. "If you say it's unflattering, that's your evaluation of it. What I experienced with him, living close to him as his scribe, led me to lose my faith. I went on the road in search of true religion, and I ended up arriving at what I arrived at. And that has been my message since I emerged from the well."

The ayatollah wanted to hear more about Salman and kept questioning Ahmed about him to the point that it seemed like an interrogation. He was especially eager to know his physical appearance.

"When was the last time you saw him?"

"At the Farewell Pass. His last words to me came after I rode down into the desert. He shouted from the top of the pass, "I hope you find what you are looking for.""

"I believe it's not inaccurate to say that you found what you were looking for."

Ahmed said, "I did."

The ayatollah leaned his back against the wall. He closed his eyes and remained that way for a minute. Ahmed was about to ask him if he was feeling ill when he reopened his eyes. "I imagine you know there are a number of documents circulating on the Internet from people who claim to have had the 'experience of time,' as they call it."

Ahmed nodded.

"Do you know these people?"

Ahmed became wary. An admission could open up an avenue of inquiry for an interrogator to pursue. He didn't answer.

After another minute of silence, the ayatollah got to his feet. "I came to check up on you and find out how you're being treated. I'm satisfied that you're not being mistreated."

Ahmed stood up. "Thank you for visiting me."

"I also wanted to let you know that your interrogation will begin tomorrow. It's normal for detainees to be interviewed, so an investigator has been assigned to you. All you need to do is cooperate with him by answering truthfully."

The next morning, Ahmed was taken blindfolded to the interrogation room. He was allowed to take the blindfold off and saw it was the same small room he was brought to when he was made to strip and change into prison clothes. He noticed a camera in a corner of the ceiling nearest the door.

The same older, square-faced man who filled out the property document was sitting behind the desk. A pile of documents two inches thick was in front of him. "Sit there," he said, pointing to a chair about a yard away from the front of the desk.

After Ahmed sat down, the interrogator stared at him, dragging it out before shaking his head in disgust. "So you are the Imam of Time?"

When Ahmed didn't reply, the interrogator stood up and walked around the desk. He was short, in his late fifties or early sixties, and physically strong with a thick neck, thick torso, and arms that bulged through his shirt sleeves. He put a beefy hand on Ahmed's shoulder and leaned to within inches of his face. His breath smelled of garlic.

"My name is Hamzeh, and I don't like the enemies of God. But I can be patient, even with the enemies of God, as long as they answer my questions truthfully." He sat back down behind the desk and picked up what looked like an ID card from the pile in front of him. He held it up. "Is that you?"

He slid it across the desk, and Ahmed leaned forward to pick it up. It was his paramilitary ID card with a photo taken two years earlier, but it showed how he looked when he was six years younger. They knew who he was, so there was no use denying it. "Yes."

Hamzeh had a list of questions in front of him and made notes after Ahmed answered them. For nearly an hour, he asked mostly biographical questions that required only yes-or-no answers. When he finished this line of questioning, he started over again, asking exactly the same questions, comparing the new answers with what he had written.

When the last round ended, the interrogator leafed through the documents in front of him and extracted several sheets, which he placed on top of the pile. The questioning turned to Ahmed's membership in the paramilitary and his activities with them in Aliabad. Ahmed explained that his primary role was to organize patriotic and religious celebrations. When the interrogator asked him about his relationship to Behrouz, he knew they had already interrogated him. He had a rebellious spirit, and Ahmed feared they had been brutal with him.

"I was married to his cousin Shadi, who is now deceased."

"Was your group mobilized when the enemies of the Revolution began their disturbances in the big cities?"

"I was mobilized following the trouble that began after the presidential election."

"Were you assigned to a barracks near Niloufar Square?"

"Yes."

"Did you go out with a motorcycle squadron to contain the enemies of the Revolution?"

"I rode out on the back of one of the motorcycles, and we drove out onto the boulevard where there were demonstrators."

"Were you in possession of a firearm?"

"No."

"Were you present when gunfire erupted?"

"Yes."

"Were you present when a young woman was shot?"

"Yes.'

"Did you see her get shot?"

"Yes, she was nearby and I saw her fall to the pavement."

"Did you see who shot her?"

"No, it came from behind me. I turned to look after the woman fell to the ground, and I saw someone running away."

"What did you do then?"

"I left."

"Why did you leave?"

"I didn't want to be a part of what was being done to the people. They were being beaten, they were being shot. I couldn't accept being part of it."

"Where did you go?"

"Home to Aliabad."

"How did you get there?"

"By train."

"Did you stay in Aliabad?

"No."

"Where did you go?"

"I went on a journey."

"Where?"

"To Arabia."

"Do you have a passport?"

"No."

"Then how did you get there? You can't leave Iran without a passport and an exit visa stamp."

Ahmed stared at him for a moment. Something about his face made him think of granite. His mind was encased in granite. "You want me to be truthful, but if I told you the truth, I don't think you would believe me."

"I'll be the judge of that."

"I've already spoken about this to Ayatollah Sohrabi."

"Speak about it to me."

Ahmed began with the dreams he had about the cave and about finding it. As with the ayatollah, he avoided mentioning Baba Koushiyar. He spoke about the light and the voice that came from the light. He described finding himself struggling in a well and learning he was somehow in Arabia.

As he spoke, the interrogator leaned back in his chair and put his hands behind his neck to get comfortable. He put his feet on the desktop so that his shoes were in line with Ahmed. He wiggled one of his shoes back and forth, sometimes blocking Ahmed from his view.

Ahmed didn't allow himself to become upset by the display of contempt. He continued for another ten minutes, at times speaking to the soles of his interrogator's shoes, at other times to the granite face when the interrogator wiggled one of his shoes so they could see one another. When he began telling about being sold into slavery and meeting Salman al-Farisi, the interrogator took his feet off the desk. His face was flushed red. He leaned forward and snarled, "Do you know what happens to people who take me for a fool?"

"You asked me to speak truthfully," Ahmed replied.

The interrogator bolted from his chair. With the flat of his hand, he hit Ahmed on the side of his head, almost causing him to fall off the chair.

Hamzeh sat back down and smiled. "Tell me more about this journey of yours. It's entertaining. Go ahead, entertain me more."

Ahmed forced himself to let go of the seething anger that shot through him and strove not to show that his head hurt. After calming himself, he continued by speaking about his desire to experience the true Islam of Muhammad and Ali. It was a fervent desire, and his journey from the cave to Arabia came about through miraculous means.

He spoke about the events that led up to his becoming Muhammad's scribe. "Salman was instrumental in bringing it about. I learned how to write in classical Arabic when I was young. He told Muhammad that I knew how to write, so I was asked to perform the duties of a scribe."

Hamzeh signaled for him to stop. "That's enough. Your fantasy is beginning to bore me." He shuffled through the papers in the file. He pulled out a sheet and placed it on top.

"Who helped you get into the well in Jamkaran?"

"No one."

"It has a maintenance door underneath. Someone had to let you in through that door."

Ahmed shook his head. "I appeared there. Before that, I was in Mecca and all of a sudden, I was inside the well, lying on a mound of paper, and it took me a while to realize where I was."

The interrogator looked like he was on the verge of exploding again. Through clenched teeth, he said, "So, we're back in Arabia. Tell me about Mecca."

Ahmed glanced up at the camera. He was certain everything was being recorded. With a sigh, he said, "It was at the time of the conquest of Mecca. Muhammad's army surrounded the valley. He had a list of people he wanted killed on sight, and I was on that list. I ended up being trapped inside the temple. I tried to block the door, but Muhammad, Ali, Bilal, and Umar broke in. Ali came at me with a sword. I was about to be killed when I appeared in the well."

The interrogator jumped up from his chair. He screamed, "Everything that comes out of your mouth is blasphemous."

He went to the door and threw it open. He made a signaling motion. Two uniformed guards, tall and athletic, came into the room. He pointed to Ahmed. "Beat the crap out of this blasphemer."

The guards set upon him, punching and kicking him everywhere except for his face. He fell to the floor and covered his head with his arms. The beating was as savage as the ones he had endured at the hands of the *basijis* at the time of the demonstrations and later from the believers outside the mosque in Yathrib, but it kept going longer.

The guards didn't stop until the interrogator shouted, "That's enough!"

Ahmed was curled up on the floor. He hurt everywhere, but he tried not to groan from the pain. Hamzeh nudged him with his foot. "Get on your feet."

The guards helped him stand. At the interrogator's signal, they put the blindfold on him. Ahmed was relieved because it meant the interrogation was over.

Before the guards took him away, Hamzeh said, "We will do to you what the holy Prophet Muhammad, may peace be upon him, wanted to do to you. He pronounced your sentence. We have that from your own mouth."

# Chapter 41

Ahmed lay on his back with a blanket pulled up to his neck. He stared for hours at the fluorescent light that always remained on and at the ventilator next to it that whirred incessantly. Lying on his back lessened the soreness in his neck and abdomen, but he felt a stabbing pain on one side and wondered if a kidney was damaged.

He tried to make sense of the brutality of the interrogation. He was imprisoned to give him time to change his mind and cooperate with the goals of the mullahs. The Supreme Leader said they would give him incentives. But where was the incentive in a savage beating? If anything, it would make him more resistant to cooperation. It became clear when he looked at it from their perspective. They were holding a noose in front of him. They wanted him to fear for his life.

But he didn't fear for his life. He only feared not being true to his purpose. The light had shown him his purpose. It led him to the cave and to the experience of time. He would be true to his purpose.

He meditated until the pain lessened. He prayed for people, including those who had harmed him. He prayed for Behrouz, Maziar, and other disciples who were likely imprisoned. Uppermost in his mind was Rayhaneh. He was grateful for the time they had together. He offered prayers of gratitude for being so fortunate to know and love her. He prayed for Rayhaneh's father and mother and for his own mother.

Two days after the interrogation, a guard opened the cell door and told Ahmed to prepare for an important visitor. A few minutes later, Ayatollah Sohrabi stood at the door. Ahmed saw from his face that he had not come for a friendly chat.

"May I enter?"

Ahmed was still lying on his back. "As you wish."

The cleric stepped into the cell, but unlike the previous visit, he remained standing. Ahmed got to his feet, but the soreness made it difficult for him to straighten up.

The ayatollah reached out to help him when it looked like he would not be able to stand up on his own. "That's one of the reasons I've come to visit you, to apologize for what happened. I told you those people could get out of hand, but they were instructed not to touch you."

"Oh, really? Perhaps it was one of the incentives the Supreme Leader was talking about." He pulled up his shirt, exposing a number of ugly yellow and purple bruises. "Take a look at all the incentives."

The ayatollah looked away. When Ahmed pulled his shirt back down, the cleric said, "They went far beyond their authority."

Ahmed wondered if the ayatollah had come to hear his final decision. He was ready with it. "What other reason is there for your visit?" he demanded.

The ayatollah glanced around the small cell. He shook his head and made a face. "It pains me to see you here. This isn't the proper place for you."

"The proper place for me is wherever I happen to be."

The ayatollah frowned. "There are people, and I count myself among them, who think you should have a much better place in the world than a minuscule jail cell. What I am referring to is the place of honor due to a spiritual leader."

"I will choose this cell over evil."

The ayatollah shook his head. "You must try to understand the world from the perspective of our leaders. They are committed to their ideal of universal peace and justice under Islam. They don't see their goal as evil. They see the promise of global Islam as good and inevitable. Since your appearance in Jamkaran, you have become an important factor in their thinking. They see you as a vital accelerant toward what they know is good."

Ahmed shook his head. "All I have to do to envision what their ideal will bring about is to close my eyes. What I see are unspeakable horrors."

"They won't let go of you easily. I want to warn you that if you don't align yourself with their vision, much worse is coming than a beating at the hands of someone like Hamzeh."

"I cannot be part of a lie."

The ayatollah's face reddened, and Ahmed wondered if he was fighting back tears. "It's against my better judgment to tell you this because it could come back to harm me, but I want you to know that they intend to destroy you. I see you as a good person, and what you've said in your sermons is good. But you threaten them. If you don't cooperate with them, they will denounce you as a false Imam. They will destroy you first by exposing you as an AWOL *basiji*. They will also accuse you of murdering a young woman during the demonstration in Tehran. Once you've been stripped of your credibility, once your message has died in the hearts of the people who once flocked to your sermons, they will destroy you here in this prison. They will not hesitate to take your life."

It took Ahmed a long moment to absorb that anyone could be so twisted. "Truth has a life of its own," he said. "It can't be destroyed with lies."

"They can invent all the evidence they want against you. You won't have any defense against their accusations."

"I don't mean accusations about invented crimes. I mean the truth of my message."

"You are mistaken. The truth of the message comes from the truth about the messenger, and that's where they will destroy you."

"You and they think that is good?"

"I don't. They do. I'm just warning you."

Ahmed was comforted by the fact that the testimonies of the disciples were now circulating. They had gone out into the world and were filtering back into Iran. It was the understanding among the disciples that if he were assassinated or faced execution, his testimony would be released. The lies would be swept away. The truth about his journey would live on, and so would his message.

When Ahmed didn't reply, the ayatollah continued, "I'm obligated to report your recalcitrance to the Supreme Leader and the members of the Guardian Council. I know they'll be disappointed, but I've been instructed to tell you they still have an incentive to offer you."

"What is that?"

"I don't know the specifics, only that if you continue to re-sist acting in accordance with the prophecies, something more is coming that involves people who were part of your group. The leaders anticipate this final incentive will make you come around to them."

The next day, a guard came for Ahmed and led him blind-folded to the interrogation room. Hamzeh was seated behind the desk with a stack of documents in front of him that was an inch thicker than during the first interrogation. He pointed to a chair. When Ahmed sat down, he noticed the bulletproof vest on one side of the desk.

Hamzeh folded his hands together and rested his chin on them. He stared at Ahmed for more than a minute. He had a severe look on his face, enhanced by dark shadows around his eyes and dark eyebrows that contrasted with the gray of his short hair and trim beard.

He shook his head and snorted, "You are the Imam of Time?" He stared at Ahmed again for a long moment. "You fooled a lot of people, given the turnout at your 'sermons.' But I wonder what they would say if they knew about this?"

He picked up the bulletproof vest and held it for Ahmed to see. "This is what you were wearing when you were first brought here, so there isn't any use denying it's yours, is there?"

Ahmed shrugged but didn't say anything.

"People think God spared you when you were shot in Hama-dan. They think it was a miracle. But we examined this vest very closely and found evidence of an impact."

He pointed to a tear in the fabric. "This is what stopped the bullet, not God."

Hamzeh stood up and barked, "I'm confident that God didn't give you this vest. So who gave it to you?"

When Ahmed didn't answer, the interrogator rushed around the desk. With his face only a few inches from Ahmed's, he snarled, "I've been instructed not to touch you, but I don't know if I'll be able to restrain myself for long if you don't answer my questions."

"I don't know," said Ahmed.

Hamzeh made a motion with the flat of his hand as if he was about to hit him, but he turned and sat behind the desk again. He picked up a photograph and showed it to Ahmed. "Do you know this man?"

Ahmed's heart sank. It was an enlargement of Bahram's identity card photograph. He tried to control his reactions, but his face gave him away. The interrogator smiled. "There's no need for you to say anything. We know who gave it to you." He pointed to the bottom of the vest. He poked his finger into an incision in the fabric. "For security, we insert a hidden identification code in each of the vests, so from that, we were able to determine to whom the vest was issued. Not even Bahram knew about this."

He picked up two photographs. "And this man. Do you know him?"

Both were of Maziar. One of them showed him at the time of the rescue at the Jamkaran mosque, standing in front of the limousine while talking to the crowd. The other photograph was an enlargement of the identity photo on the Intelligence Ministry ID that Bahram had gotten for him.

Without waiting for an answer, Hamzeh put the photographs down, picked up another, and held it for Ahmed to see. "And this man, do you recognize him?"

It was a photograph of Behrouz taken at a stadium. He had removed his sunglasses, and his cap was pushed upward so that his entire face was visible.

When Ahmed said nothing, Hamzeh stood up and went to the door. He called in two guards. They were in the room in a flash and put the blindfold back over Ahmed's eyes. After making him stand, they forced his arms behind him and snapped handcuffs on his wrists.

"It's time to teach you what you need to be taught, and in a language you will understand," Hamzeh said.

They went through a series of corridors and down a flight of stairs to another series of corridors. Ahmed was able to follow by watching the guard's shoes from under the blindfold, but he became disoriented when they rounded a corner, and he lost sight of them. A guard shoved him from behind.

When the march came to a stop, he heard a door open. He followed the shoes until Hamzeh barked at him to stop.

"On your knees," he ordered.

When he hesitated, the interrogator jammed his knee into the back of one of Ahmed's legs and pushed down hard on his shoulders, forcing him to kneel. He ripped the blindfold off and pointed to the back of the room.

It was a large room with a high ceiling. At the far end, three blindfolded men were standing on chairs under a makeshift gallows, each with a thick noose around his neck. Their hands were tied behind their backs. A line of revolutionary guardsmen stood behind the chairs.

In an instant, Ahmed recognized the condemned men. He cried out, "Behrouz, Maziar, Bahram!"

All three shouted, "Imam! Is that you?"

Ahmed trembled all over his body. "How can you allow this?" he shouted, looking up at Hamzeh. "Let them go! They've done nothing wrong. Kill me in their place."

Behrouz struggled to free his hands, but a soldier gripped his arms from behind to keep him from falling off the chair. Behrouz shouted, "Don't yield to them, Imam! Stand firm!"

Bahram cried out, "They tortured us, but we gave these demons nothing, Imam. Nothing!"

Maziar shouted, "We were true to the light!"

Hamzeh said, "Enough of this!"

He made a pulling motion. The guardsman behind Behrouz yanked the chair from under him, and he dropped to where his feet were only inches from the floor. His legs kicked, trying to find something solid. A moment later, the guards pulled the chairs from under Maziar and Bahram.

Ahmed couldn't bear to look at their death throes. He lowered his head and closed his eyes. As tears rolled down his face, Hamzeh grabbed him by the hair and pulled his head back to force him to look.

"You must watch what happens to the enemies of God and His revolution. You must remember this. You must let it burn into your mind."

As he watched the life drain from them, Ahmed couldn't bear his agony. He cried out, "O Lord, forgive them, for they know not what they do!"

Hamzeh loosened his grip but kept hold of Ahmed's hair. "We're sending them to hell where they belong," he snarled. "Nothing needs to be forgiven."

It was several minutes before the bodies of Behrouz, Maziar, and Bahram became still. Their necks were bent sharply in the nooses. The guards stared at the dangling bodies without expression.

Hamzeh pulled Ahmed to his feet. He motioned to a guardsman holding the blindfold to put it back over Ahmed's eyes. They marched through corridors, up a staircase, and through more corridors. Ahmed had trouble walking. His body drooped, and he kept falling behind so that he lost sight of the shoes in front of him. Each time he fell back, someone behind him shoved him forward. They stopped, and Ahmed saw under the blindfold that he was in front of his cell. A guard removed his handcuffs and pushed him inside.

Before slamming the door shut, Hamzeh said, "We have more of your friends in custody, many more. What happens to them will be in your hands. Remember that."

# Chapter 42

Ahmed had never before felt such heaviness. It was as if leaden hands were reaching up from the ground to pull him down. He lay on the thin blankets, at times weeping, at other times with his knees drawn up to his chest to relieve painful tension in his abdomen. He tried not to think of the executions, but the image of Behrouz, Maziar, and Bahram dangling from nooses would not leave him. It was as Hamzeh wanted, burned forever in his mind. He fought the memory by reliving the many experiences he had shared with them.

He was certain it all had to have meaning, but he was unable to think clearly about it. He could only pray for strength. More disciples were in jail, possibly in the same building where he was being held. Hamzeh left no doubt that they were being used as hostages. Were Koroush and Baba Koushiyar among them? He would have to align with the Supreme Leader's goals for them to be spared. That had to be the final incentive that Ayatollah Sohrabi alluded to.

The day after the executions, a guard opened the cell door to announce a visitor. Ahmed was lying on the blanket, still in agony over the death of his friends. The heaviness throughout his body continued to immobilize him, and he was now troubled by a burning sensation in his face, arms, and legs.

He heard the familiar voice of Ayatollah Sohrabi. "May I speak with you?"

Ahmed remained on his back, staring at the ceiling light and ventilator. "We don't have anything to say to each other," he said, without looking at his visitor.

"I want to tell you that I didn't know about it beforehand. I thought some of your followers would urge you to reconsider. I'm speaking truthfully."

Ahmed continued to stare at the ceiling. "What you mean is that you thought they had been tortured to the point they agreed to urge me to change my mind."

"No, that's not so."

Ahmed made an effort to push himself up on one elbow so he could see the ayatollah. The cleric looked fresh, like he had a good night's sleep. His face was smooth and untroubled. His clerical garb and turban were spotless and without wrinkles.

"Please believe me," the ayatollah said. "I'm tormented by what happened. There was no justification for it, especially when viewed through the lens of the law. Legal procedures were not followed."

Ahmed growled, "You told me they had another incentive to offer me. You have other people in custody. Is that the incentive? If I refuse to cooperate, then they will be killed?"

"Unfortunately, it seems that is the truth, and I say that with deep regret."

"That makes them hostages," Ahmed replied. "So you've been sent here to negotiate their safety?"

"I want to make it clear that I only learned about the executions this morning. It was something I opposed. The Supreme Leader informed me about it when I met with him after morning prayers. He instructed me to make you understand that the lives of the others will be spared provided you cooperate."

"And this is not evil?"

"Not from his perspective."

"What about yours?"

The ayatollah shook his head. "I don't know what to think. I have to confess to confusion. But what I think isn't important."

"You already know what my answer will be. I'm certain none of the people you're holding hostage would disagree with it. It's what they would expect of me."

"You're mistaken. Not all of your friends agree with your stubbornness. There's one who disagrees."

"I don't believe you. Who are you speaking about?"

"The one I am referring to is Salman."

Ahmed looked down in confusion. He wondered if he had heard right. "Salman?"

"Yes, Salman al-Farisi, or someone who claims he is Salman al-Farisi."

"Is he in custody? Is he here in this jail?"

The ayatollah shook his head. "They have him at another facility, one that's also run by the Revolutionary Guard."

It took Ahmed a long moment to absorb that Salman was now in the present time. He said, "When I parted with him, he had chosen to stay in Yathrib. When was his return?"

"It was a week before you were arrested. That's what motivated the Supreme Leader to have you taken into custody."

Ahmed scrutinized the ayatollah's face to see if he was joking. "I don't see how they're related," he said.

"The prophecies say the Prophet Jesus will return about the same time as the Imam of Time, and together they will bring the truth of Islam to the world. You are the Imam of Time. Salman is Jesus."

"Where did he appear? He would have to appear in Damascus."

"No, that's what the prophecies say. It happened at the Agha Nour mosque in Isfahan. That will do since his appearance was captured by several of the mosque's surveillance cameras. He appeared among them just as people gathered for Friday prayers. It caused quite a stir, particularly with the clerics. The Revolutionary Guard took him into custody, and the matter has been thoroughly suppressed. When the time comes, they intend to release the videos showing his sudden appearance and proclaim that he's Jesus. I've seen the videos myself. I have to admit that it's astonishing. It started with a glow, and suddenly there he was."

"Have you spoken with him?"

"Yes, I've met with him several times. It's interesting that nothing he's told me contradicts what you've told me about your experiences."

"Then you know they were miraculous."

The ayatollah shrugged. "Yes, of course, even the Supreme Leader accepts that they were miraculous. But you know that miracles can be interpreted in many ways. We interpret them as happening in fulfillment of prophecy."

Ahmed shook his head, stunned by the cynicism of the clerics. He and Salman were to play a role in advancing the goals of the mullahs.

The ayatollah said, "I met with Salman this morning, and he wanted me to convey to you that he hopes you will do the right thing. He hopes you will join with him in advancing the cause of God's religion."

"He knows he'll be executed if I refuse."

The ayatollah shook his head. "We have other uses for him. You're the ones facing execution. You and your 'disciples,' as you call them."

"You don't need to kill people who believe in me. Kill me if you must, but leave them alone."

"They would become nuisances with the potential to disrupt the Islamic system. They would continue preaching your cult of God Longing. So they must perish as well. You can save them by joining with us, because if you do, that will take the wind out of them. I can promise you we will be merciful with them because they will no longer represent a threat."

Ahmed bowed his head. He had nothing to say except that he could not go along with them.

The ayatollah watched him for a moment. "What a waste it would be to throw your life away, Ahmed. I, for one, would be grieved by this. You may not believe this, but I've grown rather fond of you. I think everything about you is good and exemplary, but you have a serious flaw, and that is stubbornness. You stubbornly hold on to what can't prevail. The future of the world is Islam. It can be no other way because it is the will of God for it to be so, and it is his will for us to bring it about. We are commanded by him to make it happen."

Ahmed looked up at the ayatollah. "I can't be part of what is false."

The cleric made a show of sadness. "This is the last opportunity for you to come to your senses. I told you days ago what they intend to do if you refuse to join with them. They will make accusations against you. They'll torture you until you sign a confession. Do you want to go through that?"

"I will experience their evil, but I will not be part of it."

The ayatollah stood at the cell door. "I warn you that I won't be able to help you. No one will." When Ahmed didn't reply, he said with impatience, "Have it your way then."

He turned and left the cell.

Ahmed spent three days without contact with anyone, not even with guards. Food trays were slid in silence through the opening in the cell door, and they were removed in silence after he pushed the tray back through. On the fourth day, a guard ordered him to put on his blindfold and took him to Hamzeh's interrogation room. The interrogator was seated behind the desk with several sheets of paper in front of him. Two guards of sturdy build stood nearby.

Hamzeh glowered at Ahmed. He pointed to a chair and pushed a document forward on the desk. "Read this, sign it, and I will go easy on you."

As he leaned forward to read the document, he remembered the camera mounted in a corner. It had a clear side view of him and a full view of the desk. After reading the first few lines, he was shocked to see that it was a prepared confession in which he acknowledged committing both crimes against God and crimes against man. The document stated that he was born in Aliabad and was a volunteer of the Aliabad contingent of the paramilitary wing of the Revolutionary Guard; he was sent with other volunteers to Tehran following disputed election results; he made illegal use of a firearm issued to him for his personal protection to shoot an unarmed woman; he fled to avoid apprehension by the authorities; after a lapse of six weeks during which he remained in hiding, he attempted to fool the people and avoid justice by entering into the sacred well in Jamkaran through surreptitious means; to carry out his deceit, he climbed out of the well and claimed to be the long-awaited Imam of Time.

Ayatollah Sohrabi had warned him of their intentions, but he was still shaken. It was a brazen lie to destroy belief in him and his message.

Rather than looking at the interrogator, he looked up at the camera. "This document is false. I didn't prepare it, and I will not sign it."

Hamzeh smiled. It was a clever smile that didn't reach his eyes. "Do you deny that you are Ahmed, born in Aliabad, and that your mother is Amineh and your father Abdollah?"

When Ahmed remained silent, Hamzeh reached into a drawer and took out the knotted cord that he had worn under his shirt ever since his conversion to Zoroastrianism.

"What is this?"

"A knotted cord."

"It looks like something the fire worshipers wear. What is the meaning of it?"

"It was given to me when I returned to the religion of my forefathers. Its purpose is to remind the wearer to live a virtuous life."

Hamzeh leaned back. "You were born into Islam. So now we have it from you that you apostatized." He waved the cord at Ahmed. "Who gave you this?"

"The High Priest Shapur."

"Where was this? In Yazd?"

"At a fire temple in Rey."

Hamzeh sneered. "There are no Zoroastrian ceremonies carried out in Rey. That fire temple is an ancient ruin. It's preserved only because it's historical."

"My conversion took place when I visited Rey with a caravan. It was there that I met Shapur and converted to the religion of my ancestors. It was he who conducted the initiation ceremony. It was I who tied the knots into the cord to signify my commitment to live by the virtues of the religion."

Hamzeh snarled, "So, we're back in time, are we? You're insulting my intelligence with your fiction." He turned to the two guards. "You heard him. Has he insulted your intelligence, too?"

They both said in unison, "Yes, commander, he has."

Again speaking to the guards, Hamzeh said, "Do you know what you're to do when a prisoner insults your intelligence?"

"Yes, commander."

He pointed to Ahmed. "Teach the apostate a lesson."

One of the guards grabbed Ahmed's hair and pulled his head back. The other slapped his face and head with the flat of his hand. Warm blood began running down from his nose to his chin and into his beard. When one guard was tired, the other one took over. Ahmed clenched his teeth to keep from groaning or crying out from the stinging blows.

After a minute, Hamzeh signaled for them to stop. When the guards backed away, he stared at Ahmed, perplexed. "This doesn't have to happen. I told you I would go easy on you if you signed this document. That's really all I want from you. Sign it, and the interrogation will be over. I give you my word." He pushed it toward Ahmed and held out a pen.

Ahmed was dizzy from the beating, and his vision was blurred. His face hurt, and some of his upper teeth on one side felt loose. He wiped the blood from his mouth and nose with his shirt. It took him a moment to focus on the document. He shook his head to show that he would not sign it.

Hamzeh shrugged. "Fine! Now that we've established from your own mouth that you're an apostate, we can move on. I have more questions for you."

He pulled a thick file folder from a drawer and extracted a document that he placed in front of him. After examining it for a moment, he held it up for Ahmed to see. It was a list of names. He began reading them. They were the names used for the authors of the testimonies of time.

"Who are these people?"

When Ahmed didn't answer, Hamzeh said, "I heard your fictional tale when I first questioned you. It was insulting to our beloved Prophet. These people have also made up stories that are insulting to our Prophet. They are insulting because they are blasphemous, and their blasphemy is being spread on the Internet. I want to know who these blasphemers are."

Ahmed closed his eyes. He could see the disciples in his mind. They had gathered with him to share their experiences of time and to record them so that they would be available to the world. They were his friends and companions. He would sooner die a hundred painful deaths than reveal anything about them.

When he didn't answer, Hamzeh shook his fist at him. "I don't have the authority to kill you, but I know how to make you wish you were dead."

When he continued to remain silent, Hamzeh signaled to the guards. One of them yanked the chair from under him, and he fell to the floor. The guards kicked and punched his chest, back, and groin. They kicked his legs and stomped on his feet. During the worst of it, Ahmed prayed for his tormentors.

When Hamzeh signaled for them to stop, the guards lifted him from the floor and propped him back on the chair. He was doubled over in pain and thought he was going to vomit. He gasped for air until the feeling of nausea went away.

"Do you think I enjoy this?" Hamzeh demanded. "All I want is for you to cooperate and answer my questions. And sign the confession. It will be much better for you if you do."

Ahmed closed his eyes and thought of the cave. He went into it as a place of refuge. He said in a soft but audible voice, "O Lord, bring them light, for they are living in darkness."

The interrogator jumped to his feet. He shouted, "You are the one living in darkness. You are the one who is in rebellion against God."

Ahmed stared at Hamzeh's furious face. He said, "My journey began in a cave not far from Aliabad. A light appeared to me, and when I asked, 'Who are you?' the light said, 'I am you, and you are me.' If you allow me, Hamzeh, I will tell you what the light meant by that."

Hamzeh leaned forward over the desk. He shook his fist and screamed with such fury that spittle flew from his mouth. "I am not you, and you are not me. I am the follower of truth, and you are not, and that is why I am the interrogator and you are the one being interrogated."

Ahmed said softly, "It is the desire of our Creator that we love one another."

Hamzeh barked at the guards, "Get him out of here!"

Before Ahmed was led away, Hamzeh said, "Everything I want to know I'll get from you one way or another. You won't be able to hide anything from me."

# Chapter 43

The interrogation continued for several weeks, sometimes every day, at other times after a lapse of a day or two. The guards who took part in the beatings were often different, but the interrogator was always the square-faced Hamzeh with his cropped gray hair and beard and dark accusatory eyes.

During one of the interrogations, he showed Ahmed photos of a dozen disciples, all of them wearing jail clothes. They were the disciples most often involved in setting up the sermons and ensuring security. They must have been arrested along with Behrouz and Maziar.

"Admit it," Hamzeh bellowed in Ahmed's face. "They're among those who wrote those blasphemous fictions."

On another occasion, he showed Ahmed photos of people who were at the temple dedication. They looked like screenshots from broadcasts rather than original photos.

"Who are these people?" Hamzeh demanded.

One of the photographs showed Koroush, another Baba Koushiyar. With their wraparound sunglasses and hats pulled low, they were difficult to recognize. One of the photos showed Rayhaneh with a small group of religious representatives. Ahmed hid his fright when he saw her. But with the large sunglasses and the hijab pulled around her face, she had a typical Shi'ite appearance, and he was certain she could be taken for any of hundreds of women. He prayed she was safe.

"Who is this woman? Answer me!"

Ahmed was relieved. If Hamzeh had to ask about them, it meant they were safe so far. When he refused to reveal anything, the beatings followed. On one occasion, the guards clamped electrical wires to his toes. At Hamzeh's nod, they gave him searing jolts of electricity. The pain in his feet and legs was so excruciating that he couldn't keep from screaming. During another interrogation, a guard whipped the soles of his bare feet with a thick electrical cable. His feet were swollen for days after, and he had trouble walking to and from the interrogation room. During the torture, he escaped into the cave. It became a mental refuge where he communed with the light and prayed for his tormentors. Praying for them gave him greater strength to endure their torments.

Between the interrogations, he remained in solitary confinement. When he was first jailed, the food was edible; now it was watery, foul-smelling, and had a bad taste. He had to force himself to eat, but the food made him sick, and he lost weight. He was sure it was another way to break his will by weakening him physically, and he endured it from within his mental sanctuary.

The interrogations ended without anyone notifying him they were finished. The guards ceased coming to his cell. As each day went by, he anticipated they would come for him again in the morning, but nothing happened. He wondered if this uncertainty was intended as another form of torture. Maybe they were preparing something else. He feared they would threaten to hang more of his friends as a way to force him to sign the confession. Hamzeh would bring him to the execution room and give him an ultimatum. "Sign or they die."

Ten days after the last interrogation, three guards came to his cell and ordered him to put on the blindfold. He followed them through several corridors. When he was told to take the blindfold off, he was in a room with hot shower stalls. He was allowed to shower for twenty minutes. He was almost speechless when the guards provided him with soap, scented hair shampoo, and a fresh set of jail clothes.

When he asked the reason for these courtesies, one of the guards said, "You will find out."

Blindfolded again, he followed them up three flights of

stairs. He ended up in a narrow room where he was allowed to remove the blindfold. It looked like a waiting room. It was furnished with benches along one wall and medium-sized portraits of the Supreme Leader and Ayatollah Khomeini. In addition to the entrance, the room had a second door with a small window. He sat in quiet thought, wondering if he should risk looking through it. Whatever was on the other side was his likely destination.

Half an hour went by before a revolutionary guard officer wearing a holstered sidearm opened the door and motioned to him. As he followed the officer through the door, he was shocked to find himself in a courtroom. Numerous television cameras with bright lights that obscured the men behind them were aimed at him. An older man with a trim gray beard, wearing a suit without a tie, was seated behind an enormous desk mounted on a platform, a stack of files in front of him. A name plaque in front of him identified him as the judge. Large portraits of the Supreme Leader and Ayatollah Khomeini were mounted on the wall behind him, flanked by flags of the Islamic Republic. Two men in civilian clothes sat behind cluttered tables in front of the judge's bench.

It was small for a courtroom, with no benches; only a single chair was placed at a distance from the judge. Other chairs were pushed against the walls.

The judge pointed to the lone chair, and with a hint of anger, he said, "Sit there. You are to remain silent unless you are asked a question. If you speak without permission, you will be removed from the courtroom, and the trial will proceed without you."

After Ahmed sat down, the judge conferred in a low voice with the two men seated behind the tables. When they both nodded, he turned toward the courtroom. "In the name of God, the merciful and kind, this court of Islamic justice is now in session."

The judge picked up a document from a thick stack in front of him. "We are present to hear evidence of the following crimes against God and the people that are believed to have been committed by the defendant." He read from the list. "The crimes against God are as follows: waging war against God, making mischief in the land, blasphemy, desecration of a holy site, and apostasy. The crimes against the people are: murder, evasion of justice, and abandonment of duty.

Ahmed had tried to steel himself for this moment. Ayatollah Sohrabi had laid out what was in store for him, but he was still shaken now that it was happening. Just as the ayatollah warned, he would be destroyed through exposure of his contemporary origin, and he would be accused of crimes he had not committed, all with the intention of undermining belief in him and his message. The presence of so many cameras meant the trial was being broadcast live or recorded for later broadcast after censors reviewed and edited the material.

The judge said to Ahmed, "Are you Ahmed, son of Abdollah and Amineh, born to them in Aliabad?" He gave Ahmed's age and date of birth.

Ahmed had no way to defend himself against the accusations. Since it was a show trial with a predetermined outcome, he decided it was best not to speak at all, but to remain in polite silence. He folded his hands in his lap. He closed his eyes and said silent prayers for the people in the courtroom.

The judge stared at him with a cold expression. "Let it be recorded that the defendant refuses to identify himself."

The judge began calling witnesses. As they were called, they came out through a door at one side of the judge's bench and sat on a chair on the platform.

The first was Omid, the leader of the paramilitary volunteers of Aliabad. He verified Ahmed's identity and gave a brief account of his membership in the militia and his role in organizing cultural and religious events sponsored by the paramilitary organization. He explained that the Aliabad contingent was mobilized following the disputed election.

"Ahmed was among those sent to Tehran to help contain outbreaks of violence instigated by demonstrators. He was assigned to a barracks near Niloufar Square."

The next witness was the barracks commander who had

given the inflammatory speech before the deployment of motorcycle squadrons to the streets.

One of the men seated behind the desks in front of the judge's bench stood up to question the commander. He was not introduced as the prosecutor, but that appeared to be his role. He held up a handgun that had a tag dangling from the trigger. He handed the gun to the commander. "Do you recognize this weapon?"

The commander nodded. "Yes, it was among those given to certain members of the barracks and also to some of the militia that came to us from Aliabad."

"Was the defendant among those issued a handgun?"

"Yes. Because of his standing in the Aliabad militia, he was given one of them."

"Is this the one he was issued?

The barracks commander turned it over in his hands and pointed to the serial number. "According to our records, this is the one issued to the defendant."

The handgun resembled the Makarov that was confiscated from the man who tried to assassinate him in Hamadan. Ahmed worried they had learned of his Tehran safe house and discovered the firearm during a search. If so, they would have found much more than the handgun. But as he watched the barracks commander examine the weapon, he thought it was more likely a firearm from their armory. It would be easy to select one and create false paperwork. Possibly it was the very weapon that killed the young woman.

"These were issued for self-defense," the commander said. "We were concerned the demonstrators would attack our volunteers. They were to be used for self-defense only."

It was clear to Ahmed where the testimony was going. A witness or witnesses would be called next to claim he shot the young woman. He closed his eyes and remembered the horror of that moment.

The next witness was the burly Reza, the motorcycle squadron leader. He glared at Ahmed as he sat in the chair near the judge. He identified Ahmed as his "motorcycle companion" during the demonstration. He confirmed Ahmed was carrying a weapon and that it was for defensive purposes only.

"Did you see him use this weapon in a manner that was not authorized?"

"I did. He was supposed to assist me in dispersing the demonstrators near Niloufar Square, but I lost sight of him. Someone alerted me that he was about to shoot. I turned to see. He was not in any danger. I shouted to him to put the gun down, but at that moment, he fired. The bullet struck a young woman who was standing off to the side of the boulevard. After that, I saw him run away down a side street."

More witnesses were called, including a forensic expert who tied the bullet that killed the woman to the gun exhibited in the court. Other witnesses testified that after Ahmed failed to return to the barracks, a search for him began. Inquiries were made in Aliabad, and when he could not be located, he was declared a deserter.

The next witness was an elderly mullah. It was the cleric who approached Ahmed after he emerged from the well. His eyes darted from side to side, and his hands trembled as he fidgeted with prayer beads. Ahmed wondered if he was there voluntarily.

The prosecutor pointed to Ahmed. "Is this the man who came out of the sacred well in Jamkaran?"

"It looks like him, but it's hard to say for sure because he was not dressed as he is now."

The prosecutor lifted a box from the floor and placed it on his desk. He took out the flowing garment of time and the black turban. He unfolded the garment and held it up for the cleric to see.

"Is this what he was dressed in?"

"Well, it looks like it, yes."

"When you went up to him to ask who he was, did he say to you, 'I am he who is awaited. I am the Imam of Time.'?"

The cleric glanced at Ahmed, then looked down at the prayer beads. He was almost inaudible when he said, "Yes."

"Is there a way to get into the well from underneath?"

"There's a small door, yes, because the petitions pile up and have to be removed from time to time to make room. We know that the Imam of Time is aware of these petitions the moment they're dropped into the well, so we can remove them later. We put them in boxes and store them in a room next to the well."

"Is the door sealed so that it will show if it has been opened or tampered with?"

"Yes, the seal has to be broken to open the door."

The next witnesses were agents from the Intelligence Ministry. They were part of a team dispatched from Tehran to investigate the appearance of the Imam. Ahmed thought that they must have been part of the investigative group that Bahram led.

One of the agents testified that they arrived that very day and examined the well from top to bottom. It appeared that the seal had been tampered with. "We concluded that he had an accomplice, someone with access to the well who resealed it after the accused entered it," the agent said, looking at Ahmed.

Obvious questions were never asked, such as whether an accomplice had been identified or why the Supreme Leader and the president would declare his appearance authentic if their investigations showed that he could have entered the well from the maintenance room. Asking such questions should have been the role of a defense attorney, but Ahmed had never been visited by an attorney. He wondered if the man sitting at the desk next to the prosecutor was his attorney. He scratched his jaw and smiled often, and yawned or rubbed his eyes from time to time. When asked whether he had questions for the witnesses, he always said he did not. Ahmed concluded that he was a prop, his name appearing in court documents so that it could not be said he had been denied legal representation.

The bright camera lights were bracketed on Ahmed the entire time. As the trial dragged on, he was saddened that countless people who had placed hope in him would now think of him as a deceiver and his sermons a lie. His only defense lay in his testimony of time. Had it been released yet? Perhaps it had been. Perhaps it was the revelation of his experience of time that precipitated the show trial. He had no way of knowing one way or the other, but if his testimony was not yet public, it would soon be. People hungry for truth would read it. They would read the dozens of other testimonies. The truth could not be suppressed; it could not be destroyed by a cold, cynical sham of a trial.

When it was over, the judge said to Ahmed, "We will make a determination about the charges against you based on the testimony presented today and other evidence. You will be notified of the verdict."

He said to the guards. "Take him away."

# Chapter 44

Alone in his cell, Ahmed awaited the inevitable guilty verdict. He prayed for the judge and the people who had borne false witness against him. He did not feel animosity for them, only sadness that they were captives of a blinding dogma. He prayed they would one day become free of it.

Five days after the trial, a guard slipped a court document through the food tray slot at the bottom of the door. It was the verdict, signed by the judge. It listed the charges against him and gave the verdict after each: guilty.

A week to the day after receiving the verdict, he learned the sentence from another court document: death by hanging. The last paragraph noted that the sentence would be carried out expeditiously due to the gravity of the crimes. As he read the document, he felt gripped by dread, but it soon faded, replaced by acceptance. He had sought understanding, and his experience of time gave him what he sought. He came to know the spirit within that prompts people to seek God, and he had been loyal to the spirit. It mattered not that his loyalty brought him to condemnation by people who had not allowed themselves to understand the nature of the spirit that was in them, too.

He let his mind drift through the important events of his life, particularly his experiences of time. The endpoint of the streams of memory was always Rayhaneh. He thanked the Creator again and again for the privilege of knowing her, even if so briefly. He was saddened she would grieve for him, but he found happiness in the certainty that an important destiny lay before her. He prayed for her and her destiny.

He let go of concerns and remembered the first time he had gone into the cave above Zarringol. He was amused that he had become so frightened that he ran away when there was nothing to fear. He remembered how the light appeared to him when he braved his fear and went back into the cave, how it filled the cave with an exquisite brightness that enveloped him.

He closed his eyes and brought the light into his mind so that it was just as vivid as it had appeared to him in the cave. He was able to sustain the image for a long time, but at some point he became aware of a luminance outside of him as well. It penetrated his eyelids, as if he was stretched out on a sandy beach in the warming sun. He opened his eyes. The luminance was there! It was just as it had been in the cave, bright and good and comforting.

He said, "Thank you, O light, for all you have given me."

The next morning, when a meal tray was usually slid through the slot at the bottom of the door, Ahmed was surprised when a guard knocked on the cell door and asked for permission to open it.

"Yes, of course."

The guard, slim, in his mid twenties, and wearing the usual trim Shi'ite beard and moustache, was holding a food tray. He had a glowing smile.

"Imam, my wife prepared a favorite dish and asked me to bring it to you."

It took him a moment to realize the guard had addressed him as Imam. Throughout his time there, the floor staff had treated him with professional gruffness. They were never particularly harsh, only demanding compliance with their orders. The guards who took part in the beatings and torture were members of the Revolutionary Guard, separate from the jail staff. They were cold people trained in the methods of torture, and he only encountered them when he was with Hamzeh. The jail staff was largely made up of people from poor backgrounds who worked out of need for a job.

"I think you will like this, Imam," the guard said as he handed Ahmed the tray. When Ahmed thanked him, the guard said,

"Please forgive me for having to close this door again, but I'm obligated to do so."

It was the same over the next few days. Various guards brought him specially prepared food, addressed him as Imam, and spoke to him in a reverent tone.

Ahmed wondered about it. When the young guard came again with a specially prepared meal, Ahmed said, "You're so kind. Is this the kindness you show the condemned? If so, it's commendable."

The guard shook his head. "We saw a glow coming from your cell, Imam. We heard words in our minds that made us understand and made us regret any harshness we've shown you."

A few days later, an older guard took him from the cell without a blindfold and led him to the shower room. He enjoyed a shower for longer than ever before. The guard gave him special soap and shampoo, along with fresh, pale blue jail clothes. When he was dressed, the guard said, "We wanted to prepare you, Imam. You have visitors arriving soon. I'll take you now to the room where you'll meet with them."

He restrained a burst of joy. The only visit he had ever received was from Ayatollah Sohrabi.

"Who are the visitors?"

"I don't know, Imam. That hasn't been shared with me. But I'm told you will be very pleased."

He waited with strained patience. The room was larger than the interrogation room and was furnished with a few chairs and a table. He looked around for a hidden camera, but could not find any trace of one.

After a ten-minute wait, he heard the sound of footsteps in the corridor. A guard opened the door and stood aside. Ahmed could not believe his eyes. Rayhaneh and his mother, wearing tight head scarves, rushed past the guard and threw their arms around him, tears flowing.

Ahmed pulled them to him. He had almost forgotten what it was like to be so close to those he loved. As she wiped tears away, Rayhaneh said, "I promised myself I wouldn't cry all over you, but I can't help it."

He kissed his mother and told her he prayed constantly for her safety. He wrapped his arms around Rayhaneh and said how much he missed her.

Rayhaneh said, "I've been sick with worry about you. Everyone has been praying for you."

Ahmed wondered if they knew he had been condemned to death. They had to know about the trial since it was broadcast, but not necessarily about the verdict or the sentence. He decided to wait before telling them.

Uncertain if they were being monitored, he put his finger to his lips to show them to speak in a low voice. He whispered, "Tell me about the others. Are they safe?"

"Koroush, Baba Koushiyar, and most of the other disciples are safe. The only ones we don't know about are the disciples who were arrested when you were."

He told them about Behrouz, Maziar, and Bahram. Rayhaneh and Amineh bowed their heads.

"I don't know about the fate of the others," said Ahmed. "They were being used as bargaining chips to get me to cooperate with the clerics, but I couldn't do it. I don't believe any of them would accept it if I joined with the mullahs. I don't know what has happened to them, but I fear the worst."

"None of us would fault you for refusing them, not even at the cost of our lives," said Rayhaneh.

"I was put on trial because I wouldn't cooperate with them. I suppose you saw that on TV?"

Rayhaneh struggled to restrain tears. "It was a cruelty. They were intent on destroying you, but I know that not everyone was fooled by it."

"The hardest part for people to understand is that I'm Ahmed of Aliabad. I can't deny it, nor would I ever deny that Amineh is my mother. But there is also the truth of my experience of time. What about my testimony? Has it been released?"

"Yes, the government has made every effort to block it, but it's still getting through. We've heard that some people have been arrested for sharing it online. People are making copies on CDs and flash drives and passing them around. So it's out there."

"When people read my testimony, they will know the truth," he said.

Instead of sitting at the table, they remained standing so they could remain close to one another. Ahmed's mother kept breaking into tears, and Ahmed wrapped his arms around her to console her.

Rayhaneh brightened. "I have something very good to tell you, my Ahmed."

Ahmed took her hands and raised them to his lips. "What is it? Tell me the good news."

She looked up into his eyes. "I'm pregnant. It was confirmed last week. Your child is within me."

Rayhaneh took his hand and placed it over her abdomen. "It's too early to feel any movement. But your child is here, growing."

"I can't wait to be a grandmother," said Amineh. "I will spoil the child for sure."

Ahmed felt a rush of joy, but he squeezed his eyes together from the pain of knowing he would never see his child. He kissed Rayhaneh's hands again and looked at her with tenderness. "I can't think of a better mother for the child."

She had to suspect he would not live to be the father of his child. He had to tell them of the verdict and the sentence, but he hesitated to shatter their joy about her pregnancy.

"It's a miracle you're here," he finally said as a way to delay telling them about his approaching end. "How did you arrange the visit?"

"You can thank Abu Sufyan," Ahmed's mother said. "His gold coins made this happen."

She had made several visits to the Ministry of Justice to ask for permission to visit, but her requests were always ignored. The day after the trial, she learned where he was imprisoned and visited the jail administrator. She showed him some of the Byzantine coins. She explained their value to collectors and hinted there were more. The administrator informed her two days later that he couldn't make the decision on his own. There were people higher up who needed to be consulted. In the end, she gave them all but five of the coins.

"I hope you're not upset that I bribed them."

Ahmed shook his head. "May they benefit from Abu Sufyan's coins."

Their time was running out. He plucked up the courage to tell them about the verdict and the sentence. Looking in turn at Rayhaneh and his mother, he said, "You know the trial was nothing more than a show." When they nodded, he went on, "The outcome was predetermined. I can't hide it from you. I've been notified that I was found guilty of all the charges. I am to be executed soon."

The women burst into tears. Rayhaneh leaned her head against Ahmed's chest. Her shoulders shook from sobbing.

"We have to be accepting of what can't be changed," Ahmed said.

"Is there no end to their evil?" Rayhaneh cried. "They destroy everything that is good. Even the temple has been destroyed. They left nothing standing. They even tore out the staircases."

Ahmed's eyes became moist. "It will be built again. And others will be built like it."

Rayhaneh reached up to touch his tears. She was quiet for a moment. "I do have some more good news for you, my Ahmed. The number of people who claim the experience of time has now reached nearly a thousand. Even the son of Yazdegerd has appeared, but it turns out he is not the emperor's son. He was appointed to the court as an adviser because of his foreknowledge. He's now in Germany. The disciples are recording his testimony, and they say that what he's revealing is astonishing."

Ahmed said. "He will tell us about what was lost."

"We're growing in strength," Rayhaneh said. "Hundreds of testimonies are being prepared."

Ahmed told her about Salman. "I always hoped he would return. They have him in prison, too. They want to use him as Jesus. They wanted to use both of us."

Rayhaneh said, "Koroush, Baba Koushiyar, and the disciples who are still free have been organizing people throughout the country. They became emboldened because of the lies of the trial. They're preaching the truth of the flame within. Everywhere they go, they draw huge crowds. I've spoken at some of these events. I spoke about what I witnessed on the boulevard."

They strove to say as much as possible during the last few minutes. The guard soon opened the door and leaned in. "Imam, I'm sorry to say that time is up."

He glanced over his shoulder toward the corridor and looked back at Ahmed. "I think I can give you another ten minutes, Imam, but no more than that."

Ahmed's mother was surprised. "Did you hear that? He called you Imam!"

He smiled with warmth. "The guards know the truth."

He gathered Rayhaneh and his mother into his arms and held them tight. He wished he could hold them forever.

When they began to weep, he wiped a tear from Rayhaneh's cheek. "You're a woman of great destiny, Rayhaneh. Your experiences were given to you for a great purpose. It's now for you to fulfill your purpose."

He said to his mother, "Rayhaneh is your daughter. Help her to fulfill her purpose just like you helped me fulfill mine."

When the guard came again, Ahmed stood back from them. Before they reached the door, they turned to look at him for the last time. Rayhaneh's face was torn with anguish. When they were gone and the door was closed, Ahmed felt that his heart had just been ripped from his chest.

# Chapter 45

Ahmed prayed for everyone but himself. He prayed for everyone: for Rayhaneh and their unborn child, for his mother, for the disciples who were imprisoned, and for the disciples who were still free. He prayed for the people who were now stepping forward to share their experiences of time with the world.

He prayed for the political prisoners still in jail, and for the ones who had been released but suffered from the physical and emotional trauma of their confinement. He prayed for the people who had harmed him: for Hamzeh and the brutal guards; for the judge and the prosecutor at his trial; for the Supreme Leader and the members of the Guardian Council.

He never found a shortage of people to include in his prayers. When he ran out of people who harmed him, he said prayers of thankfulness for the people he was certain were praying for him.

It was always a delight to see the guards. They were courteous; they had kind things to say; they continued to bring him treats their wives prepared. But as the days wore on, he could see a transformation in their faces. It became his measure of the time remaining to him because they had to know when he was to be executed. The greater their sadness for him, the closer it had to be.

When the day came, the young guard who was the first to bring him a home-cooked meal opened the cell door after asking for permission. "It grieves me to inform you that the time has come, Imam, and that I must ask you to put on the blindfold."

Ahmed complied and went with the guard. The guard led him gently by the arm to a room where he could remove the blindfold. It was windowless, without furnishings, about twice the size of his cell.

"You will be joined here soon by someone else," the guard said.

Ahmed sat on the floor, his back to the wall, and he tried not to think about anything except for the light of the cave, his source of comfort, but he couldn't help but wonder who else was being brought there. One of the disciples?

Fifteen minutes later, the door opened. A guard stood aside, and a tall, well-built man with a blindfold stepped into the room. When the door closed behind him, he took off the blindfold and squinted because of the bright ceiling light.

"Salman!" Ahmed cried.

He looked at least fifteen years older than when Ahmed parted with him at the Farewell Pass. His face was drawn, and he seemed weary to the extreme.

"Yes, it's me, Ahmed. They're going to execute us together."

Ahmed jumped to his feet and embraced him, kissing him on both cheeks in the Persian fashion.

"How can it be that they'll execute you? I thought you were cooperating with them."

"Why would you think that?"

"Sohrabi told me you wanted him to tell me to do the right thing by joining with you in cooperating with them—you as Jesus and me as their Mahdi."

"Sohrabi is a liar. I told him I didn't want to have anything to do with them and to tell you that I'm not afraid to die. He told me the same thing about you, but I knew you better. I called him a liar to his face."

They sat on the floor and leaned back against the wall. "When we said goodbye at the Farewell Pass," Salman said, "I could never have imagined it was going to end this way."

Ahmed asked him about the intervening years. Salman told him stories of battles and raids. "I got tired of all the killing, the plunder, and the rape. Before going on my journey, the most blood I'd ever seen was from a nosebleed, and there I was in the middle of a river of blood. I contributed to the river. Over time, I became very sick in my soul. But I have to admit that I only have myself to blame. I should have gone with you."

"Sohrabi said you returned inside the Agha Nour mosque in Isfahan."

"That's true. It was strange. I was in military gear at the time because we were going into battle. All of a sudden, I was sitting in a pulpit with all these people in front of me. The mosque was packed. Everyone stared at me like I was from another planet. Another thing that's strange is that I was gone for nearly twenty years, but when I came back, only two months had gone by."

Ahmed told him about the disciples. "That's how it is for everyone. For me, it was six weeks."

"Here's something you won't believe. I knew about you before my journey began. I never went to any of your sermons, but I remember hearing that someone tried to assassinate the Imam. When I first saw you in Yathrib, I knew where you were from, but I didn't connect you with the Imam."

Ahmed stared at the door. Any minute now, the guards would come for them. After a few moments of silence, Ahmed said, "Now that it's close, how do you feel about dying? Are you frightened?"

"I had trembling hands when they told me it was time. Talking with you helps. And you, how do you feel?"

"My body's afraid, but my soul isn't."

"For everything I've done, I fear for my soul."

"You don't have anything to fear. You don't believe in that hellfire nonsense anymore, do you?"

"I'm not so sure."

"The only hell is the one that we create for ourselves in this world."

"After you die, what's it like then?"

Ahmed told him about his experiences with the light, that it was loving, good, and accepting.

A few minutes later, a group of revolutionary guardsmen unlocked the door and pulled it open.

"It's time," one of them said.

They ordered Ahmed and Salman to put their hands behind their backs. When they stood up and complied, the guardsmen snapped on handcuffs and put the blindfolds back over their eyes.

A guardsman walked alongside Ahmed, his hand on Ahmed's shoulder to guide him, while another did the same with Salman. They went through a corridor, down a staircase, and through more corridors.

While they were going down the stairs, Salman said, "I never thought I'd have the opportunity to say this to you. Since I'm never going to have the opportunity again, I'll say it: I really do regret that I came up with the idea for the trench."

"It couldn't be any other way," Ahmed said. "It was like you used to say, 'We can experience the past, but we can't change it.'"

"I know, but it was my idea, and I really, really do regret it."

They were led into a room. People were talking in low voices when they entered, but the talking ceased. Though he couldn't see, Ahmed remembered what he had seen before: a scaffold at one end of the room, and chairs for the condemned to stand on, and other chairs for the executioners so they could get high enough to fit the nooses around the necks of the condemned.

Ahmed was pushed from behind. He walked forward with reluctant steps until someone pulled him by the arm in another direction. He was made to stop, and several people snapped at him to turn around.

He heard Hamzeh's voice off to one side. "Get them onto the chairs! Send the enemies of God to hell!"

While guards held him on each side, Ahmed stepped onto the chair. He heard other chairs being dragged forward, and he imagined the executioners were getting on them. Until then, he had been calm, but now he felt his chest and throat tighten and his heart beating faster.

As the thick noose was placed around his neck, he thought of Rayhaneh, and he thought of their child. Would it be a girl? A boy? He imagined holding the swaddled infant in his arms and gazing into its beautiful eyes. He wished he could be there to guide the child into adulthood. Surely it was going to be a child of great destiny.

He felt the breath of the executioner on his neck as he fit the noose. The rope was thick and scratchy where it touched his skin. When the executioner tightened the loop, it dug under his jaw where it joined his throat, and the knot pressed hard against the back of his head.

Salman couldn't have been more than two arm-lengths away. Ahmed heard him say, "I bid you farewell, Ahmed."

As the executioner made final adjustments, Ahmed thought of the light, the good and kind and warm light that felt like arms wrapping around him in loving embrace.

"A new journey begins for us now, Salman."

He stood on the chair in quiet anticipation. He was no longer fearful, only amazed that his end was at hand. Certainly, it came to everyone sooner or later, but he thought it was still amazing now that his own life was ending.

When the moment of falling came and his body struggled against death, the memory of Maryam came to him. He saw her again when she was forced to her knees in front of the trench. He thought how strange it was that she would come to him at this moment, and he remembered how she had raised her arms to the heavens before Ali's blade came down on her. Her arms raised upward became his arms upward.

As the darkness closed around him, his mind cried out, "O the light! O the light!"

# ANOTHER GREAT BOOK BY F. W. BURLEIGH

"If it were in my power, I would require every American to read *It's All About Muhammad.* Instead, I will only highly recommend it as the best way to understand the man who literally invented a so-called religion based on his own pathologies and then, through terror, ensured it spread to the entirety of Arabia in his lifetime."
—Alan Caruba